*"Just as I gigged the roan forward again, the sound of rifle
and pistol fire resounded in the distance, causing me to turn
the horse and duck low should a bullet come whistling in. I
listened to the steady pop of gunfire long enough to realize
that somewhere ahead a battle was under way, and somewhere on one side or the other of that gun battle stood Honest
Bob and my racing stallion—there wasn't a doubt in my
mind.*

*"Shoving the roan forward, we rode fast. With any luck at
all, I'd sweep in as the last shot fired, get my horses back and
run like hell. . . ."*

He's short-tempered and softhearted—the runaway, looka-
like cousin of an outlaw named Jesse James and a horse thief
trying to turn horse dealer. But wherever Jeston Nash goes,
trouble has a way of finding him. When Nash makes his way
through drunken soldiers, lying detectives, a former baseball
player and a storm of thieving and shooting to the home of the
U.S. Seventh Cavalry, his journey leads him straight to a
madman: a general named Custer who's determined to teach
Nash a lesson in glory. . . .

TRICK OF THE TRADE

PRAISE FOR RALPH COTTON'S
PREVIOUS JESTON NASH
ADVENTURES

WHILE ANGELS DANCE

"A rich adventure novel. . . . Cotton's blend of history and
imagination works because authentic Old West detail and
dialogue fill the book."

—Gregory Lalire, *Wild West* magazine

Books by Ralph W. Cotton

While Angels Dance
Powder River
Price of a Horse
Cost of a Killing*
Killers of Man*
Trick of the Trade*

*Published by POCKET BOOKS

For information regarding special discounts for bulk purchases, please contact Simon & Schuster Special Sales at 1-800-456-6798 or business@simonandschuster.com

RALPH W. COTTON

TRICK OF
THE TRADE

POCKET BOOKS
New York London Toronto Sydney Tokyo Singapore

This book is a work of fiction. Names, characters, places and incidents are products of the author's imagination or are used fictitiously. Any resemblance to actual events or locales or persons, living or dead, is entirely coincidental.

An *Original* Publication of POCKET BOOKS

POCKET BOOKS, a division of Simon & Schuster Inc.
1230 Avenue of the Americas, New York, NY 10020

ISBN: 0-671-57034-X

First Pocket Books printing July 1997

10 9 8 7 6 5 4 3

POCKET and colophon are registered trademarks of Simon & Schuster Inc.

Cover art by Antonio Gabriele

Printed in the U.S.A.

For Mary Lynn . . . of course; and for my brothers, Raymond and Daymond Cotton, two ole Kentucky horsemen who've known trails both high and low and rode good horses along the way. And in loving memory of Alton B. Cotton, Jr.—the original Quiet Jack.

Special thanks to my friend
D. Woods in Bakersfield,
for my *very own* medicine shirt
and all the *good medicine*
surrounding it.

When he told the squaws that I was his wife they made a sign to ask if I was the only one; and an expression of compassion came into their faces when he said yes, for among some of the tribes an Indian is always very much married if he is a chief of any consequence. Possibly they imagined that a white wife has the same amount of labor to perform for her husband that a chief's squaws have, and they pitied me.

—Elizabeth B. Custer, *Following the Guidon*

PART 1

Drinking with Soldiers

The General's Wife

Off to the Dakotas

Chapter

1

---

*They were a loud and
boisterous bunch. . . .*

I stood at the bar trying to remember the name of the writer
who'd said "What I know about soldiering I know about
life, for all I've learned about life, I learned as a soldier."
Who was it said that? I threw back a drink and shrugged.
Who knows? A sweat bee zoomed in and circled close to my
nose, singing in a low steady buzz. Then it zipped away
when I swiped a hand at it.

I never liked drinking among soldiers on leave. Not that I
have anything but the *highest* level of respect for soldiers,
simply that a man on leave from the military drinks for
different reasons than, say . . . a blacksmith who drinks to
wash the taste of metal from his lips, or a businessman
who stops by the tavern at the end of a long day of
commerce.

Soldiers drink to let off steam, or to get *caught up* on their
drinking, or to drink up a reserve, knowing that once they're
back in the saddle, following the guidon those long days on
the trail, all they'll have to keep them sane are the memories
of that last night in town . . . last bottle emptied, last whore
twirled. Soldiers either drink to go crazy or else to keep
from it.

I shook my head. *A hard life at best . . . soldiering.*

3

"ANYWAY," I said, shouting in Quiet Jack's face from less than two feet away, "WE'VE MADE ENOUGH HERE. WE SHOULDN'T HAVE TO HIT A LICK ALL SUMMER, UNLESS WE WANT TO."

Jack nodded, but I'm sure he hadn't heard a word, not above the roar of drunken soldiers in that small tavern.

"WE COULD EVEN GO DOWN TO THE SHORES, DO SOME FISHING . . ." I stopped and just stared at him, realizing there was no point in yelling my lungs out. All around us a sea of blue uniforms swelled and tossed beneath a cloud of cigar smoke. A billiard ball whistled through the air and took out the stovepipe in a spray of black soot. Soldiers clapped and whistled. Jack tossed them a glance, then looked down at the bar top, his hands spread along the rail.

The bartender slung a fresh bottle before us with a shaky hand, then dropped down and disappeared. Whiskey sloshed over the top of the bottle and ran down on the bar. The sweat bee came back and hovered at the edge of the whiskey spill until I swatted it away. This time I felt it hit my hand and figured I'd killed it, but it only bounced off the bar and spun away, whining louder now, its low steady buzz sounding broken and angry. *Aggravating little bastard.* I stared at it, shook my head, and sipped my rye, hoping it wasn't one of *those* kinds of bees, the kind that seemed to single you out and stay with you for days.

Jack stood looking down, drumming his fingers on the edge of the bar. I could tell the crowd was getting on his nerves—mine, too, for that matter. We'd spent the past week shouldering our way through drunken soldiers. They drank everywhere: along the roads, in the woods, swamps, outhouses, you name it. The day before, some of them had tied a whore up by one heel and left her dangling from an oak limb. We'd found her and cut her down, but she'd just cussed and spit, thrown back her hair, and taken off toward the tavern.

The Seventh Cavalry had hit town about the same time as the winter horse auction, so anybody with anything to sell squeezed the crowd for all it was worth. New Orleans had thrown open its doors in fine Southern hospitality. Officers and their wives had taken up lodging by the week. You couldn't get a decent sit-down meal without a reservation.

All the better drinking establishments back in town were full up, even though they'd raised their prices so high that a working man felt guilty going there. So we drank among the troopers, the enlisted men, men who'd gotten so wild and rank and ornery that they'd been forced to the outskirts of town. We drank and listened and kept to ourselves, each of us wondering who'd be the first to crack somebody's head with a gun barrel.

Beside us along the bar an argument brewed between a big red-faced sergeant and a swarthy little Italian private half his size. I'd nudged Jack and nodded toward them, giving him a signal that it was time to go before they squared off on one another. But just as Jack glanced toward them, the fight started.

All of a sudden the sergeant shoved the little private back and shouted, "Come on then, you little olive sucker!" His voice boomed above the roar of the crowd. "Give me everything ya got!" His chest swelled. His thick arms spread wide, parting a cloud of cigar smoke.

The tavern fell silent as a tomb. Upturned bottles and mugs came down slowly, beer dripped from mustaches, bleary eyes stared. "I'll scour you down like a washboard!" The sergeant squeezed his big fists tight and growled, advancing on the private like a stalking grizzly. I took a cautious step sideways; Jack stood watching them, and threw back a drink.

"Come on, Jack," I said just above a whisper, still slipping away. But he ignored me and poured another shot.

The little private caught himself against the bar and backed away another three feet; yet I saw no fear in his dark eyes. His boot heel clinked against a brass spittoon and he stopped there, muttering what I took to be a curse in Italian. He glanced down then back up at the sergeant. A nerve twitched in his tight jaw. *Uh-oh.* I slipped sideways along the bar in the other direction as if the floor had tilted beneath me. "Jack, damn it! Come on."

"Pride comes before a fall," Jack said, watching the big sergeant tilt his chin back and clench his eyes shut.

"I'll spot ya the first punch, with my eyes closed, you chickenshit little—" The sergeant's words cut short about the second I stopped at the end of the bar. Then his eyes flew open—wide open—just in time to see the little private spring forward like a panther, his right hand sweeping down and coming up in a high arch, swinging that spittoon in a whistling flash of brass and a spray of sour tobacco juice. I ducked low, winching at the solid thud, the loud after-ring of metal against skull bone. *Lord! He's killed him!*

"Damn, what a lick," Jack chuckled. He leaned an elbow on the bar and grinned, watching while the sergeant staggered in place. Blood and tobacco juice ran down the sergeant's face from the rising knot on his forehead.

"Who's next?" The sergeant's voice sounded distant, his eyes swam about the room. He rocked on his boot heels.

"Me, you big field ox!" a voice bellowed. A stocky corporal shot forward from the crowd, shouldered past the private, and broke a wooden stool across the sergeant's chest.

I slipped back along the bar up to Jack and tugged his sleeve. "Jack, let's get the hell out of here." The broken buzz of the sweat bee hummed in my ear.

"Why? We've had to listen to this drunken bullshit all week. We might as well watch 'em beat the hell out of each other."

Man! In a second the brawl flared and spread like fire through a wheat field, the whole tavern turning into a raging, writhing sea of blue uniforms. A soldier came falling backward toward Jack, but Jack raised a boot and kicked him back into the battle.

Amber waves of beer curled and spun behind flying mugs. Cavalry hats sailed through the air. An empty boot skipped across the bar and shattered the dirty mirror. Broken glass sprayed out across sweaty backs and bloody heads. I sidestepped a flying canteen with a trail of whiskey streaming behind it. *"Damn it to hell, Jack! This is crazy!"*

"Let me out of here," said a voice at our feet. The bartender had crawled through an opening beneath the bar. He tugged on my trouser leg with a trembling hand.

I grabbed him before he slipped past me. "Where you going? You've got to break this up. You can't leave."

"Like hell, I can't." Spit flew from his lips. "You wanta break up the Seventh Cavalry, be my guest. You can have this shit, I'm gone!" A table came sliding along the bar upside down. Jack snatched the bottle away just in time as it wiped out a stack of shot glasses, slammed the wall, and fell in pieces. I slapped glass from my duster sleeve. Jack laughed and threw back a swig from the bottle.

"Is there a shotgun back there anywhere?" I yelled in the bartender's face.

"Hell, no. Think I'd keep a loaded shotgun around this bunch?" He twisted free of my hand and crawled away toward a broken window.

I grabbed Jack by the back of his shirt. "We're getting out of here—"

But my words were cut short as the little Italian came charging the sergeant again with the raised spittoon. This time the sergeant caught him in midswing, raised him up, and flung him toward us like a rag doll. "Look out, Jack!" I yelled. But Jack sidestepped, caught the private, and slid him along the bar, leaving a wake of beer and broken glass.

Enough's enough! I drew my forty-four and fired two shots into the ceiling, stepping to the middle of the floor toward the broken window. "Everybody freeze!" I shouted with my pistol still raised, and shoved a soldier out of my way. Broken glass crunched beneath my boots. Again the tavern fell silent as a tomb. "The fight's over! I'll shoot the next man who throws a punch!"

Taking another short step toward the window, I glanced at Jack and saw him raise the bottle again, shaking his head. "Come on, *damn it! Let's go!*" There were more than a dozen of them facing me, all of them wild-eyed and liquored up. I wasn't going to shoot anybody; I just wanted to hold them at bay long enough to get Jack and myself out of there.

"Now who the hell might you be, lad?" The big sergeant wiped a hand across his bleeding forehead and spread an evil grin. The sweat bee circled in and hovered near the fresh blood. He swiped it away.

"Never mind who I am, just don't make a move." I slipped over another step, watching them.

The little private struggled to his feet and staggered over

7

beside the sergeant, the flattened spittoon still hanging from his hand, his breath heaving. "Jerka his arms offa his body, Sarge," he hissed. "Hita him witha this." He nudged the spittoon toward the sergeant.

Jesus! I shot the private a curious glance. I couldn't believe it. Now he and the big sergeant stepped together as one, cautiously but unafraid, staring into my eyes from eight feet away. Behind them the others closed ranks, advancing inch by inch.

"Naw," the sergeant said, nudging the spittoon away. "I'll crush his little head with me own bare hands. Just don't let him make a break for it."

Jack's voice said quietly, "Hold it right there, *hog guts,* he's with me." I shot Jack a quick glance, saw him throw back another drink and let out a whiskey hiss.

The big sergeant turned slowly toward him with the same evil grin. "Oh, is he now? Then who might you be?"

Jack returned the grin, only Jack's was not a grin at all, but more like a wildcat flashing its fangs. "Me? Why, I'm with him." He threw back another drink and let the empty bottle fall to the floor. "And that's all the questions I'll be answering tonight." His elbow brushed his duster back slightly, just enough to open a clear reach to his tied-down holster. I stepped over closer to him, my pistol still raised, cocked, and ready. This wasn't what I had in mind at all, but these boys weren't ready to back off an inch.

The sergeant took note of Jack's poised gun hand, but it didn't stop him. He waved a thick hand slowly to the side. "You men spread out, flank them both." Then he stepped closer, saying to Jack and me: "So, you wanta skin iron on dear ole H Troop, huh?"

"All we want is out of here," I answered, knowing Jack wasn't going to say another word. He'd drawn his line; I knew what came next. "Nobody has to die here. Y'all wanta take each other apart, that's your business. Just let us go on our way—"

"Get 'em!" The sergeant barked; they all lunged at once. Then they froze as Jack's pistol snapped out, up and cocked, jammed into the big sergeant's right eye so fast he had no time to pull away from it.

"I'll ruin ya," Jack said in a whisper, the wildcat still showing fangs.

I almost let out a sigh. That would do it. It was over now. The sergeant saw he had no way out. He'd called the wrong man's bluff, now he'd have to fold his hand. Now all we had to do—

"Hear that, lads," the sergeant said back over his shoulder, Jack's pistol barrel holding his head back at a stiff angle. "He'll kill *me*. But there's only ten shots between them. Once he shoots me, rush them both."

Rush them both? For God's sake! He's stone nuts, I thought. He's nuts, they're *all* nuts . . . and we're all gonna die here!

"Suit yourself," Jack said; and I could *feel* his finger press back on the trigger.

"Wait, Jack!" I raised my free hand chest high in a cautious show of peace. "Boys, we're all a little drunk and testy here. I admit, I mighta done wrong firing those shots, but damn it, let's not start killing each other over it."

"See, lads, we've got them and they know it. Now do like I told you, and we'll be fine."

Be fine? The man's eye bulged with a pistol barrel against it! To hell with it, then. I shot Jack a glance, saw him thinking the same as me, and felt my thumb tense on the hammer, ready to drop it and let the shooting commence.

"Te-hut!" A voice bellowed from the doorway, loud and suddenly. I almost spun and fired toward it. "Stand down, troopers," said a tall captain with a red goatee and muttonchop sideburns. His voice kicked up a notch when he saw the soldiers hesitate for a second. "I said, *stand down, NOW!"*

Jack and I both lowered our pistols as the sergeant took a step back. His right eye watered in a long stream down his thick red cheek. "Call this your lucky night, lad," he said under his breath to Jack before turning and snapping to attention.

Lucky night?

"Now what's the meaning of this, Sergeant Griebs? Were you men fighting?" The captain folded his hands behind his back, glancing from one battered soldier to the other. .

"No sir, Captain Dunlap, sir," the big sergeant said. "Just a spirited discussion, is all." Without breaking from attention, he cut his eyes to Jack, then back to the captain. "I was just telling these gentlemen—"

"As you were, Sergeant," snapped the captain. He glanced again at the red-faced troops, then to me, then to Jack, and said, "What say you? Were you men only having a *spirited* discussion?"

Jack smiled and started to speak, but the sergeant leaned slightly toward the captain and said, "Begging the captain's pardon, but will you be taking the word of this barroom ruffian over your own troops?"

"One more word, Griebs," said Captain Dunlap, "and you'll be sleeping in chains this night." He turned to Jack. "Now, sir, what went on here?"

Jack shot Sergeant Griebs a glance that held his eyes for a second, then shrugged and said to the captain, "It's true. We were just rehashing some old battles, Harper's Ferry and all such as that."

"I see." The captain looked Jack up and down. "And why then was your pistol in the sergeant's eye?"

Jack grinned. "Just illustrating a point, Captain. Nothing serious."

The captain's cheeks flashed red. "What is your name, mister?"

"I don't use one any more than I have to," Jack said. "Just to keep things simple, you know."

"He's with me, Captain," I cut in. "And he's been drinking a little."

"So, that allows him to go about *unidentified?*"

I shrugged and started to answer, but he went right on. "And why is your gun drawn? Were you also *illustrating* a point?"

"Well—" I grinned and slowly holstered my pistol. "—Only if he failed to."

A slight chuckle rippled across the drunken troops. The captain shot them a warning glance, then turned back to me. "You wouldn't happen to be Mr. Beatty, would you?"

"Uh—" I stalled for a second. "—Yes, I am Beatty . . . James Beatty. I'm a horse trader out of Missouri, just here for the auction, then back—"

He waved my words away. "I know you're a horse trader, Mr. Beatty. The rest of it . . . well, I'm sure you've said it enough that there's not the slightest flaw in it."

Huh? I shot Jack a curious glance, then looked back at Captain Dunlap. "Do I know you, Captain?"

"No, of course not." He smiled slightly. "But I have been searching for you all afternoon. There's someone outside who wishes to speak to you."

"There is?" Again I shot Jack a glance.

"Yes. If you'll follow me, please." He swept a hand toward the door.

"Wait a gol-dawded minute here, Cap'n," said the bartender, slinking back in across a floor covered with broken glass and busted furniture. "What about this mess? Is the army gonna pay for all this damage?"

The captain looked about the tavern and said very cooly, "What damage?"

"Bine-gawd! The damage they done here, Cap'n! Look at this place!"

Again the captain shot a glance about the place, smiled, and said to the troops, "Some of you men *will* help him tidy up a bit before you leave."

"Tidy up? Damn it, Cap'n, they's nearly torn the place to the ground."

"Oh, I see. Are you saying my troops have been out of line here?" He raised a finger for emphasis. "Because if they have, just say the word and I'll issue a special order and see to it you're never bothered by army personnel . . . ever again. Will that satisfy you?"

The bartender scratched his head. "Well, it ain't been all that bad, I reckon." He rolled away the stovepipe with the toe of his shoe. "Maybe a good sweeping would do."

"Good then," said the captain, turning from the bartender and gesturing Jack and me toward the door. I shook my head, nudged Jack, and headed out into the darkness, glancing over my shoulder at the red-eyed, drunk, and bloody soldiers.

A hard life at best, soldiering . . .

We walked through the moonlight across a clearing out front of the tavern, toward a covered buggy alongside the road. Jack instinctively fell back a couple of steps and slightly to the side, ready to cover me in case there was something wrong here. There was no reason for the army to be looking for us that I could think of.

"Lucky for you men I arrived when I did," Captain Dunlap said, taking note of Jack's position and speaking as he glanced back at him.

"Lucky for us all," I heard Jack reply. "I was just about to *illustrate* my point when you walked in."

My hand tensed near my holster as we stepped up beside the buggy, but I eased down when the horse took a step forward and a woman's hands in lace-trimmed sleeves reached out and steadied the reins. "Whoa," said a gentle voice from within the closed buggy, and Captain Dunlap reached out and took the buggy horse by the harness.

"Elizabeth," he said, "allow me to introduce the gentleman we've been looking for. This is Mr. Beatty—" He glanced at Jack as Jack stepped up beside me, still looking all around. "—And his associate, of course."

"Oh, Mr. Beatty, you dear man!" She leaned forward from beneath the buggy top, turning to face us in the moonlight. "What a time we've had finding you. It's as if you're *hiding out*, sir."

"Uh, no, ma'am, of course not." I felt my face redden; Jack chuckled beside me. Right off I noticed something about the woman that made me a little edgy. *What was it?* A distant aura of some sort.

"Of course not, indeed," said Captain Dunlap. Then before I could say any more, he added, "Gentlemen, allow me to introduce Mrs. George Armstrong Custer." I detected a slight flash of resentment as her gaze passed from him to Jack and me.

"Ma'am," Jack and I said in unison, our hats already off and in our hands. She stood, and Captain Dunlap assisted her down from the buggy. "Sorry if I've inconvenienced you," I added.

"Oh, I have to admit it's been quite an adventure for me. I seldom get to see this side of civilian life." She tossed a hand. "The stock dealers, the . . . how do they say it? The wheeler-dealers? Horse trading must be quite exciting."

"It has its moments," I said, blushing there in the moonlight, knowing she was only being kind. For the most part, everybody viewed horse traders as the kind of person you wouldn't trust around your pet rattlesnake. "The captain says you want to talk to me?"

For some reason I felt I could've used a drink right then. A restlessness set in on me that made me want to hurry her up, get done with her, and get the hell away. While we spoke, Captain Dunlap reached over into the buggy and took out a candle lantern. He lit it and adjusted the globe back into place.

"Yes, I want to talk to you about the horse you bought at the auction this morning . . . the one called Honest Bob? I'd like very much to purchase him from you." In the candlelight her eyes sparkled like a child's for just a second, until she saw me look into them. Then they seemed to close off, go distant and blank, shutting me out. Yet I continued to look into them; and as I did, for some reason I wished we had brought the bottle of rye with us from the tavern.

I glanced at Jack, then back to her. *"Honest Bob?"* I shook my head. "Ma'am, believe me, you don't want to buy Honest Bob."

"Captain Dunlap here has already cautioned me to be prepared to *dicker* with you." She smiled toward the captain, then Jack, then me. "Did I say that right? *Dicker?* I'm afraid horse jargon alludes me." She tossed a hand, cutting her gaze away from me, not letting me back into her eyes. What was she afraid for me to see there? *A beer would be good right now.* Nonsense, I thought, shaking the thought from my mind.

"Yes ma'am, dickering's the right word." I answered for all three of us, holding my hat close to my chest, idly running my palm along the brim. Boy, she got on my nerves somehow. But why? "Except in this case it's not a matter of dickering, ma'am. Honest Bob is not for sale. I'm sorry."

"Oh dear. I was so looking forward to trying my skill at dickering. Captain Dunlap and I have made reservations at a restaurant for that very purpose. Have you and your friend already had dinner? We would so love for you to join us."

Before I could answer, Jack's elbow hooked me in the ribs. We hadn't had a decent meal in days. "Well, ma'am, we don't want to impose." Again he elbowed me, this time grumbling something under his breath. I ran my hand across my lips. Damn, I wanted a drink, a shot of rye . . . a cold beer, something, *anything*.

"Nonsense, Mr. Beatty," Captain Dunlap said. "It would be our pleasure. Mrs. Custer has her heart set on buying the horse. At least grant her the opportunity to persuade you."

"Yeah," Jack cut in, "for the sake of good manners." Again, the elbow in my ribs, this time making me sway to the side before I caught myself. "Let's at least go hear what the lady has to say to us."

I let out a breath, wondering what it was about her that made me want to get away. *Just my own foolishness?* "Certainly, we'll join you for dinner. But I have to let you know, Honest Bob is *not* for sale. I'm firm on that." *Was it her voice?* She did have a certain flat monotonous whine. *Stop it . . .*

"I understand, Mr. Beatty," Elizabeth Custer said quietly, and she smiled a gentle smile there in the candlelight, folding her hands across her waist as if having resolved something of great importance in her mind.

Chapter

2

Something about her made me want to drink. . . .

"I don't know what's wrong with you sometimes," Jack said, riding beside me on his silver gray gelding a few yards behind the buggy. I rode a Gypsy roan we'd taken in on a trade, a hard-boned little Spanish Barb gelding who looked as if he'd blown into town on a desert wind. Jack shook his head. "The lady wants to buy us dinner someplace where the food ain't still crawling, and you act like she wants to pull your teeth with a pair of shoeing tongs."

"Be still, Jack, they can hear us," I said in a low tone. "I just didn't want to mislead her into thinking she could talk me out of Honest Bob just by buying us dinner. Just wanted to be forthright about it."

"Can't you be *forthright* on a full stomach? Sometimes I think you forget we're outlaws here . . . *desperadoes."* He swung a hand in the darkness. "Hell, if we have to be *forthright* all the time, we just as well be undertakers." He chuckled and spit, feeling better now with the promise of a good meal.

"You're saying undertakers are forthright?" I brushed a hand past my ear, feeling something circling near it. *That same sweat bee?*

"Mine better be forthright." He looked around in the

darkness. "Tell you the truth, if she wants to buy Honest Bob, you oughta sell him to her. It's probably the only offer you'll ever get. Don't know why you ever bought him."

"He's a novelty, Jack. Every horse trader on the circuit has owned him one time or another. He's a fine-looking animal."

"Yeah, but he ain't worth a sack of dirt, and you know it."

"That's the novelty of owning him. You just don't understand the finer points of the horse-dealing trade."

"The *trade?* Shiiit. Horse dealing ain't a trade, it's an affliction." He tapped a finger to his head. "It's something missing up here, is what it is. The thing it takes to make a good horse dealer is the same thing it takes to make a man wanta break up a fight between a bunch of drunken soldiers. What came over you back there, anyway?"

I grinned, feeling better myself now, away from the clamor of drunks, riding in the cool of night. Maybe all those things had played together to make me a little nervous around Elizabeth Custer. Whatever it had been, I was sure it was over now. "I had it under control. Probably coulda talked 'em out of it in a few more minutes."

"Talked them out of *what,* eating ya after they tore you apart? Them boys are so full of *army,* they piss stars and stripes. Custer's got 'em so swollen up, they have to use bedsheets for bandannas."

"Keep it down, Jack," I cautioned him. "They can hear us up there."

He lowered his voice slightly. "Well . . . it's the truth. You ever seen anybody as pumped full of themselves as that bunch? They're a killing in the making."

I thought about it a second and realized he was right. Both of us had been up at Powder River back in '68 and watched the army take a beating from Red Cloud's Sioux, the best guerilla light cavalry force in the world. But those soldiers had been young, green, and poorly outfitted, led by untried officers whose objectives were not clear.

Now talk had it that Generals Terry, Cook, and Custer would lead an expedition party into the heart of the Black Hills. They could call it an *expedition party* if they wanted to, but it didn't change what everybody knew. This was an assault force, and from what I'd just seen of the men of the

Seventh Cavalry, the Sioux would have their hands full this time. These were mostly older soldiers, hardhanded veterans of Washita and the Apache campaign. They cared nothing about a gun pointed at them. Hell, they enjoyed it. *A killing in the making.*

I thought about it as we rode on through the darkness, seeing the glow of the candle lantern circle the buggy in a halo of golden mist. "Why do you suppose she wants Honest Bob?" I asked quietly, still thinking about the Sioux up there in their promised land awaiting the bugle's blare and the coming storm.

"You called him a novelty horse. Maybe she wants him for her novelty husband. From what I hear of Big George Custer, he'd backhand a grizzly through a barbed wire fence. They say that crazy bastard once—"

"Jack, damn it, *please* keep your voice down. Don't start telling *Custer* stories right now. You *want* the lady to hear ya?"

He chuckled. "Hell, it ain't nothing she don't already know, unless she's as crazy as he is. Did you notice that blank-faced stare? Reminded me of a plaster doll. Bet she can't buckle her shoes without him reading it to her from an army manual. Yep. I reckon ole Georgie boy keeps her brain-screwed and cross-eyed crazy."

I stopped the Gypsy roan in the middle of the road, crossed my wrists on my saddle horn, and kept nodding my head as he spoke. Jack stopped beside me. "She ain't a bad-looking woman, but I've never seen a flatter expression in my life. Think maybe she's dull, a little simpleminded? A man like Custer might marry a woman like that just to make sure he's always the center of attention. He probably figures nobody would show any interest in her while he's off kicking ass on the high plains somewhere. Maybe he thinks as long as he keeps her head spinning and her pantaloons—" His words stopped short and he looked away at the candle lantern bouncing along into the distance. "Why're we stopped here?"

"Because I ain't gonna have them hear you bad-mouthing her or her ole man, that's why." I shrugged. "So get it all out of your system, and if we ain't lost 'em by then, we'll go on and get something to eat." Had Jack felt as uncomfortable around this woman as I had? I started to ask him, but decided not to right then.

"I ain't bad-mouthing him, or her, either. Just offering a little food for thought here." He gigged his silver gray gelding forward and I fell in beside him, following the candle's glow.

No doubt about it, something about Elizabeth Custer's voice made me want to drink. It was not an unpleasant voice, but it droned on endlessly. And no matter what she said, it never seemed to be going anywhere, never seemed important. I kept catching myself wanting to finish her sentences for her just to get them over with. Words spilled from her lips and disappeared, but they didn't stick with me, didn't impress me in the slightest. How did her husband stand it? He travels a lot, I reminded myself, nodding as she spoke.

No sooner had we sat down at the table in a private dining room just inside the town limits, I'd ordered a bottle of wine and nearly finished it *by myself* before our food arrived. Jack and the captain only sipped their wine; Elizabeth Custer nursed a cup a tea. It was all I could do to keep from ordering a bottle of bourbon and throwing the cork away. She went on and on! Didn't she ever have to stop and breathe?

When the four of us had finished our late dinner, I tapped a linen napkin to my lips, laid it alongside my empty plate, smoothed it down with my hand, and emptied my glass of wine with one long gulp. Then I poured another glassful and said, "Begging your pardon, ma'am, but I don't think you understand what you'd be getting into, owning Honest Bob." I pitched back a gulp of wine, then another, and added, "I couldn't sell him to you in good faith. I'm sorry."

Throughout the meal all she'd talked about was buying the horse for her husband. The more she'd talked, the more I'd swallowed glass after glass of wine. It wasn't like me, drinking that much. I could feel it by the time I'd pushed my plate back.

Across from me, Jack laid down his knife and fork across a steak bone and leaned back with a wineglass in his hand, settling down now that he'd gotten his belly full. Captain

Dunlap offered him a cigar. Jack took it, thanked him, bit off the tip, and adjusted the cigar in his mouth. I saw a glint of devilment in his eyes when he said to Captain Dunlap, "So, Captain, what did you do before you joined the army?"

Now that Elizabeth Custer wasn't talking I managed to sit the wineglass down and take a breather. Lord, she was wearing me out.

"Well, actually . . ." Captain Dunlap started to answer, then caught himself and smiled beneath his raised brow. "Pardon me, sir, but I'm afraid I've heard *that* little joke before."

Elizabeth Custer turned from me to the captain. "Oh? What joke is that?" I studied her face as she spoke, and as if on cue, picked up my glass, tossed it back, emptied it, and poured another without taking my eyes off her. Jack was right, there wasn't much there. I couldn't understand it. A pretty woman, but with no shine of life in her eyes or expression. *A plaster doll?* Yet there had been a vibrant sparkle there earlier for just a second when we first met. Where had it gone?

The captain tossed a hand. "Oh, Elizabeth, you don't want to hear it."

She batted her eyes slightly. "But yes, I do. I enjoy a good joke, as long as it's appropriate." I looked at her and threw back a drink. *Please tell it, for God's sake!* I felt like screaming, "Somebody keep this woman from talking before I drink myself into a stupor here!"

Jack's eyes darted back and forth between them, a smile playing at his lips. He saw something was wrong with me. He had to.

"Well, then," the captain said, raising a finger for emphasis. "He asks me what I did before I joined the army . . . I tell him. Then he'll say, 'But what have you done *since?*'" The captain chuckled and tapped a napkin to his lips. I took a deep breath and kept my hand back from the wineglass. "A harmless little quip," the captain shrugged. "Quite humorous, actually, the *first* time I heard it."

Jack's smile broadened toward Elizabeth Custer but she only stared for a second with no expression, absolutely *none*, then said, "Oh, I see . . . *humorous,"* and turned back to me. My fingers crawled forward across the tablecloth, then stopped and climbed the stem of the glass. Couldn't she see what she was doing to me?

"Not everybody gets it," Jack said quietly to Captain Dunlap as Elizabeth Custer started in on me again about Honest Bob.

She'd already told me the story twice during dinner, how her husband had watched me buy Honest Bob for three hundred dollars off the auction block. All he'd spoken about the rest of the day was how much he'd love to own such a fine-looking animal. Although she'd never seen the horse, she checked around, found out who had bought it, and had Captain Dunlap help her find me. Her plan was to surprise the general with it when he joined his troops at Fort Lincoln, before he started his expedition into the Dakotas . . . and so on and so on.

I drank and drank, nodding along with her as she spoke, knowing it by heart now but still seeing no point to it.

I hated bursting her bubble, but buying Honest Bob was a bad idea; and when she finished her story the *third* time, I looked her straight in the eyes and told her so . . . again. This time she looked crestfallen. But she took a deep breath, and I truly believe would've started all over had I not raised a hand and stopped her.

"The fact is, ma'am, I'd be greatly concerned, sending your husband off into Indian country on a horse like Honest Bob."

"Oh?" Her blank expression turned curious. "And why is that, Mr. Beatty? As a dealer I should think your main concern is simply making a profit, is it not?"

"Elizabeth . . ." The captain admonished her gently.

A waiter appeared at my side, and I glanced up as he eyed the second empty bottle in surprise, removed it, pulled out another, and filled my glass. I cleared my throat quietly, glancing back and forth between her, Jack, and the captain. Jack blew a thin stream of smoke and grinned at me.

"Well, ma'am," I said, "it's true horse dealing is a profit-driven trade, but there's some things I can't—that is, *won't*—do for the sake of making money." I sipped my wine gently, trying to control myself, then sat it back on the white tablecloth and pushed it slightly out of reach.

"I didn't mean to imply anything untoward about your profession, Mr. Beatty. I hope I've given no offense. But I would like to know why you would refuse a reasonable offer. Are you greatly attached to this animal?" She'd offered me five hundred the first time she told her story, then added two hundred with each retelling of it.

"Noooo, ma'am. No attachment here." I reached out, took the glass, and drained it. *She's killing me . . .* "The fact is, I only bought him on a whim. You see, Honest Bob is not an *honest* horse. He's woodenheaded and untrainable. Nobody's ever been able to teach him anything and make it stick, not for more than a day or two. He's got every bad habit you can name, and he picks up another every time somebody else owns him." I glanced at the captain and had to squint to focus on him. "You've seen his type, Captain, I'm sure. One day he's the best horse in the world, the next day he's a stall kicker, a wood cribber. He shies, bolts, bites, wheels, and rears—"

"Of course." He nodded, waving my words away, and lowered his eyes toward Elizabeth Custer. "Take heed here, Elizabeth. I think Mr. Beatty is trying to save you great disappointment."

But she only shook her head slightly. She'd have to hear an in-depth explanation, so I prepared one quickly as she asked, "Then why on earth would you have purchased such an animal?"

My face reddened a bit as I caught Jack's smug grin, but I smiled, raised my wineglass, and studied it as I said, "Ma'am, Honest Bob is a running joke among the horse-dealing crowd. He's such an impossible horse, it's become an honor to own him for a while. It sort of tells the other dealers that I'm a good sport." I sipped the wine and smiled again. "But nobody can straighten Honest Bob out—" I shook my head. "—Nobody. He's been handled *too* wrong for *too* long."

What I'd said was true, except in my case there was more to it than just showing other dealers I was a good sport. Honest Bob, for all his problems, happened to be one of the most beautiful horses I'd ever seen. Call it vanity, foolish pride, but I could just picture myself one day riding onto the auction circuit atop Honest Bob—a horse no one else could handle—his tail high, sunlight glittering off his mane. What a trick that would be.

"You don't know my husband the general, Mr. Beatty. He has a reputation as an *extraordinary* horseman, and he *soooo* admired Honest Bob."

I feared having to hear the story once again, but she stopped herself, her eyes pleading as she leaned slightly forward. "Please tell me you'll sell him to me, for the general's sake, for the sake of his morale?" She almost placed a hand on my arm, but she caught herself and folded her hands instead. I cut a glance to Jack and saw him watching closely as I pulled the bottle to myself and filled my glass. The captain looked embarrassed and stifled a quiet cough with his fingertips.

An awkward silence passed, then she said in a lowered voice, "Very well. I'll pay you . . . one *thousand, five hundred* dollars?"

"Eliza-beth!" The captain almost rose from his chair. I studied her eyes as she held my gaze.

"Everybody knows what an outsta-anding man the general is, ma'am," I said quietly, stifling a wine belch without taking my eyes from hers. "But selling you Honest Bob is out of the question, at any price. I'm sorry."

"I see then," she said softly, lowering her eyes and picking absently at the linen napkin beside her plate. Somehow she took it personal, I thought. This whole thing had been an attempt at her proving something to herself, and she'd failed. Somewhere in those caged eyes, I saw that her failure in buying the horse ran to some much greater failure she felt within herself. Whatever she thought her shortcoming to be, I'd just cinched it for her. I felt uncomfortable.

"Then I suppose I'll return home unaccomplished this evening, Mr. Beatty." There was hurt in her voice, and she folded her hands on her lap beneath the table, raised her face, and smiled graciously through her defeat. *Jesus* . . . I felt low, started to reach for my glass, but stopped myself. What the *hell* was it about this woman?

"Well, Elizabeth," said the captain, "no one can say you didn't try. Although I still think Mr. Beatty is being quite a gentleman, not taking advantage here. When someone tells you a horse is bad, it pays to listen."

"Two thousand dollars, Mr. Beatty," she said firmly. "And no one will ever say you didn't try to warn me against it." She turned to the captain. "You will bear witness that Mr. Beatty told me beforehand how difficult this horse can be."

"Ma'am, difficult is not the right word. You never know when Bob'll get in one of his moods. He's been handled hard. He'll turn cold-jawed all at once, and the best hands in the world can't bring him around." Again I felt my fingers want to crawl toward the glass, but I stopped them. "He'll kick, bite—"

"Of course," said the captain, cutting me off. "I'll confirm Mr. Beatty's straightforwardness in the matter." He turned a tilted gaze on me and I squirmed a bit in my chair. Jack chuckled quietly and puffed the cigar, gazing off to the ceiling. It was starting to appear rude of me at this point. I'd given her every reason in the world not to buy the horse, but she still wanted him. Was I just being contrary because she got on my nerves?

This was no way to treat a lady, especially one whose only intent was to do something special for her husband, who would soon ride off into the fury of battle. *What was I thinking here?* I shook my head and let out a breath, the wine doing something strange up there in my head.

"Mistress Custer," I said, offering a whipped smile, "If the army ever needs someone to procure horses, I'd certainly recommend you for the job." The room tilted a bit as I moved my head. I sat up rigid to keep my mind clear. "It goes against my better judgment, but if you insist, the horse is yours."

"Then . . . then you'll do it? You'll take two thousand dollars for the horse?" In her excitement her eyes let down their guard for just a second and they sparkled as before. This time, she *did* reach across and clamp her fingers on my forearm. I shot the captain an embarrassed glance and saw his eyes take on a skeptical expression.

"Well, no, ma'am, not for two thousand." I gestured my hand toward the table before us. "In appreciation of your hospitality, I think *seven* hundred dollars will be sufficient. After all, you know how much I paid for him. I wouldn't want to leave a bad impression here."

She looked relieved. What would she have done to rake up two thousand dollars had I taken it?

The captain's eyes softened toward me. He smiled. "Well done, sir. And if I may say, I've never seen a horse dealer conduct himself in such a honorable manner."

"Some of us *do* consider ourselves to be gentlemen," I said with a deep breath, hearing a trace of a wine slur in there. Jack rolled his eyes upward and looked away.

"Oh, Mr. Beatty, you can't know how much this will mean to the general. When he came back from the auction telling me about the horse, I just knew—"

"Please," I said, nodding, raising my hand, stopping her from telling the whole story one more time. Now that the deal was done, I didn't want to hear about General George Armstrong Custer or how much owning Honest Bob would mean to him. *I could drink myself to death here.* From what I'd heard of the man, he and Honest Bob might make a perfect pair, one as unpredictable and headstrong as the other. "Your husband does have a good eye for horses. Honest Bob is a strikingly handsome animal; aside from his shortcomings, he's got a lot of possibilities."

"And, *oh!* I can just see the look on his face when you bring the horse to him. He'll simply beam."

"Whoa now, ma'am." I cut her off. "I won't be bringing the horse to him. Delivering him wasn't part of the deal."

"But, but . . . how else will I get the horse to him? I can't take delivery here; he might see what I'm doing. It would spoil everything. I just assumed you would bring it to Fort Lincoln for me."

"Did you say you're going to Fort Lincoln? Up to the *Dakotas,* ma'am? Up in the Sioux Nation?" It had to be just the wine, but I coulda sworn I heard arrows whistle through the air.

"Yes, I'm leaving here tomorrow for Virginia while the general goes back to Washington before joining his command. Then I'll leave for Fort Lincoln before he does and meet him when he gets there. I'd hoped to have the horse there by then."

"No, ma'am." I shook my head. "If I said anything to give you that impression, I apologize. I cut the price right to rock bottom to show good manners . . . but, my goodness. I can't deliver the horse to you."

"So," said Captain Dunlap. "You get seven hundred for the horse, but the rest you make on delivering it? Perhaps I spoke too soon in judging you, Mr. Beatty."

"No," I shook my head. "I'm not trying to bump up the price for delivery, Captain. The fact is, now that I know where the horse is going, I wouldn't take him there for any amount of money." I felt their eyes on me, pressing me, and I squirmed a bit. "Maybe you could detail a couple of soldiers to transport it up there."

"You can't trust them to keep it a secret, Mr. Beatty." Captain Dunlap laid both palms flat on the table. "Our expedition was supposed to be in confidence, but it appears everyone from here to California has heard about it. Besides, we have no stock cars to spare. No. I'm afraid you'll have to call it off, Elizabeth." He sighed and dealt me a less than pleasant glance.

"Yes, then." I thought I heard a slight quiver in her voice as she turned her eyes from us for a second. "I'm afraid I've done all I can."

I looked at Jack, tapping my fingers lightly on the tabletop. He shook his head slowly. *No way,* his eyes told me. "We've got a lot to do, amigo," he said quietly.

"Very well, Mr. Beatty," Elizabeth Custer said, turning back and smoothing her hands along the edge of the tablecloth. I saw that her eyes had misted, but she blinked them and continued. "We've agreed on seven hundred dollars for the horse. Now let us see what amount of *dickering* it will take to get him delivered. I *must* have the horse at Fort Lincoln shortly after I arrive there."

Dickering? There'd been no dickering here. She'd simply worn me down. I'd talked myself into letting her buy the horse, then lowered the price to boot.

"Ma'am, maybe I ain't making myself clear." I stopped for a second, shook my head to clear it, then asked, trying to get it straight in my mind, "You really are going to the Dakotas? The Black Hills? Sioux country?"

"Certainly, why?"

I glanced back and forth between them again. The captain's eyes sharpened. "Uh . . . nothing, I suppose, just curious, ma'am. Sounds a little dangerous, is all."

"No, it really isn't," she said, and as I looked into her eyes, once again they drew distant and shut me out. "Most of the wives will be there. We'll have a steamboat and everything . . . and, of course, our own dear Seventh Cavalry to protect us."

"Well, then," I shrugged. "I'd call that as safe as a walk in the park." No matter what she said or did, or tried to do, there was nothing going to get me up into the Dakotas. *Nothing.* Not even if she went into a crying fit, I thought, throwing back another belt of wine.

"It would be so wonderful of you, Mr. Beatty. And not to mention patriotic." Elizabeth Custer clasped her hands together; I watched and threw back a long drink. "It would mean so much to the general. If you could have only seen his face when he came back from the auction. He said to me, 'Libbie, I've just seen the most splendid horse . . .'"

Jack grinned, leaning forward and nodding, encouraging her to go though the whole story one more time, word for word. I sat my empty glass down, pushed it away, picked up the bottle, leaned back with it, and resolved myself to hearing the story *one more time,* but not really listening as she rattled on and on. It made no difference what she said. She could drone and whine all night.

Her words grew distant as I threw back shot after shot. I recalled seeing her husband from afar yesterday at the auction barns. In the crowd of army brass and dignitaries, although he'd jutted his chin as high as the rest, he'd appeared smaller than the others somehow, small and all alone, occupied by some dark and troubling thought. I wondered what it was, and pictured him as I'd seen him then, a man who looked out of place there among the wheels of war and commerce.

Custer had looked like a barroom tough who'd stolen an officer's dress uniform and donned it for the day, one that fit him well, yet did little to distinguish him as either an officer or a gentleman.

I watched Elizabeth Custer flutter with excitement as she spoke. Jack and the captain seemed to hang on her every word, Jack appearing interested simply to aggravate me, the captain perhaps because it was expected of him.

A hard life at best . . . soldiering.

I thought about it for a second, trying to picture it all in my mind as she droned on with her story. I wasn't about to go. *Noooo way.* But if I did, how would it turn out? I shook the thought from my bleary mind and drank and drank, listening as Elizabeth Custer droned on and on like a mud dauber building a nest. General George Armstrong Custer and Honest Bob, I thought. Was the army ready for that?

Chapter

3

The hair of the dog that bit me . . .

I had no idea how or why, or even *when,* but I awoke the next morning stunned by the realization that somewhere in the course of the woman's babbling and my drinking last night, I'd finally agreed to take the horse up to Fort Lincoln to her. *Aw, Jesus.* This had been no dream. I'd really done it. My head thumped like a war drum.

I smelled the strong aroma of coffee outside the tent, and when I'd pulled on my boots and stepped outside the fly, Jack looked up from the fire sipping from a steaming tin cup. "Any man sleeps till daylight is either rich, sick, or lazy." In the east, daylight cut a thin silver line on the horizon.

"I'm neither," I said, rubbing my face, stepping over beside him, picking up a tin cup, and rounding my finger in it. I tested the handle on the pot before picking it up, then poured myself a cup and eased down beside the fire. A damp warm breeze blew in across the swampland, smelling earthy and bittersweet. "But what I am is a hungover idiot, Jack . . . a straight-up fool."

"Yep, I'd have to say so." Jack laced his coffee with a shot of rye, corked the bottle, and put it away. He sipped and let out a hiss. "Of course, you can always claim you were drunk. I'll back you up on it, say you're unable to control your drinking, been drinking all day . . . was out of your mind."

"That wouldn't be a lie," I said. "I don't know what got into me. You know I don't ordinarily drink like that. She caused it some way or another." I scratched my head. "Hope I ain't going into some kinda phase where things start getting out of control."

"Don't know about any *phase,* but I always say, a man oughta either drink like a fish or not at all. It's that *moderation* that gets ya in trouble when you come upon somebody like her. You got to do something to be able to stand them, and when you ain't used to holding a stiff bellyful of booze, you end up on your face."

I looked at him. "You mean . . . you've had that happen?"

"Aw, yeah. But I know when I'm around somebody like that, and I just distance myself from them, keep them at arm's length, so to speak. You sat right there and took that story over and over, full blast. Lucky you've got any mind left at all." He shook his head.

So did I. "Well, I reckon I'm stuck with it." I rubbed my temples with my fingertips. *Man oh man!* "Why didn't you stop me, Jack? You know I didn't want to do it."

"Then you shouldn't said you would, drunk or sober. I can't always tell when you've lost your mind. I ain't a doctor."

"She just went on and on, over and over, about how much 'He just loved that horse,'" I said in a mock voice. "Shit. It's a month there and a month back, that's if we make *good* time and nothing goes wrong."

"For seven hundred dollars, we can't afford anything going wrong." Jack shook his head and leaned forward, stirring a stick in the glowing embers. "It's not enough to make it worth our trouble. You let that *dull* little woman out-dicker ya."

"That's crazy, Jack. She don't know the first thing about horse dealing."

"Oh?" He cocked an eye toward me. "She got everything she wanted, price *and* delivery. It don't matter *how* she did

29

it. She did it. Now we're stuck with it, unless you want to crawfish out of the deal."

I let out a breath. "I reckon I'm stuck with it."

"Sure ya are. I spent the night thinking about it, and I already figured we're going. So I've accepted the fact and put it out of my mind. I'm ready when you are." He grinned.

"What's that supposed to mean?" I asked.

"Nothing." He shrugged and looked back into the embers. "I remember a story about Custer from back in the war. Wanta hear it?"

I just looked at him. "You've spent the night thinking about George Custer?"

"No, it just came to me. Wanta hear it?"

"Everybody's got a *Custer* story," I said. "Looks like I'll soon have one, too." What I knew of George Armstrong Custer is what I'd read in *Harper's Weekly* and what I'd heard of him from those who'd known him during the great civil conflict. I'd pretty much decided he was an overbearing, self-willed maniac who'd happened to be at the right place at the right time and made quite a name for himself early on in his career.

Jack nodded and went on. "Seems the commanding generals had a chance to get the drop on a regiment of Southerners, but they'd stalled on crossing a river, worried about how deep it might be. Custer was just a young captain then, but after the big brass spent over two hours discussing the river, wondering how to find out how deep it was, he got tired of waiting on them, jumped on his horse, and rode right out into the water." Jack cut a hand out before him. "Got out in the middle, stopped his horse, raised his arms, and yelled back, 'Here's how deep it is, Generals. Can we go now?'"

"If that's your story, I already heard it," I said, sipping my coffee, studying the low flames dancing in the breeze.

"Thought you'd want to hear it again, since I've got none to tell about little *Elizabeth* Custer . . . not yet, anyway."

I stared at him, wondering if it could've been true. Could she have known what she was doing? Could she have strung me along? *Naw, no way.* I shook the thought from my head. Jack sat watching me, as if seeing it work itself out in my mind. He chuckled and sipped his laced coffee. "Yep," he said, "she got ya. In more ways than one." He raised a finger. "Never get involved with an unfulfilled woman."

"Unfulfilled woman? Jack, you don't know nothing."

By daylight we'd broken camp and ridden into town. This being the last day of the auction, Jack and I made the early sale line, sold off a couple of brood mares and a Morgan cross, then swung our horses and headed over to the rail station. Nobody showed any interest in the Gypsy roan, so I figured on riding him myself for the time being. The horse had little going for him, no flash, no showy high-headed gait, nothing to attract attention to himself other than a flankful of brush scars and a restless front hoof. He couldn't keep that left hoof still for a second, always raising and dropping it, scraping it back and forth.

I led Honest Bob and a big racing stallion named Foxfire. I'd waited a long time to own a thoroughbred stud like Foxfire, and now that I had him I wasn't about to let him out of my sight. He'd have to make the trip with us.

Our idea was to pick up tickets in advance for the next train out of New Orleans following the troop train. Since I had agreed to deliver the horse, I wanted to get it over with as soon as I could, then get home and forget about it. We figured on booking the horses into freight, resting on the way up to Memphis, maybe catch a few hands of poker on the way, and before we knew it this whole thing would be over and done with.

But when we got to the station, the platform swarmed with soldiers end to end. "Now what?" Jack slumped in his saddle and stared at the crowd; and we sat in silence among the noise for a few seconds until Jack let out a breath and said, "They'll be three days getting this bunch out of town, another week cleaning up after them." He bit a plug off a twist of tobacco, put it inside his jaw, and worked it into place. "Looks like we're stuck here till then."

"Huh-uh," I said, "We'll ride up to the next stop or all the way to Memphis if we have to. We can wait there. I've had it with soldiers." Fifty feet down the platform, I caught sight of Elizabeth Custer and a colored woman making their way through the crowd, the colored woman in the lead, using a raised leather valise like a battering ram to part a way for them. Elizabeth Custer didn't see us, but I nudged Jack and nodded toward her.

"Yep. There goes one happy little soldier's wife," he said. "A truly *intoxicating* woman." We watched them weave through the flurry of blue uniforms and step onto the crowded northbound train. Jack chuckled as the two women disappeared in to the crowded car. "The proud new owner of Honest Bob—one horse that hell wouldn't have."

Through the open windows officers sat poised as if at attention, staring longingly out at ladies in bustled dresses who lined the platform. "It ain't as if I forced him on her, Jack," I said, feeling a little guilty for some reason, watching the women smile and wave little lace hankies beneath raised parasols. Some of them tapped the hankies to their cheeks and tried to look brave. "You know, I really *did* want to keep ole Bob for a while."

"Sure you did."

I just looked at him, then looked away, farther down the platform at enlisted men who bent whores backward in one last deep kiss and shoved money down their bosoms. "I hate to think of Custer riding that horse into battle."

"Sure you do."

I looked at him again. "Jack, why are you acting like I was up to something? Like I *did* want to sell her the horse . . . that I'm only acting like I didn't want to?" I swatted a hand at the sweat bee hovering near my shoulder. "If I was up to something, I could've stung her for two thousand dollars, couldn't I?"

"Not the way that little lady deals horses, you couldn't. I never seen nothing like it. She talked *herself* up to two thousand, then got *you* to talk her down to seven hundred." He shook his head. "I swear, amigo. That's a strange way to do business, drunk or sober." Jack rubbed his throat and gazed away. "If you wanted to impress her, you shoulda quoted some Shakespeare. It'd been cheaper."

"Impress her? I just wanted her to shut the hell up. I didn't go there to sell her a horse . . . but once I did, I didn't want to take advantage."

"Somebody *takes* a little advantage on every deal. If they didn't, nobody would ever sell nothing. I'd just like it to always be us, if that makes any sense to ya."

"Shit." I saw what he was doing, just getting under my skin, needling me. "I'm gonna hear about this for the next month, I reckon."

"Not from me, you ain't. I'll never mention it again. I'm just glad we got the opportunity to do something for one of our boys in blue . . . and his dull wife."

"Don't call her dull, Jack," I said. Then I caught the snap in my tone of voice and added quickly, "She can't help it if she's not the most exciting woman in the world. Besides, if you hadn't been poking me in the ribs, we never woulda even gone to dinner in the first place."

"Ah, I see, it was all *my* fault." He chuckled. "If I could only break this bad habit of needing to eat every few days . . ."

"It'd sure be terrible if Honest Bob throws the general during a big battle or something, wouldn't it?"

"Don't worry about it," Jack said, still gazing off. "Honest Bob'll break Custer's neck long before the Sioux ever get a chance to kill him. You mighta just stopped a whole war from ever happening. Don't it make ya proud?" He chuckled under his breath.

"If I did, it would." I looked all around at the crowd and added: "But I didn't. These boys are cocked, packed, and primed for a bloodletting. Nothing'll stop 'em this time. It ain't like it was at Powder River."

A small band played brassy and loud. Colored kids danced barefoot on rough planks. Above the station a wide flag snapped back and forth high in the wind. "I reckon not," Jack added quietly.

Stock cars stood full of enlisted men who pressed their faces between the rail planks and let out catcalls to the gathering of whores. "Feed 'em and lead 'em," I said to Jack, and when he looked around as if he hadn't understood me, I added, nodding over my shoulder, "These two horses, Jack. Looks like we'll have to feed them till we can find room on a train somewhere."

"Yep." He pushed up his hat brim, and as a conductor called out and the train blew its whistle, we turned with our four-horse string and headed away, weaving our way through the crowd, Jack in the lead and me following leading the horses.

Soldiers sat on open flatcars with their legs dangling over the sides, waving at the crowd as I rode past. Big Sergeant Griebs stood red-eyed with a bandage wrapped around his head and a hand on his hip, barking orders at his men as they squeezed aboard a crowded stock car and milled like sheep looking for a spot wide enough to sit down. I ducked my head slightly, hoping he wouldn't recognize us, but as Jack started past him, Griebs grinned and stepped back, blocking our way. "Say now, laddie, don't I know ya from somewhere?"

"I doubt it," said Jack, returning his grin. "I've never been there."

Griebs chuckled, hangover sweat running down his red face as he looked us both over. "I never forget me a face, laddie."

"You'd do well to *forget* mine," Jack said, stepping his silver gray to side around the big sergeant.

"Theya the ones whata gonna shota ya last night, Sarge!" The little Italian private called out from the stock car. His wiry arm reached between the rail planks, pointing at us.

"Aw, yes! Now I remembers ya!" The big sergeant reached out and slapped Jack's silver gray on the rump as it walked past him. The horse snorted, tensed, and stepped out. Jack reined him up, turning him to face the sergeant.

"You're the one who poked a pistol in my eye last night!" The sergeant shook a finger at Jack. I stopped and spun my lead rope around my saddle horn, wondering what came next. Soldiers called out, reaching their hands toward us through the planks. But the big sergeant let out a booming laugh and spread his arms wide. "And what a gay ole night it was, eh, laddie?"

If he saw the dark warning in Jack's eyes, he took no heed of it. "Yeah, I sure enjoyed it," Jack said, his duster seeming to spread back on its own, clearing itself from his pistol butt. If the sergeant even took note of it I couldn't tell.

"Awww, but didn't we all . . ." Sergeant Griebs rocked back on his heels, his big arms still spread, gazing up as if thanking heaven.

"Hey, remembera me? Remembera me?" The Italian called out, but I ignored him, keeping an eye on Jack and Griebs, and drawing the two-horse string closer to me.

"T'was a night *unlike* all others," Griebs said. Then he tapped a finger to his bandaged head and roared with laughter. "And I got me eleven stitches in the noggin to prove it." The stock car roared with him. I eased down a bit and saw Jack do the same. He cut a quick glance to me, then back to Griebs. Griebs's expression turned bewildered for a second, and he asked, "But tell me now, why were you gonna shoot me, if I might inquire?"

Jack smiled slightly and backed his horse a step. "Just on general principle, Sergeant."

"That's a good one," Griebs bellowed, slapped himself on his thick knee. "Here that, lads? He would've shot me on *general principle*. What a stunning line that would've made on my marker." He struck a finger across the air as if reading. "Here lies Sergeant Latimeer Griebs, *Shot on 'general principle.'*"

The soldiers whistled and hooted. No problem here, I thought, nudging my horse forward, freeing my lead rope. Just hungover soldiers still feeling their whiskey. The sergeant looked up at me and pointed a thick finger. "Now *you*—let me get this straight—*you* were with *him?*" His finger wagged from me to Jack, then back to me. "And vice versa? You two were together last night, weren't ye?"

"Yep," I said. "I tried to break up the fight and you got a little salty about it. Remember?"

He worked on it for a second scratching his bandaged head, then chuckled, "Awwwww, yes, now I do. But *why* would you go and do a thing like that? It was our last night in this wonderful town, you know."

"I remembra you, I remembra you!" The Italian called out, shaking a finger toward me.

I smiled and shrugged, still ignoring the Italian. "Call me crazy, Sarge, but I got tired of all the racket. You boys got a little out of hand."

"Then there you are. The noise was more than you could bear." He laughed, half turning his red face toward the stock car, again spreading his thick arms like a bandleader. "Hear that, lads? *Vice* was going to shoot out my eyeball because *Versa* thought us to a wee bit out-of-hand." He pinched his thumb and finger together. The stock car roared. "Perhaps he had himself a wee bit of a headache." Soldiers stamped their boots, whistling and yelling. "You look none the better this morning," he said, studying my face. "Are ye searching for a hair of the dog that bit ya?"

I almost ran a hand across my face, realizing last night must have left me with a hangover pallor. "Because if ye are, I know *that* dog—know wherst he lives and who sicced him on ye." He patted a hand on his tunic. The bulge of a whiskey flask stood out on his broad chest. I shook my head no; he shrugged and dropped his hand.

"But tell me true, laddie—" Griebs turned back to Jack with his finger raised. "—Would you have shot me dead, then, for making so much noise?" He winked with an ear cocked forward, waiting for Jack's answer. The soldiers fell silent.

"Deader than hell," Jack said, smiling, the tension now gone and his eyes only watching the sergeant curiously.

Griebs seemed frozen for just a second, considering it, then cocked back his raised finger and shot it toward Jack as he stamped a heavy boot down. *Gooood man, then!*

A loud cheer went up from the soldiers. The Italian shook a fist and screamed like a banshee. Griebs jumped up and down, slinging his thick arms, laughing as whiskey sweat flew from his face.

We doffed our hat brims, smiling as we turned our horses and stepped them away. "But you lads left too early last night," Griebs called out to us. "I would've bought the next round, you know."

We rode on, and he called out, "If you're ever around Lancaster Square, tell 'em you know Big Red Griebs. Tell them I'm fine, and working for the Lord's own army . . ."

Jesus. I raised a hand and waved back toward him, shaking my head. They would fear no river's depth, these men of Company H.

And all the way, as we made the long pull from New Orleans to Memphis, I thought now and then of General George Armstrong Custer. I pictured him riding out in the river as a young man while the higher officers stood beneath a tree talking about it. What had they thought of this brash young captain flaunting his bold nature? I thought of the brief flash of excitement in Elizabeth Custer's eyes when I agreed to sell her a horse that I'd already told her nobody would want, nobody in their right mind, anyway.

"The *new* army," Jack said, sitting at a crossing watching the caboose grow smaller in the distance. Across the tracks a one-legged man leaned on a crutch and snapped a lingering salute at the fading troop train. "I wouldn't soldier again for nothing, would you?"

"Nope," I said, nudging my horse forward. "Not for nothing."

A breeze fluttered against the man's empty pinned-up trouser leg as we crossed the tracks and rode past him. He looked up at us, wobbling slightly on his crutch, raising a stained and shaky hand, palm up. "Would you sport an ole veteran a drink . . . for Old Glory?"

I reached into my vest pocket for a coin, but Jack stopped me with a glance. "Hold on," he said under his breath. Then he raised his voice turning to the man. "I've seen you around, mister. You didn't lose that leg in the war."

"Like hell, I didn't." He stiffened on his crutch. "You don't know me . . . not from Adam. I took one through the knee at Peach Orchard, by God."

"No you didn't, so quit lying. If ya wanta drink, I'll buy ya one." Jack raised a finger. "But don't lie about it, all right?"

The man rubbed his nose and looked down with a sheepish grin. "Well, hell . . . maybe I didn't. But I *was* in the army, and I *did* lose me a leg, and I *do* need me a drink."

Jack smiled and pulled out a dollar bill. "What army was you in, ole buddy?" He handed the bill down, but held it a second as the man reached for it.

The man thought about it, cutting a bloodshot glance back and forth between us. "Whichever one you boys was in," he said, snatching the bill quickly and shoving into his pocket.

"That's what I thought." Jack nudged his horse forward. "Never met anybody yet who didn't want to part of a war once it's over." I nudged my horse along beside him, flipped the man the coin, and watched him catch it with a snap of his shaky hand.

"That was hardhanded of you, Jack," I said.

"No it wasn't, not unless I'd been wrong—which I wasn't."

"But you coulda been. You just took a guess."

"No I didn't. I knew he was lying when he said it. He was just putting on a show, saluting that train for us." Jack spit a stream of tobacco juice. "Shit, anybody with half sense coulda seen through it."

"I didn't."

"Oh?" Jack just smiled, adjusting his reins across his lap.

"I hate it when you start acting like this."

"Like what?"

"Like you know something you *really* don't."

"But I did know it, or I wouldn't have done it."

"Bull . . . you was *tricking* your way through it, that's all. You shamed that old man, making him admit he was lying."

"If he hadn't been lying he wouldn't been ashamed. So he shamed himself. I just called him on it. If he'd lost his leg in the war, he wouldn't been the one ashamed, *I* would. So there." He stared ahead with a smug grin.

"You don't know no more than anybody else, Jack, so quit acting like it."

"Yeah? Well I knew he was lying. And I knew you were having thoughts about Elizabeth Custer . . . last night at dinner. I saw you wondering about her."

"There you go." I let out a breath. "Thought you wasn't gonna mention last night, ever again."

He grinned. "Just this once. I saw you warming up to that boring little woman, staring into those plaster-doll eyes, maybe wondering just what it was that—"

"Whoa, now." I shook my head and almost laughed out loud. "Jack, you was doing all right till you said that. Of all the times you've been *wrong*, you have never been more wrong than you are right now. *Elizabeth* Custer? Jesus! If you wasn't my friend I'd be offended. You said yourself, she's dull. Said she has a face no man would remember the next morning. To be honest with you, Jack, I thought she was a little homely looking."

"Yeah?" He raised an eyebrow. "You never said so before."

"Well, I just now realized it," I said, ducking my head a bit, hoping he couldn't tell I was lying.

"Ha! You don't know *what* you think of her, do ya?"

"Maybe not."

"See. That means you *are* thinking about her. I saw how you looked at her. You was interested, don't deny it."

"I *do* deny it. Think what you want to think, but the fact is, all I wondered about was why I was so uncomfortable being around her. I reckon any man might wonder something like that."

"That's where it started. But don't tell me you ain't thought of her since then. I know you have."

"Well . . . a time or two, maybe." I shrugged. "Nothing like you're thinking though. You're wrong on that."

"All right, then, I'm wrong," he said, giving in too easily.

I shook my head and tried to dismiss it, knowing he was just egging me on. But the rest of the day I kept thinking about Elizabeth Custer, hearing her tell her story, hearing it drone over and over in my mind. I could see her hands, gentle and delicate, and her hair, finely brushed and kept. I saw how her eyes could be vibrant and alive one second, then withdraw in an instant to some remote place inside her.

She was an officer's wife, used to the rigors and the sway and pull of military life, used to the chain of command, to the bow and curtsy of lower rank and to the line of authority above all else. An unfulfilled woman? I thought about it, picturing these things I remembered about her. *Not homely, not homely at all.* Why had I even said that? But as I thought these things then and would think of them again over the coming week, try as I might . . . for the life of me, I couldn't picture her face.

PART 2

—◆—

Swimming Wild Rivers

Horses to Keep

Medicine Shirt

Chapter

4

That's what I call traveling . . .

I stepped down off the loading plank, leading the roan and the two-horse string. Honest Bob had bits of splinter stuck around his mouth from chewing through a wood slat inside the railcar. Longer splinters clung to his mane. "That horse would eat through an oak tree," Jack said, following me down the plank, leading his silver-gray. "Maybe the Custers want to go into the logging business."

A chilled evening breeze swept in from the northwest, licking at loose edges of tar paper on the back of low-roofed shacks strewn out along the rail yard. Wooden crates and barrels lay stacked against the rear of the shacks, covered with tied-down tarpaulins. The smell of curing hides filled the breeze. A goat stood tearing off long strips of tar paper, chewing it like tobacco as it turned a lazy gaze to us. A string of black saliva swung from its chin.

Bismarck.

Before us in the near distance lay the Missouri River, the smell of muddy water rising up, mingling with the musk of the hides. Wood smoke curled from rusty stovepipes, drifting in swirls above the rooflines.

Only two weeks ago we'd sweated in the heat of New Orleans. Now this, I thought, gazing all around, turning the

43

horses, waiting as Jack stepped down the plank. Behind us, beyond the rear of the buildings, the sound of a twangy piano rattled along the street like a man gone mad in a shed full of empty cans.

After traveling that week from New Orleans to Memphis, having to stop daily at some point and wait as another loaded troop train scuttled past us, we'd spent two days by rail from Memphis to St. Louis, another three days to Chicago, two more to St. Paul ... I shook my head. It didn't seem natural covering that much ground in that short a time. Now we'd taken the Northern Pacific west until it ran out of track.

Across the yard, a man wearing a shiny cream-colored high-crowned Stetson stood watching us, leaning against a shack with a pipe hanging beneath his long mustache. At his feet lay a saddle and a blanket roll. Evening sunlight stretched his shadow long and thin. We'd played poker with him from Memphis to St. Louis, to where he *said* he was going, but I'd seen him again when we switched trains in Chicago. Now here he stood on the edge of nowhere, just staring.

"I see him," Jack said under his breath as I cut a glance toward the man. Jack slung the saddle from his shoulder onto his silver gray. "He's on us, no doubt about it." He looked over at the man fifteen yards away, and spoke to me in a lowered voice. "Damned lawman of some kind or other." He made the cinch and jerked it tight. "Told me he was a cattle buyer when I ask him. Cattle my stinking foot."

"What did you expect him to say, Jack? 'Yeah, I'm a lawman?' Then ask if we were outlaws? Then we'd say, 'Why *yes,* of course, we are!' Where would that have left us?" I spoke as I slung the saddle from my shoulder onto my roan gelding and made the cinch. Behind me, Honest Bob took a mouthful of my duster and pulled me back until I reached a hand around and smacked his nose.

"Bob's got you feeling a little testy, don't he," Jack said.

"I just don't want somebody dogging us the whole trip. For two cents I'd walk right over and ask him just what the hell he's staring at."

"For a lawman, he sure don't mind making his presence

known." Jack dropped his stirrup, tested his saddle, and looked over at the man with me. "Look at him, staring a hole through us."

"He sees *us* . . . we see *him*. No need to be bashful. Hold the horses, Jack." I reached to hand him my reins and the lead rope. "I'll see what this is—"

But before he could take the reins, Honest Bob reared straight up letting out a high-winded neigh, dragging me up off my feet. The reins to the Gypsy roan fell to the dirt. The lead rope snapped a coil around my wrist before I could turn it loose.

"Whoooa-boy!" I swung away as he came down bucking sideways, the racing stallion being pulled along, me between them. To keep from being crushed I stuck an arm out holding off the stallion and swung my leg up and hooked it over Honest Bob's neck, my hand still coiled in the rope. "Jack! Damn it!" Now I hung there, upside down by one leg, both horses moving sideways as Jack grabbed the stallion by the nose. Honest Bob thrashed and lunged, sawing and slinging his head, batting me off the stallion's side like a rubber ball.

"Damn," Jack said, catching Bob by the nose and holding the horses apart until I dropped to the ground. "What are you trying to do here?" Beside him the Gypsy roan stood watching, scraping his hoof, his reins dangling to the ground.

"Nothing, Jack, he got me!" Uncoiling my hand and scooting across the dirt from between them, I jumped to my feet, slapping dust from my trousers. "That crazy son of a bitch just went nuts! Did you see that?"

Jack chuckled. "All I saw was you hanging by a leg. Thought you'd taken up circus riding."

My face reddened. "It ain't funny." I looked around quickly to see if anybody had seen it; only the ticket clerk sat staring through the window. The man in the Stetson had disappeared. "Jack, he's gone!"

I glanced around as my hand went to the empty holster up under my arm. *Empty?* I spun toward the horses, looking all around on the ground for my forty-four. There beside Jack, the man stood holding it by the barrel. They both smiled,

Jack now holding both horses by the lead rope, but his eyes never straying far from the man's hand near his tied-down holster.

"Looking for this, Mr. Beatty?" He raised the gun butt to me and I took it, shook it off, and shoved it up into my shoulder harness.

"Thanks," I said quietly, watching him as I stooped down, picked up my hat, and slapped it against my leg.

"And to answer your question—" He offered a tight smile back and forth between us. "—No, I'm not a *lawman* . . . so put that out of your minds. And as far as what I was starting at . . . it's this beautiful stallion. A thoroughbred, eh?" He took a step sideways and ran a hand down Foxfire's muzzle.

I hadn't seen Jack caught off guard in years; but he looked as stunned as I felt. "Mister, nobody can hear *that* good from that far away." I squinted at him.

He shrugged. "They're both striking animals, but this one," he patted Foxfire and dropped his hand. "I think I've seen him race somewhere, haven't I?"

"Maybe," I said, "but I ain't talking horse racing, I'm talking, *how* did you know what we said?"

He tapped a finger to his head, smiling behind the thick mustache. "I'm a mind reader. Would you believe it?"

"No more than I believed cattle buyer," I said, shaking my head slowly. "Care to try again?"

He let out a breath. "You were partly right, though. I used to be a lawman . . . a police detective back in Louisville, Kentucky. Ever been there?"

"Well, I—Wait a minute. How come I ask you a question, but end up answering one myself?"

"Old habit," he said, raising his hat brim slightly and running his hand under the edge of it. "Call it a trick of the trade. We all have those, don't we?" I tensed as his hand went out of sight for a second, and he must've noticed it. He brought his hand out slowly with his fingers spread enough to show us there was nothing there. "Does it bother you, my having been a lawman?"

"There you go again, another question," I said, smiling a little. There was something about this man that made you *want* to like him, something that made you want to *trust* him . . . almost. But there was something else about him that told you to keep your distance.

He turned to Jack. "Is your friend always this cautious around strangers?" Jack didn't answer. "We *did* share a few hands of poker after all . . . we were introduced."

"Yep, and you won most of them, Mr. Gateholder," Jack said. "More of your mind reading?"

"No, it's *Gaither* . . . Roland Gaither, but my friends call me Roe. I hope you will."

"It's your first trip out here, ain't it, *Mr. Gateholder?*" Jack turned his back on him just a little and adjusted the lead rope at Foxfire's muzzle. Honest Bob stood with his head down as if thinking up something crazy to do next. *Ornery bastard.*

"It's *Gaither,* please. And you're right. It's my first time this far west. What gave me away?" He glanced up and down himself.

"Asking too many questions, wearing a brand-new hat." Jack grinned. "Reading people's minds. It's best to buy a *one-way* ticket out here the first time, just in case things don't work out for you."

"Oh? Is that a fact?" His expression stiffened a bit.

"Yep." Jack turned back to him. "Correct me if I'm wrong, but you was right on the verge of offering to buy us dinner, wasn't ya?" He nodded beyond the rear of the rail shacks toward the rutted street, toward the sound of the rambling piano.

Roland Gaither's expression eased. He raised a brow as if impressed. "So, you do some *mind reading* yourself."

"I like to keep my hand in," Jack said. He spun the lead rope into a half hitch around his saddle horn and dusted his gloved hands together. "While we eat you can tell us that since you're going the same place as we are, why not ride along with us. Does that sound about right?"

I smoothed my reins and drew the roan close to me—the only horse of the three who'd kept his head, I thought—and I watched Roland Gaither's eyes study Jack in a way that Jack wasn't supposed to see. But Jack saw it; I saw it, too. "Well now," he said, spreading his easy smile, the kind of smile a former police detective might use just to let you know he, *too*, liked to keep his hand in. "It looks like you've figured me out." He swept a hand in the direction of the piano music.

Jack returned his smile in the same easy manner, but I'd seen this smile before. It wasn't his open *who-gives-a-damn-for-anything* smile, nor was it the wildcat showing its fangs. This one was harder to describe, sort of like the smile you give the preacher when you know the preacher's lying, but you like his preaching all the same. "No," he replied as we started off across the dusty ground, "but I'm working on it."

The saloon was so crowded, a bartender served beer and food through a broken window. A swaying line of men stood there milling, laughing, and cursing as the line pressed ever forward. One of them grinned through crooked teeth and announced to the others that *no* gawdamned army could tell him where he could go, and no gawdamned painted *injun* could keep him from going there. "Not when it comes to *gooooold!*" His eyes and mouth formed high lingering ovals on the word *gooooold!*

Dinner was overcooked hash in three wooden bowls, and when it was shoved to us, we ate it with big wooden spoons outside, stooped down, leaning against the side of the saloon while our horses fed on cracked corn four feet away. Honest Bob bumped his muzzle against the Gypsy roan, trying to crowd him away from the corn. But the roan only stiffened, looked at him, and snorted, then dropped back to eating without giving an inch.

Wind whipped at our collars. Down the side of the building, two old men and an Indian woman squatted beside a mule strapped with mining gear. They eyed us closely and lowered their voices between themselves. Then the Indian woman stood, walked over to horses, stuck her hand out, and ran it along Honest Bob's neck. "Careful, ma'am," I said, watching her. "That horse is crazy. He bites and kicks."

But without looking at me, she whispered something in Lakota close to Honest Bob's ear, and he nuzzled her like a kitten. Smiling at me, as if to show me I didn't know what I was talking about, the woman turned and left, and I had to stand up and settle him to keep him from trying to leave with her.

When I sat back down, Honest Bob nipped and threatened the racing stallion, and stepped in close to me with his ears laid back and a strange look in his eyes. He sniffed toward my bowl, then blew wet flecks of corn in my face and stepped back slowly, sawing his head up and down. He watched me as if seeing me for the first time—as if I might be a wolf come to kill him.

Jesus. I shook my head and tightened my grip on the spoon in case I had to whack his nose with it. "What was that all about?" Jack eyed the woman as she walked away.

"Who knows," I said. "Probably doesn't see horse this nice every day up here."

"I've never seen a horse act like him," Roland Gaither said, nodding toward Honest Bob as he took a bite of hash and wiped a hand across his mouth. "One minute he's fine, the next he acts like a lunatic. Are you sure it's a good idea, selling him to a general?"

I stopped chewing long enough to nod and say, "He'll be all right." I swallowed and added, "I hope, anyway. It wasn't my idea."

We'd told him why we were here, about Elizabeth Custer buying the horse, figuring there was no reason to lie about it. This was one of those rare times when honesty seemed better than an alibi. Besides, I'd thought, how could we lie to him anyway with him being able to read our minds? *Could he really do that?* I looked over at him.

"Now this one, this *Foxfire.*" He pointed at the big racing stallion with his spoon. Hash dripped. "I could see how any general would be proud to own such a fine stallion. I'd like to own him myself. How much does a horse like that bring, Beatty?"

I looked up at Foxfire, sucked a tooth, and said, "It don't matter. He ain't for sale."

"But if he *was?*" He cocked an eye at me.

"He ain't, so that's that." I said, dipping up another spoonful. "But as far as *looks* go, I can see why Custer wanted Honest Bob. He's a beautiful animal . . . smart, too." I shrugged and ate. "Might even be just as fast as the stallion. But he's crazier than a snake on a griddle." I shot a glance toward Honest Bob and saw him biting on a loose board along the side of the building.

"But a fast horse, huh?"

"Can't really say. I doubt if anybody's been able to ride him flat out enough to know. Nobody knows where he came from till he showed up on the auction circuit. Every dealer twix hell and Texas has owned him one time or another . . . never for long. He either tears down their barn or bites somebody's ear off. I kinda wanted to try my hand with him."

"Really? Why?" Gaither asked with a puzzled expression. I shrugged and spooned up my hash.

"Speaking of horses," Jack said, picking a tooth with a thumbnail, "how'd you plan on getting to Fort Lincoln on foot? It's a long day's walk and a hard river crossing."

Gaither smiled. "I suppose it was foolish of me, but I thought it'd be better to buy a horse once I got here instead of bringing one along." He gestured a hand about the bustling street. "But as we see, horses are going to be in short supply around here."

"Yep, it was foolish," Jack said. "What kind of *cattle buyer* travels without a horse?"

"You fellows don't believe that's what I am, do you?"

"I can't picture anything on hoof being for sale up here for a while," I said. "The way this place is filling up, they'd be more apt to buy than sell."

"Exactly. I'm here to *sell,* this time," he said. "Thought I'd try to land a big contract with the army . . . feed the troops until the hostiles are rounded up, then feed the Indians, too."

"Thought all them kind of deals got handed down by congressmen over a few drinks at a fancy whorehouse."

"Well . . ." Roland Gaither stalled long enough to take a bite and swallow it. "Ordinarily that's probably true. But I figured with the expedition forming up here, there'll be a lot of big brass. Thought this might be a good place to get to know some of the *right* people."

We just nodded, neither of us believing him. "Meanwhile," Gaither said, "Could I impose on you to lend me a mount until we reach Fort Lincoln? I could ride Foxfire, perhaps?"

I considered it for a second, then said, "I'll put you on the roan, and I'll ride the stallion. Foxfire might take some getting used to, and I wouldn't put anybody on Honest Bob—" I grinned. "—Except General Custer, that is."

"Much obliged, then." He stood up with his empty bowl and adjusted his tied-down holster on his hip. "How far is it over to Fort Lincoln?"

Jack and I stood up also. "Not too far, just over the river. But from here on everything's a week more or less, depending on what shape the river's in and how soon we can get ferried across it."

"I see." Roland Gaither reached for our bowls. "This is a whole new experience for me. Lucky I ran into you two." We handed him the bowls and watched as he turned and walked around the corner toward the door of the crowded saloon.

As soon as he was out of sight, I leaned near Jack and said, "What do you suppose? Think he really reads minds?"

Jack cut me off with a raised hand. He glanced at a dirty window behind us and turned me away from the building. "Look at me when you speak," he said, standing right in front of me.

"What are you, a schoolteacher now?" I chuckled and glanced around at the dirty window. Jack turned me back to him with a hand on my shoulder.

"Just do like I say in case he's watching." He glanced over my shoulder with a hand shielding his mouth.

"Well, Jack, I reckon if he reads minds he'll know what we're saying."

"Umm-um." Jack bowed his head, shaking it slowly. *"Please,* tell me you didn't believe that mind-reading crap. Sometimes I wonder about you. Maybe you *are* going into a phase."

I felt a little embarrassed. "It ain't that I believe it, it's just that he *did* know what we were saying back there. I reckon he might have some kind of—"

"He reads our faces, damn it!" Jack spoke through his gloved fingers close to my face. "Any idiot coulda figured that out."

I blinked a couple of times to let it sink in. "That's what I was gonna say . . . he just read our expressions and figured what we were talking about, is all."

He eyed me skeptically. "I'm glad you caught it right off." He turned with me, and both of us stared out at the street as we spoke, two men watching a great parade. "If this ole boy's a former detective, he knows a lot about reading people. We'll have to keep an eye on him till we find out what his game is."

"Why not just leave him here?"

"Because if he really is dogging us, I'd like to keep him close at hand, so we can reach out and swat him if we need to."

"If he's dogging us, he's going about it in a funny way." I scratched my jaw. "I'd hate to kill him then find out he really is a cattle buyer."

Jack grinned. "Then go find a cow and see if he buys it. Meantime, it won't hurt to have an extra gun with us, as long as he don't end up pointing it at us. Anywhere there's men on the move, there'll be some hard cases wanting to rob them." He grinned. "It's getting to where traveling ain't safe. So let's watch him close."

"Got ya," I said, still looking at the parade of man, mule, and manifest destiny passing before us. On the other side of the street a young man in a ragged bearskin coat sat on the edge of the boardwalk looking over at us. He wore a dirty blue bandanna tied around his head and held an eight-gauge fluted-barreled wad loader propped between his feet. His chin rested on the tip of the barrel. Dangerous, I thought. Then I looked away as he took note of me watching him and raised his head slightly.

When Roland Gaither came back around the corner of the saloon, he carried a bottle of rye in one hand and a cork in the other. Wind licked his long duster tails sideways as he offered the bottle to Jack. "Thought this might cut the dust some," he said.

Jack nodded. "Knock one back, then." And he watched as Gaither raised the bottle, took a drink, and let out a low hiss.

"There now," Gaither said, wiping his free hand across his mustache. Jack took the bottle, threw back a drink, and offered it to me. I passed on it, raising a hand, and went about untying Foxfire from the lead rope. Inside the saloon, the piano slowed into a peaceful ballad, but then a loud protest went up from the drinkers. The whole building shook, and in a second the madman was back, rattling like crazy in a shed full of empty cans.

Chapter

5

———◆———

Off toward the river . . .

When Roland Gaither and I finished making up our saddles, his on the Gypsy roan, mine on Foxfire, we left the stir and the whir of the crowed railhead and started off toward the banks of the Missouri to spend the night. Come morning we'd find passage across.

Now that we'd gotten up to the Dakota Territory, I felt a little better about everything. How hard could this really be? Cross the river, deliver the horse, rest a day, then rail on back to my place in Kentucky. Might even meet the general, us sitting there with our legs crossed, leaned back . . . *a good cigar, glass of bourbon.* Why not?

Time had passed quickly coming up here, shooting along the steel rails at speeds of up to twenty-five, sometimes *thirty* miles an hour. You couldn't beat that. And now that I thought about it, was it really hurting me, going a little out of my way to help a woman do something nice for her husband? I pictured Elizabeth Custer's blank innocent face as we heeled our horses forward.

"Pssst, hey, ole buddies," said a voice, and as the three of us turned our heads toward it, the young man in the bearskin coat came heeling his red mule up behind us. "Mind if I ride with yas to the river? You *are* going to the river . . . huh, aren't yas?" He spoke in a quick, sharp tone, his voice lowered, as if anything he said must be kept secret. A bandoleer full of thick, hand-twisted shotgun wads hung around his shoulder. I eyed the large fluted barrel of the eight-gauge hanging from his hand.

"Who are you?" I shot Jack and Roland Gaither a glance as I spoke. They reined down, turning their horses with mine.

He smiled—more like a tight nervous twitch. "Just passing through, same as you fellows." He shrugged, and the barrel of the shotgun waved upward a bit, sweeping across us. "Don't mind telling yas, though, it's best to travel in numbers around here. I've been hit once already, coming up." He gestured toward the south with his shotgun, again the fluted barrel swinging past us. I almost ducked. "A big outlaw Indian name of Rain in the Face and a couple of his boys—"

Cutting him off with a raised hand as the shotgun yawned right at my face, I said, "If you're gonna talk, I wish you'd do it with an empty hand."

"Huh?" He looked genuinely confused.

"That barn burner." I nodded toward the shotgun. "Stop pointing the damn thing at us. It's distracting as hell."

"Oh." He glanced at the eight-gauge as if he just realized he had it with him, then laid it across his lap. "Heck, it's not loaded, see." He cocked back the hammer and pulled the trigger. I flinched at the metal on metal click. Had it been loaded, I judged it would've cleared away a tar-paper shack and cut a drainage ditch halfway across the street.

"Who the hell are you, young man?" Jack stepped his horse closer.

"Name's Tommy, but everybody calls me Shotgun Tom. I've been waiting all day for somebody headed down to the banks. I've been moving about cautiously since they way-laid me the other day."

"I bet," I said, looking him up and down. His footwear was a pair of spent hobnail boots, one with a piece of wire wrapped around it to keep the sole from flapping. His trousers were threadbare in both knees. Gnats swarmed at one shoulder of his bearskin coat. One landed on his lip and he spit it away.

"Yeah." He nodded. "I'm as bold as the next, but three on one? I tell yas, I ran until I dropped. Left my spindle, my pick, and shovel . . . everything I had." He swung an arm as if pushing something away. "Go on, take it, it's yours! Then I got out of there. You blame me?"

We shook our heads as he heeled alongside us, still talking as we turned our horses and continued on. "Figured if somebody came along I'd ride with them down to the river . . . if not, I'd just sit right there until hell turned to a hiccup, see what I'm saying here?"

"Sure," I said, grinning, glancing at Jack and Gaither. Jack rolled his eyes upward and looked away. Gaither looked at Shotgun Tom the same way he must've looked at a thousand other down-and-out drifters during his days as a peace officer. "You can ride along with us, but keep that wad loader down while you're talking."

"I will, you bet." He looked around me at Jack and Gaither. "I guess yas got yaselves plenty to eat back there, huh?"

"You hungry, Shotgun Tom?" I asked without looking at him. "If you are, there's some jerked beef in my saddle-bags."

"To tell yas the truth . . . I *could* eat."

I heard his belly growl just thinking about it, and I reached back as we rode, fished out the jerked beef, and pitched it to him.

He snapped it out of the air and tore off a bite in one motion. "Thanks," he grunted, chewing the hard beef like a starved wolf; by the time we'd reached the banks of the Missouri, he'd downed that chunk of jerky and the other two I'd carried since we'd left New Orleans.

It hadn't been long since the river had been out of its banks, so when we got there, we stayed back above a shoring of tangled driftwood, and made a low campfire among swirls of limp wild grass where the ground was solid but still soft to the boot heel.

Darkness had set in beneath a thin quarter moon by the time we boiled coffee and made a line for our horses between a maple stump and a willow tree just outside the small circle of firelight. North of us in the distance along the riverbank, other campfires glowed in the night where travelers like ourselves would rise up at the first streak of gray dawn and gather at the steamboat crossing. South of us, blackness lay like a bottomless pool beneath an endless sheen of starlight.

Shotgun Tom kept his red mule right beside him and tied his reins to the clump of wild grass where we pitched our saddles and bedrolls near the fire. "I imagine the farther west ya go, the darker it gets, huh?" He looked around at the wide night.

We looked at one another without answering. Even with the army running patrols, we agreed to each of us standing a two-hour watch throughout the night, and between Jack and me it went without saying that regardless which of the other men were on watch, one of us would stay awake and keep an eye on things. We didn't know either of these men. While there was safety in numbers, *two* was the only number we knew we could count on.

After a silence passed, Shotgun Tom said, "So, what about you fellows?" He gulped hot coffee without letting it cool first. I winced at the sight of it. "Yas don't look like prospectors and that." He darted a glance at each of us, holding the tin cup with both hands, the wad loader across his lap.

"Cattle buyer," Roland Gaither said grudgingly, as if it bothered him to answer at all. He hadn't seem overjoyed at the young man joining us, and hadn't spoken a half-dozen to him during the ride. I figured it was because he'd cracked a blackjack over too many heads resembling Shotgun Tom's.

"I'm a horse dealer," I said, leaning back against my saddle with my coffee steaming in the night air. Jack studied the low flame of the campfire, stirring it with a stick, and offered no answer at all.

"Businessmen, huh?" Shotgun Tom sniffed and ran a hand under his nose. "That's me, too, once I strike it big, you know. Mostly I've only played baseball until now. But I tell yas, if a man ever strikes—"

Gaither had stirred forward as Tom spoke, staring at him with a bemused expression. Now he cut him off, saying, "Stovine? Tommy Stovine?"

"Yeah, that's me, used to be, I should say." He shrugged

and went on talking. "—a good vein of gold, it's *Katie bar the door* from then on." He slid a hand through the air. "I'm talking stocks, bonds, investments, and that. Shoooot, I'll know how to handle big money once I get it. It's the *getting* it that's taking up all my time."

Gaither had moved forward slowly, as if in awe, getting a better look at Shotgun Tom's face in the flicker of firelight. Jack and I glanced at each other, then watched Gaither rise halfway to his feet. "My God, man! You really are! You're *Fastball Tommy Stovine!*"

Shotgun Tom cut him a dark glance. "Say, now, mister . . . I don't go by that name anymore. Now that I'm on the frontier, I prefer *Shotgun* Tom."

Gaither didn't seem to hear, pointing a finger as he moved closer. "The Louisville Grays, eighteen seventy-three? Grays against the Red Stockings? You're pitching to a big Irish galloot, Spay Nelligan?" He slapped his hands together. "Man, what a game!" His voice rang along the riverbank.

Jack ducked his head slightly. "Jesus, Gateholder, keep it down. We might have Indians prowling around out here."

"Oh, sorry." Gaither looked embarrassed and leaned back, adjusting his forty-four on his hip. Then no sooner had he settled, he snapped forward again. "But do you men realize who this is? It's *Fast-ball Tommy Stovine.*"

"I told you, I don't use that name, Mr. Gateholder," Shotgun Tom said. Something white hot flashed in his eyes. His thumb slipped over the hammer on the eight-gauge and tightened there. *Had he loaded that thing . . . ?*

"Okaaaay," I said in a soothing tone, "let's all settle in here. We'll call each other what we want to be called. Nothing to get upset about, right?" I glanced from one to the other of them. Gaither evidently saw the same look I'd seen in Tom's eyes and it froze him in place, his hand near the tied down holster. *"Right, gentlemen?"* I raised my voice a notch, wondering if he'd loaded that shotgun, and if so, how prone was he to dropping a load on a man for miscalling his name.

I glanced at Jack for support, but now he'd leaned forward himself with a curious expression and a raised finger, and he said in a hushed tone: "Knickerbockers, eighteen seventy-one? I read all about it. Heard you knocked the cover plumb off the ball!"

Shotgun Tom looked down smiling. "I wouldn't say I knocked the cover off it . . . but I *might* have." His thumb dropped from across the hammer, then his hand left the shotgun and drifted back up, joining his other around the coffee cup. "They hung that bat up and wouldn't let nobody else use it for the rest of the year. Then somebody stole it or something . . ."

Shit. I leaned back against my saddle and flipped the edge of my blanket over my legs as Shotgun Tom went on. Gaither stooped back down with his hands on his thighs, hanging on Tom's words. Jack leaned forward, grinning, his eyes widened like a kid's at a carnival. *Baseball* . . .

Through a veil of sleep I heard, as he rattled on, the roar of a crowd and the crack of a bat, somewhere high above the banks of the muddy Missouri. At one point, I saw Shotgun Tom standing out there somewhere, wearing a baggy baseball uniform. He stood slightly crouched, leaning forward, one hand behind him resting on his hip, turning a baseball back and forth. He stared straight ahead toward home plate like an eagle studying distant prey.

Then Gaither's voice sliced into my sleep, saying, "So what? Doesn't every good ballplayer carry a flask of whiskey or something during a game?"

"Yeah," Tom answered, "but the Baseball Player's Association decided to clean things up, and I was an easy target. Besides, I wouldn't cooperate with the owners when it came to throwing a game. They hate that, you know."

His voice faded as I slipped farther back inside the dark tunnel of sleep, and somewhere deep in the night as black faded to gray and the flame of the fire turned to glowing embers, I heard the low nicker of Jack's silver gray, followed by that of my Gypsy roan.

"Come on, wake up," Jack said in a lowered voice, shaking me back and forth by my shoulder. "They've got our horses."

What? I rolled to my feet, blinking sleep from my eyes in

the gray dawn. My hand snatched the forty-four from my holster. Across the fire, Shotgun Tom stirred and rose to his knees, the wad loader in his hand. "Where's Gaither?" I spoke in a whisper, hearing a thrashing sound in the wild grass a few feet past where we'd tied the horses.

"Dead probably," Jack said, stepping back, crouched, his pistol out and scanning the swirls of grass. "He stepped over to check the horses ten, fifteen minutes ago. Ain't came back."

Shotgun Tom rose up quietly and backed around the campfire toward me. "It's him. It's Rain in the Face! You can bet on it."

"Easy," I whispered. "Stay with us."

We crept over the few feet between the camp and where the horses had been, and Jack leaned down, pressing his fingers to the ground, squinting off into the parted grass. "It ain't Indians," he whispered. "They don't leave this much to track."

I spun toward a thrashing sound and saw the Gypsy roan raise his muzzle and blow at us through the morning mist. "You're right. Indians would've gotten them all . . . us, too." I looked all around as I moved over to the roan and took up the dangling reins, looking him over while he scraped his hoof in the grass. Maybe they'd thought the roan wasn't worth stealing. "Where the hell is Gaither? If he's dead, where's his body?"

"I don't know," Jack said, stepping over past me into the grass, searching all around for his silver gray. He shot me a glance that said he was thinking the same as me. Maybe Gaither had stolen the horses. *Why?*

"Whoever got them, they haven't been gone long. Let's get to it. I'll get after them on the roan. You and Tommie swap out the mule and follow my tracks."

I led the roan over as Jack jerked my saddle up from the ground. "Don't do something foolish when you catch up to them," he said, tossing the saddle on the roan's back. "Just pin them down with your rifle until we get there, okay?"

I didn't answer. He grabbed me by the arm and said: "Okay? Wait for us? Don't go charging in and get yourself shot."

"I'll try," I said, rounding my arm loose. "Just keep to my tracks and listen for rifle fire." Reaching under the roan, I grabbed the cinch and made it, tightened it, and stepped back. "If they get across the river we're sunk. I wouldn't trust this roan to cross it, and you wouldn't have a prayer on that mule." The roan shook out his mane and scraped his hoof.

Tom said behind me, "If it's Rain in the Face, he'll kill us whichever side of the river we're on."

I said over my shoulder, "Don't get yourself overimpressed, Tom. There's been people trying to kill us all our lives . . . most of them's dead. Get your mule ready and stay on my tracks." I offered a tight smile, hoping it would calm his apprehension. "This shouldn't take more than a couple hours." I looked at Jack.

"I could go," Jack said. "They took my silver gray, after all. You and Tom could follow *me* and—"

"Forget it," I said. "I'll take care of it. You oughta know that."

"I know. I'm just thinking about your *phase* here."

"Forget my *phase*, too." I stepped into the stirrup and swung up. "I ain't letting go of that racing stallion, phase or no phase." It flashed across my mind: *what about Honest Bob?* I pictured Elizabeth Custer's face, drawn and saddened as I stood before her telling how I'd lost her husband's brand-new horse. *Jesus.* "Catch up to me as soon as you can. If not, I'll meet you at Fort Lincoln."

He grabbed the roan by the bridle, stopping me from turning toward the tall grass. "Don't go shooting it out with them. You know you ain't much when it comes to shootouts."

"Thanks, Jack." I paused for a second, let out a breath, and swatted a hand at the sweat bee as it whined past my nose. "I won't *shoot it out,* if I can keep from it. But if I can, I'll slip in and steal 'em back." I jiggled the reins to get him to turn them loose, but he hesitated.

"Damn, I hate doing it like this," he said, looking up at me.

"Jack. Time's slipping here. I'll steal them back." I jerked a little harder on the reins and the roan threw his head back

Ralph W. Cotton

and forth against Jack's grip. "Maybe there's lots of things I *ain't much at,*" I said with a cool stare, "but is there any better horse thief than me?"

"Sorry," he said, letting his hand slip from the roan's bridle and stepping back. "Good luck, amigo."

I turned the roan toward the break in the wild grass and tapped my boot heels to him. "Did he say *'horse thief?'*" Tom asked Jack as I rode away.

"Yeah," Jack said. "But it's just a figure of speech."

Chapter
6

Nobody steals my horses. . . .

Roland Gaither might be a lot of things, but surely a horse thief wasn't one of them, I thought, slipping quickly through the tall grass on the Gypsy roan. It bothered me having to leave Jack trailing along behind, but there was nothing else to do if we wanted our horses back. Keeping a close watch all around me for any sign of Indians, I followed the fresh part in the grass until it ran out into a stretch of shale and dirt higher up, a mile above the riverbank.

Whoever they were, they weren't headed for the other side of the river, and judging the fresh hoofprints in the soft ground, they couldn't be more than a few miles ahead. Probably not even worried about being followed, I thought, figuring the roan had just strayed off somewhere when they turned him loose. *Not worth stealing?* I tapped my heels to him and he bolted forward, breaking sideways into a fast canter for a second, then straightening out into a fast, steady clip. He seemed to like it out here, cutting across open ground with the wind in his mane.

We held a fast pace for another mile or so, the roan running low and quietly as if knowing the business at hand. When I'd stopped for a second and leaned down to study the prints, the sound of a horse spluttering its lips in a nearby stretch of cottonwoods caused me freeze there against the roan's side. With no coaxing from me, he turned in place, slow and silent, until his whole body stood between me and the stand of trees. *Good horse.* I wanted to whisper to him but dared not. Then, after a few more anxious seconds, I slipped down and belly crawled away from him.

No Indians would've allowed a horse of theirs to make a sound if they lay in wait to ambush me. And if it was a horse they'd just stolen, they would have led it farther away rather than take a chance on something like that happening. *Who then? Gaither?*

From behind the shelter of a cottonwood deadfall I waited until I heard the sound again, followed by the clop of hoofs coming slowly toward me. As the sound came closer, I peeped carefully around the log at ground level and saw the hoofs of Jack's silver gray stop and mill in place. He perked his ears as I stood up slowly, gazing all around. Nothing else stirred in the still morning air.

"Easy, boy." Holding out my hand to him, I coaxed him closer until I caught hold of his reins, then we sidled over to the roan, where I crouched between the horses, using them both now for cover. But after waiting a few minutes, hearing nothing, seeing nothing, I slipped up onto the roan and gigged him back along the fresh set of tracks, leading Jack's silver gray behind me.

One down, two to go, I thought, knowing now that *no* Sioux or Cheyenne warriors in their right mind would have let the big gelding get away from them. *Unless they're setting a trap!* "Whoa!" I sat back hard on the reins, pulling the roan up so sharply Jack's silver gray got past me for a second.

The horses turned in a tight circle as my eyes scouted every possible drop, draw, or blind of cover around me. It crossed my mind to turn back now that I had Jack's silver gray in hand, but I didn't want to break away from a warm trail and take a chance on losing them by the time Jack and I came back.

My advantages were considerable here, if this wasn't some kind of Indian trick. Whoever had the horses wasn't as good a horse thief as me or he'd never have lost the silver gray. Wherever he was headed, he'd have a hard time shaking me. I had a good lead on a fresh set of tracks, plenty of ammunition, and now a couple of good horses I knew I could rely on. This wasn't the time to give up the chase, not even for a minute. *Naw, sir, push ahead . . . dog them till they drop.*

But just as I gigged the roan forward again, the sound of rifle and pistol fire resounded in the distance, causing me to turn the horses and duck low should a bullet come whistling in. None came. I listened to the steady pop of gunfire long enough to realize that somewhere ahead a battle was under way, and somewhere on one side or the other of that gun battle stood Honest Bob and my racing stallion—there wasn't a doubt in my mind.

Shoving the roan forward, we rode fast, swinging up wide around the sound of the rifle fire farthest from the river. Whichever side had my horses, I wanted to keep them between me and the river, close them off, and with any luck at all, hold them down with my rifle until Jack caught up to me. If that failed, my only other hope was to charge in as the last shot fired, get the horses, and run like hell. The gunfight might be just the break I needed.

The firing lulled by the time I got around it and closed in. The sound of an Indian yipping like a coyote came up from the river bank as I rode up and down across the rolling pitch of the land, batting my heels against the roan, pushing hard, my rifle arched out to the side. Topping a rise, the river came into view a hundred yards ahead, early sunlight glittering on the brown muddy water.

Halfway to the middle, three riders bounded up and down in the swift current, their horses drifting sideways toward the other bank, pulling Honest Bob and Foxfire along behind them. *Damn!* I pushed harder, watching the current carry them farther and farther away.

"Beatty, thank God it's you! Help me," said Roland Gaither's voice from behind a large rock as I shot past it and slid the roan down to a halt. As both horses rocked down on their haunches, I slipped back off the roan's rump. Coming into a kneeled firing position, I glanced quickly at Roland Gaither and saw his pistol out at arm's length, covering a man six feet away. His other hand pressed against a circle of blood on his side.

"No, don't do it," the man said. "Please, don't—" But his voice was cut short by a blast of Gaither's forty-four as I sighted out on the riders drifting farther away. Laying slightly off on the upstream side of their mounts, they seemed to slip through a world of sunlight on broken glass, and I had to blink to clear my eyes before I squeezed off the first round and watched the middle rider melt off his horse's side and sink down into the churning current. In front of him, the other Indian stiffened and swayed along his horse's side but then righted himself and hung on, leading my horses behind him.

"Fine shot," Roland Gaither said beside me, his voice sounding weak.

"No, it was terrible." I squinted around at him, jacking another round up in the chamber. "I aimed for the one leading the horses." Whether he knew it or not, Roland *Gateholder* had some tall explaining waiting ahead of him. But I wouldn't say anything now, not with him and his pistol so near me, not while I needed to knock out that Indian who was leading my horses off to God knew where.

I honed in, holding my breath, tracking him downstream in my sights, my sights rising and falling with him, catching the thrust and sway of the river—*steady now*—squeezing on the trigger with the sight leveled on the center of his back. *That's it,* right between the two long braids whipping back and forth like snakes. *No! Wait!* The two-horse string drifted in my sights just as my finger squeezed the trigger and I jerked the rifle away as the shot exploded.

"Damn it to hell!" I lowered the rifle and rubbed my watering eyes. I couldn't risk another try, not with the rough swells of current and the glare of the morning sun. If it came right down to it, I'd rather *anybody* have Foxfire than see him sink like a stone in a spread of bloody water.

"He's gone," Gaither said beside me as I let go a deep breath and shook my head. "We'll never see that racehorse again." He stood silent for a second, then added, "Or Honest Bob either, for that matter."

I looked at him, saw his pistol hanging from his hand near me, and I snatched it from him before he could stop me. "What the hell?" He staggered back a step with his hand still pressed to his bloody side, his fingers red with it.

"What was that for, Beatty?" His voice sounded steady but strained.

"You're wounded," I said. "What good is this to you?" I shoved his pistol down in my belt, stepped forward, eased him down against the rock, and tore open his shirt to see the wound. *A simple flesh wound, in and out, clean, right above the hipbone.* No problem, I thought. But then I looked deep in his eyes and said in a lowered tone, "Yep, you're dead here. Looks like an hour, maybe two at the most . . ." I pressed my fingertips against the wound to stay the bleeding as I jerked the bandanna from around my neck. "Sorry, Gaither. Anything you feel like saying before it gets too late?"

"Get the hell away from me!" He shoved me back, snatching the bandanna from my hand and dabbing it against the wound, examining it. "Do I look like an idiot to you? What are you two doing? Seeing if I had something to do with stealing your horses? For Christ sake, man, I used to be a policeman. I risked my life coming after them for you."

"Yeah? Well why didn't you say something while they were *getting* stolen? You could've woke us up!"

"Sure I could've . . . and gotten us all killed! *'Yoo-hoo, fellows, guess what? Got some Indians in the grass here,'"* he said in a mock voice. "That would've been *real* smart. What would you have done?"

I bite my lip for a second, not sure what to make of it, not having time even to think about it. Across the river the two riders closed in on the far bank, my two horses getting farther away from me by the second. "Forget it then." I stood, glancing across at the endless rolling land full of countless places a man could hide a couple of horses for the next hundred years. "Can you ride?"

"Yes," he said, struggling to his feet as I reached a hand down to help him. "But I've never swum a river like *this* before."

"Good, because you're not starting today. Take the silver gray and head back for Bismarck. My friend'll be along the trail. Tell him to follow me. You and Tom head back on the mule. If you pass a homesteader or two on the way, they'll patch you up and help ya."

"Huh-uh," he shook his head. "Not on your life. I'm

going with you. You're not leaving here thinking I might have had something to do with this." He pointed a bloody finger at me, limping over to the silver gray. "I'll hear your apology when this matter is settled."

"What you'll hear is my partner busting a forty-four cap on your ass when you have to tell him you got out there and drowned his horse. Now do like you're told! He'll need his horse to catch up to me. I figure they're either headed to the Black Hills or the badlands . . . either one's a good three-hundred-mile ride or more."

"I'm through arguing with you, Beatty. Give me my gun and let's go." He took a short step toward me, then froze when I drew his pistol from my belt, cocked it, and pointed it at him.

"I'm through arguing, too, Gateholder. Now get your ass on that horse. There's no time for this."

"Shiiit." He looked away and spit. "All right, I'll head back. But this is no way to treat a person who's only tried to help."

"You *ain't* helping unless you do like you're told." Across the river my two-horse string climbed out of the water shaking themselves off, their noses pulled forward by the Indian at the end of their lead rope. "Now get out of here." I glared at him, jiggling the pistol barrel toward Jack's silver gray.

"Go to hell, then, Beatty." Gaither struggled up the side of the bareback silver gray. I watched until he rode off a few yards, then I stepped up into my saddle, shoved my rifle down in its scabbard, snapped the safety strap around it, and kicked the Gypsy roan forward, down toward the water's edge.

Life ain't meant to be *this* hard, I remember thinking, looking out, down at the swirl of current. The sweat bee circled in and whined near my ear until I slapped it away and backed the roan a few feet up the rise of the bluff. The horse shook and wrung his head, blowing a deep breath as if loosening up for what lay ahead. So far this horse hadn't shied from anything. I rubbed him along his neck and stuck my hat inside my shirt. Across the river a thin strip of dust rose up in the distance—my horses growing farther and farther away.

Here goes— As soon as the reins slacked forward, the roan shot forward in a hard sprint without a tap from my spurs. Then his body arched into a lunge, his hoofs turning silent beneath me as I braced forward, low, and we sailed out off the bluff twenty feet above the muddy Missouri. For a second that seemed like forever, we flew out and down, down to the thrashing current, the roan's hoofs stretching out, pawing in midair.

Then the water slapped shut around us like a cold hand as I took a quick bite of air and held it, and we swept sideways in the undercurrent, the roan struggling upward toward the surface, me clinging to him, the reins slack but still in my hand. The trick to withstanding the current would be to keep the horse's head slightly upstream against it. If the roan turned downstream with the hard current, we'd go under.

So when we surfaced, I let go of my breath and drew the reins high and upstream. But only for a precious second to get the horse righted, then I gave him the lead, keeping the slightest tension on the upstream rein, letting him work it out for both of us. Slipping my weight half off him on the upstream side, the same as the Indian had done only moments before, I clung to the roan's side, not too far down, lest my weight cause his hoofs to be swept from under him. From now on it was up to the horse. I could only coax him, keep him pointed, and hope he wouldn't spend himself out.

Like the riders before us, we rose and fell, drifting downstream three yards for every yard we gained toward the far bank. A high swirl of water rose up beneath us, surrounding us with the sucking pull of a whirlpool. Behind us, the sound of a pistol exploded from the bank, and I turned for only a second, just long enough to see Gaither waving his arms. *What the . . . ?*

Beside him now stood two old men, both of them jumping up and down, waving their arms and calling out words I couldn't hear above the sound of the water. One of them waved a long pistol and pointed his other hand upstream. As I turned back away from them, I caught sight of something up there fifty yards away, bobbing and swaying at the bank. *A cargo barge? "Son of a bitch!"* I yelled aloud out there, struggling across the big Missouri, and I glanced back once just to make sure I'd truly seen it.

Gaither and the two men moved along the bank toward the barge, pointing and calling out to me. Water lapped up in my face. I spit it away. *What do they think? That I can turn around and come back?* Below the surface, the water tugged at my boot well until I felt my boot give way and leave my foot.

Water swept over me again, but I held on to the roan's mane and tightened my knee across the saddle. Once, a rolling pile of driftwood swirled in, brushed against my leg, and nearly snagged me. Somehow the roan steered clear of it and moved on, never giving in to the constant draw of the whirlpools or the crushing grasp of the current.

I spit water and gazed up at the sky for a second. *Why me?* The other two hadn't had this many problems. There'd been no whirlpools full of driftwood come along to engulf *them!*

Finally the bank swayed before us, dropped out of sight behind a swell of brown water for a second, then reappeared. Cold seeped deep inside me, grasping my stomach like icy fingers. But the Gypsy roan never faltered. He pressed through the cold muddy water with a strong, steady rhythm until I felt his hoofs scrape rock beneath me. He struggled to take hold as the river swept us sideways along the bank.

Closer to the bank, I forced myself back up on the roan and searched for a place to climb up. *They hadn't had this much trouble . . . naw, sir!*

We slipped along quickly, bobbing up and down, going deeper and staying under longer with each plunge, until all at once I felt the horse jolt to a sudden stop beneath me. His hoofs took solid purchase just as I strangled on a mouthful of water thick with mud. I gagged and slumped down his side the second he stepped up from the deep water into the shallows.

"Good boy," I said, choking, coughing, dropping the rest of the way off his back, and shielding my face as he shook himself off. How the hell had they done it so slick and easy, those two. They'd slipped out of the water farther up by a good fifty yards. Now they'd gained a good half hour on me by the time I rode upstream and picked up their tracks. And what the hell was Gaither doing, coming on over here?

I slung water from my hair and wobbled on one bare foot, the toe of my sock wagging in the shallow drift like a fool's tongue. Halfway back across the river I watched the large cargo barge rise and fall, moving ever closer as Gaither stood holding one hand on the side rail, steadying Jack's silver gray with his other.

Chapter

7

———◆———

After a cold swim . . .

I'd walked upstream, found the tracks, and stood there wet and cold, *shivering* mad, watching the big wooden barge bump against the bank almost exactly on the spot where the hoofprints came up from the water. "Lord have mercy, boy," said one of the ragged river men, looking me up and down as he jumped off the raft with a coil of hemp rope on his thick shoulder. "You oughta see your face. It's blue as a baboon's backside! Be lucky you don't catch your death, jumping in the Missouri this time of year. The hell's wrong with you?"

"Never mind me," I said through a tight jaw, staring past him straight at Roland Gaither from beneath my sagging wet hat brim. "Thought you were heading back like I told ya. How'd you know there was a ferry barge there, Gateholder?" My voice was a low rasp. He took note of my hand on my pistol butt.

"Hold it, Beatty. Don't even *let* yourself think I knew anything about a raft being there. I wasn't about to leave you alone over here, no matter what our differences are." He pointed a finger. "But I can only take so much of this low-handed suspicion of yours before I—"

"Here now! Here now!" The other boatman stepped up

from the keel and between the two of us, looking over at me on the bank. I'd unwrapped my riding duster and put it on while waiting for them to cross. It still dripped on my boot toe and my bare foot.

"What's going on here?" The one who'd jumped off with the line quickly spun it around a rock and stepped over in front of me.

I looked past him at Gaither. "How *did* you know? Old habits? Another *trick* of your trade? Or some more of your *mind reading?* Because if you really can read minds, you better take a quick look at mine right now." I started to jerk the pistol from my shoulder harness, but the boatman jumped in front of me.

"Are you *crazy,* mister? How the hell could he known we'd be here? Me and Ed don't know ourselves, one day to the next. We heard shots, came running, saw him trying to keep you from *drowning* yourself, I reckon . . . and we brung him over. Now that's the whole of it."

I stared into the old man's eyes. "It's the damn truth," he added. "Me and Ed here hop back and forth all the way from Bismarck to Fort Rice, then haul back up by mule team. We got no gist of where we'll land every time. We's only trying to do what was right here. Man said Indians skinned ya for ya horse. Damn lucky you're both alive, is what."

I eased my hand, nodding at the old boatman. "You're right. Thanks for your help. I'd appreciate it if you go back and bring over two men and a red mule. They'll be along in an hour or so." Then I looked back at Roland Gaither, saw him take out his pipe and pack it with his thumb. He stared back at me, raised it to his lips, and lit it while the raft swayed gently beneath him. "Now that I see you're dry, warm, and comfortable," I said with a sharp edge to my voice, "I'll just be getting on my way here . . . *by myself.*"

"Don't worry. We'll go back, pole up the other bank, and wait fer 'em," one of the men called out while I turned and walked my roan up the bank, following the tracks left by the two horse thieves and my two-horse string.

"Thanks," I called back over my shoulder, and in a second I heard a loading plank hit the rocky bank and heard the hoofs of Jack's silver gray step down it.

"Beatty, I'm with you on this whether you like it or not," he called out, catching up with me as I walked up the bank, favoring my bare foot on the rocky soil. "They'll bring the others over. Meanwhile, we'll run down the horses. What's so wrong with that?"

I slowed down just enough to let him fall in beside me. Then I asked without turning toward him, "Why'd you shoot him?"

"What? Shoot who? *Oh,* back there?" He nodded back across the river as we topped the bank, leading our horses. "Because he shot me." He shrugged. "There's another dead man back there. I shot him for *shooting* at me. Does that make sense to you?"

"I don't know. Something about this whole morning don't seem right to me," I said. "Seems to me you've got more twists and turns than an Arkansas road map."

He stopped in his tracks and said as I turned facing him, "Look, Beatty, for some reason you and I haven't exactly hit it off. Maybe it's my past occupation, maybe it's the way I talk . . . hell, maybe it's the way I part my hair, I don't know. But I told you I'm sticking until we get those horses back, and I intend to do it. In the meantime, the best thing we can do is put our differences away and do what needs doing."

"They're put away for now," I said, turning and stepping up to the crest of the riverbank. Before us lay rise after rise as the land rolled away to the end of vision. I looked down at the fresh tracks, then out before us, and let out a breath.

"Ready when you are," he said beside me, the sound of saddle leather creaking as he stepped up into it.

I looked around at him. "Where'd the saddle come from?"

"They lent it to me. Said it'd been lying around on the raft, doing nobody any good."

"Lent it to you, just like that?" I snapped my fingers and swung up on the roan.

"That's right, just like that. Care to go back and ask them about it?"

I grinned a wry grin, adjusting my reins, nodding toward the open land ahead. "You'll have to keep up with me out there. Ever rode this kind of plains before?"

"No, but how'd I do on my first river crossing?" He chuckled and gigged the silver gray along beside me.

"This ain't no Sunday outing," I said. "Think you can handle it? With a bloody side?"

"It's just a graze. Where do you think they get detectives from in Louisville, Madam Wanda's Charm School?" He snatched up the silver gray's reins and flagged his fingers at me. "Now give me back my pistol and let's get going."

I hesitated, then drew his pistol from my belt and pitched it to him. "Don't make the mistake of pointing that iron at me."

He caught it and checked it, shaking his head. "You remind me of some of the hard cases I dealt with back in Louisville, always thinking somebody's out to get them, suspicious, distrustful. It'd be easy to think you've run afoul of the law somewhere, Beatty." He pushed up his hat brim and stared at me.

I stared right back. "Think what you want to think . . . just don't let your thoughts get the better of ya."

In minutes we'd closed back in on their trail, our horses stretched into a good steady clip. If we could hold this kind of pace we'd soon ride them into the ground. I knew Jack's silver gray could do it; what about this Gypsy roan? Ahead we caught a glimpse of the riders topping a rise and disappearing down the other side.

"Will they try to ambush us?" Gaither called out, pulling the silver gray in close beside me.

"No," I called back to him. "Not if we can keep them hard-pressed. There's two of them and two of us. They'll try to stay ahead of these rifles, unless they meet up with others somewhere."

"What if they do?" He looked concerned.

"Then they will *stop* and make a stand." I looked at him riding beside me. "But that's when we'll take my horses back. Simple enough?"

He didn't answer as I slapped the reins to the Gypsy roan. The silver gray fell back a bit, blowing hard as the roan surged forward. *Does this horse ever get tired?* Its pace picked up as if he'd been waiting for me to ask more of him, and we pressed on hard and steady, headed up a long stretch of grassland with the morning sun turning warm on my back.

It was nearly noon before we stopped. When we did, we slipped down from the horses and eased forward on foot to the edge of a coulee where the hoofprints dropped off. Five yards back from a narrow gully the hoofprints had started turning as the riders prepared to slide the horses sideways down the six-foot muddy wall. They knew this coulee was here, I thought, glancing all around. They were ready for it. I crouched down and stepped close enough to peep over the edge and down at the three or four inches of water six feet below us. Mud still swirled where their horses had stirred it up only moments earlier.

"What do you think?" Gaither asked in a hushed tone behind me, holding the horses.

I eased back a couple of steps and turned to him. "We're close. They're worried about us." I stooped down, took off my hat, and wiped my hand across my brow. "Bend down here with me a few minutes," I added, looking up at him as I took my reins from him.

"Why?" He caught the caution in my eyes, and asked as he stooped down beside me, "Shouldn't we keep on them if we're this close?"

I nodded toward the edge of the narrow coulee and let my eyes trace it off to our right, in the direction they'd taken. "If there's a turn somewhere over there, they'll be standing up on their horses' backs right now, sighting their pistols on us from ground level."

"I see." He stooped down closer to the ground. "Now what? We're stuck here?"

"Nope. We just wait a few minutes to show 'em we ain't easy. They'll get the message and start getting restless. Then we'll flank this coulee and force them to either fight or make a run for it."

"And if they fight?"

"That's what I'm hoping for. We can't dog them forever. They've done their horses in, but ours are starting to falter, too." I let out a breath, pushed up my hat brim, and tried to relax for a minute. "We're about to wrap things up here, I'm thinking. They ain't moving or we'd hear them splashing through the water."

He stared at me with a bemused look in his eyes. "You sound awfully cocksure of yourself."

I shrugged. "It ain't the first time I've run down stolen horses. It generally works about the same way each time. The *hunter* always has the advantage, as long as he keeps the *hunted* in sight, and at arm's length. This ain't the time to go charging in. This is time to let 'em wonder awhile."

"I'm impressed," he said, taking out his pistol, checking it. "Where did you learn all this?"

I smiled, not about to admit that most of this I'd learned the hard way while being on the other end of the chase. "Horse dealing ain't just about grooming mane and slapping rumps. There's times when ya actually have to work at it."

I looked up at our horses and took stock of them. They were both lathered and blowing hard, but the silver gray much more so than the Gypsy roan. I noticed that while the silver gray milled in place, the roan stood still as marble and hardly made a sound except for the deep rush of air in and out of his lungs.

"Sit tight," I said to Gaither, then slipping back to my saddlebags, took down a set of rope hobbles and slipped back with them. He watched me hobble the horse's front hoofs and turn back to him checking my rifle. "If we find them waiting in there, I'll slip across the coulee and get behind them. You wait until you hear me fire, then hit them from this side . . . got it?"

He nodded and gripped his rifle barrel with both hands.

"Okay. Now we go to work. Follow me."

"Wait." He took hold of my forearm. "Were you once an Indian fighter? Is that it?"

"No." I rounded my forearm free. "Some of my best friends are Indians. Are you coming?" I turned away shaking my head.

We belly crawled along, a few yards back from the edge of the coulee, keeping our horses in sight but no longer hearing their heavy breathing. Then we lay flat in the cover of grass, our ears turned toward the slightest sound of man or beast there in the stillness. After several minutes had passed there came a faint sound of a hoof clicking against rock off to our right. I looked at Gaither and nodded toward it.

In a few seconds the sound came again. This time his eyes told me he'd heard it, too, and we struck out toward it, belly crawling to the crest of a rise that looked down on a wide turn in the coulee twenty yards below us. There, barely visible through the grass, we saw a dirty hat move at ground level and the glint of sunlight on a pistol barrel. A few feet away from that man, we saw another pistol barrel move and disappear.

I looked at Gaither and winked, feeling a little smug about being right. They were there all right, just as I'd predicted, standing on their horses' backs, peeping out over the edge, wondering where we'd gone and why we hadn't came charging along the coulee toward them. They'd soon find out.

Leaving Gaither there, I backed away, turned, and crawled back until I passed the a turn in the coulee—the spot where we would've been riding into their pistol fire— and I slipped over the edge there, crossed the six-foot width of it, and slipped up the other side as quiet as a snake. *So far, so good.* I lay there for a second, letting my mind catch up to my heartbeat, then crawled along the other side until I knew I was well behind them.

Before starting toward them with my pistol in one hand and my rifle stretched out before me, I glanced all around and happened to notice the twitch of a horse's ear at ground level a few yards away. *Whoa, now, who's this?* I lay still for another few seconds, then eased toward it, knowing that any minute things could get real tricky.

The two riders knew we were here. They wouldn't wait forever to see what we had in mind. If there were others hiding over there, Gaither and I would be suddenly out-numbered here on the open plains with two winded horses. These things I thought of as I inched closer to the flicker of the horse's ear until I found myself gazing down at Honest Bob and Foxfire hidden, down in a shallow basin, alone.

Okaaay! With no more than a quick glance over toward the edge of the coulee and a cautious glance around the rim of the narrow basin, I lifted myself in a crouch and moved fast, down between the two sweat-streaked horses, raising a hand to each of them, stroking and soothing, keeping them quiet as I unspun the lead rope from around a jut of rock and started to back them away. But then I stopped.

Lying there beside the rock was a leather braided lariat and a rolled-up doeskin shirt. Beside them lay a dirty canvas possibles bag dark-stained with fresh blood. I touched my finger to it and felt it was still damp. Had my rifle shot gone through the other Indian back at the river and wounded the one in front of him? Was that why the other had swayed and nearly fell from his mount? *Lucky shot.*

I *had* to take their belongings, just for the sake of my time and trouble. These two had thought so little of us as to leave their belongings lying back here, figuring we'd ride along that coulee and into their pistol fire. To hell with them, I thought, grinning to myself, scooping up the items and wadding them up under my arm—*teach them whose horses to steal.*

Above the basin, back out of sight in the tall grass, I turned the lariat into a one-rein harness on Foxfire and pitched the bag and shirt across him for a saddle. Slipping up on his back, I kept him at a quiet walk, leading Honest Bob until I knew we'd passed the turn in the coulee, then back a good twenty yards from the edge of it. "Hope you can jump," I whispered, rubbing Foxfire's shoulder. Glancing back at Honest Bob, I added, "You son of a bitch, if you don't go along with this, I'll leave you here and *hope* they eat ya." He stared at me wild-eyed, sawing his head up and down, leaning back against the lead rope.

Here goes . . . I braced, took a breath, and slapped my boot heel and bare foot to Foxfire's sides. He shot out like a comet, snapping me back for the split second it took Honest Bob to realize he had to either come along or get his head yanked off.

I heard a voice call out from down the coulee at the sound of my horse's hooves, but I let out a loud yell, kicking toward the edge, and felt Foxfire lunge up and over it, my arm back holding the lead rope, feeling Honest Bob go up with us. Midair, I turned the lead rope loose and rocked forward and back as Foxfire's hooves touched ground. My hat blew away as we raced up alongside Honest Bob. I snatched the end of the lead rope whipping up and down beside him, and had just started to turn both horses toward Gaither when I saw him stand up with his pistol pointed at me from twenty yards away.

"It's me!" I shouted, but not in time to keep him from pulling a round that whistled past my head. Behind him, from the coulee, I heard more shouts. Gaither ducked down to his knees but fired another shot at me as I yelled at the top of my lungs, "It's me! Damn it to hell—" The bullet grazed my shirtsleeve. I flinched, circling both horses. "—You're shooting at me here, *damn it!*"

Now bullets whistled past him from the coulee and past me as I ducked and kicked the horses out wide of him. There I dropped with my rifle out and fired past him, trying to offer him some cover. But he jumped up from throwing the hobbles off the horses and fired another round at me as he pulled them away. *"Damn it! He's trying to kill me!"*

"Gaither! It's me. Are you crazy?" A bullet thumped near the horse's hooves beside me. *Jesus!* I jumped straight up, waving my arms as he ran, pulling the silver gray and the roan along with him, bullets from the coulee spitting past him. He stopped long enough to get a good look at me before I dropped back down. All right, I thought, now he knows it's me, maybe— Another of his bullets thumped the ground. "Damn it to hell, man!" I looked up just in time to see one of the shots from the coulee hit him and spin him around like a rag doll.

"Aw, man." I jumped up on Foxfire and punched him toward where Gaither hit the ground, Honest Bob snorting and jerking against me on the lead rope. Bullets whistled. Gaither stood up staggering, his gun hanging from his hand, his hat gone, blood running down the side of his head. I spun Foxfire, reining him down, and reached a hand to Gaither even as he tried to raise his pistol. "Don't shoot me, Gaither, Jesus, man! Are you nuts?"

"Beatty?" His voice sounded thick, bleary. Another shot spun past us. I grabbed him by the shoulder, pulled him up across my lap, snatched the reins to the silver gray and the roan, and turned Foxfire away, leading the other three horses. *Why couldn't anything go right?*

When we'd topped a low rise and dropped down out of

the line of fire, I rolled Gaither off my lap and heard him grunt as he hit the ground. With my rifle ready, I jumped off the horse, and *then,* leading all four horses, went back to the crest of the rise and looked back fifty yards at the winding edge of the coulee. There hadn't been a shot fired since I'd ridden away. *Out of ammunition?*

"What's the problem, boys?" I yelled to them. "Out of bullets there? I got plenty here, if you wanta come get some."

A full minute passed until finally the white man's voice called out, "You stole my damned shirt! We'll remember you! You killed one of my friends . . . shot my other friend here in the back. We'll come looking, you can count on it."

"Yeah?" I yelled back, watching, ready to raise my rifle and aim it if he poked his head up. "I stole your possibles bag, too, and your dandy braided lariat, so there! Anytime you want to come get your stuff back, just ask for the meanest bastard at Fort Lincoln. I'll be the one wearing your doeskin shirt."

After a pause the voice called out, "Asshole!"

I slumped, chuckling a little to myself, feeling better now. The familiar broken whine of the sweat bee buzzed near my ear. I slapped at it, calling out, "That'll teach ya to steal *my* horses."

Chapter

8

———◆———

Rabbit on a stick . . .

"**W**hat was I supposed to do, Beatty? I had no idea it was you. I'm waiting to hear you start shooting from behind them, then here comes two horses flying over the gully—somebody screaming like a maniac." Roland Gaither shook his bloody head and held a wet rag to the side of it. "My head hurts something terrible."

"Bet it does," I said, and I paused for a minute, holding a sizzling rabbit on a stick over a small fire. By midafternoon we'd followed our own tracks halfway back to the banks of the Missouri, then stopped to eat alongside a wide shallow creek, hoping Jack and Shotgun Tom would catch up to us. Once they joined us we could head on up to Fort Lincoln and be there by nightfall. "But after calling out my name a *half-dozen* times, didn't you get some kind of idea it just *might* be me?"

"I told you, I couldn't hear you with the pistols firing on me. Couldn't even *see* you with the sun behind you." He lowered the rag, squeezed it, and pressed it back against his head. "When you dropped and fired the rifle at me—"

"It was to cover you . . . damn it!"

He shook his head slowly. "I could have sworn it was some kind of Indian saddle on the racing stallion. How

82

would I know it was a shirt? How'd I know you decided to *rob* them?"

"Rob *them?*" I shook my head. "That really beats it all." I drew the rabbit close to my face, blew on it, and pinched off a piece to see if it was done. Beside us the creek sparkled and swirled. "Don't take this the wrong way." I broke off a hindquarter of rabbit meat and pitched it to him. "But you really oughta think about going back to Louisville or somewhere."

He caught the piece of rabbit and stared at me. "Thanks." I didn't know if he meant thanks for the meat or the advice.

I took a bite of rabbit and talked as I chewed it. "See, you're a person whose intentions ain't easily understood. Out here, a man in question is a man in trouble . . . if you get my drift."

He started to say something but I stopped him with a raised hand. "Not that I'm judging you, ya understand. It's just that the things you say don't quite square up and tally out with the things you do. That makes people uneasy around ya."

He looked at me with a flat stare, chewing on his piece of rabbit, and said, "Is that why you won't give me back my pistol?"

I grinned, laying the rabbit on a tin plate, and stood up wiping my hands on a bandanna, the same one I'd used to wash the blood off the graze across my forearm. "I told you, you must've lost your gun back there while you was out of your head." I picked up my rifle and turned to the horses beside us.

"I seem to recall you taking it from my hand," he said, "and putting it *somewhere.*" He looked all around.

I considered it for a second, then said, "Naw, I don't remember nothing like that." I spread my duster open and shook it. "See, no gun here anywhere. I'll look around for it, though, first chance I get, once we get to the fort . . . and if I find it, I'll sure give it back."

"What if we run into more trouble on the way?"

"We won't," I said. "The odds of us running into trouble twice the same day is . . . what's the word?" I hesitated for a second, then said, *"As-tro-nomical?* Yes, I believe that's the word—" I raised a finger. "—astronomical."

He just stared and ate in silence while I looked the horses over good. Sure, I had his pistol. *Shouldn't have given it back to him in the first place.* I'd pried it from his hand, and on the way back had shoved it down in my saddlebags. Too many things didn't add up about this man, and I wasn't leaving myself open. If I was wrong, I could live with it. But until we hooked up with Jack again, I wasn't letting Roland Gaither out of my sight, not for a second.

As Gaither sat staring at me, there came a low rumbling sound across the land above the creek bank, and though it was a sound I'd known since the days of the great civil conflict, it took me a second to recognize it. When I did, it struck my senses like a bolt of lightning. "Oh, shit!"

"Thunder?" Gaither asked, seeing the look on my face as I snatched my rifle from its scabbard.

"Thunder, *hell.* It's horses." I ran up the creek bank far enough to look out across the rolling plains. *Aw, naw!* Two hundred yards away, no fewer than nine horses topped a rise and sped toward us, dead on our tracks like a pack of bloodhounds. An older-looking Indian rode lead. Around him rode a half a dozen young warriors and two white men.

"What is it?" Gaither called out to me.

"War party," I called back to him, and he was up, snatching at the horse's reins as I slid and tumbled back down the bank.

"Give me my gun!"

I snatched it from the roan's saddlebags and pitched it to him. The roan sensed my urgency and swung against me. I scrambled into the saddle with the lead rope to Foxfire and Honest Bob in my hand.

"No more trouble today, huh?" Gaither had jumped atop the silver gray and spun it in place. "Now what?"

"Follow me," I said, kicking the roan out. We splashed across the shallow creek and up the other bank, then circled above it. I cut left for a few yards, turned the roan sharp, and headed back down, pulling the two-horse string. The thunder of hooves moved closer.

"The hell are you doing?" Gaither called out, seeing me head back down to the creek.

"Backtracking," I yelled. "We'll ambush 'em when they cross, then bust them up and make our getaway."

"Are you sure about this?" Gaither splashed in behind me, crossing the creek. I'd already slipped from the saddle and pulled the horses behind a spill of rock that form a deep crevice in the bank.

"No, I'm not," I said. "But it's all I can come up with right now."

He dropped down and pulled the silver gray in beside the others. The horses milled in a tight circle. "What if they don't go for it?" His breath heaved in his chest.

"Then we're dead, I reckon, short and simple." I pushed my hair back from my eyes and steadied my rifle across the cover of a rock. The hooves pounded closer. "Get as many as you can before we cut out of here." The sweat bee zoomed in and spun around the back of my hand. I brushed it away.

"Has this ever worked before?" He dropped down beside me, checking his pistol.

"Shut up," I said. "Here they come." Above us, their horses topped the bank and headed down, coming at a hard run right out across the creek and up the other side, still in our tracks. No sooner had the lead rider topped the other bank, he spun his horse and looked back down, seeing what we'd done, but seeing it just a second too late. We opened fire on the others while they were still strung out behind him, climbing the bank.

My first shot hit a rider in the side from ten yards away, spinning him up off his horse. I jacked the lever and kept firing, Gaither's pistol exploding beside me. A horse reared up on the rising bank and flipped backward, but the rider rolled free and sprang to his feet, running at us, a horse pistol blazing his way. Gaither stopped him cold with one shot and kept firing along with me until the riders had broken and ducked for cover. Some of them pounded on up the bank; others ran straight down the middle of the creek. Three lay dead in the water.

"Okay, move out before they get settled!" I pushed Gaither toward the horse behind us. We'd hit them hard, but it would take them only a second to regroup and be upon us. Gaither turned, standing, and reached for the silver gray's reins. But the older Indian had taken position from the crest of the bank, and three rifle shots spun down around us almost as one.

"Holy—" We ducked back down. I managed to get a shot off toward the puffs of smoke above us, then ducked when a ricochet whistled off a rock. He had us pinned. *Why couldn't nothing to like I wanted . . .*

Gaither got off two quick pistol shots, then ducked. Now the others had shaken off our surprise attack. Shots popped in from down the bank alongside the creek. Our horses crowded the cover of rock, whinnying and pulling against the reins. "We've had it," I said. "They'll shoot us to pieces."

"Great." Gaither's voice took on a sarcastic snap. "You've gotten us killed with your *ambush* idea." He popped bullets from his belt and reloaded.

From atop the crest, the older Indian waved an arm back and forth, and the firing stopped. "Maybe not," I said. "He's stalling them down for some reason." I glanced around at the horses, then at Gaither. "Either that or he's signaling them to take better position."

Gaither's eyes met mine. "You don't really *know* anything do you, Beatty. You just sort of play one hunch after the other and hope for the best."

I glared at him as I thumbed bullets into my rifle; before I could say anything, the older Indian called down to us, "Horse stealer. Give back the horses you stole."

"And my shirt, Rain—" The familiar white man's voice called out from downstream. "—Don't forget about my shirt . . . and the other stuff."

"Send out everything you stole from him," said the Indian's voice.

"I see why they quit shooting," I said to Gaither in a quiet tone. "They don't want to take a chance on hitting these horses. Maybe we've got some room to dicker here." Looking up toward the crest of the rise, I called out, "These were *my* horses to begin with. He stole them from me."

"But once he took them, they became his," the Indian replied. "Now it is you who have stolen them, horse stealer. Send them out with the bag and the other things."

"Yeah, then what? You gonna let us leave here alive?"

A silence passed, then he said, "No. We will not do that."

I shot Gaither a glance and saw him wince. Then I called out up the crest, "Well, that ain't much of a bargain for us, is it?"

Another silence passed. "No, it's not. Send out the horses anyway."

"No," I said. "You can't have it both ways. If you're gonna kill us anyway, we'll just keep the horses here." I lifted the big Parker-made glades knife from my *only* boot and held it up for a second, flashing it in the sunlight. "See? I'll cut their throats. They'll die with us . . . unless we figure a way to work something out here."

"Don't listen to him, Rain," the white man's voice called out. "You can't trust him. It's a trick of some kind."

"Be still, Walker!" The Indian's voice boomed down from the rise. Then another silence passed and he said to me, "How can we settle this?"

A rustling sound came from along the creek bank and I knew some of the others were moving closer. "First of all, tell your boys to pull back. I don't like being snuck up on while I'm trying to talk."

The Indian's arm rose and waved his rifle back and forth, and the sound along the creek bank stopped. I glanced at Gaither and said, "So far, so good. As soon as I get something going here, be ready to grab the horse. We'll make a run for it."

"Get something *going*? Like what?"

"I don't know," I said, squinting at him. "Whatever I can."

"He called you Rain," I called up to the Indian. "Are you Rain in the Face?"

"Yes," he answered. "Now what is your way of settling this?"

"Okay, here's the deal. We'll take these horses a hundred yards upstream. When we know you're not following us, we turn them loose and run like hell. They're all yours."

Laughter rippled along the creek bank, then a rifle shot spit off the rock in front of me and whistled away. I ducked down beside Gaither. "All right," I yelled. "That was just *one* idea. There's a dozen other ways to do it—"

"No, I think we kill you *and* the horses," Rain in the Face called down.

"Like hell!" yelled the white man. "Them horses are worth a lot, and I want them."

"Then fight him for them, Walker." Rain's voice boomed along the creek bank. "He has a big knife, you have a big knife. Let the winner take the horses and go."

"Now just a damn minute, Rain. I've been riding hard all day, ain't et nothing, got hardly any sleep last night. I don't think I oughta be—"

"If you're scared, just say so," I called out, ready to work on him now that I heard him hesitate. "We don't want you soiling your trousers over it." Gaither gave me a doubtful look. I shrugged. "If it's the only way out, let's take it."

"I ain't afraid of you, you bastard. I'm just saying it don't seem fair is all, me being worn out."

"Enough, then," Rain in the Face said. "Fight him for the horses, or we will kill them all."

A tense silence passed, then Walker said, "Well, I don't think I should, to be honest about it."

"Then let us finish here and be gone," Rain said, and again I heard the rustling along the creek bank.

My heart sank for just a second, but then in a last desperate effort, I called out, "What about you, *Rain?* Why don't *we* make a few passes back and forth? Are you a chickenshit like your friend there?" I held up the big knife and turned it in my hand. "Got a handsome glades knife here, finest knife in the southland. Made by a feller named Parker down in—"

"Silence! It would no contest for me to take your glades knife and cut the voice from your mouth with it."

"Yeah?" I saw it going my way and pressed hard. "Not before I lift your loincloth and make a gelding out of ya." I shot Gaither a glance and lowered my voice. "I'll talk him right into it, you watch."

He just stared at me. "You're actually going to *fight* him with a *knife?"*

"Do I look that stupid to you?" I asked. "I'm gonna shoot him and get the hell out of here."

Since my eyes had opened that morning at dawn, I'd hit the ground at a full run: been robbed by horse thieves, shot a man I didn't know, been shot *by* the man riding with me, came near washing away in a cold river, lost a boot, lost my hat, and . . . what else? That's about it, I thought. That, and now a big Indian stepping sideways down the creek bank with a long shiny trade knife hanging from his hand, ready to carve me open like a spring hog.

On the other hand, I hadn't drowned, thanks to the Gypsy roan. *Not a bad horse, that roan.* The bullet wound was no more than a graze, my horses were back with me . . . for the time being, at least. All I had to do was get close enough to put a bullet in Rain in the Face, grab a horse when Gaither came charging out, and we'd be off.

"There has to be a better way," Gaither said, gathering the reins as I stood slowly and stepped around the rock, my glades knife in my left hand, a pistol stuck down behind me in my belt.

"If you've got one, I'm all ears," I said back over my shoulder to him. Along the creek bank, Walker and another scraggly looking white man ventured out, flanked by the Indians, all of them moving in for a good view. "If you don't, then shut up and get ready."

I slashed the glades knife back and forth in front of me, getting the feel of it, loosening my shoulder, moving sideways in a wide circle, feeling the two inches of cold water beneath my feet. The trick would be to draw attention away from Gaither long enough for him to make a break when I snatched out the pistol. The big Indian circled with me ten feet away; his long knife swung once, quickly, back and forth, cutting a figure eight in the air. "I think I oughta tell ya, Rain, once this glades knife gets started, there'll be no stopping it." I tossed the knife back and forth, one hand to the other, crouching. "It takes on a mind of its own—"

"If he reaches for the pistol behind him before I am through with him, *shoot* him," Rain in the Face said to the warriors gathered around the creek bank.

Hunh? The hair on my neck stood out; I tossed them a quick glance, saw traces of evil grins sweep their faces. How did he know? "Looks like you've been grabbed by the short hairs, don't it," said Walker, grinning. He gigged the white man beside him. They both laughed.

Seeing the question in my eyes, Rain in the Face said, moving closer, "I learned the treachery of white men long ago." The knife spun on his finger by the brass hilt ring, then stopped. "You will die today . . . it is up to you to choose whether you will do it with honor."

I swallowed the lump in my throat and crouched lower, circling slower with him, now six feet away. *Honor?* There was no honor at stake here. This came down to living or dying, nothing more, nothing less. I'd go for that pistol in a heartbeat if it would keep me alive, but for now the element of surprise was blown out the window. We were here breath to breath, two men drawn to the spilling of blood. I resolved myself to that then, to that and that alone, and I cleared my mind of all else and said, "Then let's get to killing."

He led with his left foot, coming in, splashing water, swinging the knife low and up, then back straight across, but feigning with it, feeling me out, seeing how I shied, how quickly and how far my reflexes would take me back. But I'd anticipated him, knowing he'd test me first, so I didn't jump back as far or as fast as I would've liked to. Instead, I moved away to the side on my right foot, coming up out of my crouch. Then I crowded him, jabbed, and pulled it back, me testing *him* now, seeing how quickly he moved and recovered, watching for any weakness, any bad habit that would cost him his life. I saw none.

He settled in quickly, moved with me, his eyes never leaving mine, crouching lower. *French trapper-style,* I thought, taking a step back, swinging the big blade back and forth as if in practice. His raised slightly and lowered his knife hand an inch. Then without so much as flexing my arm or cocking my wrist in warning, I came in fast, splashing down on my left foot, pivoting, swinging the big glades straight up and around, then back across him at chest level, barely missing him.

He bowed back at the waist, only enough to miss the blade, and snapped back with a short hard jab, almost before I had a chance to catch my footing and shift away. This one was no feign. This one sought flesh. He'd just learned a little about me, enough to know this wasn't my *first* knife fight. I'd just learned a little about him: he didn't like backing off. He'd risk a cut first. This was going to be a bloody one. Seeing it, I tossed the knife back and forth, one hand to the other, getting ready again.

The others saw it too. They widened their circle in anticipation. A hushed gasp sounded from them. "Stick him, Rain," said Walker. "Do him like you did Joe Plum."

We settled in, circled closer, crablike, three feet apart, eyes on eyes, each of us drifting his knife right-handed. Our blades cocked back a little, our left hands cupped, extended like shields. His shoulder flinched, dropped an inch, and he jabbed hard, stepping in on his right foot, then back as my knife sounded past his hand in a quick slice of air. I'd watch his right shoulder. Would he drop it again? A weakness? A signal before he made a move?

Without settling, he thrust again. This time I moved just as his right shoulder dropped, pivoted in beside him as his blade hissed past me. On his backswing he exposed his left shoulder, and I stepped in, slashed back and forth, fast, and felt my blade open his flesh on my backswing. But his thrust came back around and I felt it lick me as I jumped back. The son of a bitch! He'd given me his left shoulder. Suckered me in. *Gave it to me—had let me cut him.*

But it had cost me. A cold burn ran from my side down across my hip bone in a half-moon gash. Yep, he wanted it to be *real* bloody. No quick kill here. *Where the hell was Gaither? Make the move, man!*

"Got him *good*, Rain!" Walker spoke, his voice in awe. "Now open him up. Gut 'im." I shot a glance toward the rock cover, but saw no sign of Gaither.

Warm blood spread down my thigh. Blood ran down his left arm and dripped from his fingers as he settled back in his crouch. I circled with him even closer, not knowing how bad he'd cut me, not even able to consider it right now. I stepped back, faking a slight limp. Let him see me weakened, I thought. Give him reason to make a bolder move, like a panther on wounded prey . . . then kill him, kill him quick and hard. A dull thud like the beat of a funeral drum pounded deep in my forehead.

Our eyes locked on one another. He laughed under his breath and slung blood on me from his left hand. When his shoulder dropped an inch I was ready, and chopped his swing away with my knife blade. Steel rang. He spun a full circle, coming around with the blade out. I felt another cold half-moon burn across my ribs, but jabbed for his right chest and found it, a hard jab that stuck him solidly, but shoved him back off my blade. He staggered from it, going back with a deep grunt. I'd hurt him; now I had to pounce fast, the prey becoming the predator in an instant flick of steel.

But midlunge I cramped deep in my stomach and stopped short, just long enough for him to recover and catch his stance. *Jesus, Gaither! Do it! Make a move!* My left hand clamped my side for a second, squeezed it against the pain, and made sure nothing had spilled out of me. I took a breath, clenched my teeth, swiped the big knife back and forth, and stepped forward, braced. He charged in swinging steel.

A fast deadly dance began.

We clashed steel to steel, the sound of it ringing back and forth like church bells from some ancient hallowed realm. A slash hissed across my left collar bone, shooting a chill down me. My blade came up before he recovered and opened him under his arm. He spun full circle, switching the knife to his left hand, the blade running along his forearm, swinging a fist, followed by a streak of steel. Then he backhanded it into a stab, nicking my shoulder as I ducked away, and we rammed one another chest to chest, each of us grasping the other's wrist with our free hand, our hands slick with blood.

Our knives hovered above us, straining downward, force checked by force. We staggered, turned slowly, leaning into one another in the shallow trickling stream, a fountain statue in honer of man's lower nature. "Turn him to me, Rain! I'll finish him!" Walker called out above the click of his rifle lever.

Without taking his eyes from mine, the Indian slung me back and raised a bloody hand toward Walker. "Stay out . . . of this," Rain in the Face warned him. His breath pounded in his broad chest. We circled once more, apart, wider now, both of us breathing hard, the fountain come undone. We'd warded one another off, withstood one another's blows, tested, marked and maimed one another— had shown one to the other some dark truth by which men live, by which men die.

Now *time* stepped in, the interloper, the third combatant

in our circle of death, making its presence felt more and more with each beat of our pulse, each spill of blood from our open wounds, and each of us knew that given its way, *time* would decide who, if not both, now looked upon the face of his slayer.

Water splashed. We circled and jabbed, swung and fell back, each looking for an opening, a weakness, but finding only the dark resolve of the other impenetrable, the rendering of *will* intact beneath the severed substance of flesh. "You die well . . . for a white man," he said.

"I ain't . . . dead yet, you son of a bitch." Gesturing him toward me with a roll of my knife blade—"Come on, let's . . . round it on out."

The creek bed beneath us trembled slightly. *Hoofbeats? Not Gaither's, though. Why hadn't he made a move?* I felt the first surge of dizziness sweep through me and shook it off, watching Rain in the Face drop his shoulder slightly, moving in. His face had gone pale. As pale as mine? His eyes showed the same weakness I felt churning low in my stomach. The sweat bee swung in and hovered before my eyes. I brushed it away with my bloody knife as it tried to tap its snout to the blade. "Get away . . . you little bastard."

Beneath my feet the tremor of hoofbeats grew stronger.

"Soldiers coming, Rain," Walker said. "Finish him! *Now!*"

I heard the horses bolt from the rock cover, saw Gaither spring out on the silver gray, leading the racing stallion behind him. An Indian raised a rifle, but the silver gray plowed through him and pounded off up the creek bank. Gaither didn't even look around for me. The roan charged out on his own with Honest Bob's lead rope tied to the saddle horn. An Indian snatched at the reins and missed. "Damn it, Rain!" Walker fired a shot at Gaither, then stepped close to Rain in the Face. "He's getting away! There's soldiers coming! Kill this bastard! We gotta go!" He swung the rifle toward me, but Rain in the Face shoved the barrel away.

I heard rifle shots from atop the creek banks, saw an Indian fall. Rain in the Face kept his eyes on mine. "No . . . we finish this first." More shots spun in from above us along the high end of the bluff. Walker cursed and disappeared into the brush. Water splashed up near the Indian's feet. The stream beneath us ran red with our blood.

"Suits me." I raised my knife, laid the dull edge on my forehead at my hairline, and slashed it across. "Come and get it." Behind him, the warriors fell back, firing at the top of the bluff, then disappeared, seeming to melt into the brush along the creek bank.

He crouched and came forward. "You still have . . . the pistol," he said, his voice weak but taunting me. "Now you can use it."

"Yeah?" I reached my bloody left hand around, drew the pistol from my waist, and pitched it at his feet. "Now *you* can have it." I adjusted the blood-slick knife handle in my hand and crouched lower. "Let's finish it."

A shot slapped into the water between us. I heard voices yelling from atop the bluff. He looked down at the pistol lying there, water spilling over it in clear trickling braids. I saw it cross his mind, but then he backed off a step and slapped the knife blade against the palm of his bloody left hand. "Another time . . . horse stealer. I have killed you . . . but you will not fall. I hold your spirit here until we meet and finish this." He slapped the blade against his palm again.

From atop the bluff, Jack's voice called down to me: "Step away, I've got him." I shot a glance up the bluff, saw Jack aiming his rifle down at Rain in the Face, then I shot a glance back at the bloody Indian and saw the questioning look in his eyes.

"No! Don't shoot," I yelled. My voice sounded weak, and yelling caused me to sway. A strange tight smile drew across the Indian's face. He stepped away, faltering, a hand going to his chest, and vanished into the brush as I sank to my knees. The roan ran in, pulling Honest Bob behind him. I caught him by a stirrup and tried pulling myself up, but my hand went limp and the sky spun above me. The last thing I remembered was Jack calling out to me as I fell back into the cold embrace of the shallow stream.

Chapter

9

After a bloody battle . . .

I'd ridden with an old man named Cletis Avery during the last days of the great civil conflict, and he'd once told me that in a knife fight between two men of equal skill and strength, neither man would walk away. He'd also said that in a *serious* knife fight, a man never knew the extent of his wounds until he died from them. His words came back to me as I opened my eyes and looked up at Quiet Jack kneeled beside me on the bluff high above the creek bank.

"One hell of a fight," he said, seeing my eyes open; and when I tried to rise up, he pressed me back down to the ground. "Lay still awhile till the stitches set up. What the hell's wrong with you anyway, knife fighting with that big Indian? Don't you know better than to do something like that?"

"Whe— where are the horses?" I tried bending my neck enough to look down, but a sharp chill ran deep in my side. "Are . . . the horses . . . all right?"

"Yeah, now lay still. Everything's all right but you. You're cut all to hell."

"Is he coming around?" A voice asked from within the group of soldiers gathered around me. Shotgun Tom stuck his head between two of them and looked down.

A man in buckskins and a broad straw hat stepped forward, kneeled down beside Jack, and pressed a wet rag against my chest. "Aw, yeah. This boy's gonna be all right." He grinned at me beneath a wide waxed mustache. "Ole Rain put it on ya good. Cut you everywhere but the soles of your feet. Hurts, don't it?"

"Yeah . . . it hurts some." I knew Rain in the Face had taken some bad cutting himself, and I wondered if he hadn't fallen somewhere in the brush along the creek bank. "Is he . . . dead?"

"Rain, dead?" He stood up chuckling while the others smiled down at me. "Shiiit, that ole buck is too damn mean to die . . . not from a little carving match, anyway. You musta been out of your mind, trying to take him on. We've got ya some broth heating up. Gotta get your blood back up some before we move you. You lost a bucketful, you know. We can bleed that mule if you wanta drink some of his."

"The broth . . . will do," I said, feeling a little queasy, trying to turn sideways but the tight deep burning in my stomach keeping me from it.

"You got in some pretty good licks of your own," Jack said, looking me over. He held something small dark and bloody close to my face. "Here's ya souvenir."

"What is it?" I looked at it, and he dropped it on my chest. It felt cold and sticky on my naked skin.

"Part of that Indian's finger," Jack chuckled. "Hope it ain't the one he picks his teeth with."

A shiver ran across my bare chest. "Please . . . get that . . . damn thing . . . off me, Jack," I spoke in a faltering voice. "For *God's sake.*"

"Yep, he's feeling better now." He patted my bare shoulder. "He's starting to gripe about everything." He looked up at the soldiers and smiled, then picked up the stub of Rain in the Face's finger, looked at it, and chuckled before moving it away.

"Good, then," said a voice behind the others. They stepped aside as a young lieutenant came closer and looked down at me. He wore a smug grin, putting a lot of chin into it. "I have some questions for him." He shot Jack a glance and added, "Both of you, for that matter."

Questions? I looked back and forth between him and Jack as Jack stood up shaking his head. "Not now, Lieutenant. At least let the man get some strength back. I've told ya everything there is to tell ya. You saw the man fighting for his life down there."

"Yes, but for all we know that could have been a family quarrel." He smiled, a tight military *don't-give-me-any-civilian-crap* smile. Then he added, looking back down at me, "We've found some of the stolen crackers and canned peaches in his bag. I think an explanation is in order. He also carries a Lakota medicine shirt."

Gaither stepped in now and said, "I told you, Lieutenant. He took those off the men who stole the horses. I'm a former detective from Louisville, Kentucky. You can feel free to verify any of this once we reach Fort Lincoln."

I gazed up at Gaither, wanting to ask him why he'd stayed out and let me get the living hell cut out of me, but the weakness moved back across me in a great wave and I felt myself drifting off again.

"Jack . . ." I managed to get a hand over and tug at his boot top.

"Yeah? What is it?" He kneeled and leaned close to my face.

"Tell . . . him I'll answer his questions."

"What's that?" The lieutenant leaned slightly forward. "What did he say?"

Jack stood back up and leaned near him. "He said, tell you to go straight to hell, Lieutenant, *sir.*" Muffled laughter rippled through the soldiers. *Damn it, Jack. Why make things worse . . . ?*

They'd laid me in a stolen supply wagon the patrol had recovered from along the banks of the Missouri earlier that day, and on the way to Fort Lincoln, I asked Jack about why he'd said it. "Because," he replied, "I didn't know what you were apt to say, the shape you were in. Figured I'd piss him enough to keep him stewing till we reached the fort. Maybe you'd feel better by then."

"Makes sense," I said, raising a little on my elbows, looking back at the three horses tied to the back of the wagon. Gaither rode a few yards behind on a spare army gelding. Beside him, Shotgun Tom pitched a baseball up and down in his palm.

"Once we get to the fort, I reckon the Custers will straighten things out for us." I spread a weak grin. "Do we really look like cracker thieves?"

Jack shrugged. "These boys are pretty tense. According to that scout, a bunch of young Indians have been picking the fort clean. They even lit out with this wagon loaded full of crackers and canned peaches. They're stealing everything that ain't nailed down and heading up to the Black Hills. Something big must be getting ready to happen up there."

"Reckon that's where the horses were headed if I hadn't stopped them."

"No. They would've gone somewhere and been sold. They say Rain in the Face has been riding with a couple of back-shooting white boys, the Walker brothers, Rance and Ebb. They helped him break jail, and he's turned outlaw with them. He's hanging around here wanting to get a piece of Tom Custer."

"Why?"

He shrugged again. "Tom Custer arrested him, threw his ass in jail before he could say scat. Must've made him look bad. From the looks of *you,* I'd say Tom Custer's got his hands full if they ever meet. Rain swore he'd cut his heart out."

I shook my head and gazed out across the darkening land. "How'd you learn so much in such a short time?"

"Ever seen a scout who wasn't tired of talking to nothing but blue uniforms day after day? He gave me the whole nickel run down and who's who, and why. Said all the brass is running in circles snapping at their own tails because they can never find Sitting Bull or any of the hostiles. Reckon that's why the lieutenant has such a tight jaw. They go looking every day for hostiles and can't find 'em. You ride in here, and before you even reach the fort you've managed to shake down a whole tree full."

"Well . . . that's their problem. I'll be glad to get Honest Bob delivered and get shed of this place come morning." Even talking seemed to drain away my strength. I felt myself fading.

"Morning, nothing. You'll be lucky if you can ride in a week. You still don't realize how bad that ole boy cut ya. You was out for over an hour. They've put over two hundred stitches in you. Lucky he didn't slice nothing up inside ya. What came over you, anyway? Gaither said you had a gun hidden in your belt, but you never even tried to use it."

"I don't know, Jack. At first it was because they knew I had it and would've shot me if I went for it. But then something came over me. I got caught up in it or something. Just couldn't go for the gun—didn't *want* to go for it."

He gave me a curious look, then said, "Maybe you'd lost too much blood already and it messed up your thinking."

"Yeah, that's . . . probably it," I said, feeling my consciousness drift and fade once more while watching the land fall away into darkness behind us. Then I lay back down and stared up at the stars starting to come forward from deep in the dark firmament above us, and I wondered what the Indian had meant about keeping my spirit until we met again and finished it.

We rode on, Jack's voice growing more and more distant until once again sleep overcame me. In my sleep, the sound of steel ringing against steel resounded in my mind. The face of the big Indian moved in close to mine, so close I could smell him, could see the tiny beads of sweat on his brow. His knife blade whistled past me, leaving a trail of silver fire behind it, and the blade of my glades knife met it on the backswing midstroke, sparks spraying up as the big blades clashed together and hung between us, each of us pressing, forcing the knives toward one another's faces. Then the sparks died into blackness, and in the blackness the blade sank deep in my chest, leaving me gasping for air.

Hands reached out from the blackness and raised me up—the hands of angels, I thought—carrying me across dark clouds that swirled beneath me. And when they laid me down again, a dim light shone above me for a second, then it drew away, turning smaller and smaller, into a tiny pinpoint, then disappeared. . . .

At the sound of a rooster crowing somewhere, my eyes opened and I saw Jack lean forward. "You awake? Man! You must've been worse than I thought." It took a few seconds to realize that we'd left the wagon. My hands rubbed back and forth on the coarseness of an army blanket tucked under my arms.

Fort Lincoln? Yes, we'd made it. But when I ask Jack about it, he said, "No, the fort's a mile away. We're guests of the Seventh Cavalry. The fort's too small to accommodate all the enlisted men, so we're bivouacked out here with them." A breeze lifted and licked at the canvas ceiling of an army tent. "Can you eat something?"

It all came back to me now, our horses getting stolen, the knife fight. I let out a breath. "Yeah, I can eat something, *anything.* Could drink some coffee, too."

"Here, take mine. I ain't even touched it yet." He grinned, looking relieved now that I'd come awake. "I'll go get some more and bring ya back a plate of breakfast with it."

"Thanks, Jack." I rose slightly on my elbows and wrapped my hand around the steaming cup of coffee. Jack folded a pillow and shoved it beneath my shoulders. When he'd left, I lay there sipping the coffee, looking all around the medical tent in the grainy light of morning. There was only one other patient in the tent, and I heard him moan softly in his sleep across the tent. Someone stepped through the fly of the tent and slipped toward me without a making a sound.

"Ran into trouble out there, huh?" A young private looked down at me, asking in a confidential tone, with many more *unasked* questions in his eyes. His face became more clear as he stopped at the foot of my cot.

"Nothing a body can't handle," I said, trying to smile as I sipped my coffee. The man in the cot across the tent moaned once more. The private nodded toward him, then said, "That's Barlinger, a dispatch rider. Two days ago he got jumped by some young bucks outside of Bismarck. They tried scalping him, but they botched the job. He looks like hell. I believe the surgeon must've lost his eyeglasses when he sewed his scalp back on." He circled his hand around the top of his head. "It's all lopsided and that."

"That's too bad," I said; then I just looked at him until he cleared his throat and took a piece of paper from inside his shirt.

"I just was wondering if maybe you'd . . . ?" His other hand fished out a pencil stub from his trouser pocket.

"What?" I cocked an eye.

"Sign your name here? Say something like, 'To my good pal, Samuel.' No, just make it 'Sam.' That'd be even better. 'To my good pal, Sam.'"

I stared at him with my coffee cup half raised. "You want my autograph? Who do you think I am, President Grant?"

"Heck, I know who you are. You're the man who went toe to toe with Rain in the Face and lived to tell about it." He spread a proud smile. They say you gutted him *good.*" As he spoke, the pencil and paper came closer and closer, until I sat the coffee cup on a small nightstand and took them from him.

"I don't know if I was the gut*tor* or the gut*tee.*" Before thinking about it, I scribbled the words on the paper and handed it back to him. "To tell you the truth, I don't believe I coulda lasted another minute if the army hadn't showed up."

He looked the paper over, grinned, folded it, and put it in his shirt. "This goes back to Albany with me. I'll have my pa put it a frame. I've already got a pretty good collection. Got one from a man who eats broken glass, nails and such. Got one from a man who tried to go over Niagara Falls in a wooden barrel—of course, they stopped him. But later on, I snuck into the lunatic asylum where they took him and got his autograph." He grinned and patted his shirt. "This one goes right beside them."

I just stared at him. His head craned forward another inch. "But tell me, Mr. Beatty. How does it feel, being in a knife fight like that? Was ya scared? Did it hurt, getting cut?"

I looked at him for a second, then let out a breath. "No, I wasn't afraid . . . didn't have time to be. And no, it didn't hurt, not at the time, nothing like you'd think, anyway." I nodded toward the moaning man across the tent. "Nothing like that poor sumbitch must've. It just felt like somebody ran a hot icicle across me. Hurts like hell now, though." I nodded at the bandage around my chest and stomach.

"Wheeew." He sucked in a breath and trembled slightly.

"I bet it does. Our chief scout Lonesome Charley sewed you up. He said you never so much as whimpered."

"I was out cold," I said. "I'll have to thank him first chance I get."

"Yeah, but still, all that sticking with the needle, your belly laid open like that—"

"Right, Private," I said, cutting him off. "It's not something I want to think about just now, if you know what I mean."

"But, if you had it to do over—"

"That will be all, Private Barnes," said a voice before the young soldier could finish. I saw the shiny brass buttons of a tailored tunic first, then looked up at the face of a young captain who'd stepped in and now stood before me with his hands folded behind his back. He smiled, a *military* smile. "Captain Dee Hirshfield, Officer of the Guard, at your service, sir," he said.

"Good morning, Captain. I'm Beatty . . . James Beatty. Just telling the private here how lucky I was that your boys came along when they did."

"Indeed you were." He paused a second, then said, turning to Private Barnes, "Are you still here? Who is your sergeant? Griebs, isn't it? H Troop? I suggest you find him and tell him you're dying to spend the day tending horses for Ole Nutriment."

Big Red Griebs. I pictured him the day I'd seen him at the train station in New Orleans, sweating out a hangover.

"Yes, *sir.*" The private's heels clicked once, then he snapped a salute and blew out of the tent like a dust devil.

Captain Hirshfield turned back to me. *"Ole Nutriment* is a fellow named Burkman." He cocked his head for a second, glancing down at my bandaged chest. "He takes care of the general's personal stock." He tapped a finger to his head. "Like *most* men who spend all their time with horses, he doesn't have a whole lot of sparks jumping in his brainpan—if you know what I mean—but excellent when it comes to animals, dogs, horses. I'm sure you know the type." He spread a smile. "So, then . . . you're a horse dealer, Mr. Beatty?"

Men who spend all their time with horses? Ha! "Yeah," I answered in a flat tone.

"Good, then." There was the same term, *Good, then,* and the same jutted chin I'd seen on the young lieutenant. Hirshfield continued, "According to Lieutenant Rumley, your friend told him you came here to deliver a horse to General Custer?"

"That's correct, Captain. The fact is—"

"Then I suppose you have some paperwork to verify it?" He leaned slightly forward, slicing my words off slick as a straight razor, but with no more sting to his tone than a taste of smooth whiskey.

"Well . . ." I almost searched myself. "Paperwork for what?"

"Come, come, Mr. Beatty. Certainly you have a bill of sale or something. You didn't come all this way on a lark, did you?"

I thought of the copy of the bill of sales for Honest Bob in my saddlebags. "I've got one, but I'm sure it got soaked crossing the river."

"And of course, you decided to *swim* the river rather than take a steamer across, like most *normal* people would have."

I found myself starting at him the way I'd stared at the young private. "Wouldn't it be easy enough to just ask Mistress Custer? She'll tell you everything you need to know."

"Of course. And I intend to this evening, as soon as I hear she's returned to the fort." I raised a brow, and he added, "She and some other ladies spent last evening on a riverboat. They'll be back this evening. Meanwhile, it's my duty to find out everything I can about this situation. You should be able to understand that."

I let out a breath and slumped back on the pillow. "Sure, why not."

"Good then. Why don't you start from the beginning, Mr. Beatty—" He flipped out a leather-bound journal and tapped the end of a pencil to his tongue. "—Tell me everything." Across the tent, the scalped dispatcher moaned and rolled over in his sleep. By the time I'd finished telling him the whole story for the third time, Jack had stepped back inside the tent carrying a tin plate full of food and another cup of coffee. He stopped and glared at Captain

Hirshfield before walking over. "Amazing, simply amazing," Captain Hirshfield said, shaking his head as he put the journal away. "You have to appreciate that I have troopers who would give their *left testicle* for the chance to kill Rain in the Face."

"Well, if they ever meet up with him, I'm sure they'll find him obliging."

"Yet you simply pitched him a pistol, correct?"

"Yeah, but like I said earlier, there was more to it than that. You had to be there."

"I'm sure." He turned and saw Jack standing there with the food and coffee. "At any rate . . . we'll visit Mistress Custer this evening. Until then, rest and get your strength back." He smiled, but it was a smile that didn't encourage a lot of trust.

Jack started to step in with the food and coffee, but the captain stopped in afterthought and raised a finger. "One more thing. When you had this *knife fight?* Did you hold your weapon sort of like this—?" He drew his fist back close to his side and held his other hand cupped above it. "—Or was it more of an old-fashioned saloon position? Like this?" He changed his hands a bit, and looked at me. The look in my eyes must've embarrassed him. After a second of silence he cleared his throat and said, "Never mind, just curious."

When he'd left the tent, Jack laid the plate on my lap, sipped at the coffee, and nodded toward the tent fly. "I wish you hadn't told him about pitching the Indian a gun."

"Why's that?" I asked, blowing on a spoonful of steaming gravy before sipping it.

"Because it's against the *law,* if they want to get picky about it. I think they're really steamed about you letting the Indian get away."

"Then let them be steamed," I said, laying down the spoon and reaching for the coffee. Jack handed it to me and I threw back a swig, feeling the stitches in my belly tighten. "I'm seeing Mistress Custer tonight, and we're out of here come morning."

"That would suit me all to hell," Jack said. "But you ain't going nowhere for a while. So you might as well rest and take it easy."

"Can you two keep it down over there?" The voice of the scalped dispatcher groaned across the tent.

"Sorry," I called over to him.

Jack's voice dropped. "What's wrong with him?"

My voice dropped also. "Some Indian kids tried to scalp him. He's all screwed up." I shook my head.

"Ouch," Jack said. "I bet he is." His raised his voice and called over to the man, "Ole buddy, can I get ya something? Some water?"

"Is there a doctor around?" His voice sounded full of pain. He rose up on one elbow and looked around bleary-eyed.

Jack stepped over to his cot. "No, but just tell me what ya need. I'll be glad to get it for you."

"How—how does it look?" He raised a hand carefully and cupped it above his ragged hair. Stitches lined his swollen forehead. I winced just seeing it.

"Oh, I don't know . . ." Jack said. He cocked his head from one side to the other, getting a close look. "Did you always part your hair on the right side, just above your ear?"

"Oh *Goddddd!*" The man moaned and sank down into the cot.

Chapter

10

⊷◈⊶

Finding time to heal . . .

Midmorning, Jack excused himself when an old army doctor came around to examine my wounds. While the doctor poked and swabbed and picked at the stitches in my lower belly, I heard a band strike up outside. "Sounds like somebody important just rode in from the fort," the old doctor said, glancing up for a second toward the brassy sound coming from the far end of the camp. "Now if we can just get General George Armstrong Custer to show up, we'll soon have ourselves a dandy little war up here." Shaking his head, he lowered it back to attending my wounds.

"Maybe that's him riding in now," I said.

"Naw. They'd be playing louder than that if was for him. He's still up in Washington getting his ass chewed out by some of Grant's flunkies, I imagine. He took a *stand* and blew the whistle on them thieving bastards in the Indian Bureau. I'm surprised it wasn't his *last* stand." The doctor stopped and cackled. "The *White House* is one place he shoulda scouted out real good before charging in." He leaned back to tending my wounds and said under his breath, "Poor stupid bastard."

Not knowing if he meant Custer or me, I craned my neck

a bit, looking down at the top of his bald head. "How am I looking, Doc?"

The sweat bee circled in. He brushed it away with his fingertips. "Looking better than I expected, for a man crazy enough to pick a knife fight with ole Rain in the Face."

"I didn't go looking for it," I said.

"Humph. Anybody comes to this part of the country is *looking* for it. Where are you from, Beatty?"

". . . Missouri," I said, stalling for just an instant before I answered.

He caught the stall and cocked an eye up toward me. "Voice sounds more *Kentucky*. But either way, it figures. They say a Missourian's just a Kentuckian been kicked in the head by a mule. Either one would goose a wildcat if they caught it with its back turned." He chuckled under his breath and dabbed at my wounds. "The word going around camp is that you stabbed ole Rain clear through the heart, but he kept on fighting." He chuckled louder. This time it ended in a wheeze and he supported himself with a hand on my leg. "I tell ya—" He caught his breath. "—If bullshit was a nickel a ton around here, I'd be a millionaire."

While the doctor collected himself and leaned back to my wounds, the Indian's face swept across my mind. I heard the low hiss of streaking steel, saw the blade open his shoulder to the bone—could feel the solid thud in my hand as the point of the knife sank in his chest.

"Well, I didn't do too bad, Doc. I'm still alive." The picture broadened as I saw it, gazing up at the ceiling of the tent licking in the breeze. Rain in the Face lay slumped atop a horse somewhere, moving across swell after swell of endless grassland, his arm hanging down the horse's side, dripping blood. *Jesus.* Where had he found shelter? Who tended his wounds?

"Reckon I can saddle up come morning and get myself out of here?" I asked, looking down at the doctor's bald head.

"Sure," he said, "if you don't mind busting these stitches and bleeding to death in the saddle . . . or infecting— swelling up like a balloon till your tongue won't even fit in your mouth. A fight's never won until the wound is healed. Ever heard that in your wanderings?"

"Aw, come on now. I never get infected. Wounds ain't never as bad as they look, are they?"

He grunted without looking up. His fingers brushed across an old bullet scar on my side, another across my ribs. "In your case, apparently not. Must be a rigorous trade, *horse dealing.*" There was a skeptical tone to his voice.

"It has its moments." I cleared my throat and added, "I'll ride real easy-like and not get in no hurry. That'd be no different than laying around here. A man that ain't moving forward ain't getting much done. Ever *heard* that in *your* wanderings?"

He stood up adjusting his eyeglasses. "You've lost a dangerous amount of blood. Your body is doing its best to replace it. You'll have to stay down for a while if you don't want to die." As he spoke, his voice faded away for a second. His lips kept moving, but the words didn't reach me. A flash of steel whooshed across my mind and I saw the face of the Indian, until I blinked and shook my head. "So it's up to you. Do what you will," the doctor concluded.

"Thanks, then," I called out in a shaky voice as he turned and walked over to the scalped dispatcher rider. *Smart-assed doctor.* I planned on getting everything straightened out tonight and being on horseback come morning regardless of what he said.

The sounds of people around and about outside the tent had me restless. A warm breeze licked at the top of the tent as I lay listening to the dispatcher groan, slicing his breath to keep from screaming, while the old doctor poked and dabbed at his red swollen forehead. I knew I couldn't stand it much longer, lying flat on my back all day. So when the doctor left, I swung myself up on the side of the cot and had started to get up when Shotgun Tom stepped into the tent followed by a young officer wearing a thin mustache, and a solemn-looking younger man dressed in buckskin.

"Dammmn, Mr. Beatty," Tom said. "Should you be up like that?" I just looked at him, noticing that he wasn't wearing his bearskin coat or his ragged boots. Instead he carried a new wool overcoat draped across his arm. Now he wore a new pinstriped shirt, new wool trousers, and a pair of shiny new Wellington dress boots. His hair was trimmed and slicked back.

"What'd you do, strike gold on the way here?" I looked him up and down. The officer stepped around beside him with his hands folded behind his back. The younger man stood back and seemed to brood about something.

"Aw, heck, Mr. Beatty—" Tom smiled, looking a little embarrassed. "—Captain Custer here helped me acquire these things. I brought him here to meet you."

"That's true," said the young officer. "Doesn't our boy look dashing, though." He spread a hand, sweeping it toward Tom, then extended it to me. "Captain Tom Custer at your service, sir. This is my brother Boston. Any friend of Tommy Stovine is *certainly* a friend of ours." He turned to his brother. "Right, Boston?" The younger man lifted an eyebrow and looked away without answering.

I just nodded, then looked up at Tom. "Glad things are going your way." Turning my gaze back to Captain Custer, I added, "Suppose you could help locate me a good pair of boots, a shirt, maybe—they don't have to be brand-new."

He smiled. "I'm afraid that's unlikely. They're short of nearly everything at the fort. I had to send Boston over to Bismarck late last night to fetch these things. Right, Boston?" Again Boston Custer only lifted a brow and looked away.

"Oh." I slumped a bit.

"But I have to tell you what an extraordinary thing you did, fighting Rain in the Face. Most of the officers say you're a complete idiot for doing something like that. But I don't; neither will my brother the general once he hears about it."

"Nice of ya to say so, Captain."

He nodded and leaned down a bit toward me. "Rain in the Face didn't happen to say anything about me, did he?"

"Well, no. But we were both kinda busy. I heard he's out to kill ya, though." Glancing past him, I noticed a thin smile twitch on Boston's face, then disappear.

"Yes, I'm afraid that's true." Captain Custer's eyes took in the bandages on me. He took a deep breath that seemed to dismiss the subject, then turned to Shotgun Tom. "But the main thing is . . . our young ballplayer here is all right. Eh?" He patted Tom on the back and picked a piece of lint off his shoulder. "I'll become his career manager once he's fulfilled his military obligation. Hope the ole pitching arm's feeling okay."

"Yeah, it's fine." Shotgun Tom blushed, rounding and stretching his right arm. "It was terrible last night when we first got here. My shotgun went off, killed my poor mule and an army horse."

"Yes, but fortunately you weren't hurt. What's a mule and plug horse, more or less?"

"It was *my* horse," Boston Custer grumbled in a low tone. Captain Custer smiled down at me, ignoring his brother. "We're getting our ballplayer here a fine bay gelding from the fort this afternoon, as soon as it's washed, shod, and curried. Can't have him riding a dirty horse, can we?"

I stared at them both for a second, nodding, once again seeing lips move but hearing no sound for a second. *Weaker than I thought.* Then I forced myself to say, "Glad ya'll stopped by. But if ya don't mind, I'm feeling a little tired here. Maybe I better lay back down."

"Oh, of course," the captain said, cutting me off. "We must let you rest and get your strength back. Just wanted to meet you and let you know we're taking good care of your friend here, right, Boston?" *Again!* Boston only lifted a brow, this time folding his arms with a long sigh. *What was bothering him . . . ?*

"That's . . . more than kind of you, sir," I said. "Do you mind if I have a word with him alone?"

"Of course, take your time." Again he patted Shotgun Tom on the back before he turned and shoved Boston Custer toward the tent fly. "Come, come, Brother Boston—" He slapped him across the back of his head. "—Let's find you some *big* holes to dig."

Once he'd stepped out through the tent fly, I lowered my voice and said to Shotgun Tom, "It's none of my business, but do a lot of careful thinking before you go marching off with these boys."

He winked, lowered his voice, and said, "I've got news for them. Once I get up where there's gold to be dug, I'm quitting the army."

"It's hard to *quit* the army. What about him managing your baseball career?"

"If I *had* a baseball career, I wouldn't be looking for gold in the first place, would I?" He smiled, cocking his head, winked again, and backed away to the fly.

"Oh . . ." I just sat there for a few minutes after he'd left, dozing perhaps, and listened to the breeze lick across the top of the tent. *Baseball.*

I shook my head—*here goes*—braced myself against the pain in my side, and pushed myself up on trembling legs. The sweat bee droned near my face as I stepped into my dirty trousers, pulled on my one boot and my one dirty sock. For want of a shirt, I threw a blanket around me, walked over beside the dispatch rider's cot, and reached for a walking cane leaning against a nightstand.

He glanced around at me, and I said, "Thought you were sleeping and didn't want to bother you."

"How in the hell can I sleep? My head's on *fire* . . . every five minutes you've got somebody traipsing in here talking about everything from *goosing* a wildcat to *sports,* to *knife* fighting, for God's sake!"

"Sorry," I said. Then I asked, "Do you mind if I borrow this cane for a couple of hours? You won't be needing it, will you?"

"Needing it?" He looked at the cane and laughed under his breath, a strange dark laugh, nearly hysterical. "I get *scalped!* They give me a damn *walking cane.* Can you believe this lousy army?"

I shook my head. "No . . . I've never been able to understand the military. But do you mind if I borrow the cane?"

"Why?" He shrugged, looking me up and down with an air of exasperation. "Your *hair* looks *fine!"*

"Well, anyway . . ." My hand jiggled the cane a bit, then drew it to me. I was going to use it whether he liked it or not, but it seemed only right to ask first.

"You're the maniac who gutted Rain in the Face, huh?" He asked as I shifted my weight onto the cane and almost turned to walk away.

"I'm *not* a maniac." I stopped and gestured my free hand up and down my bandages. "Besides, do I look like I gutted anybody?"

"It don't matter." He sighed and brushed the sweat bee

away from the stitches on his forehead. "It's already around camp how you cut him from asshole to appetite. One of the men told me about it last night when he brought me supper. Said I better keep an eye on you. Then he said I should feel a little better, just knowing you sliced up an Indian."

"Well, do you?" I tried to look at his eyes without noting the terrible red swollen stitches across his forehead.

"Shiiiit," he hissed, turning away and slumping into the cot.

I turned, limped away, stepped through the fly of the tent and out into the camp where I stopped for a second squinting my eyes against the glare of sunlight. Before me, the band had broken up and the musicians drifted away, their polished instruments glittering in sunlight. Bright blue uniforms moved about between long rows of tents and ammunition wagons where enlisted men labored with their sleeves rolled up. They scurried back and forth like beavers as the officers' brass and yellow epaulets flashed toward them, but then they sank down on the crates as if in a trance once the officers had passed by.

Above a far row of tents, Old Glory stretched and batted in the wind, making a sound like the crack of a heavy whip each time it billowed back against itself. Beyond the camp, endless swells of grassland rose and fell. With eyes turning toward me and voices whispering back and forth at my passing, I hobbled across the beaten-down grass toward the ring of a hammer on an anvil.

"That's him," a voice said in a hushed tone, and two privates with their sleeves rolled up dropped a wooden crate in the dirt and sat down on it. "Let's take a break," one said to the other. Their eyes turned with me as I limped past them. I felt my face redden, wishing I'd also borrowed the scalped dispatch rider's boots before I left the tent.

Ahead at a rope corral near a grease-stained livery tent, Gaither stood up from a wooden bench and craned his neck toward me. As I limped on, a big sergeant stood on a nail keg speaking to a group of young soldiers in ill-fitting uniforms. He held a pistol by the barrel in one hand and a square piece of hardtack in the other. "If there's no hammer available," he said to them, "you must *improvise*. Use your pistol or rifle butt to break it up—" He tapped the pistol butt against the hardtack. "—Then eat it in small pieces. Any questions?"

"Vat means dis *improvizee?*" a young man asked in a heavy German accent.

"Damn it to hell!" The sergeant's face turned blue-red. "Does anybody in this *United States Army* speak *English* anymore?"

Gaither smiled as I limped up to him outside the rope corral. Nearby, a big soldier worked at an anvil with his sleeves rolled up. He stopped and ran a forearm across his forehead. "Good to see you up and around, Beatty," Gaither said.

Without returning his smile, I said, "Any reason why you didn't do like we said back at the creek bank?" Gesturing a hand up and down my bandages, I added, "If there is, I'd sure like to hear it."

"Hold on, Beatty. You're not blaming me for what happened out there, are you?" He spread his hands. "My God, man. I kept waiting and waiting for you to pull the pistol. But you seemed intent on fighting to the death. When I heard the cavalry coming, I decided you were dead anyway, so I did what anybody would do: I took off. What came over you, anyway?"

"I wish people would quit asking me that," I said, rubbing my jaw, thinking about it for a second, realizing what he said was true. "Him knowing I had that pistol changed everything. Being a mind reader, I figured you'd see what I was thinking and make a break for it."

"I don't know about you, Beatty." He shook his head, reached down on the wooden bench, picked up a new cavalry hat, and put it on. "I don't think you really wanted me to stop that fight." The gold braiding band had been removed from the hat, making it look not much different from any you'd buy in a store.

"See you got yourself a hat," I said. As I spoke, a weak, queasy feeling drifted through me. My vision blurred for a second, then cleared.

"That's right." He ran a thumb along the brim. "It was just lying around on the livery wagon, the braiding missing, nobody using it, so why not? These soldiers are most accommodating."

"Sure they are," I said, glancing around the camp. Everything took on a distance; a sheen of sweat lined my forehead.

"Oh," he said, "do you have something against soldiers?"

"No, some of my best friends are soldiers." I ran a hand across my bare head, looked down at my dirty sock, and adjusted the blanket across my shoulders. "I've lost a lot of stuff. Suppose they'll spare me a hat and some boots?"

The big soldier had walked over from the anvil, rolling his sleeves down. "Looks like you're short a boot there, young man," he said. His voice boomed. At first I thought he was shouting at me. Then I realized he was just a loud talker. "If you walked very far like that, you'd just go in a circle." He extended a thick hand toward me. "I'm Burkman, but everybody calls me Ole Nutriment. You must be Beatty. I'd sure like to shake your hand."

"Why, sure." I looked him up and down, shaking hands. "Suppose there's any spare boots and a hat around here?"

He didn't seem to hear me. "I took care of the general's new horses . . . fed 'em, watered 'em, picked their hooves, and all like that. Good-looking horses, except that one acts a little peculiar. Kept trying to step on my foot."

"Thanks," I said. That's Honest Bob. He *is* peculiar. But he's the only one that belongs to the general. The rest are mine. Now about some boots—"

"Nobody told me. What should I do now?" His voice boomed.

"About what?" I glanced at Gaither, then back to him.

He shrugged, struggling with something that couldn't quite work itself out in his mind. "As far as I know it is. He's s'posed ta been here by now, you know."

I winched and shook my head. What the hell was he talking about? Then it dawned on me. The man was deaf. "Are you hard-of-hearing?" I asked in a raised voice.

"What?" He glanced at me, then at Gaither, then back to me.

I leaned forward and said louder, "You can't hear me, can you?"

"Can I what?"

Jesus. I looked at Gaither. "He can't hear shit, can he?"

"Apparently it comes and goes," Gaither said. "He was hearing fine earlier. Says he got hit in the head by a wagon tongue years ago."

"How's that?" Burkman's voice boomed. "Wait a minute." He palmed himself hard on the side of his head and wringed a finger in both ears. "There, got rid of that anvil ringing. What'd ya say?"

Jesus. I rubbed my forehead and stared down at my dirty sock.

"I was just telling Beatty that your hearing comes and goes," Gaither said.

"Yep, but I can hear now. It ain't nothing that'd get me thrown out of the army." His eyes flashed back and forth. "So no need in telling anybody, right?"

"Right," I said. "Are there some spare boots around here, maybe a hat, a shirt?"

"Naw." He waved a hand. "Ain't nothing like that around here. Might talk to Sergeant Griebs, though. He has a way of getting things other folks can't."

"Oh? How's that?"

He sniffed and ran a thumb beneath his nose. "Ain't for me to say. I just tend horses. So don't worry about the general's horses, or your own, for that matter. I treat all horses the same. The general's all the time telling me, I shoulda been a horse instead of a human." He grinned. "I love that man, you know. He's been like my daddy, brother, *friend—*" He rolled a hand. "—And all such as that in one. There's some here who speak ill of him, but by God, they better never let me catch them at it." His hand slipped instinctively to his hip, where his pistol would have been had he been wearing one.

I turned to Gaither. "Have you seen Shotgun Tom? Seen all the new stuff he's got?" Ole Nutriment shuffled back to his anvil grumbling something under his breath.

"Yes," Gaither said. "Once they found out who he is, the Custers haven't let him out of their sight. They've moved him to the officer's quarters at the fort and talked him into enlisting."

I shook my head, looked around the fort yard, and saw Jack walking toward us. "There you are," he said when he got close enough to be heard. "Am I gonna have to knock you in the head to get you to stay in that tent?" He took a wadded-up shirt from under his arm and pitched it to me. "You ain't getting no better till ya stay off your feet a few days."

"I'm all right." I leaned on the cane and shook the shirt out with my free hand. "If a man lets a little cutting get him down, what's he gonna do if something *really* bad happens?"

Jack and Gaither just looked at each other. Burkman stood watching me examine the wool shirt. "Jesus, Jack. This looks like a dog mighta slept on it." Short white hairs fluttered away when I shook it.

Jack shrugged. "Might have. I don't know where it came from. It's been in my saddlebags for a few months. Ain't had a chance to get it washed."

"Thanks, but I've got the doeskin shirt I took from the horse thieves." I glanced at Gaither's new hat. "I don't seem to acquire stuff as easy as *some* do." A couple of soldiers had started past us, but they stopped and listened and looked down at my bare feet, then at my bloody bandages as I threw the dirty shirt over my shoulder. "You oughta see Shotgun Tom. He's got a new striped shirt, new trousers, *brand*-new boots—" The weak queasiness swept through me once again. I wavered a bit and steadied myself on the cane.

"I saw him," Jack said. "I'm happy for him. The boy needed a little streak of good luck."

My face reddened a bit. "I'm happy for him, too. But damn it! How come everybody's getting new stuff but me?" I gestured a hand toward Gaither. "Ex-policemen . . . *baseball* players. They get all kinds of stuff for free. I can't even *buy* what I need." The soldiers watching us looked back and forth at each other, then back at me. One of them scratched his head beneath his cap.

Another wave of weakness swept over me, this time seeming to force me into a narrow tunnel back away from everything. "Easy," Jack said, seeing me sway on the cane. "You know nobody gives a damn about a horse dealer." He stepped close and steadied me with a hand on my arm.

"Come on, let's get you back to the tent before you pass out."

"Need some help?" The soldiers stepped in with Jack, reaching for me at the same time.

"I'm all right," I said, trying to brush their hands away. But even as I spoke, I felt the ground sway back and forth beneath me.

Chapter

11

———✦———

A knock on a lady's door . . .

Somewhere along the way back to the tent, my knees had buckled and I'd lost consciousness. The last thing I remembered was Jack catching me and hefting me up like a sack of grain while I babbled about boots and hats and other stuff. Then a cool darkness had surrounded me, followed by a ringing silence. When I woke up, shadows of sunlight through the tent lay long across the dirt floor, leaning from the west. My face and chest were beaded with cold sweat, yet I told myself I felt much better, and swung up on the side of my cot.

"When are you gonna start listening to somebody," Jack said, sitting beside my cot, slicing an apple and eating it as he spoke.

"Don't start on me, Jack," I said, letting go a breath and combing my fingers back through my hair. For a second I sat waiting for the surge of weakness. When it didn't come, I felt relieved, raised my arms chest high, and said, "See, I'm all better here. Just needed a little sleep, I reckon." I thought about how I'd acted earlier and said, "Hope I didn't make too big a fool of myself out there."

He spit a stream of tobacco juice on the dirt floor, chuckled, and said, "Naw, no more than usual. Some of the soldiers are taking up a collection to get you a pair of boots."

"Aw, Jesus." I rubbed my forehead. "Tell them not to do that, Jack. I've got money to buy what I need. Couldn't everybody see I was out of my head?"

"If you couldn't, how could anybody else?" He stood up, picked up a pan of water from the nightstand, and sat it beside me on the cot. "Get washed up a little; you smell like a billy goat. Hirshfield's coming back for ya in a few minutes. Gonna take ya to see Elizabeth Custer."

"Good. Maybe I can get paid tonight and get out of here first thing come morning."

He cocked an eye. "You just don't get the picture, do ya? You . . . are . . . *wounded!* Badly wounded. You're half out of your head, and all you're gonna do is kill yourself if ya don't settle down. The doctor was by and said if you don't act like you've got some sense, he ain't fooling with you no more."

"All right." I raised a hand. "I'll take it easy a couple of days. Just tell them not to buy me no boots."

He shrugged. "You know how soldiers are. Once they decide to do something, you might as well stay out of their way. Ran into the big sergeant we met in New Orleans."

"Griebs?" I dipped my hands into the pan of water and rubbed my face. "Any hard feelings there?"

"Naw. He's happy as a lark. Said tell ya to come see him and his boys once you're able. When he heard about the knife fight, he won three dollars betting you'd live through the first night." Jack grinned. "Said he prayed all night for ya."

I stopped washing my face and raised my brow toward him; he shrugged. "Hell, you know how soldiers are. They bet on everything while they're waiting for orders. Ant fights, knife fights, an egg toss, it's all the same to them. Now they're betting day to day whether or not you *stay* alive."

"Yeah? I don't suppose you put any money on it, did you?"

His face reddened. "I mighta thrown off a couple dollars, if you must know."

"Jesus." I shook my head. "Which way?"

"That ain't none of your business." He shifted in his chair. "Which way you think I'd bet? That you'll live, of *course.*"

"I see. Is that why you're so concerned in keeping me bedridden?"

"I'm gonna act like I didn't hear that." He pitched me a towel and spit a stream of tobacco juice. "Want me to go with you to see the Custer woman?"

"Naw. I'll be all right."

"Good. Then I'll be at the livery tent when you get back. Griebs is supposed to bring by some rifle ammunition to sell. Try not to piss Hirshfield off. I don't think he likes you much."

"I'll try," I said. Looking around as I dried my face, I noticed the scalped dispatch rider's cot was empty. "Where's he at, out looking for a mirror?" I chuckled a little.

"He's dead." Jack's words brought me to a stop, and I let the towel down from my face.

"Dead? But— But he seemed better when I left this morning, fussing, cussing. I even borrowed his cane." My stomach felt a little queasy again.

"Yep. But he's dead. So it looks like you get to keep it."

I looked up at him, saw the grim expression in his eyes as he added, "Are you starting to get the picture?"

Right at dusk, Hirshfield and I arrived at the fort, him on horseback and me driving a mailman's buggy the army had purchased in Bismarck. The doctor had bound me good and snug with gauze wrappings before we left, and I sat poker straight on the buggy seat. Along the way we passed a long uneven line of recruits marching through the dust in their ill-fitting uniforms. A sergeant bellowed and cursed as they turned their gaze toward me, looking longingly at the faded letters U. S. Mail on the side of the buggy.

"Not exactly *seasoned* just yet, are they," I said to Hirshfield riding along beside me.

"They'll do," he replied, "by the time Custer's men are through training them. His sergeants have a knack for whipping men into shape pretty quick."

Beside us in the dust, a sergeant yelled, "Damn it! When I say *left*, I *mean* left! Your left heel should strike the ground at the *same time!*"

"Vat is dis *zame dime?*" a voice called out.

"Jeeeesus R. Christ!" The sergeant screamed.

I shook my head and chuckled under my breath. "Then God bless them and the fine work they're doing." Hirshfield reined his bay gelding forward and stayed five yards ahead of me the rest of the way without saying another word until we rode through the gates of Fort Lincoln and turned toward a row of neat frame bungalows.

When he'd secured his horse at a hitch rail, I eased down from the buggy and followed him, limping along on my cane. The row of bungalows stood like sentinels between the fort yard and a row of much larger houses. *Officer's row.* Once there, we stood on the porch of a freshly painted two-story house where the Custers lived, Hirshfield with his hat cradled in his arm, me absently running a hand back across my bare head once I'd raised it there and realized I no longer *owned* a hat.

"Hated hearing about the dispatch rider," I said absently as he reached out and worked the brass door knocker. My free hand drifted down the front of my dirty shirt, smoothing it. "He seemed like a good enough sort."

"He was. They all are," he said in a clipped tone. "We all hated hearing it—" He glanced at me, then turned back to the door. "—But it's a soldier's duty to die." Then he added in a resolved tone, "Lousy Indians."

"Yeah? Of course, if ya'll wasn't here, I reckon it wouldn't have happened. It ain't like the Lakota invited you here, you know."

Without facing me, he said to the door, "But we *are* here, Beatty. And we're going to be here from now on. The Lakota might as well get used to it." He looked me up and down with a smug toss of his head. "We're here to make the country safe for folks like you."

"I'm only came here because I had to," I said, rubbing my dirty sock foot against my boot.

"Didn't we all." He looked away and let out a breath.

When the door opened, the same colored woman I'd seen

at the rail station in New Orleans looked at Hirshfield, then looked me up and down. "Mistress Custer is expecting you. I'll just tell her you're here," she said, her finger gesturing us inside. Her eyes lingered on me for a second before she hiked her long dress and turned away.

"Thank you, Martha," Hirshfield said as she left. Cutting a glance and a thin smug smile at me, he added, "I see our *charity* committee hasn't outfitted you yet."

My face reddened. From the other room I heard the colored woman's voice speaking hushed and fast, talking about me as if I'd just stepped through the door and thrown a handful of cockroaches on the wall. Now the whole house must be *burned* and rebuilt.

"I wasn't about to bring that dirty man in here," the woman's voice whispered.

Jesus. I rolled my eyes upward. Beside me, Hirshfield stifled a laugh by clearing his throat against the back of his hand.

"It's all right, Martha," said Elizabeth Custer's voice above the swish and rustle of women's garmentry. Her footsteps sounded light, almost musical, coming to us from the other room.

At the sight of her, Captain Hirshfield snapped to attention so rigidly I almost did the same. His heels clicked—something mine wouldn't do if I wanted them to. "Ma'am, begging your pardon, ma'am. With your permission . . . this gentleman has—"

"Come now, Captain, at ease." She dismissed his formality with the toss of her hand. "Enough *boots and saddles* for one day. Everyone in my house is off duty for the evening." Even as she smiled most graciously, I noticed the flat blank expression. Her mind could've been a thousand miles away.

"Yes, ma'am," he said, standing down at ease, but not too much.

"And I see you've brought dear Mr. Beatty to me . . . how wonderful!" She took a step back, folded her hands, looked me up and down with that her vacant gaze, and smiled. "Why, Mr. Beatty, I heard about the terrible thing that happened to you. Are you getting along well?"

"Well enough, thanks." I felt a little guilty about the

dispatch rider dying from a scalp wound and me still alive, walking around stitched together like a rag doll.

She looked at my feet. "But, my! You seemed to have stepped out of your boot."

"Yes, ma'am, you could say that. But I brought your horse as promised. So if you'll explain our arrangement to the captain here . . ."

"Then, he *really is* here to deliver a horse?" Hirshfield asked in a way that implied everything I'd said up to this point was nothing but a barefaced lie. I stared at him, picturing *me* wearing his shiny boots and him running away, zigzagging across the yard, my pistol blazing and bucking, kicking up chunks of dirt around his bare feet. *Men who spend too much time with horses. The turd.*

"Ohhhh, Mr. Beatty!" She reached out as if to slap me on the arm, but then stopped herself. "It was supposed to be a *surprise.* Now everyone will know it." She mimicked a look of exasperation. "And I thought I could rely on you." *That flat blank stare . . .*

"Well, ma'am, things ain't gone real smooth since I left Bismarck. And you know how inquisitive these *boys* can be." I slid the captain a sharp grin, emphasizing the word *boys.* He stiffened a bit, and Elizabeth Custer saw it.

"Now, Captain, you mustn't take offense. Mr. Beatty is the kind of person we can only describe as *earthy.* In fact, he tells an army joke that Captain Dunlap finds quite amusing. How does it go?" They both looked at me. "Tell the Captain, Mr. Beatty, please."

"It wasn't my joke, ma'am." I looked back and forth between them.

"Of course, it was someone *else's* joke." She tossed a hand. "Who knows where jokes stem from? But it goes something like this: you ask a soldier, 'What have you done since you joined the army?' Then when he tells you, you say 'Oh, I see, you haven't done a thing since you've joined the army—'" She placed a hand on one hip and tossed her other one, smiling. "—Just nothing at all . . . since . . . you . . . joined . . . the . . ." Her voice trailed, seeing the look on Hirshfield's face as he glared at me. "Did I tell that right?" She looked confused. "Oh dear, I didn't, did I?"

I ran a finger around inside my shirt collar. "No, ma'am, but it wasn't me who told that joke. It was a friend of mine, that is, a fellow I know." I shrugged. "Well, I don't really *know* him, he just happened to be around. Truth is, I never liked him much."

"Anyway," said Elizabeth Custer, "that will be all, Captain. I'll have a word with Mr. Beatty in private now."

The captain stiffened again. "Ma'am, if I might say so, perhaps you'd like me to stay for the sake of propriety."

"Nonsense, but thank you. We'll be fine here. Martha will prepare tea." I knew she'd mentioned Martha being only there for the *sake of propriety*.

"Very well, ma'am, as you wish." He stepped back with a courteous nod and caught the doorknob in his hand. "I'll bid you good evening—" He shot me a cold stare. "—I'm afraid I've found *much* to do since joining the army."

Oh well. I raised my arm and dropped it to my side, turning from the door on my cane, back to Elizabeth Custer, dreading whatever repercussions that little joke might bring about. "Ma'am, if you don't mind my saying so, I wish you hadn't said I told you that joke. They're gonna be on me like flies on—" I stopped short of saying that unwholesome substance a fly might be on, and shook my head. "I just wish you hadn't."

"Have you any news on the general's whereabouts?" Her voice changed the second the door closed behind the captain; so did her whole demeanor. She turned pensive, anxiously wringing her hands. Her eyes widened, alive, alert now.

"Your husband's whereabouts?" I stared at her. "Well . . . no, I haven't. That is, I wouldn't have, would I? I just brought Honest Bob here like I said."

"I'm a strong woman, Mr. Beatty; nobody has to hide anything from me. If you've heard something, you would tell me, wouldn't you, please, no matter how terrible it is?"

"Yes, ma'am." I reached inside my duster and took the damp bill of sales. The ink was too smeared to be read. She gasped and stepped back at the sight of the folded paper. "But I haven't heard anything, except that he's not here yet."

"I see." She calmed down, dropping her hands to her sides.

"I'm afraid the bill of sales is ruined."

"Oh?" Her eyes grew blank again for a second.

"But we both know what we agreed to. So if you'll go ahead and pay me the seven hundred dollars, I'll be able to leave in a couple of days without causing you any inconvenience. The horse is being taken care of by *Ole Nutriment* right now. I hope you and your husband will be pleased with Honest Bob. Be patient with him; maybe someday he'll be a fine riding horse."

"Mr. Beatty, I don't give a——about that stupid horse. He can go to blazes for all I care."

I shook my head, stunned to hear such a word come from her lips. Who was this woman, and what had she done with Elizabeth Custer? "Ma'am, I don't know what to say."

"There's nothing to say." She turned away from me, tapped a finger to her eye, then turned back. "We're having trouble, the general and I." She pushed back a strand of hair; it fell again. "I know I shouldn't tell you this, although I'm sure you've heard of it already, the way gossip flies around here. I knew about you killing Water in His Hair no sooner than I arrived this morning."

"Uh . . . ma'am. His name's Rain in the Face, and I didn't kill him, he and I just had a——"

"Oh, what's the difference what his name is. All their names sound so silly, anyway." She tossed a hand. "But the rumors about the general and I are true—all true."

"I just got here last night, ma'am. Haven't really been in the position to hear anything—not that I'd care to, that being a private matter and all."

She didn't seem to hear me as she went on. "He's done some bad things in the past, and I've overlooked them. But this time he's gone too far. I can never forgive him." She turned as Martha the colored woman stepped in from the other room and cleared her throat.

"Missus Custer, you come on away now, ya hear. No need in you telling this *dirty* man nothing." She looked down at my damp, grimy sock, then up at my face, her dark eyes full of fire and sharp objects.

Elizabeth Custer swallowed a knot in her throat and said over her shoulder, "Martha, be a dear. Go out back and kill us a chicken, please."

"Ain't no *chickens* in that backyard. Ain't nothing but a goose stirring around out there."

"Marrr-tha." Her voice sounded tight, strained, and quivering. "Then . . . go . . . out . . . back . . . and . . . kill . . . that . . . *goose, PLEASE!*" The strand of curly hair bounced and trembled against her temple.

"All right, then, but I hate to." She shook her head, grumbling as she walked away.

"Look, ma'am," I said, raising a hand. "She's right. You shouldn't be telling me anything about your and the general's trouble. "I'm just here and gone . . . once you pay me, of course. And listen, if cash is a problem, I'll gladly take a promissory note, I mean, if you can't trust the *military,* who can you trust? I think you're gonna like that horse a lot." I wanted out of there.

She looked down at her folded hands on her stomach. "He's a father now, you know."

"Oh, no, ma'am, that's impossible." I smiled. "You see, Honest Bob is a gelding."

"Not that——horse, Mr. Beatty. My husband, the general! He's a father!"

That word again! Did she even realize she was using it? She looked back down at her hands on her stomach. I stood stunned for a second, then it dawned on me and I snapped forward on my cane, putting my free hand on her forearm. "Oh, I see! *Congratulations,* then! Here, let's get you off your feet."

I tried guiding her to a nearby chair, but she slung my hand off her arm. Pain shot along my side. "Are you an imbecile, sir?" She jumped back from me; tears streamed down her face. "The general has a child by an Indian woman, an *Indian woman!*" She clenched her fists at her side, trembling.

Ho-o-o-oly Jake . . . She swooned; I'd thought she was going to faint. "Ma'am, I don't know what to say." My voice dropped almost to a whisper. I wanted out of there . . . bad! But I couldn't just turn and leave, leave her there with tears streaming down her face.

How long had she known this? Not long, I figured. How long had she kept this inside her? *Jesus.* It must be killing her. Out here, away from her family, no one to confide in . . . this poor woman. *Not homely, not dull. Just hurt, and hurting alone.* It came to me now why her eyes had a way of turning flat and caged at times. It was an art she'd cultivated, a way of keeping her secrets, a means of pulling away from the rest of the world and taking refuge inside herself.

"There's nothing to say, Mr. Beatty." She tried to take control of herself, but it wasn't working. "I—I hoped that getting the general a nice present—a good *horse*—would lessen the tension between us, but it has-n't . . ." Her voice started out strong, then cracked and trailed into weeping. For some reason, she'd allowed me inside her secret place. Why? Because I was so far removed from her world that I represented no threat? That I meant nothing?

Outside the bow and curtsy of military protocol, talking to someone like me was no different from talking to the wind. I realized it and said, "Aw, ma'am, I'm so sorry. I just wish things like this never happened." I raised my arms just to drop them to my sides, just to offer a little gesture of sympathy, but she fell forward against me, sobbing on my chest. My cane dropped and rattled on the floor. The pain in my chest nearly took my breath, but I managed to stay afoot. I looked at my dirty outstretched hands . . . and what else could I do but pat her trembling back as gently as I could.

"Things'll work out for ya'll somehow," I whispered near her ear. "Just have faith, and I know they will." I thought of pulling my bandanna from my back pocket, then remembered it hadn't been washed since the day I'd swabbed Gaither's bloody head with it.

"I try, Mr. Beatty. I try so hard. To . . . be . . . a . . . good wife. You just don't know." She sniffed my shirt and I knew she must've smelled the dog odor on it. But she stayed against me, finding some comfort there, I supposed.

"I know, I know," I said, consoling her, patting her back, rubbing my hand up and down it. Man! I wanted out of there so bad, I would've given her the horse and paid a year's feed bill. The pain in my chest and side rose and swelled.

Over in the doorway to the other room, Martha cleared her throat, and I looked over and saw the same fire and sharp objects glitter in her dark eyes. Her right hand hung at her side. In it the long neck of a dead goose wobbled as she bumped it idly back and forth against her leg. Its head lay cocked at a crazy angle, its eyes bulging, it beak open a half an inch. *Man!* I wanted out of there *bad!* Its wide orange webfeet hung straight down toward the floor, paddling gently back and forth, as if trying to walk on air.

"Mr. Beatty? Are you all right?" Elizabeth Custer stepped back and looked at me. The pain had broken my forehead into a cold sweat. "Here, let's sit you down. My goodness." She draped my arm over her shoulder and led me to the next room. "Martha, you could *help,* you know."

"Hunh-uh. I ain't touching no dirty man, smelling like a *ca-nine.* I got this *goose* to fool with." She jiggled the dead goose.

"Marr-tha, *please?*"

"All right, then." She glared at me, but did step in and help guide me into the parlor and over to a small wingback chair where I spent the next hour. It was most uncomfortable for me, sitting there, feeling a trickle of blood beneath my bandages, but I listened to poor Elizabeth Custer spill out her personal problems. I listened, nodded, sipped my tea, and tried not to remind myself what a bad spot this was for me to be in. No man would appreciate having a total stranger—a horse dealer at that—hearing this sort of thing, especially if that man was a general in the U.S. Army. Yet there I sat, one knee crossed over the other, the tip of my damp, dirty sock hanging long off the end of my toes, lapping back and forth a little each time I adjusted myself on the seat of the wingback chair.

"You must think me a fool, Mr. Beatty," Elizabeth Custer said after telling me her and the general's problems, "going on like this to a perfect stranger." She tapped a lace handkerchief to her cheek as she sat her teacup down. "I've never told this to anyone except Martha, of course. I don't know why I've burdened you with it. Please forgive me." From two rooms away I heard the chop of a knife against a butcher's block, and now and then a grunt or a grumble.

"Nothing to forgive, ma'am. You just needed to get it

said, I reckon. Sometimes maybe there's things you can say to a stranger that you wouldn't reveal to your closest friend." I hadn't the slightest idea what I meant by that, so I cleared my throat and sat my empty cup aside. Martha had offered me a glass of sherry, but I turned it down cold, remembering what a powerful effect this woman had had on my drinking back in New Orleans. "Are you feeling some better now?"

She sighed and offered a weak smile. "Yes . . . yes, I am. You've been such a dear. And to think of all the trouble you've gone through, bringing me the horse, killing that wretched Indian, getting stabbed. How can I ever thank you for your kindness?"

I smiled, feeling the weakness stir once more in my stomach. "Well, ma'am, it's all a part of the service. Look at it as all figured into the *seven hundred* dollars—which if you wanted to pay me tonight would be just fine. That way I wouldn't have to disturb you for it in a couple of days when I leave." I tossed a hand, sort of a casual *it's-only-money* gesture. "Hate to even bring it up. But I need to get back to the tent now. I'm not feeling so good."

She didn't seem to hear a word I said. "You know, as I look back, I realize our troubles started long before this. Back when we were first married. The general has always placed his career above everything . . . always so—so *driven* . . ." And on she went for another half hour, until I finally felt my chin creep down toward my chest and I snapped my head up, blinking my eyes.

She took note of my drifting away on her, and said, "Listen to me rattle on, and you, poor man, you must be in terrible pain."

"No, ma'am, I'm fine here, although to tell the truth, I think I'm bleeding again." I pushed myself forward and up, stifling a groan. "So if you'd like to go ahead and settle our account tonight?"

She raised a finger, saying, "You know, I believe that all things happen for a purpose, and I can't help thinking that our meeting was *no* coincidence. Oh, I know I came looking for you to buy Honest Bob, but don't you feel that sometimes forces bring people together for a reason, I mean a *real* reason, one that we aren't even certain of at the time, but later come to realize?" She spoke as she guided me toward the door. "I truly believe that the Lord often uses each of us to act as *angels of keep* for one another. See, I think your coming here serves some higher purpose than perhaps either of us is yet aware of."

"Well, ma'am, I'm not exactly what you'd call anybody's *angels of keep.* To be honest with you, I'd like to get on back to the tent and attend to my wounds—"

She cut me off with a raised hand as she reached for the door. I hadn't noticed how open and unguarded she'd been until once again her eyes took on the caged depth and shut me out. "Now, Mr. Beatty, don't tell me you had any way of knowing you'd arrive here at a time when I was so distraught I— Well, I'm afraid to say what I might have done if you hadn't arrived when you did."

Was she playing with me here?

Now the door was open and I was half out it, no closer to my seven hundred dollars than I had been when I'd got there. "If I've been of help, ma'am, I'm real glad . . . and the only thanks I need for it is the price we agreed upon that night you—"

"Oh, but that's the wonderful thing about acting as one's angel. We'll both benefit from it. In fact, look at you already. Sure, you've had some misfortune. But I couldn't help but notice how sober you are. Perhaps these are things that needed to happen to you just to get back on the right path."

Sober? I stopped and stared at her a second. "Ma'am, I haven't drunk a drop since the night we left that restaurant."

She clasped her hands together. "See? Isn't that wonderful! And the way you turned down the sherry when Martha offered it to you. That took willpower. Perhaps my having faith in you bringing the horse here has helped a great deal. Sometimes taking on the mantle of responsibility makes us—"

"Ma'am." I shook my head a little, the pain glowing red hot in my side. "What I mean is, I haven't *wanted* to drink since that night. Believe me, if I'd wanted to, I would have."

She patted my forearm. "I know, I know. And that will get better and better in time. For now it's best to try and not think too much about it." She rolled a hand. "You know, look for other things to do, keep your mind occupied. Soon your wounds will heal. You'll look back on all this as if it's a bad dream. Just keep saying to yourself, 'every day in every way, I find myself growing stronger and stronger.' You'll see, it works." She smiled.

I let out a long breath and ran a hand across my forehead. "Yes, ma'am. Meanwhile, if you would, please, I'd like to get my money from you tonight. I've had a long day here."

She studied me closely as if considering it for a second—or pretending to—then said, "I see. We shouldn't have talked so much about the drinking, should we? Now I fear we've brought it to mind and your cravings have emerged, is that it?"

Nothing I said was going to register with this woman. "Ma'am, it's late. Just . . . give . . . me . . . my money . . . please." Only then did I realize she was on one side of the threshold and I the other.

"See, look at you." She jutted her chin. "You're in no condition to drink." The door eased forward between us an inch, then another and another. "Be strong, Mr. Beatty. Take it one step at a time. Believe me, in the morning you'll be glad you did."

Jesus. My head spun walking toward the livery barn, wondering if she seriously considered me a falling-down drunk, or if all this was her way of putting off paying me my money. *Every day in every way, I find myself . . .* Man oh man, I thought, is this woman really that trite, that lost and vacant, or was she just playing me like a cheap fiddle? Come morning, I was leaving whether Jack or the doctor or anybody else liked it or not. I hoped she'd give me my money first, but if she didn't, I was leaving anyway, writing it all off as a bad venture. This woman was beyond me. I might as well admit it.

On my way to the livery barn, I caught a glimpse of Captain Hirshfield standing on the porch of a frame house where three officers sat studying a chess game in the glow of a lantern. He looked toward me, checking a pocket watch in his hand, as if he'd been timing my visit in the Custer household.

PART 3

——◆——

Face of the Enemy

Riding Broad Circles

Leaving Custerland

Chapter

12

Planning a cakewalk . . .

The sound of the sweat bee hummed near my ear, growing closer and louder until I finally reached my hand up and swatted it away. "You awake?" Jack's voice came from some distant place and opened a thick veil of sleep surrounding me. I opened my eyes and saw him leaning toward me, and realized that once again I was on my cot not knowing how I got there. Above me the wind licked at the ceiling of the tent.

"From now on you're gonna listen to the doctor or I'll crack your head with a gun barrel," he said.

I rubbed my face and didn't try to sit up. "How— How long have I been out?"

"Two days," he said. "You've been drifting in and out, talking out of your head, knife fighting with that Indian." He let out a breath. "I've been a little worried. Started to think you wasn't gonna make it."

"Two days?" I rubbed a hand across my jaw and felt the course beard stubble. "You mean, for two days I haven't even known where I am?"

"I waited for you at the livery tent the other night till I got worried, then I lit out and met the lieutenant on the trail, bringing you back. Said he found you wandering around in the dark back at the fort. Your side was bleeding again. Doctor sewed up some busted stitches."

"Jesus." I turned my head toward him. "I really was hurt bad, then, wasn't I?"

He shook his head. "What the hell you think everybody's been trying to tell ya? You saw what happened to the dispatch rider, and he wasn't near as bad off as you. You damn fool. When you lose that much blood it affects your mind for a while—" He grinned. "—If you've got any *mind* to begin with."

I lay there for a second, taking stock of what had happened the past few days, trying to recall how I'd felt, how things had looked to me, how I'd been thinking. I pictured myself as a man in a trance, wandering here and there with no real purpose, a sleepwalker who thought he was awake. Now, as I looked up at the flapping tent ceiling and all around the tent, I noticed how much clearer everything appeared. I was getting better. I let out a sigh and rose up on the side of my cot. "Boy, Jack. It's been a rough one."

He leaned forward to press me back on the cot, but I raised a hand. "No. I'm all right. This time I mean it. Everything looks different now. Don't ask me how, just different. But I'm okay now."

"I sure hope so," he said. "Look, I brought you these." He reached down and picked up my saddlebags with one hand and a new pair of boots with his other. "Couldn't find a wide-brimmed hat, so I had to get this." He picked up a tall silk top hat and laid it beside me.

"A top hat?" I just stared at it.

"It's the best I could do for now. You don't *wanta* know what those boots cost."

"These will do, then," I said, not wanting to hurt his feelings.

"The Custer's colored woman took your shirt to wash."

"No kidding?" It struck me as odd.

"Yep. Elizabeth Custer's been here four or five times. Seems real concerned about you."

"Did she seem *concerned* enough to go ahead and pay us for Honest Bob?"

He cocked his head. "I figured you got paid for him the other night."

"Not at all. She skipped around the subject every time I brought it up." I took a deep breath and let it out. "I don't think she heard a word I said."

"Naw, she hears all right. It's just her way of getting what she wants. She's still out-dickering you. Can't you see that?"

"You're wrong, Jack. The woman's got problems. Things I can't even tell you about. Personal things."

He cocked an eye. "Oh? The two of you sharing secrets now, are ya? Things a man can't tell his *partner* about?"

I just stared at him as he rolled a hand and added, "Because if you and that *homely,* boring, uninteresting woman, whom you have no regard for whatsoever, need a little private time alone—"

"Okay, Jack." I cut him off. "I lied about thinking she's homely. But listen to this . . ."

I took a glance about the tent, then lowered my voice and told him everything Elizabeth Custer told me about her and her husband's marital problems. The last thing I told him was that until she'd heard of the general's affair with the Indian woman, she'd seriously thought her husband was unable to father a child. "So now I must face the fact that it has never been my husband's problem, but rather my own." She'd paused for a second, then. "I'm barren," she'd said with finality, and remembering her telling it to me, I recalled the pain in her eyes as she looked away from me with an expression of total failure.

"Jesus, Jack, why did she tell me such a thing? Or any of it for that matter."

"I don't know," he said quietly, staring in disbelief for a second. Then of all the things he could've asked, he said, "She actually said *that* word?"

I stared at him for a second, let out a breath, then said, "Yep, three or four times . . . bold as a sailor about it. But forget that. That's nothing. The strange part is, why on earth did she tell me?"

"Are you sure she really did? You've been out of your head, you know. Maybe you just imagined it?"

"No. She sat there and spilled out all their problems. And her housekeeper heard her tell me." I squinted, then said,

"See why it's best we get out of here as soon as we can? I don't like getting caught up in stuff like this, especially with folks like these. It's just a matter of time before the general finds out that some *horse trader* knows all about his personal affairs. How's that gonna set with him?"

"What about Honest Bob?"

"She said she doesn't care one way or the other about the horse now, so I figure we take him back with us and write this whole thing off as a wasted trip."

Jack sat rubbing his chin. "We came all this way to deliver a horse she *had* to have. Now we're going home with that same horse on a lead rope behind us. Nothing's any different, except you get cut all to hell for your effort." He winced and rubbed his brow.

"I know, I know. It's all been a waste of time. Shoulda known better than fooling with anybody who's part of the army. Now I figure we need to cut out and forget the whole thing. As soon as I get something to eat and get—"

"Hunh-uh." Jack cut me off, shaking his head. "We ain't leaving till the doctor says you're able to go."

"Jack, listen to me. I'm all right now. Since when did we ever hang around a place because a doctor said we had to?"

"This is a little different," he said. "It ain't like we've got a posse breathing down our necks. This is just a matter of you staying clear of that woman for a couple more days. Once the doctor yanks the stitches out of your side, we'll move on. But not until."

"Right, *stay clear* of her." I tossed a hand. "You said yourself she's been here checking on me, washing my shirt. What if she comes around wanting to tell me *more* stuff I shouldn't be hearing?"

"Just make up excuses, don't be around her. If she decides she still wants Honest Bob, *I'll* sell him to her. You stay scarce. Meanwhile I'll try to buy a wagon, something you can ride in as soon as the doctor gives ya the okay."

"I hate leaving here in a wagon. I'll stay clear of the general's wife, but when we leave here I wanta ride out the way I rode in—with a horse stuck twixt my boot heels."

"That's the spirit," a gruff voice called out from the fly of the tent. Griebs stepped inside, followed by the Italian corporal and a man in a straw hat and long riding duster.

Jack and I watched the three of them walk over to my cot. Griebs took a battered pair of boots from under his arm and pitched them down at my feet. "I've won enough money off ya to pay for these boots and four quarts of whiskey, lad. Everyday somebody bets me you'll die, and every day I take their money." He rubbed his thick thumb and finger together in the universal sign of greed, then let out a booming laugh.

"He done taka alla my money." The Italian shrugged.

"Glad you're winning," I said to Griebs with a wry smile.

He winked beneath a bushy red eyebrow. "I knows ya are, laddie." Then he swept a hand toward the man in the straw hat and duster. "This is Mr. Brazelton with the *Harper's Weekly*. He'd like a bit of a word with ya."

"If you're up to it, that is," the man added, sticking out his hand to me. "I'm here covering the expedition, but I also would like to do a few human interest stories around it. So when I heard about you and the knife fight . . . I said, now there's an interesting feature if ever I've heard one."

When we'd finished shaking hands, he ran his hand down his duster and looked back and forth between Jack and me, beaming.

"It's not really something I want to talk about," I said.

"He cutta the shit outa that Indian," the Italian chimed in.

"Aye, that he did," said Griebs. "I've known this lad since new Orleans, and I said even then, now there's a young lad with some *grit.*" He clenched a fist and swiped it through the air.

Brazelton smiled, then said to me, "Well, perhaps later when you're feeling better. We could find a quiet spot and go over the story."

"We'll see," I said.

"Good, then." He beamed again, putting that same familiar jut of chin into it, and tapped a pencil to his lips. "But if you could just tell me—"

"Why did you just say that?" I asked him in a curious tone.

"Say what?" he asked.

"You said *'Good, then.'* I've heard everybody saying it ever since I got here. I just wondered—"

"Aye, laddie," Griebs said waving a hand. "It gets on a body's nerves after a while. Everything is *good, then, fine, then,* or *dandy, then.* It's something General Custer says. Now the whole lot of them are saying it."

Brazelton scratched his head. "Come to think of it, I don't recall ever using that expression until I arrived here."

"Enough, *then,* gentlemen," Jack said, stepping between me and the others. "We need to let him collect himself. He's had a rough time of it."

Brazelton leaned around Jack and said down to me, "Will you be going along on the Black Hills expedition? I'm sure the army could use someone with your kind of *yarrrk—!*"

His words twisted into knots as Jack's hand spun a turn in his necktie and jerked his head down. "I don't like saying nothing twice," Jack said, leaning close to Brazelton's face, Brazelton's face turned blue around his bulging eyes. His broad-brimmed straw hat fell to the dirt.

"Easy, Jack!" I reached to grab his arm, but he turned loose of the necktie, and Brazelton's neck snapped back up as if made of rubber.

Griebs and the Italian looked at each other and grinned.

Brazelton staggered back and his free hand tugged at his collar. "Of course . . . I understand," he gasped. "As soon as you feel like talking—"

"I'll let you know." I nodded, and we watched as he stepped backward to the fly of the tent.

"You forgot something," I called out to him, sweeping a hand down and picking up his hat. I dusted it and held it out.

"No, that's all right—" He raised a hand toward us. "—You keep it. I have another. I heard you need one, anyway."

We just stared at him as he slipped out through the fly of the tent. When he was gone, Griebs and the corporal laughed out loud. "Aye, but you lads are *jewels* to behold." He spread his arms toward us and laughed, then opened a button on his tunic and slipped out a whiskey flask. "Would you honor me with a wee nip of the ole *start and stumble?*" He jiggled the flask toward Jack.

"Did you fellows happen to hear what we were saying when you came in?" I asked as Jack threw back a shot and ran a hand across his mouth.

"Oh, you mean about finding a wagon?" Griebs grinned in a way that made me wonder if they'd heard anything more. "Good luck, is all I can tell ya. We came here seventeen wagons short and had to buy up everything with wheels on it. I doubt you'll find four-wheel transportation for sale within a hundred miles." He gazed away for a second, rubbing a hand across his beard as if considering something. "Of course, I might arrange for you to borrow the mail buggy you rode to Fort Lincoln, if you can keep quiet about it and not mention my name should you run into a patrol along your way." He grinned and winked.

"No thanks," I said. "I don't wanta get hung for stealing government property." I reached for the flask, but Jack moved it away and handed it back to Griebs.

"You'd only be *borrowing* it as far as Bismarck, wouldn't ya? From there ya can take the rails." Griebs shook the flask and threw back another shot.

"Yeah, but forget it," I said. "It's a bad idea."

"Suit yourself, then." He shrugged, then leaned in close to my face and winked. "And as far as any designs you might have on little Libbie Custer, we didn't hear a word—" His voice dropped lower. "—Not a word." He swung a glance to the corporal. "Eh, Dammio?"

"Thata right. We notta hear a thing."

I looked at Jack, then back at them. "Whoa, now. I've got designs on the general's wife? That's not at *all* what we were talking about."

"Of course not, laddie." Griebs grinned, nudged Dammio in the side.

"We notta think nothing like-a that," said Dammio. "Ifa we did, we die before we breathe-a word of it." He pinched his thumb and finger together and tapped them against his lips.

"Did that reporter hear anything?" Jack reached for the flask as he asked Griebs.

"That I can't say." He handed him the flask and watched him throw back a shot. "But you've no cause to worry about us. You know what a stiff penalty it is, drinking on duty? I would lose me stripes, a month's pay, and spend a week in the drunkard's barrel. So let's call this little drink a token of trust between us."

"Thanks," Jack said.

"Besides, I give less than a blue tinker's damn about General *Hard-ass* Custer. H Troop serves under Captain Benteen." He took back the flask, tipped back a shot.

Jack eyed the two of them. "So, you're not exactly loyal subjects of General Custer?"

"Ah, make no mistake." Griebs wagged a thick finger back and forth for emphasis. "As soldiering goes, I'd side with our young *brevet* general at the gates of hell, just to show him I could." He shrugged. "But soldiering aside, I keeps tabs on when he retires, so I can retire the same time." He spread a dark grin. "I plans on moving me into a house close to his, so every time I sees him on the street, I can beat the green living shit out of him."

The corporal leaned in and tapped himself on the chest. "Anda I helpa him do it."

Jesus. I shook my head. "But I don't want you even *thinking* there's something untoward going on between me and Libb— I mean, the general's wife."

"Ah, laddie, we know little Libbie would not cast eyes on the likes of a horse dealer. But who can blame a man for trying?"

"But I'm *not* trying."

Griebs leaned in and patted a thick hand on my shoulder. "Come now, let's face it, the little woman is sweeter than a breeze over lilac, isn't she, though?" He chuckled under his breath.

"Not to me she's not." I shot Jack a glance, then looked back at Griebs. "She's homely, if you'll pardon my saying so . . . and—and she thinks I'm a drunk. Yeah, that's right. So, there's nothing at all between us. Nothing at all, never could be." I caught myself waving a hand and shaking my head as I spoke, and saw that Griebs and Dammio were grinning, shaking their heads along with me.

"You've got it bad for her, don't ya, laddie. I don't know when I've seen a man so smitten."

"Stop it, Griebs, that's not true." I rose slightly from my cot, but Jack pressed me back down. "All I want to do is stay away from her. I came all this way to bring her a horse. Now I don't even know if she wants it or not. I just want out of here."

"Aye, laddie, if ya say so. Meanwhile, Dammio and me wanted to see if the two of ya would want to make a whiskey run with us this evening. It would get ya up and around and keep your mind off the pining of your heart." He grinned.

"Thought there was no whiskey allowed within five miles of the camp?" Jack said. "How far are you riding?"

Griebs shrugged. "Five miles, of course. There's a camp of tamed Indians three miles from here, couple miles past it we meet a sutler out of Bismarck. He can get ya anything ya want. Sells whiskey that would peel paint off a fence post."

"Can *he* get us a buggy? Legally, that is?" Jack cocked an eye at him.

"If anybody can, it'd be him. But I wouldn't count on it."

Jack looked at me. "It's worth a try. Maybe *I'll* ride along with them. What do you think?"

I cocked an eye at Jack, then looked back at Griebs. "How will *I* get there?" I asked. "I can't sit a horse."

"Oh, we'll be taking a wagon. This is no small load of provisions we're going after."

"You don't need to go," Jack said. But I ignored him.

"What about getting caught?" I asked.

"There's little danger of that," Griebs said. "We'll be bringing back many an item for the officers and their wives. Things they can't get at the fort. Everybody sort of turns their heads when I make a run." He spread his big hands. "It's a common practice except when hard-ass Custer is around. Some of the officers rely on *Griebs's Express* to provide their womenfolk with the little things that make life bearable out here." He grinned, paused for a second, and said, "To be honest, I could use a couple of good riflemen along—not that I foresee any trouble. This should be a cakewalk."

"Then, sure," I shrugged, "count us in."

"Are you sure you're up to doing this?" Jack asked me, eyeing my bandaged chest.

"Sure, I'm sure. Jack, I'll go nuts hanging around here. If it's the only way we're gonna get a buggy to travel in, I say we go see about it." I looked back and forth between him and Griebs. "Besides, like the good sergeant here said, 'It's a cakewalk.'"

Chapter
13

---◆---

Looking through a bead of dew . . .

Now that I had two hats and two pairs of boots, I pulled on the pair of boots Jack had brought me, carefully slipped into the doeskin Indian shirt, dusted off the top hat, and placed it on my head.

"You oughta think about it some before you go traipsing out there this evening," Jack said as I stashed the rest of my belongings under my cot.

"It'll be good for me, getting out and around a little." I grinned and took up the walking cane, and Jack and I left the hospital tent and walked to one of the enlisted men's mess tents for a noon meal of boiled potatoes, brittle hardtack, and salt pork fat. Some of the soldiers stood up and cheered my recovery when we walked in.

The sides of all the mess tents had been rolled up to allow a stirring breeze to blow through them. As we ate, we smelled the aroma of roast elk, sweet potatoes, and some sort of rich cobbler pie coming from the officer's mess tent. Their tent stood across the way and pitched on a slightly higher level of flatland. Once, when I glanced over there, I could've sworn I saw Shotgun Tom seated in the middle of a long table of officers, looking like a picture of Jesus at the Last Supper.

I wasn't about to complain, but the food *we* ate had a harsh, stale taste to it. Although I hadn't eaten in two days, I only ate enough to appear grateful, then pushed the plate back and said to the gathered soldiers, "I've got to be careful for a couple of days. Don't want to crowd myself." I smiled and patted my stomach near the bulge of bandage beneath my shirt. Jack ate like a horse.

"So there you are," Roland Gaither said, walking into the tent and over to us. "Glad to see you're feeling better."

"Thanks," I said, sipping coffee that tasted of soap, salt, and some kind of disinfectant. "Have you ate yet?"

He glanced at the food left on my plate, at the sweat bee circling in and tapping its snout to a stringy chunk of salt pork. "Uh . . . no," he said. "But I'm fine. Had a large breakfast."

I grinned. "Are you sure? There seems to be plenty, right boys?"

The soldiers nodded in unison as I ran a hand across my mouth and stood up from the long wooden table. Jack stood up, too, stifling a belch, and as we turned to leave, one of the soldiers stepped forward and said, "Mr. Beatty? Do you mind telling us how hard it is, fighting a *wild* injun?" The question struck me as strange, and while I paused there, another soldier said, "What we mean is, it ain't nothing like fighting a *tame* one, is it?"

I winced, trying to think of what kind of answer would suit that kind of question. A picture of me and Rain in the Face crossed my mind, both of us lunging, swinging a handful of sharp steel at one another, our flesh sliced deep, spilling our lifeblood into the shallow peaceful stream that ran across a broad stretch of earth between his people and mine. "It ain't something I want to ever do again," I said, my voice sounding a bit hollow to me.

"He don't like talking about it," Jack said, stepping along with me as I walked away. Gaither fell in beside us, and we walked over to the rope corral behind the livery tent where Ole Nutriment stood bent over his anvil. He struck his hammer against a glowing piece of metal, turning the metal with a long pair of tongs after each ringing blow.

"Well, gentlemen," Gaither said, hooking a thumb in his belt, "you might be interested to know that I've met with a couple of agents from over in Bismarck, and it looks like I have a good shot at landing a beef contract with Indian Affairs."

We looked at him as we walked along. "No kidding?" I said. "You sure didn't waste any time once you got here." I still couldn't picture him being a cattle buyer.

"Well, that's the way this business works," he said. "The key to it is moving fast. Get the right person, strike the right price, settle the figures and terms on paper, and there you are." He smiled and spread a hand. "Probably no different than horse trading, eh?"

"Naw," Jack chuckled. "In horse dealing, you let the buyers talk you up in price, then you talk them back down, then you travel a thousand miles, deliver the goods for free, and they end up not paying you."

Gaither's voice dropped a bit. "I'm sorry things haven't gone well for you. Maybe you'd like to throw in with me for a while. I can always use some venture capital."

I stopped outside the rope corral and turned facing them with my cane up under my arm. "Oh? I reckon this hasn't turned out too bad, all things considered. No offense, but I don't want nothing to do with these army *sweet deals*. I know how the government beef program works."

"Now see here, Beatty. This is not one of those kind of deals where the agents and I make money off screwing the Indians, if that's what you're implying."

I grinned. "Naw, of course not. But if they overcount your cattle by a few hundred head and they overpay you for them . . . and you happen to drop a stack of dollars on the floor while you're leaving, whose fault is it? Hell, mistakes happen, huh? Ain't that the very thing Congress just investigated out here? Only I believe it was *corn* instead of cattle, wasn't it?"

"You're impossible, Beatty. Forget I said anything. I don't think I'd want your venture capital. You think everybody is out to beat somebody else." He turned and said to Jack. "I don't know how you put up with it. Is he always so cynical?"

Jack grinned. "Aw, yeah. But the thing is, he's usually right when it comes to government deals, anyway. Government won't even take its pants down unless it knows somebody's gonna get screwed. You oughta know that. Being a former policeman, you're bound to have seen some *sweet deals* going on."

Gaither stood silent for a second, then shook his head. "I feel sorry for you two. I wouldn't want to live in the world you live in. There's plenty of fine, decent people running this country and these government programs. Sure, there are some bad apples, but they're few and far between. This is a good straightforward deal, and I'll see to it *personally* that it stays that way." He tossed a hand. "I've already gathered nearly seven thousand dollars, much of it from army officers who, like myself, are eager to see this thing go well. The fact is—"

"Damn." Jack cut him off and spread a sheepish grin. "I didn't know you felt so strongly about it. You're right. There are some good folks out there running things." He nodded toward me.

"Absolutely," I said. "We just a little carried away sometimes. Don't pay us no attention. What the hell do we know?" I shrugged.

Gaither let out a breath. "Well . . . I didn't mean to go into a spiel there. It just gets to me sometimes, everybody blaming the government, calling all our leaders crooks." He smiled. "If you would change your minds, you're welcome to invest with me. Just let me know something pretty soon, though. Like I said, the key to my business is to move fast and get it done."

"Sure," I said. "We'll seriously think about it."

"It really ain't a bad proposition," said Jack.

"Yes. I think we all stand a chance to make an honest profit here," Gaither said. "Now if you'll excuse me, I have some other folks to talk to. Everybody wants in on this, it seems."

"Good, then," Jack said and we watched as Gaither turned and walked away. Then Jack turned back to me. "Well, it looks like I was wrong and you were right. He just cinched it for me."

"Yep," I said, watching Gaither's duster tails sway behind him in the breeze. "I just knew that son of a bitch wasn't no *real* cattleman."

* * *

I saw Jack walk back to the coral from the livery tent, leading his silver gray. He carried my saddle on his shoulder, then dropped it on the ground and stood watching me as I walked among the horses until I found the Gypsy roan, slipped a lead rope his head, and led him out. "Where'd you find your horse?" I asked, tying up the corral rope behind. The roan nudged my shoulder and tapped his hoof on the ground. "Easy boy." I rubbed his muzzle.

"I paid him a couple bucks to keep him over with the officers' stock," Jack said, running a hand down his horse's neck.

"Did he say where Foxfire and Honest Bob are?"

"Yeah, he had them both taken over to the fort. Said they were too fine animals to be out here, even with the officers' stock."

"Yeah? Then he throws this ole roan right in with these army plugs." I patted the roan's withers; bust bellowed.

Jack chuckled. "Well, let's face it. That ain't the best-looking horse ever came around the pike."

"He ain't let me down since I got him," I said. "These Spanish barbs will surprise you, looks aside." I bent over, raised the roan's right front hoof, checked it, and let it down, then stepped around to check his other.

"Careful with them stitches," Jack said.

"I'm all right, Jack. My stitches are healing up. I've got my strength back."

"Good thing, too, you're gonna need it. Look who's coming here." He nodded in the direction of the livery tent, and when I looked over there, Libbie Custer came walking toward us leading a tall bay rigged with a sidesaddle. A long linen cape swayed behind her in the warm breeze. When she saw us watching her, she flipped back the hood of her cape and touched her free hand to her hair.

"I wish she hadn't came here," I said to Jack under my breath, even as I smiled and raised my silk top hat.

"But here she is," he said, "and here I go. You're on your own, *mi amigo.*"

"Wait, Jack, damn it." I turned, but he'd already stepped up on his silver gray. "Don't leave me here alone with her," I hissed. "What if folks see us and get the wrong idea?"

He nodded at the bustle of soldiers fifty yards away in

camp, all of them looking busy as a young captain strolled by. "If they ain't already, I doubt if they will. It ain't like she's carrying a bottle of wine and a picnic basket." He turned the silver gray and heeled off toward the livery tent, passing her and tipping his hat.

Well, shit . . . I stood there holding the lead rope to the roan as Libbie Custer called out from fifteen feet away. "There you are. I went by the hospital, but the doctor said you were up and around, doing fine, evidently."

"Uh . . . yeah. I feel much better, thanks. What brings you this way? Not just to see about me, I hope?"

"Oh—" She swiped her free hand, then touched it to a ringlet of hair the breeze swept across her face. "—I should tell you no, to keep from flattering you . . . but *yes*, I did come here specifically to see you." She stopped three feet from me as I took off my top hat and held it against my chest. Beside me the roan blew toward the tall bay and stamped a hoof. The bay perked its ears and sawed its head a bit. "Don't have your hat off. You'll catch something in the breeze."

"Yes, ma'am." I placed the hat back on my head.

"Besides, look at you. You've taken on a flare for frontier dress."

"Hunh?"

"And you look quite fetching: the hat, the Indian shirt . . ." She swept a hand toward me; I glanced down at the shirt and touched the breastwork of tiny shells and antelope bones.

"Oh, well, I'm a little short of clothes right now."

"Speaking of which—" She reached inside her cape, took out a folded shirt, and handed it to me. It wasn't the one I'd gotten from Jack, and I commented on it as I turned the shirt in my hands.

"No. I'm afraid the other was beyond washing. Do you own many dogs, Mr. Beatty?"

"No, ma'am, it was just a spare shirt that had been laying around."

"You needn't explain," she said. "At any rate, I hope you like this one."

"Yes, ma'am. It's a fine shirt. But where? I mean, how? That is, I hear stuff is hard to get around here."

"Not for an officer's wife, Mr. Beatty." When she said

that, I noticed her eyes take on that familiar withdrawal, and she turned and faced the breeze coming off the open land. After a moment's pause, she said, "Don't you *so* love this beautiful country? Isn't it lovely here?

"Yes, ma'am, it is." And I stood there in silence with the shirt and my cane under one arm and my other arm cradling the roan's head while he sniffed at the breastwork on the Indian shirt, finding in his breath the remembrance of places and things gone past the here and now, and long faded to memory. Yet the scent of those things lingered deep in the leather and breastwork and spoke to his higher senses. I envied him that.

But this woman wasn't here to talk about the land—even my senses knew that much. "Mr. Beatty," she said at length without facing me. "I said some things the other night— Things I shouldn't have said. I hope. That is . . . I truly wouldn't want you to get the wrong impression of the general."

"Ma'am," I said in a quiet tone, knowing she couldn't face me right then, not until I said something to break the awkwardness for her. "Nothing you said to me was untoward in any way. And no mention will ever be made of it." As soon I said it, I felt a little ashamed. I'd already told Jack about it. "It was just a bad day for you, and you needed to talk, ma'am."

"Yes. Yes, that's all it was." She let out a breath and turned, almost but not quite looking me in the eyes. "He's a wonderful man, my husband. Charming, dashing, courageous. If you knew him, you'd agree."

"Yes, ma'am." I felt my expression go as blank as hers.

She noted it and said, "But it's true, you would. You mustn't let the things I said the other night influence you."

"Of course not, ma'am." I smiled, and she returned it.

"Please call me, Libbie . . . or Mistress Custer, if you prefer—" She smiled; her eyes flicked across mine, then away. "—Anything but *ma'am*. It makes me feel so *elder* to you."

I smiled also. *"Mistress* Custer, then."

"I have received word the general will be arriving at the fort tomorrow. I want to pay you for the horse and thank you for your kindness."

I nodded. "Then you want Honest Bob after all?"

"Of course. I think the general will be thrilled. This morning I went to the officer's stables and looked at him." She smiled, but there was a sadness there. "I thought the dear animal would kick down the stall and follow me home."

I chuckled. "Don't say I didn't warn you, ma'am—I mean, Mistress Custer. He's got some bad habits. Stall kicking is only one of them."

"Yes." She brushed a loose ringlet back from the breeze and stood silent for a moment as if out of anything to say.

"So, I guess that's that. You did mention paying me?"

"Oh, yes, I did." She smoothed back her hair against the breeze. "I would have had the general give me the money today had I known you were up and around. But if you'll come by the house early tomorrow, your seven hundred dollars will be waiting for you."

I nodded, suddenly feeling better about the whole trip, and now gazed out across the open land myself. "You're right about this land, Mistress Custer. It's beautiful beyond words." Out toward the perimeter where guards were posted, two officers in straw hats stood watching enlisted men set up a tripod for a ground transit. A leaf of paper left fluttered from one of the officer's hands and he bounded after it as it skipped and tumbled away. "Too bad it can't stay this way."

"Oh, but it can and it will, Mr. Beatty. Once these hostiles are under control, once this land is settled, once we've established civilization here, this place will be even more beautiful. Oh, but I can just see it looking out there, gentle hamlets dotting the plains . . . row after row of houses with white picket fences, as far as the eye can see." She looked at me and blushed. "Of course I realize this shan't all happen overnight."

I just stared at her. "I hope not, ma'am."

"My husband doesn't share my vision. He sees it as someday being a large park, a wildlife refuge. A placed to be preserved as it has always been, in honor of our heritage—once we get rid of the Indians, of course. *Custerland National Park,* he says we'll call it."

Again, I just stared at her and cocked my head curiously.

"Oh, yes. And he sees it someday being a place where people can bring their entire family and spend the summer, riding trains back and forth through exhibit after exhibit of wild animals . . . perhaps even some wild animal rides, if there's a way to train the remaining buffalo by then. He's quite a visionary, the general."

"Custerland," I said under my breath, gazing out where the soldiers worked at the transend. "Custer Land." I said it a different way, trying to get the feel of it, trying to picture it. But nothing came to me except an old bull buffalo spiking tourists on his horns and slinging them high in the air. I shook my head.

She clasped her hands together. "I must share a little secret with you, Mr. Beatty." I almost raised a hand to stop her, but before I could, she continued. "I'm a writer. And I keep a journal about all this." She swept a hand taking in the whole endless rolling land. "Yes. I write about this land, how it looks now and how it will someday look."

I didn't know what to say, so I just said, "So, you're a *writer?*"

She cocked her head and looked at me. "You say *'writer'* as if you have something against writers."

"No, ma'am." I shook my head. "Some of my best friends are writers."

"Really?" Her eye took on an excitement. "You know some writers? Anyone famous?"

My face reddened. "No, I don't really know any . . . just a figure of speech. But I think it's admirable that you write."

Now she blushed slightly. "It's only a dream at present, but I shall keep at it until someday, who knows? Someday I could well be another Mary Shelley."

"Nothing wrong with having a dream," I said. "Someday I hope I'll see a book you've written."

"It will be quite some time, I'm afraid. Everyone says, write about what you know, and to be perfectly honest—" She tossed a hand and offered a weak laugh. "—I don't know anything."

"I'm sure that's not so, ma'am. You're married to a famous man, you're well traveled, you meet heads of state. I'm sure you know a lot . . . a lot more than many of us."

"Perhaps you're right." She tapped a finger to her lips,

considering something, but then she seemed to dismiss it. "But the things I'd like to write about are the very personal inner thoughts and experiences of a person. Dare I say it? I want to write about love and romance, somehow express these things in a bead of morning dew as it glistens in sunlight on the peddle of a yellow rose . . . show the hands of two young lovers when first they touch, seen through that bead of dew."

Jesus. Again, I just stared at her, then I said, "Well . . . that might take some practice, but meanwhile, as long as you're at it, I reckon you can always write about you and your husband."

She sighed. "Yes, I suppose."

The roan stood beside me raising his head into the breeze, letting it lift and lick at his mane. I glanced at him and patted his neck.

"Do you have a wife, Mr. Beatty? Children?"

"No, ma'am, it's just me. I once had a wife, but it didn't work out for us." Her question took me by surprise and I'd answered her quickly before having time to stop myself. It was not like me to mention either my past *or* my personal life to anybody. Yet I'd just mentioned both in a single breath.

"I'm sorry," she said. "But you *have* been in love, then?"

"Yes, ma'am, a long time ago . . . at least, it feels like a long time." *Why was I telling her this?* "I fell in love with a young woman back after the war. We married, but her father did everything in his power to break us up. Finally he did." I shrugged. "The pressure got to us, I reckon." I wasn't about to mention that it involved a shoot-out, a posse, a near hanging, a jailbreak, and a killing.

"That's terrible, Mr. Beatty. And you've never found someone to take her place?"

"No. I've never *looked* for anyone, to be honest with you." *What the hell was wrong with me, telling her all this?* But even as I warned myself to stop, I pulled the roan's head down from the breeze, rubbed his muzzle, and said, "I figure if a man's lucky enough to love one good woman in his life for a while, and have her love him in return . . . well, he ought not expect any more than that."

"Oh, Mr. Beatty," she whispered.

I stopped for a second but couldn't seem to keep myself from saying, "I still love her, always will. Can't help hoping that wherever she's at, she's happy . . . and that maybe in some way she still thinks about me sometimes." I looked past the Gypsy roan out across the gentle round sweeps of breeze across the wild grass.

"I—I know how you must feel," she said in a soft tone, and as I turned and looked at her, she quickly looked down at the ground and added, "That is, I know it must be terrible going through life with no further expectations of ever loving someone. That must be painful."

What a strange thing for her to say, I thought. "Yes, well—" I cleared my throat against the back of my hand. "—I try not to think about it. I stay busy traveling a lot, always at my trade, you see." I smiled and patted the roan.

She smiled, but it looked a little forced. "Oh, you *men.*" She put a hand on her hip in mock exasperation. "You simply refuse to let things get the better of you."

"That's us, all right . . . hard as nails." We stood looking in each other's eyes, there in the warm breeze off the rolling plains, each knowing that somehow we'd just stepped outside ourselves and touched one another. Like two hands touching through a bead of dew, I thought. For a second as the breeze pressed me forward, I wondered how it would taste, kissing this woman's lips. This warm beautiful woman, I thought, whose very aura drew me to her, whose eyes held a depth of understanding like no eyes I'd seen, whose hair shone like silk in the—*Jesus! Stop it!* I shook my head to clear it.

As if having been joined as one in the same thought, she, too, shook her head slightly and touched a hand to a loose ringlet of hair. Once again the expression in her eyes withdrew back to that place inside her. Was it lonely in there? "Well, then," she said. "Until tomorrow, Mr. Beatty?"

"Uh, yes. Until tomorrow."

Chapter
14

An evening on the rolling plains . . .

Three miles out of the camp, Griebs shot a young buck deer. We stopped long enough to dress it out, cut some steaks from it, wrap the rest of it in canvas, and load it behind the wagon seat. After cooking the steaks over a small fire, we ate as we traveled on toward the Indian village a mile ahead. At the edge of the village a crowd of old woman and young children stood waiting for us, their dark caged eyes studying the wagon bed as it rolled into their midst. Their expressions told me they'd heard Griebs's rifle shot earlier, and now they waited to see if the sound of it meant food for someone's belly or news of someone's loved one felled on these endless plains.

"How come there's no men here?" I asked Griebs as he closed his horse up near the wagon. Between him and the throng of milling Lakota, Corporal Dammio sat his big bay horse with his rifle propped up and his finger inside the trigger guard.

"If it's young warriors you're worried about, they've all drifted up to join Sitting Bull." Griebs reached down in the wagon bed, pulled up the bloody bundle of deer meat with his thick hand, raised it, and pitched it toward the crowd. "There's some old men here, but they refuse to show themselves." The bundle of meat hit the ground, raising a low stir of dust. The Indians stepped back and stared down at it.

I looked about the village, at long rows of ragged teepees mended in spots with patches of army blankets and strips of tent canvas. On one I saw the faded letters *U.S.*, and on another an advertisement for agricultural equipment. Standing among the teepees here and there were sheets of rusting corrugated tin bent over walls of rough-cut lumber and held down by bailing wire.

"This is what the government has to offer," Jack spoke under his breath and nodded toward a mound of empty flour sacks and rusty tin cans on our right. Flies swarmed.

Griebs grinned, speaking to an old woman as he pointed to the bundle of deer meat and rubbed his stomach. With no expression, she pulled away from the hand of a younger woman on her arm and stooped down to gather the bundle. The younger woman glanced up at me with a flash of humiliation that she swallowed when our eyes met for a second. Then she and a young boy of seven or eight years leaned down to help. "Why the hell did we have to come through here?" I asked Jack almost in a whisper.

"Probably the army's way of promoting *goodwill,*" Jack said in a low tone.

Others stepped forward and helped gather the bundles of meat, and as the bundles disappeared into the crowd, the little boy pointed up at me and scolded me in Lakota. I looked all around, feeling my face redden. "What's he squawking about?"

Griebs chuckled and spit, then said, "He says you're the white man who shot his father. He wants to take your scalp."

Aw, Jesus. I ducked my head, thinking of the two Indians I'd shot back at the river. One had rolled off dead into the water; the other had rode on, wounded. Which one was the boy's father?

The boy berated me, pointing his dark tiny finger while the crowd murmured behind him. Then Griebs spoke to them in their tongue, loudly and harshly, and the young woman's hand reached out and snatched the boy back.

"What did you say?" I asked him, seeing the crowd draw back and quieted at the sound of his words.

He chuckled, and he and Dammio moved their horses forward, parting the crowd. "I told them to get him back or you'd make a *good* Indian out of him."

"Damn you, Griebs." I stood halfway up from my seat, but Jack's hand caught my arm and pulled my down.

Griebs spun his horse close to me and said, grinning, "Listen to me, laddie, they only understand *tough talk.* Ya can't mollycoddle savages. They misinterpret it."

I just stared at him, then down at the crowd as they pulled back and drifted away, some of the old women hugging the bundles of meat against their bosoms. I caught the eyes of the young boy on me for a second, looking through me, I thought, seeing me forever as some dark terrible force that had laid harm to his family. Pulling my high top hat low on my forehead, I looked away. Jack slapped the reins to the mules and we rode on.

To clear the face of the Indian boy from my mind, and to keep from thinking of that whole village of stark-eyed refugees of war, I told Jack about my meeting with Libbie Custer—about the strange feeling I'd had out there with her in the warm breeze.

Jack sat listening, the reins dangling in his hands. His silver gray and the Gypsy roan walked along behind us reined to the wagon gate. Ahead of us, Griebs and Dammio rode one on either side of the trail, keeping an eye on the rise and fall of the land around us.

"What gets me is that I *told* you so, and you denied it," he said when I'd finished talking. "'Naaaaw,' you said. No interest there. Called her homely, dull, said she wasn't the kind of woman you'd ever—"

"I never said any of that, Jack, *you did.* I just said she got on my nerves a little, is all. Now that I've got to know her, I can't help it if I feel a little attracted to her. She's a beautiful woman."

"Yeah, a beautiful *married* woman . . . a general's wife, don't forget."

"She ain't happy with him, Jack. I can tell that."

"Boy oh boy." He flicked the reins on the team of mules to keep them moving steady. "You let her play you around on the horse deal, and now you're listening to her sad story."

My face reddened. "She ain't giving me no sad story. She ain't said a word about how unhappy she is. But that's how I can tell she is." I thought about that and scratched my head under my top hat.

"Listen to yourself," he said, and he chuckled a little and shook his head.

"Jack, damn it. What I'm saying is, she's lonely . . . she doesn't love him. She doesn't love *him,* and she's afraid she'll never love anybody else. She's stuck with who she is— with who *they* are. That's why she puts up a front, hides her eyes, says things that sound foolish just to keep the world at arm's length." I took the canteen from him and threw back a drink of water.

"And you got all of this on your own? From her just telling you about a bead of water on a rose petal, or some such thing?"

"A bead of *dew,* Jack. Yes, that's where I got it, that and her saying she knew how I felt, being alone . . . never expecting to *not* be alone." I looked around at the shadows growing long across the tall grass, at the sun glowing low on the rim of the earth. "Don't it seem like we've gone a lot farther than five miles to you?"

"Yeah, some," he said. Then he shot me a glance as Corporal Dammio turned his horse and started back toward us. "But I've to warn ya as a friend, it'd be one damn *bad* mistake to go bumping your roscoes with a general's wife, especially one as crazy as George Custer."

"I wish you wouldn't talk that way about her. Besides, don't you reckon I know how dangerous it is?" A silence passed as we gazed ahead, then I said, "He'll be here sometime tomorrow. I'll pick up our money, we'll go our way, and she'll go back to being the general's wife. Whatever mighta sparked between us for a minute or two will be all forgotten. That's how things go."

"Um-hmm." Jack looked at me as Dammio drew closer. "How's your stitches holding up?"

I patted my doeskin shirt. "I'm fine. I could have these things plucked out and go on about my business anytime."

"Good. Maybe we oughta go ahead and leave tomorrow,

whether we can get a buggy or not. Think you can sit a horse as far as Bismarck?"

"Sure. But don't be thinking I'm going to do something stupid if we stay." I threw back another drink of water as Dammio reined his horse around alongside us. "I shouldn't even have mentioned it to you."

"The hell you shouldn't," Jack said.

"Excusa me," said Dammio. "You-a have-a the private conversation here?"

"Naw," Jack said. "Just going over our traveling plans. Why?"

"Griebs saya to tell ya, we gotta problem. Thata sutler, he shoulda beena here by now." He looked a little worried and pinched a thumb and finger together. "We no understanda it. Griebs saya maybe you ride aheada with him." He pointed at me. "Me anda him stay here witha the wagon, eh?"

Jack drew back on the reins and wagon brake, then looked up at the corporal as we stopped. "You thinking something might've happened to the sutler?"

"Maybe. We done comea three miles more thana we should. He shoulda be here."

Jack and I stood up dusting the seat of our trousers before stepping out of the wagon. "Cakewalk, huh?" he said.

"I don't thinka we got nothing to worry about," said Dammio, reining alongside us as Jack and I walked back to our horses. "Butta ya never know."

Jack unhitched the reins to his silver gray. I checked my Henry rifle and loosened the reins to the roan just in case I needed to free him up and make a run for it. "If ya'll ain't back in twenty minutes, I'll come looking," I said.

Jack stepped up on the silver gray and swung his rifle from the scabbard. "Pull the wagon off the trail. If ya need us, fire two shots back to back," he said.

When Jack rode up to where Griebs sat waiting alongside the trail, Dammio stepped up into the wagon seat and reined the mules off into the waist-high grass beside the trail. I followed him, scanning the land with my Henry rifle cradled in my arm. The sweat bee circled in and whined near my cheek. I slapped myself on the jaw, but missed him and heard him buzz away. "Thisa army isa always the *hurry up and wait,* eh?" Dammio asked in a quiet tone, stepping down from the wagon and squatting down beside the wheel with his rifle over his knee.

He didn't seem concerned that we were out in open country, four men on the edge of a wilderness that stretched to the end of vision. "Mighta as well make-a yourself comfortable." He gestured for me to join him there on the ground, and I did. If he wasn't too concerned, neither was I.

"So, Corporal Dammio, has this happened before? Maybe the sutler's got a late start. Maybe his wagon broke down?"

He grinned. "Sure, thisa coulda be. We no starta worrying yet, eh? I finda out a long time ago, not to worry until-a you see arrows sailing past you. Thena you gotta no time worry."

I nodded. "You been in the army long?"

"No, buta it seems like *long.*" He checked his rifle, raised it, sighted some imaginary enemy on the distant horizon, and pretended to fire at it. Then he lowered the rifle and patted a hand on it. "I joina the army foura years ago." He paused as we searched the silence of the land, hearing only the rustle of an evening breeze. Then he added, "The army she's-a been good to me. Make-a me a citizen, teacha me to speaka the English, teacha me a trade. All I gotta do isa protecta this United States, and she'll protecta me."

"Protect her from what?" I nodded back in the direction of the Indian village. "Protect her from the people she rightfully belonged to?"

He shook his head. "I don'ta know what'sa right or wrong about the Indians. I only know thata I sneaka onto a ship and hide for-a two months to getta here. I walka the city streets, picka the garbage, do-a the things even the Irish won'ta do, just so someday I can-a say to my *familia,* 'thisa United States, she'sa my home now, because-a I do-a my part for her.'" He pinched his thumb and finger together. "So, nobody ever come to me and say, 'Dammio, you do-a this, you do-a that,' and make-a me bow down like a peasant."

I looked away, checking the land. "Well, I hope it works out for you better than it did for the Lakota."

We sat in silence for nearly half an hour, then I got up,

walked back, and unreined the roan from the rear of the wagon. "I thinka we better wait," said Dammio when he saw me getting ready to step up in the stirrup.

"I've waited as long as I said we would. We should've known something by now." But just as I swung up in the saddle, Jack came up over a rise in the trail, and I watched as he rode toward us. When he got a few yards from us, he cut his silver gray off the trail and rode on to the wagon. "Where's Griebs?" I asked, looking past him up the trail.

"I don't know. One minute he was right behind me, the next he was gone." Jack and I both turned to Dammio. He stood up with a concerned look in his eyes.

"It'sa not like-a the sergeant to be late. We better go looka for him."

"Any sign of the sutler?" I asked Jack.

"Not a trace." He gazed out toward the crest of a rise fifty yards away. Beyond it the sun lay low on the darkening horizon. "If we're gonna look for Griebs, let's do it quick. I don't like the feel of this." He looked at me atop the roan and added, "You okay on that horse?"

"If I ain't, I know how to get off." Stepping the roan over beside Jack, we both watched as Dammio mounted and swung his rifle across his lap.

"I'ma gonna be ina big trouble, if we don'ta take the wagon back with us."

"We'll make one sweep for Griebs," I said. "If we don't find him, we're out of here. To hell with the wagon. Let the army—" My words were cut short as a bullet thumped against the side of the wagon, followed by the crack of a rifle from the crest of the rise. We spun our horses, but before we could even dismount, a shot whined in from the other direction and Dammio threw a hand to his shoulder.

"Cross fire," Jack shouted. "Hit the grass!" He dropped from his saddle with his rifle in his hand, swung himself up around the silver gray's neck, and downed it into the tall grass. Dammio dropped from his saddle and did the same with his horse. I slipped from the roan as bullets pelted the wagon and the ground.

"Jesus, we're surrounded!" I yelled. Not wanting to risk busting my stitches, I slapped the roan's rump to get him out of the fire, but instead of running, he spun a circle and bellied down like the other two horses. I dropped behind him and fired my rifle across his side. Dammio kept a steady fire in one direction, Jack and I in the other. Stems of grass sliced by bullets whipped around us. "We can't hold out here, Jack."

"Howa many you figure?" Dammio asked Jack as he jerked cartridges from his ammunition pouch.

"Four," Jack said. "Two on each side of us. They'll have to slow down to reload. When they do, we make a break for it."

A bullet clipped the high rim of my top hat and spun it up in the air. I rolled away to the side and fired a shot toward the rise, unable to aim amid the tall grass.

A succession of rapid pistol fire boomed from the rise, then the rifles fell silent from that direction. We all three looked at each other, then turned and fired at the rifles on our other side. In a second, rifle fire started again from the crest of the rise, but this time no bullets came in on us. Instead, the firing seemed to be above us and aimed at the other two rifles. "Think it's Griebs?" I yelled, but Dammio only shrugged and kept firing.

"Wait, hold your fire," Jack said, raising a hand slightly. We lay there for a second as two more rounds from the rise fired above us toward the other rifles. Then there was only silence, and in the distance beyond the rise, the sound of horse's hooves running away.

From above the rise, Griebs's voice bellowed, "That'll do it, lads. Now draw up whilst I bring in a prisoner." We glanced at one another as we stood and saw Griebs stepping down the rise, shoving a skinny white man along before him. As they came closer, I recognized the man as Walker, the one whose shirt I wore. He held one hand against the side of his head, his other out to the side for balance while Griebs goaded him forward with his rifle barrel. "Double-crossing bastard," I heard him say to Griebs.

"Don't be a sore loser." Griebs chuckled and poked him in the back until they came the rest of the way to us.

"What's he talking about, Griebs?" Jack looked up from raising his silver gray from the ground. Dammio and I did the same, and stepped over to Griebs and Walker while the horses shook themselves off.

"He's talking about me setting him and his weasel brother up for the kill," Griebs said, raising his rifle barrel and tapping Walker on the side of his head with it. "Not too smart, are you, Ebb, *lad,*" he said.

Ebb Walker sneered, looking up and down my doeskin shirt. "That's mine and I want it back, you son of a—"

"Here, now." Griebs tapped a little harder; Walker flinched and raised a bloody hand to the side of his head. "Don't make me cheat the jailers and shoot you where you stand."

"What's this about, Griebs?" I stared at him. "There was no sutler coming to meet us here, was there? You brought me out here to give me up to this rat?" I felt my neck heat up. My hand went to my pistol under my arm.

"Now, now, laddie," Griebs said to me. "Don't jerk a knot in your bowels. Sure, I mighta let the word out that you would be riding with me this evening. Might have even led this little snake to believe I would be bring ya to him. But you're alive, he's on his way to the jailhouse—" Griebs's eyes widened. "—And *gl'hory be,* lad, we'll fetch up and split the thousand-dollar reward the army has posted on him for stealing government property." He smiled and spread his thick arms. "Now, who but a dear ole Irish sergeant would do such a thing for ya?"

I glared at him. "I don't like it, Griebs, not a bit."

"Anda neither do I," Dammio said stepping forward with a hand clasping his wounded shoulder. "You gotta me shot this time, you biga tub-a shit!"

"Easy now, lads." Griebs shoved Walker to the side and faced us, his rifle raised and drawn back like a club. "You should be thanking me for it." He trained his stare on Dammio. "You've been broke since last payday, so don't tell me you're not hard put for spending money." He turned to me. "And you, Mr. Beatty, tell us now . . . would ya rather face Walker like this, or would ye prefer meeting him and his friends along the trail whilst you and your friend head back to Bismarck in a buggy rig?"

"He's got a point," Jack said as I glared at Griebs.

"There, then." Griebs grinned, grabbed Ebb Walker by the collar, and shook him like a rag doll. "We all make a little something off this miserable hide."

"Still seems like a damn dirty trick," I said, stepping back a foot.

"Yeah," Walker sneered at Griebs. "You said I'd get my shirt back. Said as far as you cared, I could take him to Rain in the Face and let him cut his heart out. Said—"

Griebs cracked him a sound lick with the rifle barrel and sent him to his knees against the wagon. Then he turned to me saying, "Aye, it might sound a little coarse and under-handed to ya at present, but it'll settle with ya once we take our share of the reward. Don't go thinking too harshly of me."

"I don't want the damn money." I spit on the ground and stepped aside.

"Even better, then." Griebs beamed and raised a finger. "The world loves a man with a high sense of morality." He chuckled, reached down, and yanked Walker to his feet.

Jack stepped in close to Griebs. "Ever pull another stunt like that on us, I'll kill ya, Sergeant. Make no mistake about it." His voice sounded calm and quiet, but it caught Griebs and kept him staring with uncertainty until Jack turned from him and stepped up into his stirrup.

Chapter

15

The thing about outlaws . . .

A three-quarters moon lit our way back to the camp. We swung wide of the Indian village, lest the sight of Ebb Walker in our custody provoke more bad feelings. Once more I sat in the wagon, only driving it now as Jack rode along beside me. Ahead, Dammio and Griebs argued among themselves, Dammio's shoulder wound cleaned and dressed, his left arm in a sling and his right hand throwing angry gestures at Griebs as he spoke. But Griebs only chuckled and shook his head. Behind me in the wagon, Walker sat with his hands tied behind him and one leg tied to the side of the wagon. "I couldn't treat a dog this way," he said. Then when Jack and I paid him no attention, he raised his voice a notch. "Hear me? I said I couldn't treat a dog this way."

"We heard ya, Walker," I said. "Now stick a rag in it. It's hard for me to find sympathy with a man who was about to ambush me. You're lucky Griebs didn't kill ya."

"Lucky? Ha. You ain't seen how they treat prisoners, have ya? 'Specially ones like me who lives with the Lakota. 'Specially when they all know me . . . and that asshole Tom Custer can't wait to get his hands on me. Them damn

Custers are all dogs. They wasn't born one at a time—they was born in a litter!"

I smiled at Jack, then said over my shoulder, "Bet they'll drag you out and rip you apart like a possum skin when we take ya to 'em."

"Don't make fun, mister. If it wasn't for you shooting my friends, stealing my shirt and horses, none of this woulda happened."

"Those were *my* horses, you thieving son of a bitch." I reached a hand around to smack him, but he ducked away from it. "And if it wasn't for you stealing them, I wouldn't have got cut from one end to the other." I swung back again, missed again, and almost fell from the wagon seat.

"Whoa, now," Jack said, swerving his horse slightly and pushing me back onto my seat. "You're gonna keep on till you pull something loose."

"That's right," Walker said. "Wouldn't want nothing to happen to ya before Rain gets another chance at ya." He snickered under his breath.

"Jack," I said loud enough for Walker to hear me, "you wanta drive this wagon a few minutes while I carve a couple pounds off this bastard?" I jerked the glades knife from my boot well and slashed it back close to Walker's face.

"Sure. Just don't let his blood get all over me. This is my last clean shirt."

"Hold on now, damn it!" Walker's voice sounded shaken. "I never seen men you can't even talk to without they get so upset by it."

"You have now," I said, "so keep your mouth shut."

Jack nodded down at me, then fell his horse back a ways to check the trail behind us. After a moment of silence, Walker said, "You know ole Rain ain't in too good shape hisself. You cut him bad."

"Yeah?" For some reason, hearing it from one of the Indian's friends made me feel a little better about it.

"That's right. He was laid up three or four days over it. Walked around in a stupor, talked out of his head. Lost too much blood, I reckon."

I pictured it, knowing how he felt, knowing how all men had felt since the beginning of time while their wounds healed. I heard the sound of his blade hiss across my mind, heard it connect with my blade in a ringing of cold steel. For some reason, I thought of the steel itself, saw it coming out of the ground, dug up by gnarled hands and carried away into the future of man, and I wondered for a second how man had come upon the knowledge of such a substance, and how he had ever directed its use.

"It should've been you instead of him, Walker," I said. "But *you* were too chickenshit to fight for what *you* stole."

"Shiiit, don't tell me about stealing. You whites steal everything you get your hands on, even the land."

"Us whites? You're forgetting what color you are."

"I know what color I *used* to be. But I'm a redskin now, same as any of them out here. So don't chastise me for *stealing* when you and your kind stole the land you're riding over."

"Not me. I ain't stole nothing. I'm just passing through."

"Aw, and that makes it all right? Think if you ain't dirtying your hands with it, you ain't guilty of it? Then damn your ass straight to hell. I've got a *right* to take your horses!"

"Then I've got a right to keep your shirt!" I raised a hand, took my doeskin shirt by the shoulder, and shook it, as if showing him it was mine. Ahead of us, Griebs and Dammio looked back as Walker's voice and mine raised higher in the quiet night. "Settle down," I said back to him, "or I'll hang a rifle barrel over your head." I thought about the crazy-quilt pattern of stitches across my body and added in a lowered tone, "You ain't *never* getting this shirt back."

"Then, by God, you ain't never getting your horses back, either."

I chuckled and jiggled the reins to the mules. "I've already got my horses back. They were mine to begin with, and they're mine again. I've got the scars to prove it."

"Shit, you ain't seen scars yet. Maybe you've got the horses now, but you won't have for long. Take 'em on up country with your boy *Custer*. We'll see whose horses they are. Rain'll be waiting for ya like a demon in your nightmare. You think he's carved you up before, just wait till—"

"That's it! I've had it with ya!" I turned, sweeping up my

rifle from beside me and poking it back at him like a spear. He ducked away and I swung it like a club, still missing him and banging the side of the wagon with it.

"Whooa, what's going on here?" Jack had returned beside the wagon and he caught my rifle barrel as I drew back for another swing. "Sounds like two kids arguing over marbles." He looked me up and down as he turned loose of the rifle barrel. "You doing all right?"

I let out a breath and settled down. "Yeah, I'm all right. Just got fed up with his crap—" I nodded back toward Walker, who was huddling against the side of the wagon. "—Telling me Rain in the Face is waiting for me *like a demon in my nightmare.* Ha!" I spit off the side of the wagon and ran a hand across my mouth.

Jack looked back and forth in the light of the moon from Walker to me. "Hell, every white man's got an Indian in his nightmare. You just happen to know yours by name."

I slapped the reins to the mules and felt them bring their pace up a bit, and Walker and I settled down and rode on the last few miles without talking. Close to midnight, we rounded the last turn in the trail and caught sight of the torchlights and campfires among the dark rows of tents whose peaks stood straight and perfect against the purple sky. "Who goes there?" a voice called out as we neared, and ahead of me Griebs gave a reply.

Walker scooted up close behind me on the rough wagon bed and said in a low tone, "Pssst. What do you say, ole buddy? Just let me go? Before it's too late? I didn't mean nothing, saying them things back there. Hell, these boys are gonna kill me."

"They're not gonna kill ya, just jail ya, get you out of circulation for a while."

"That's the same as killing. I'm Indian now, don't you see? Jail will kill me . . . if *they* don't."

"You ain't Indian, you're as white as I am, whether you like it or not. Besides I ain't got no say in it. You're Griebs's prisoner. So shut up about it."

As the guards came in and circled around Griebs and Dammio, Griebs cut his horse around and jogged it back the few yards to the wagon. He looked down at me and said in a quiet tone, "Just for the record, lad, I told them it was you who captured this snake."

"You what?" I stood up halfway from the wagon seat. "I told you I'm no part of this . . . don't want the money."

"I know, I know." He raised a hand as if to soothe the situation. "But for practical purposes, go along with me here, laddie. They might try to hold up the reward, me being a military man and all."

"You should've said something earlier. I ain't going along with this."

"Aw, but surely you will, laddie, just for a while? Just to help me out?" He leaned in his saddle, closer to me on the wagon seat. "Lest they get picky and ask what Dammio and I were doing out there . . . and I be forced to tell them you stole this wagon and we caught you at it." He grinned, his eyes shining in the light of the three-quarters moon.

"See how they do it?" Walker spoke in a low voice behind me.

I stared at Griebs, feeling anger boil in my chest. "You'd do that? You'd jackpot us?"

He feigned an expression of regret. "Aye, but only if ya give me no choice, lad."

"You dirty son of a bitch," I said as the guards came back toward us with their rifles at port arms.

Jack rode up from behind us and stopped his horse beside the wagon. Seeing the look on my face, he said, "What's going on?"

Without answering him, I glanced down at Walker in the wagon bed. "See," Walker said. "You can't have it both ways . . . you can't be around shit and not catch the smell of it."

Jack and I stood inside the command tent in the weak glow of a candle lantern watching Captain Tom Custer lean close to where Walker lay against a tent pole. For twenty minutes he'd asked about everything from stolen crackers to the location of Sitting Bull's hostile forces, but Walker was having none of it. I couldn't help but smile when Custer stood up and stamped a boot on the dirt floor. "Do you realize you could be hanged for consorting with the enemies of this nation?"

"They ain't my enemies. This ain't my nation," Walker said, and he raised his cuffed hands and whipped his forearm across a trickle of blood running down his chin.

"Want me to bust him again?" a scout in buckskin asked, then took a step forward to go ahead and do it. But Custer stopped him with a raised hand.

"No! We'll have no more of that." He leaned toward Walker again and asked, "At least tell me this. Has Rain in the Face said anything more about me?" Behind Tom Custer, Boston lifted a brow and spread a tight smile. *What's wrong with him . . .?*

Walker lowered his face and said, "No. Only that when he gets his hands on ya, he's gonna cut out your heart and eat it."

"Outlaw bastard!" The scout stepped in and booted Walker in the jaw before Custer could stop him.

The two Crow scouts stood by the tent fly like ancient centurions. They looked at one another, nodding and laughing with their mouths wide open. "Kick the shit off of him," said one.

"I've had it with him," Custer said, dusting his hands together. He looked at the Crow scouts and said: "Bloody Knife, you and Curly go tie him to a field cannon until tomorrow." He winked at them and added, "Be *real* careful with him, you understand?" Their eyes lit cruelly and sharply like war dogs. One of them growled low and licked his lip.

Ebb Walker struggled to his feet on his own, slinging free of two soldiers' hands reaching for him. He glared at Custer, then at the Crow scouts. "I don't give a damn in hell if ya kill me. I druther die a redskin Lakota than live like any lousy white man here." His eyes swung to mine as the two soldiers grabbed his arms from behind. "See what you've done? Alls I wanted was my medicine shirt back and my horses you stole from me."

"Take him away," Custer said, and as the soldiers dragged him through the tent fly, the two Crows turned and fell in behind them. It had sickened me to see Walker beaten like an animal, and it must've shown on my face. But Captain Custer read my expression wrong. "Don't let him get to you, Mr. Beatty. The man's an outlaw, unfit to live. They all act like that once their luck runs out. They blame you, blame me, blame *society* in general." He smiled and shook his head. "Blame everybody but themselves. You probably don't know those kind of men, but I do." Behind him, Boston Custer closed his eyes and shook his head slightly.

"What'll become of him?" I asked, gazing deep into Tom Custer's eyes, wanting to judge if he would tell me the truth. "Will he go to jail all in one piece?"

"Of course." Custer folded his hands behind his back. "We're only scaring him a little, telling him we'll give him to the Crow scouts." He shrugged. "Oh, some of the men might get heavy-handed with him, but that's to be expected, isn't it? The main thing is, you've taken one more hostile ne'er-do-well out of action, and for that you've earned the reward of one thousand American dollars." He smiled. "Not bad for a day's work, eh?"

I started to say something, but Griebs raised a thick hand and patted my shoulder. "You have to admire this man, Captain Custer. Not only does he capture the heathen . . . he worries about their well-being afterwards!"

"Cut it out, Griebs." I moved my shoulder from under his hand, and faced Custer. "About that the reward, Captain. How soon can I expect to get it?" I shot Griebs a dark glance. His expression turned curious.

"Oh . . . let's say a week, just to be on the safe side. Paperwork, you understand. Where would today's army be without its blessed *paperwork?* Is a week satisfactory to you?"

"Well, the fact is, we're leaving here come morning if I can finish up my horse business." I stopped long enough to cut Griebs a sharp glance. "But if it's all the same, I'd like the reward money to be sent to that Indian village just down the trail." Griebs' face swelled red; Jack chuckled beside me. I added, "They can use it for food, blankets, whatever they can buy in Bismarck—"

Custer cut me off with a raised hand. "I'm afraid that's impossible, Mr. Beatty. We can't give them American currency. They would only waste it. Besides, the government provides their every need."

"Jesus. Have you been out there . . . seen that place?"

"No, but let me assure you the peaceful Indians are not

slighted. Unfortunately we have to sparsely supply them, or else they share their rations with the hostiles. We can't have that, now can we?"

"Indeed not, sir," Griebs cut in. "I think Mr. Beatty is just tired and needs to think things over just a wee bit."

"Then can I just leave an address in Missouri and have the full thousand dollars sent to me?" I asked Custer, and shot a slight grin to Griebs. His face looked ready to explode.

Tom Custer considered it for a second, rubbing his chin with his thumb and finger. "Well. I don't see why not. Perhaps if you had someone here you know and trust, they could always receive it and forward it on to you. . . ."

"Aye," Griebs said, "and I'd consider it an honor to be that person." Now *he* shot *me* a piercing glance. Again Jack chuckled beside me.

Custer turned to Jack. "Something keeps amusing you, sir. Might I asked what it is?"

Jack grinned. "I always get a kick out of watching everybody try to do the right thing by one another."

"Oh, I see." Custer looked bewildered for a second, then turned to me. "Good, then. I'll leave it to you to arrange the care of your reward money. Just be sure to let me know before you leave."

"You bet, Captain." I lifted a gaze toward Griebs, then looked back to Tom Custer as Jack and I backed away, turned, and left the tent.

"Wait, Beatty," Griebs called out, running up beside us as we walked through the darkness toward the livery tent. "What sort of shenanigan are ya pulling here?" He started to grab my arm but thought better of it when he looked into my eyes.

"You're getting screwed, Griebs, short and simple. You brought me into your game without me knowing. Now I'm cutting you out of *my* game, whether you like it or not."

"We had a deal!" He looked at Jack. "Didn't we? Tell him we did."

"Don't talk to me about it, Griebs," Jack said. "I've already told ya, I'll kill ya without batting an eye."

"We had no deal," I said. "You just had us on a spot for a while. We got off it when you gave your version of me capturing Walker." I cut a smug grin. "Unless you want to go back now and tell the captain you were lying."

His bushy eyebrows leveled into a straight line. "That's low and underhanded of ya. I shoulda had no dealings with a damn horse trader. You're all full of trickery! The whole damn lot of ya!"

"Yeah? Well go write your congressman about it," I called back to him as Jack and I walked away. "Meanwhile, if you want your part of the reward, you better go think of some *really* good reasons why we'd want to be your friends."

"Why, you bastar— I mean, *sure! Right ya are, lads!* I still like the both of yas, ya know. We can work this out . . ."

"You mean it about leaving come morning? You're feeling well enough to ride?" Jack spoke as we walked on toward the medical tent. Off to our right, Walker lay huddled against the wheel of a cannon. In the glow of a low fire, we saw the two Crow scouts prod him with their rifle barrels. One of them kicked him in the ribs.

"Yep," I said. "I'm able to ride now. This little trip tonight proved it. But even if I ain't, I'm leaving here tomorrow if I have to crawl to Bismarck and take a goat cart back to Missouri."

"I know what you mean," he said, glancing back at Walker as we walked past. "There's one thing we gotta do first, though, right?"

"Right," I said, and we walked on toward the soft glow of candlelight on the side of the livery tent.

Chapter

16

———✦———

A matter to be reconciled . . .

After eating some warmed-over stew Ole Nutriment had made before turning in, I left Jack at the livery tent, went to my cot in the hospital tent, and dozed for nearly an hour. When I awoke, it was with Jack's hand shaking me on the shoulder and talking in a whisper. "Come on, wake up. Time to go to work." His voice sounded thick with whiskey. I could smell it on his breath from three feet away.

I rose up and looked around the long dark tent in the glow of a candle lantern Jack held up in his hand. "Okay, okay, I'm awake." At the far end of an empty row of cots, Corporal Dammio snored like a broken steam whistle. "How'd it go?" I asked.

Jack wiped a hand across his forehead. "The one called Curly is the drinkingest sumbitch I ever seen. He's still on his feet. The other one just went over to the mess tent to wake the cooks and bum some coffee. You best get going."

"You couldn't get them drunk?"

"I did the best I cou-ould," he belched and wobbled slightly. "It's up to you now, unless you just want to shoot them and be done with it."

"Naw. I'll take care of it. Stay here and try to get your head clear. They'll be asking questions come daylight."

"Damn 'em, let 'em ask."

"Jesus, Jack. They've drunk you plumb under the table."

As I stood up, he sank down on the cot and let his arms fall out on both sides. His hat crumpled up and covered his face. "Just do it, and let me know how it went," he mumbled.

I shook my head, took my glades knife from my boot, put out the candle, and slipped to the back of the tent. Outside the tent, I lowered the rear fly and tied it shut, then slipped along in a crouch through the first gray wisps of dawn toward the cannon where Walker lay tied. The camp was silent as a tomb. Ten feet from the cannon, I waited for a second, watching from behind a stack of firewood until I was sure only one of the Crow scouts sat guarding Walker.

With my glades knife out in front of me, I dropped flat on my belly and crawled like a snake across the ten-foot stretch of beaten-down grass, feeling the cool dew soak into my doeskin shirt. When I drew close up behind the Indian, Walker's black swollen eyes looked past him and caught sight of me sneaking in. I froze and raised a finger to my lips.

"What you look at, Walker?" The scout called Curly spoke to him, but as he spoke, he started rising up and turning toward me. I sprang to my feet holding the glades knife by its wide blade. As his face came around, I swung with all my strength and smacked him across the forehead with the big brass handle. It made a sound like someone dropping a watermelon from a rooftop. But instead of the Indian falling as he should have, he turned a full circle with the blow and staggered in place with his knobby knees batting together beneath his loincloth. Then he grunted and just walked away across the wild grass like a sleepwalker, with his arms hanging straight down his sides.

"Damn! That didn't kill him?" Walker whispered as I reached down and slashed the rope holding his handcuffs to the cannon wheel.

"I hope not," I said, whispering, stepping back, pulling him to his feet, and shoving him away from the dim firelight. "You're out of here, Walker, now git."

He stared at me through swollen eyes, dark blood caked on his jaw and in his hairline. "Is this a trick?"

"I don't play tricks. Now get going." I shoved him again; he staggered and caught himself.

"What about these?" He raised his fists and shook the handcuffs.

"Can't help ya there. But you're free. Now go."

"But . . . a gun? A horse? How'll I get past the camp guards?"

"Shit! I can't do it all for ya. You leaving or not?" I looked around quickly to make sure we hadn't been seen.

"I'm beat all to hell," he hissed in a whisper.

"Don't blame me, you dumb son of a bitch—" I waved my arms to shoo him away. "—Take off, run!"

"All right, then." He turned, crouched, and gazed about the grassland. "But don't expect me to be grateful. This don't change nothing. You've still got my shirt and horses." He looked at the doeskin shirt and lunged at me with his cuffed hands. "Give me my damn shirt!"

I jerked back a step and swung the knife handle past his head. "Go, or I'll knock your head off."

"I'm gone, then," he said, and as he crouched again like a man ready to start a footrace, he added, "I didn't steal them horses from ya, you know. I stole 'em from three white men. One was the feller with the thin mustache—the one what was with you when you took my shirt."

I stared at him, stunned. *Gaither!*

"It's the damn truth," Walker said. "I stole 'em from him. So *you* stole 'em from me."

"Get out of here, now." I raised my pistol from my holster and cocked it.

"Okay!" He trotted off sideways, calling back to me as he disappeared into the early morning haze, "But I'm getting my shirt back. Sitting Bull touched that shirt with his own hand, made it bulletproof for me . . ."

The Crow scout was still knocked out, walking in a wide crazy circle when I turned and slipped back to the hospital tent. No sooner had I stepped inside, the sound of the morning bugle blew reveille, and within seconds the sound of men coming awake and stirring about filled the silence of morning. I was standing in the middle of the tent when Dammio rose up with a groan and pushed himself up from his cot. "Thisa army gotta no mercy," he grumbled, turning toward me.

Not wanting to be caught coming in right after Walker escaped, I leaped over, landed on the cot against Jack, and pretended to be asleep. I heard Dammio walk down the middle of the tent, then heard him gasp, "Oha! *My God!*" as he stopped near my cot.

I opened my eyes, feigning sleep, and looked up at him. He stared down, stunned, at Jack and me on the same cot, then threw a hand over his mouth and ran out of the tent. *Jesus!* My face reddened; I stood up and shook Jack by the shoulder. "Get the hell away . . ." He groaned and slung an arm.

Outside, angry voices begin calling back and forth. Boots pounded through beaten-down swirls of grass. "The son of a bitch is gone!" someone yelled. I took off my shirt and boots and sat down on the empty cot next to where Jack lay snoring toward the sky. A young private came running with his rifle at port arms. He glanced around, then left. Then a minute later, Griebs stuck his head through the tent fly, looked at me, at Jack, and all around the tent.

"What's going on out there?" I asked him, stifling a yawn and rubbing my head.

"Ebb Walker's gone! Come quickly, lad . . . bring your friend."

"Gone? He better not be gone." I sprang up from the cot, grabbing my shirt, but sat back down and let out a breath as Griebs disappeared, leaving the tent fly flapping behind him. *Conniving asshole.* I grinned to myself as Jack opened his eyes and shook his head. We'd see how Griebs liked this little turn of affairs.

"Did you . . .?" Jack glanced, rubbing his eyes.

"Yep, I did." I slipped my boots on, checked my mending wounds, pulled on my doeskin shirt, and dropped my top hat on my head. "Now let's go greet the new day."

Outside, squads of troops ran in every direction, following their leader, cutting and turning behind him like herd animals. Officers jogged back and forth, hitching their sabers up against their sides. Down by the mess tent, Curly, the Crow scout I had smacked with my glades knife, hung against a tent pole with one hand, his whole right leg covered with a white substance that oozed down his leg and steamed in the cool morning air. Beside him, his partner, Bloody Knife, stood with his rifle at port arms, shoving back a big cook who ranted and raved.

"Look at this, Jack." I smiled, shaking my head. "And Libbie tells me she doesn't know anything to write about."

"What are you talking about?" He cocked his head at me. "Now it's *Libbie*, hunh?"

"Forget it." I nodded toward Griebs and Dammio walking toward us at a quick clip. Griebs's jaw was swollen and his cheeks were spotted red above his beard. From the look on his face, he must've figured out what we'd done. "This oughta be good," I said to Jack out the corner of my mouth. Then I raised my voice to Griebs as he and Dammio came closer. "What's the deal here? Can't the Seventh Cavalry manage to hang on to one measly prisoner?"

"I'm on to you, laddie." Griebs raised a thick finger and pointed it at me. Behind them, Captain Custer came running up, shoving his shirt down in his trousers and hooking his galluses over his shoulders.

"What're you talking about, Griebs?" Jack stepped slightly between us with his hand on his pistol.

"I'm talking about him turning Walker loose, is what!" Griebs stood with his big fists clenched at his side, and leaned, looking around Jack at me. "You did it, didn't ya? Don't lie, now!"

Captain Custer stopped right behind Griebs as I spoke. "Sure, Sergeant Griebs. After all the trouble I went to capturing him, I just said, 'Okay, Walker, you go on home now.' Even you oughta know better than that."

"He's right, Sergeant," Captain Custer said, stepping in. "This man has more reason than any of us to hold on to the prisoner. Now what happened here?"

"I don't know, sir," Griebs said. "One of the Crows went for coffee, the next thing we know, the other came staggering in across the mess tent and stepped in a kettle of mush." He pointed at me again. "This man had something to do with it, rest assured."

"Enough of that, Sergeant!" Custer snapped at him, then

turned back to Jack and me. "Just for the record, where were you two?"

Jack shrugged. "Just for the record, I got drunk and passed out in the hospital tent."

Tom Custer cut his gaze to me; I also shrugged. "Same here. If you don't believe me, ask Dammio."

Griebs and Custer cut their eyes to Dammio. "Well, what say you, Corporal?" Custer asked him. "Were both these men in the hospital tent all night?"

Dammio looked embarrassed and fanned his hands. "I don'ta like-a to say, Captain. I don'ta judge-a nobody."

"The hell's wrong with you?" Griebs cocked an eyebrow. "Captain Custer asked you a question. What were these two doing last night?"

Dammio's face turned beet red. "Alla I gonna say is, they were asleep when I wake up. Whata they do last night isa their business. I don'ta ask, and they don'ta tell me." He stepped back, holding his hands out at arm's length.

Jack looked from Dammio to me with a curious expression. I just shrugged. "What I want to know, Captain, is how come a man can't turn a prisoner over to a whole camp full of soldiers without them losing him?" I looked from Custer to Griebs, keeping myself from smiling.

"We'll find him," Custer said. "You can count on that. Meanwhile, I hope you understand, this puts a *hold* on your reward money."

"Bullshit!" I feigned an angry tone. "I did my part. I caught him. It's the army's fault if they can't hold on to him."

"He's right, Captain," Griebs said, cutting me off. "How does it look if we fail to honor our—"

"Did I ask for your opinion, Sergeant?" Custer raged at him. "I'm not sure what's going on here. But nobody gets anything until I sort this all out! Understood?" A fleck of spit spun from his lips. "My brothe— I mean, *General Custer* will be arriving today, and I won't have us looking like *fools!* Do you understand me?"

"Aye, sir," Griebs said, stiffening to attention. Past them, the two Crow scouts walked away, one with his arm looped over the other one's shoulder, steam still rising from streaks of hot mush on his leg. They both stared back at me with eyes like warning labels on a bottle of poison.

"Now both of you come with me . . . let's find the prisoner!" Custer bellowed, and Griebs turned and walked away with him. Before Dammio followed them, he shook a finger at me, leaned close to Jack, and said: "Youa keepa an eye ona your friend here . . . better sleep witha your ass against the wall anda your handa over your mouth."

"What the hell does he mean by that?" Jack asked me as Dammio turned and jogged away behind the other two.

"Beats me. You know soldiers." I shrugged, not about to tell him about what had happened in the tent. Instead I told him what Walker had said before he left, about stealing the horses from three white men—one of them sounding an awful lot like Gaither.

"But why?" Jack fell in beside me, and we headed for the livery tent to get our horses and ride over to Fort Lincoln. "I can't see Gaither wanting to steal your horses . . . and where would the other two white men fit into it? He was alone when he got off the train."

"As far as we know, he was," I said. "And as far as finding anything out from the other two white men, they're both conveniently dead, back along the bank of the Missouri River."

"Well, whatever he had in mind, we won't have to worry about him. Now that he's got himself a *good thing,* working up a government contract, I reckon he's making himself scarce to us. If he's collecting investment money, he needs to be seen around more *influential* folks than a couple of horse traders."

"Yeah," I said, "and now that Shotgun Tom's living the life of a baseball player, we ain't seeing much of him, either."

"Well, ya can't blame the boy. He's found himself a *good thing,* too. He'll ride it as far as it takes him, if he's smart."

"I reckon," I said. "Seems like everybody's got what they want up here except us horse traders, eh?"

Jack grinned. "Yeah, us and the Indians."

"Well, I ain't even gonna think about it. Let's go home."

"Now you're talking," Jack said.

Chapter

17

———◆———

A quiet chat with the general . . .

It was midmorning by the time we left the camp, owing to Captain Hirshfield showing up with his clipboard, wanting a blow-by-blow account of all that happened, how I captured Ebb Walker, what he had to say on the way in . . . even how *I thought* the man might have gotten away when two of Custer's best Crow scouts had him covered. "Beats me," I'd said, watching him write everything down while the doctor clipped the stitches from my wounds and pulled them out with a long pair of tweezers. Each length of thread felt as if it was dipped in ice water and kerosene as it slid through my skin.

When the doctor had finished, I pulled on my medicine shirt and turned to Captain Hirshfield. "Are we through?"

He paused with his pencil against his chin. "Yes, I believe I have all I need for my report."

"Good, then." I turned to the doctor. "I want to thank ya for all your help, Doctor."

He brushed a hand. "Aw, don't mention it, Missouri."

I looked at Jack and nodded toward the fly of the tent. But before we left, Hirshfield said, "Missouri? I didn't know you were from Missouri, Mr. Beatty. You never mentioned it."

"Yeah, so? You never asked."

"Of course." He grinned and scribbled something on his paper. "All these things need to go on report. The general is very particular . . ."

I thought about Hirshfield and his clipboard while Jack and I made our way to Fort Lincoln. "Think there's enough trees in this land to provide all the paper it'll take to write about it?"

"What?" Jack gave me a bemused look.

"Nothing," I said. "Just getting a picture of all the paperwork involved in an expedition like this. Seeing Hirshfield someday telling his grandkids about the part he played in the Black Hills expedition."

"Thinking it'll go down in history, huh?"

"Yep, don't you? Big George Custer at the lead, saber flashing, Indians running, his men riding them down." I shook my head. "It's a damn shame, but that's how I see it. This is the Indian's last stand, Jack, mark my words on it."

"Reckon you're right." He spit and gazed ahead, and we rode the rest of the way to Fort Lincoln in silence.

I noticed something different as soon as we rode through the gates at Fort Lincoln. The place had taken on a whole new air, an energy that just hadn't been there before. Everywhere we looked, soldiers ran back and forth at a *quick* time pace. Even the officers moving about did so as if they were on the verge of breaking into a trot. Their voices bellowed out to sergeants, the sergeants barked at the troopers, and the troopers just barked at one another. Throughout the fort even the cannon and stacks of equipment seemed to stand at attention.

Two privates raced past us so close that our horses shied back a step. "What's going on?"

I called over to Jack a few feet away, but a corporal in a sharp-creased uniform heard me and said, "The general's here. That's what's going on. Get those horses out of the way!" He reached out with a yellow glove folded double in his hand and slapped at Jack's silver gray. Jack reined the horse away and glared down at him. "Move it! Move it!" He drew back to swing again, and I saw Jack drop his right boot out of his stirrup.

"Touch this horse, Soldier, and I'll hang a spur across your jaw." He spun his silver gray in place, sidling it toward me with his heel cocked and ready. The soldier didn't even seem to hear him as he walked on, shouting at a short column of troops carrying crates of ammunition. Sweat stains streaked their shirts front and back. "And keep yourselves looking presentable," he bellowed at them.

"They've all gone nuts," Jack said to me, and we reined our horses on, weaving a careful path over toward the Custer house back on officer's row. Once we got behind the line of small cottages the commotion settled, and we looked back at the soldiers running like antelopes back and forth in the front yard. "I'll wait here for you," Jack said. "Try not to take all day."

"I'm in and out," I said, handing him the reins to my Gypsy roan.

I walked up to the door and knocked with the brass knocker, then after a second when no one answered, I looked around at Jack and shrugged. "Knock harder," he called over to me.

In another second I did, this time noticing that the door was slightly ajar, and that knocking had opened it an inch or two more. Inside, the sound of women's voices came from farther back in the house. "Hello," I said, speaking in through the crack of the open door. Still no one came, and I opened the door a little farther. "Hello . . . anybody home? Mistress Custer? General Custer?"

Still no answer. Now I couldn't help but peep through the door, and as I did I saw that the place looked as if it had been ransacked by a pack of coyotes. *Jesus!*

"What's wrong?" Jack asked, seeing the look on my face when I glanced back at him.

"The place is a wreck." I shrugged, spreading my hands, then turned and stepped inside the door. Furniture lay overturned on the floor, the globe of an oil lamp lay broken in pieces, a rug had been flipped over halfway, and water piddled on it from a spilled vase of flowers. "Hello." This time I called out as I stepped forward—getting a little concerned. Farther back in the house, the women's voices stopped suddenly, then one whispered, "No, I didn't . . . didn't you?"

"Mistress Custer?" I said, stopping there halfway across the floor of the parlor.

"The general's not here," Martha's voice called out through the house.

"It's me, Beatty. Is everything all right here?"

"Oh, him," Libbie Custer said in a hushed tone.

"I'll shoo him out of here—"

"No, wait, I'll see him. Get some of this cleaned up, please."

I heard her coming through the house and meant to hurry back to the doorway, but she stepped into the parlor just as my hand reached for the doorknob. "Mr. Beatty," she said, trying to look calm and cordial despite walking through the crunching sound of broken glass. "Whatever must you think, coming into all this." She spread her hands to take in the mess. Her voice sounded shaky. Her cheeks were red, one of them a bit puffy, I thought.

"Sorry, ma'am. I shouldn't have come in . . . just got a little worried. The door was open." My eyes swept about the place. There was no way to pretend I couldn't see it. It reminded me of the tavern the troops had busted up back in New Orleans.

She put on a brave smile. "Oh, that husband of mine. What will I do with him? He's such a scamp."

"Scamp?" Martha's voice said from the other room. "Um-um, Lawd have mercy."

"Martha, be a dear?" Libbie called over her shoulder. "Please straighten up the kitchen?" Her voice rang high and thin, barely under control.

"I already am," Martha called out.

She turned back to me, pushing back a strand of hair with a nervous hand. "He— He gets so excited when he's been away. He simply frolics all over the house." She managed to toss her hand in a casual manner and smile, stepping past me and closing the door behind me.

"Frolic, *huh.*" Martha grumbled under her breath, still being heard. "He was mine, I done frolicked his ole bony back with a rolling pin . . . *frolic that.*"

Libbie's eyes widened. "Mar-tha *PLEASE!* Will . . . you . . . just . . . straighten . . . up . . . *THE KITCHEN?*"

"Don't be hollering at me . . ." Martha's voice trailed into a low rumble. "Oughta wash his face with a butcher knife. Carrying on like something crazy . . ."

Libbie Custer pressed her fingertips to her lips and stood there for a second with her eyes closed.

"Ma'am, maybe I'll just come back in a few minutes."

"No, please." She waited another second, taking a deep breath. "Mr. Beatty . . . I must apologize," she said, opening her eyes and stepping forward, having herself all collected now. "I'm afraid I have nothing prepared . . . no tea, no—"

"Ma'am, that's quite all right." I raised a hand. "Just stopped by to get the money for the horse, and I'll be on my way. Hate bringing it up, under these circumstances."

"Oh, don't be silly, Mr. Beatty. The general and I both act like a couple of children when we get together. We *dance,* he pitches me in the air, throws things around . . ." She managed a see-through laugh and tossed a hand again. "It's simply *wild.* I must write about it someday."

"I hope you do, ma'am. And tell it just like it is." I let my eyes look into hers, seeing if she got my meaning.

She cocked her head. "But of course, I'd have to be honest about it, wouldn't I, for history's sake?"

"Sure." I nodded.

"Now, then. Payment for the horse." She folded her hands across her stomach and tilted her chin up a bit. "I've discussed it with my husband, and he said to tell you—"

"Whooa, now." I cut her off. "Discussed it? Ma'am, you bought the horse. That was *your decision.* I brought it here under that understanding. We're a long way past *discussing.*"

"You didn't let me finish, Mr. Beatty. Yes, I *bought* the horse. Everything is fine. The general loves the animal. He went over earlier and checked him out thoroughly. But he said to tell you to come to his office and he would pay you." She stood there rigid, staring straight ahead, and I sensed how small and unimportant it must've made her feel, wanting to do something nice, surprise him, and now he'd taken it all away from her. *He* had to be the one handling the money transaction instead of her. It had to be humiliating. *Some surprise.*

"I understand, ma'am," I said in a quiet tone. "I'll just go by and see him."

I started to turn to the door, but she said, "It is better this way, don't you suppose? He *is* the horseman in the family, after all."

"Yes, ma'am. I understand."

"I mean— A horse is not the sort of thing a woman should surprise her husband with, do you think? The general said he appreciated it, but that it was . . . well—" She shrugged. "—A foolish thing to do, he told me . . . don't you think so?"

Her eyes misted over; she stared straight ahead past me into the wall. "I'm real sorry, Libbie," I spoke gently, reached behind me and opened the door.

"I meant what I said about writing all this down." She swept a hand, taking in the room in its disarray. "As soon as this expedition is over, while he's getting medals pinned on his chest, I'll be writing about all this. The bad parts as well as the good."

"I hope so, ma'am." My tone must've sounded a little unsure.

"No, I mean it. You're coming here this morning has inspired me." She smiled and wagged a finger. "See, you really are my angel of keep. You thought it was foolish when I told you that, but it's true."

I reached out, took her hand, and squeezed it gently. "I'm nobody's angel of keep, Libbie . . . but if I ever was, I'd rather be yours than anybody I know."

I turned her hand loose but she held on an extra second. She started to say something more but stopped herself, let go of my hand, and watched me as I opened the door, stepped through, and closed it behind me.

"Well?" Jack had stepped down from his horse, and he handed me my reins when I walked out to him.

"Boy oh boy, Jack." I shook my head. "It just ain't getting any easier . . ."

I told him what had happened, and I thought about Libbie and her husband and the whole Black Hills expedition as we walked along, leading our horses through the tangle of soldiers and equipment on the way to the general's office. "It just dawned on me," Jack said, "we're both gonna die up here."

His words struck a chill up my neck, and I stopped short and looked at him. "Now that's hell of a thing to say."

"No—" He cut me off, raising a hand. "—It's true. It just came to me. We're gonna die of old age up here waiting to get paid for that damn good-for-nothing Honest Bob."

The chill lessened; I let out a breath, shaking my head. "You can say the damnedest things."

"Listen. You said everybody was getting something out this but *us?* Here's how it'll go. Gaither'll get rich selling the government beef, Tom'll become a celebrated baseball player, Libbie Custer will get rich writing books about her husband being a lunatic, Custer will get a medal of honor for wiping out the whole Lakota Nation . . . and here we'll be, old and gray, still waiting to get paid and get the hell out of here."

"We're going, Jack, believe me. The minute he lays the money in my hand, we're blowing out of here like a bad wind. I just hate seeing poor Lib— I mean, *that woman* be so miserable."

"That woman, huh?" He spit, nearly hitting a passing soldier on his boot. The soldier grumbled the word *asshole* under his breath, but kept going. "I've watched ya go from *Mistress Custer* to *Libbie;* now you've jumped all the way to *that woman.* Anything go on back there that you ain't told me about?"

"Put it out of your mind, Jack. She's just a beautiful woman with a lot of problems to work out for herself. I'm just a horse dealer trying to practice my trade—or I was, anyway, till I got roped into this Custer craziness."

We stopped outside a small frame building where two guards stood at attention on the front porch. Above us a flag flicked in the breeze. From inside the building a harsh voice ranted and raged, then a young lieutenant came out with his hat under his arm and a look on his face like a man who'd just had his neck scalded. He marched stiff-legged off the porch and started shouting at two privates as he crossed the dirt street toward them. "Maybe I'll just wait out here," Jack said, pushing up his hat brim.

"Don't you want to meet the general?" I eyed him as I handed my reins.

"No. I'm afraid he'd start that loudmouth crap with us and I'd have to kill 'im. Only person I want to meet is a bartender. You go on; I'll go find something cold to drink and meet you back here."

"You're not gonna get something to *drink* around here." I gestured a hand.

"Wanta bet?" he said.

Walking into the frame building, I bumped headlong into the journalist Henry Brazelton, and we both staggered back a step, then caught ourselves. "Why, Mr. Beatty," he said, smiling. "Good to see you up and around. I still want to talk with you, you know." Sweat ran long, jagged lines down his face. A bead hung from the end of his nose.

"Sure, first chance we get," I said, just putting him off. Right away, I noticed it was terribly hot and stuffy in the small foyer.

"Fine, then," he beamed, running a hand across his wet forehead. "If you're here to see the general, I hope you have better luck than I. It's been over an hour, and I'm afraid this heat has me wiped."

"Oh?" I glanced around the narrow foyer. "Well, you won't catch me waiting that long."

"Right you are." His smile broadened. He patted my shoulder, then turned and walked out the door. I looked around again and had started to take a seat on a long wooden bench when I saw a wrinkled notepad lying on the dusty floor. *Brazelton's?* Picking it up and thumbing it open, I saw his name and address inside the cover. But when I stepped over into the doorway and looked for him, he was already out of sight among the throng of soldiers and teamsters filling the street.

Behind me a door opened. "The general will see you now,' said the voice of a young lieutenant as I turned toward him. His face was tilted down to a stack of papers in his hand. He studied them through thick eyeglasses as he stepped past me hurrying, almost in a run. "Go right in," he added, leaving his words hanging behind him as he disappeared out the door.

"Yes, come in, come in, come in," a loud voice boomed from inside the office. Stepping in, closing the door behind me, I saw the general standing behind an ornate wooden desk. His back was turned from me, and he faced a large map on the wall with his hands folded behind his back at parade rest. "Sorry to have kept you waiting," he said. Then before I could speak, his hands unfolded; one of them snapped out and tapped a finger soundly on the map. *"There,* sir! *There* lies the future of this nation. Our destiny, if you will!"

He stood tall, thin, and broad shouldered, his dark blue tunic tailored to fit like a layer of skin. His long hair shimmered with dressing oil and lay covering his collar line. I shot a quick glance around the small office, taking note of a human skull with a large rock imbedded in it. It sat on a stack of papers, facing me on top of the desk. I made up my mind to be straight to the point with him and tolerate none of the guff I figured was coming.

"General Custer, I'm Mr. Beatt—"

"Yes, indeed you are! And it is my pleasure meeting you, sir!" He cut me off, swinging around, throwing his hands behind his back once more, and stepping around the desk toward me with the sharp grace and motion of a mountain cat. "Mistress Custer tells me you've already spoken with her in my absence, and she is quite *taken* with you, sir!"

"Well . . . uh—"

"Set down, sir! Come come! Please, have a seat!" His hands clasped around a box of cigars and flipped it open. "Have a cigar!" *Jesus* . . .

We'd shaken hands before I realized it, and now I was seated in a wooden high-backed chair holding a thick cigar before I'd managed to say a word. General Custer lit my cigar, then stepped back, looking down, taking note of my doeskin shirt and the top hat in my hand, and said, spreading his arms, "My, but haven't you become the essence of the noble plainsman!"

"Well, I'm a little scarce of clothes right now." I drew on the cigar, laid the top hat on the floor beside my chair, and sat holding Brazelton's notepad on my lap.

"Traveling light, eh!" He raised a finger. "That is the only way to travel, to my thinking! You are dressed rugged—" His pointing finger turned into a fist. "—Yet stylish, in a rakish sort of way . . . if you don't mind my saying! I find that a man who doesn't *dress* sharp usually *isn't* very sharp! Wouldn't you agree, Hank? I hope I may call you *Hank."*

Hank? I ran a hand down the front of my shirt. "I ain't really put a lot of thought in it. But, General, my name's not Hank." I pointed the cigar at him for emphasis.

"You *'ainnnn't'* put a lot of—" He threw back a laugh. "Oh, my! We're gonna get along fine! I can already tell!" He spun on his boot heels, threw his hands back behind his back, and circled around behind his desk. It was obvious the general had no idea in the world who I was; and as I glanced down at the battered notebook in my hand, it dawned on me. He thought I was Henry Brazelton.

"Now, then! Where to start?" He dropped down in his chair before I could say a word, and brushed his palms across the top of his desk as if clearing away all other business. Then he cocked his head, "Oh, I know," and he reached out and tapped the human skull paperweight on the desk. "I'm sure you're curious about this tough-looking fellow."

"General, I better tell ya—"

"Well, this happens to be the skull of some ancient fallen warrior, found on excavation in a remote South-American jungle. I don't mind telling you how delighted I was to receive it as gift from my very dear friend—"

"General! Hold it!" I had to yell slightly to cut him off. "Do you think I came here to write about you?"

He shrugged one shoulder. "Well, I'm sure you want to get the *whole* picture, the men, the Indians, the land. You've already spoke to some of the wives, of course . . ."

I shook my head as he rattled on; then I stopped him abruptly, saying, "General, I'm not Henry Brazelton. I'm Beatty . . . James Beatty? I'm here about the *horse*. The *horse?*"

He sat staring at me for a second with a bemused expression, then squinted his eyes shut and shook his head. "Oh, Beatty . . . about the horse."

"Right," I said, putting the cigar in my mouth and slumping in the chair.

His whole demeanor changed. He stood up, reached across the desk, snatched up the skull paperweight, put it a drawer, then straightened his tunic as he walked around the desk. "Right indeed." His voice had gone lower now, no longer the snappy voice of an energetic officer out to impress a news reporter. No. Now he was a man whose wife had a bought a horse without his say-so, and sitting before him was the man responsible for his apparent displeasure.

"Beatty." His voice dropped even lower as he stopped beside my chair and looked down at me from beneath a narrowed brow.

"Yes, Beatty." I nodded and puffed the cigar.

He snatched the lit cigar out of my mouth, walked back around his desk, and dropped it into a brass cuspidor. It landed with a muffled ring, then sizzled and died. "Who let you in here, *Beatty?*"

I just looked at him, wondering what the army would to do me for hanging a chair over his head right there in his office.

Chapter

18

———◆———

Negotiations in good faith . . .

Ordinarily I might've dickered and dealt, bargained and begged, and done anything else it takes for a horse trader to get rid of a horse. Maybe that's what General Custer expected; I don't know. But since Honest Bob was not a horse I'd wanted to sell in the first place, it came to me, sitting there listening to Custer rant and rave, that once he'd spent himself out, all I'd need do was take my horses and leave. Just chalk this trip up to *experience* and put it all behind me. This was a domestic battle between him and his wife. Certainly nothing for me to be involved in.

". . . And just what kind of man sells a woman a horse without her husband's permission to begin with, *Beatty?*" He'd been rambling on and on about what evil snakes horse traders were—even found a way to make a horse trader responsible for Napoleon's defeat at Waterloo. Only when his fist came down loudly on his desk did I lean forward in my chair.

"General, believe me. Had I known it was going to cause this much trouble I *never* would have sold her the horse—"

"Ha! I'm supposed to believe that? From a man who impersonates a reporter just to weasel his way into my office?" He gestured toward the notebook on my lap. "I believe you'd do anything to make a sale, Beatty, regardless of what problems it caused!"

I shook my head. There's was no point in trying to explain that even if he paid me for the horse I'd be losing money, considering all I'd gone through. "This is not mine," I said, raising the notebook from my lap. "This is Henry Brazelton's. He left it in the foyer. I found it, is all." I let out a breath. "And as far as selling Honest Bob . . . let's just forget the whole thing. I'll gladly release you and your wife from the deal—"

"Release us? That implies that we've somehow failed to uphold our end of an agreement."

"No, sir," I said, although that was exactly what had happened. "It just means there's been a misunderstanding and I'm trying my best to make things right. I said to begin with that it would be a mistake buying Honest Bob."

"Honest Bob. My goodness, man, have you no shame, palming that beast off on an unsuspecting female? I checked that horse over this morning. He's actually ripped down every board in his stall and ate—I say, *ate!* his water bucket!"

Rather than let the whole conversation do a complete circle and start all over, I said, "I understand. So let's just call it quits, General."

"Quits, I'll say." He leaned back and tapped his fingers on the chair arm. "Although that certainly lets you off the hook and leaves me with a problem. My wife is terribly upset at my stepping in and taking over. Ruining her *surprise."* He raised two fingers on each hand and wiggled them for emphasis. "Now you think you'll simply ride off into the sunset, no loss, no gain, while I have to put up with all—"

"Damn it, General—" I should've bitten my tongue instead of saying it, but the words spilled out. "—She only did it thinking it would *please* you. Can't you see that? Don't you see how she feels?"

His face went flush of all color. He rose from his chair rigidly and slowly, his knuckles white, gripping the chair arms. "How . . . dare . . . you . . . to . . . *presume* to have . . . any idea . . . of my wife's feelings, sir."

"Easy, General." I rose with him, wondering if I'd have to fight him.

"If I weren't in the uniform of my country, I would trounce you within an inch of your miserable life." He stopped short halfway around his desk. I backed off, sweeping my top hat from the floor, letting Brazelton's notebook fall.

"I'll just get my horse and leave, General." I backed closer to the door, still keeping an eye on him.

"You'll . . . do . . . no such thing!"

I stopped and stared at him. "But you just said—"

"I know what I *just* said. Now, I'm telling you, if you go near those horses I'll have you shot . . . *shot,* sir! I'm trying to conduct a military campaign with Washington breathing down my neck, and here you come interfering in my personal life, as if you have some sort of understanding, some familiarity with my *wife!"*

"General, you've got me all wrong! I shouldn't have said what I said, and I apologize. Let me just take my horses and go."

"I think not, Beatty. You sold my wife a *fine* riding horse, and *by* thunder, I'll honor the agreement. Now you march your ragged arse out of here and have that blasted animal ready and fit for a *general* to ride by the time we leave here in three days."

"Three days? That's impossible! I can't break a lifetime of bad habits in three days."

"But you will have, sir. If not, I'll ride the other one, this *Foxfire,* I believe you call him."

I shook my head slowly, feeling the sting of what he said. "I won't stand still for this, general or not. You ain't about to ride my racing stallion into an Indian battle. We'll settle this man to man if we have to. Damn your uniform." I reached a hand down and started rolling up my sleeves.

"Damn my uniform, you say? Good, then! That is all the reason I need to . . ." His voice trailed to a whisper, and he reached up and unbuttoned his collar. Stepping sideways to an open window without taking his eyes from mine, he called out to the guards on the front porch. "You men, take a break. Go have some coffee." I heard them speaking between themselves for a second, then heard their boots pounding off the porch. "Now, I'll just trash you soundly and teach you some manners."

He stepped toward me, his fists raised into a high guard, a classic gentleman's fighting stance. I almost smiled. "I think I better warn you, General, your fancy West Point training ain't gonna take you very far here." I dropped down into position, my left fist out and low, my right tucked back close to my chest. It would be quick, I thought, feign a couple of lefts, get him watching them, then hammer a hard right into his tilted jaw. Then two lefts, another right while he staggered back. I almost felt sorry for—

My head snapped back three times before I realized I'd been hit. *Jesus!* My nose swelled up like a tree frog. He stepped to the side and effortlessly shot a sharp left into my jaw. I staggered around and backed against the edge of his desk. "Now you've done it, *Georgie boy."* I slung my head to clear it. Blood flew. "Now I'm gonna have to hurt yo—"

Again, three quick ones in my face. Where'd they come from? "Perhaps I should've warned *you,* sir. I was first in class at fisticuffs. Maybe you'll think twice next time before meddling in a man's personal—"

I shot a good one in fast. "Try to keep my horses, you arrogant son of a—" But it glanced off his guard, went high, and hammered him on the forehead. He flinched back a step, opened his guard, and I hooked him in the stomach hard enough to mash his navel on his backbone, I thought. But hitting his stomach was like hitting a steel washboard, and he only let go a puff of air, then came in jabbing like a railroad piston.

I couldn't get away from the punches, so I went back over his desk and circled toward him as he came around it, throwing my arms out around his waist before he got another shot at me. "Oh, a wrestler, hey?" He grunted as I lifted him off his feet. "Good, then! Another of my specialties!"

Oh God!

He locked his boot heels around my ribs, reached down my back, and pulled us both forward. He hit the floor rolling backward, unlocked his heels, and managed to pitch me over him upside down into a shelf of books. Books tumbled; pages fluttered. He sprang up, grabbed both my heels as I thrashed upside down trying to right myself, and stood there like a man using a posthole digger, bouncing my head up and down on the floor. "You will learn to keep your nose out of . . ."

And there we were when the door flew open. "George! For heaven's sakes! Stop it!" Tom Custer, Captain Hirshfield, and Shotgun Tom stood staring in disbelief. Hirshfield's clipboard fell to the floor.

"Gentlemen! Do come in!" He turned loose, and I tumbled to the floor like a bundle of rags. As he straightened his tunic and pushed his sleeves down, I crawled hand over hand up the side of the bookshelf, my breath heaving in my chest. "Don't mind us. We were just sharing some defense techniques." He took me by my shoulder, raised me up, and even dusted a hand across my shoulder. He wasn't even out of breath! "Mr. Beatty is quite a scrapper, it appears."

"You . . . had . . . enough?" They watched me wobble over and hang against the side of the desk. My nose looked as large as a cucumber between my watering eyes. They stared, Hirshfield reaching down and retrieving his clipboard.

"—I mean, *General,* are you all right, sir?" Tom Custer asked, looking his brother up and down.

"Why certainly, Captain," General Custer said, smiling, tugging down the waist of his tunic. "You might've considered knocking first."

"Sorry, General," said Tom Custer. "But there were no guards at the door, and we heard such a racket."

"Yes," the general said, "and yet as you see, all is well here." He swung a finger toward me. "Mr. Beatty was just leaving. He has a horse that needs his immediate attention."

"Begging the general's pardon, sir," Hirshfield said, stepping forward with his clipboard extended. I'd stood up to leave but stopped as Hirshfield cut a glance toward me. "Our Mr. Beatty here has been the talk of the camp ever since his arrival. It's all in the report there."

"Do tell." General Custer took the clipboard, flipped over a page, scanned it, and flipped over another. "My, my. A knife fight? With Rain in the Face?" He glanced at me with a renewed interest, then continued on.

For some reason, I felt closely pressed there among three union officers, and I said as Custer read the report, "My friend is out there, expecting me back any minute." I had no idea what difference that was supposed to make.

Hirshfield smiled. "Oh, we met him on our way in. He asked us to tell you he'd wait for you over behind the livery barn. He and Mr. Brazelton seemed to have found a way to pass the time."

Custer leafed through the last pages of Hirshfield's report and sighed, looking up at the others. "You gentlemen will excuse us, please."

Hirshfield looked surprised and started to speak, but Custer shot him a glance that silenced him. "What about this young man?" Tom Custer asked, gesturing toward Shotgun Tom. "He's the baseball player I mentioned."

Custer looked Shotgun Tom up and down. "Yes, Tommy Stovine! Always a pleasure to meet an athlete of your quality."

Shotgun Tom started to step forward to shake hands, but Custer stepped away and circled back behind his desk. "Of course, we always have room for an outstanding young man like Tommy Stovine. Rush him through the enlistment process with my personal approval. We'll talk later."

I could tell Tom Custer had more to say, yet he only glanced at Shotgun Tom, then back to the general. "Very good, sir." And he nodded toward the door, and he and Shotgun Tom turned and left.

Hirshfield lingered, a concerned look on his face. "Perhaps you'd like me to stay, sir, and explain my report?"

"That *will* be all, Captain." Custer's voice sounded stern.

"I don't know what he says about me in that report," I said to Custer as Hirshfield closed the door behind him. His boots marched out across the foyer, then across the porch. "I came here to deliver a horse. All that other . . . well, it's just the crazy stuff that can happen to a person, I reckon."

"You might have mentioned that you've only recently recovered from some terrible wounds." His voice had gone soft, almost apologetic.

I shrugged. "What's the difference?"

"The difference, sir, is that I would not have taken advantage of a man in your condition. How does it look? A strong, strapping man like myself beating the daylights out of some weak, helpless—"

"Now hold on, General." I started rolling my sleeves up again. "You mighta had the best of me there when they stopped it. But we've got all day to finish up anything that needs finishing here."

He sank in his chair and let out a breath. "Sit down, Beatty. Let's forget this whole unfortunate incident. I have to admit, I've had a lot on my mind of late, Congress dragging me over there when I should be *here* preparing for the campaign."

I just looked at him, let out a breath, and eased down on my chair as he continued. "That little thrashing I just gave you? Call it letting off steam, I suppose. No hard feelings, I hope?"

"Well . . . I reckon we both got a little too tense for our own good. Just don't go thinking you got the best of me." My face reddened a bit, for indeed he *had* just gotten the best of me, had handled me as if I were a schoolboy.

"Aw, of course not. I dare say, any man who will fight Rain in the Face in a knife fight, and capture one of the Walker brothers, certainly has nothing to be ashamed of. After all, look at me." He spread his arms. "What *civilian* would stand a ghost of a chance against me?"

I decided not to say anything. Okay, he'd licked me. It wasn't a life-or-death battle. *If it was?* The question flashed across my mind, then left. "All right, then," I nodded. "Let's let bygones be bygones. I'll just excuse myself, take my horses, and leave."

"Tell me, Beatty—" He cocked his head to the side, steepling his fingers. "—Now that I see you're not some unmanly *coward*. Now that I think perhaps there is more to you than meets the eye. Just what exactly were you intentions, coming up here?"

"What?" I didn't understand what he was asking, and I must've looked confused.

"Come now, *seven hundred* dollars? To bring a horse all the way up here? I happen to know Mistress Custer offered you three times that amount for the horse, yet you so graciously refused it."

I spread my hands slightly. "I—I just felt like she wanted it so bad. I knew the horse had problems—"

"Yes, and perhaps had some idea that my wife had

problems as well?" He pointed a finger at me across his desk. "I'm no fool, Beatty. I graduated at the head of my class. It's becoming obvious to me what you had in mind. A beautiful woman? Alone up here while her husband is off defending our nation? If I ever so much as catch you breathing the air in front of my house, I will show you another *specialty* of mine." His eyes glistened.

I just stared at him beneath my lowered brow, my nose throbbing. "We're getting ready to fight again, ain't we."

He smiled, a smug smile. "For your sake, let's hope not. No. I believe you've received an adequate lesson on speaking out of turn to an officer and a gentleman. But you *will* have that horse ready to ride when I lead this expedition, and you *will* have him as bridle wise as any horse in our stables.

"Hunh-uh." I shook my head. "Like hell, I will!"

"Like hell, you won't!"

The soldiers had already started to line up outside the mess halls for their noon meal as I led my Gypsy roan over to the livery barn, my nose throbbing, my right ear feeling twice its normal size. Maybe if I'd been in better shape, I thought. After all, the knife fight had taken a lot out of me.

"Good Lord," Jack said, looking up from beneath the shade of a sycamore tree behind the livery barn as I walked up to him. "What in the world happened to your face?" Beside him sat Henry Brazelton with a half-drunk smile hung on his face.

"Nothing," I answered in a flat tone and dropped down beside him.

"Nothing?" He looked me up and down.

"That's what I said." I stared out across back of the fort where soldiers hitched a team of mules to an old cannon. "Looks like we're gonna be here a day or two longer."

Jack groaned and pulled his hat down on his face. "Don't tell me you didn't get paid."

"I didn't." I let out a long breath. "Not only that, I told Custer I'd have Honest Bob broke and ready to ride by the time the expedition leaves here in three days."

Jack reached his hand over. Brazelton stuck a half-full bottle of rye in it. Jack looked at it and swished it around.

"You sell her a horse for next to nothing, deliver it for free, now you're gonna train it for them?" He threw back a drink and let out a whiskey hiss. "I hope you also explained that the horse comes with a lifetime guarantee . . . should anything happen to him in the next hundred years, either we or our heirs will replace him at no additional cost."

"Cut it out, Jack. I don't like it no more than you do."

"Beatty, you didn't happen to see my notebook while you were at the general's office, did you?" Brazelton leaned forward with a rye glow in his eyes. "I seem to have misplaced it."

"Yep, as a matter of fact I did see it. Found it on the floor after you left."

"Thank heavens. For a moment I was afraid it might have found its way into Custer's hands. I say some things in my notes that don't exactly cast him or some of the other *high brass* in the best light."

"Then brace yourself, Brazelton," I said. I left your notebook lying on the edge of his desk."

He groaned. Jack put the bottle in his hand. "How could you do that to me, Beatty?"

I shrugged. "Everybody has to look after their own stuff, Brazelton. You oughta know that." I looked over at him, making sure he saw my swollen nose. "Think he'll read it, knowing it's your personal notes?"

"Wouldn't you, if you were him?" Brazelton asked, then threw back a drink and licked his lips. "I shudder to think that *George* Custer has anything to hold over my head."

"Then start shuddering," I said, pushing myself to my feet and dusting my seat. "I've got a horse to train."

Chapter

19

———————

Business, strictly business . . .

Just to test out the situation, Jack and I went to Foxfire's stall inside the livery barn. If nobody tried to stop us, I'd slip a lead rope over his neck, walk him out of there, out through the soldiers, and head straight for Missouri with him. I didn't owe General Custer a thing. But the second I reached to open the stall door, a rifle lever clicked and two armed soldiers stepped out of the shadows toward us. "Wrong horse, sir," one of them said. "The horse you're looking for is down in the breaking stalls, out back by the training corral. This horse is on its way out to the camp with the general this evening."

"My mistake." I stepped back from the stall door, turned, and said to Jack as we walked back out of the barn. "Can you believe this? He already *knew* he was going to hold Foxfire and make me train Honest Bob for him. Already had his guards in place. We've been suckered, Jack."

"Not necessarily. It was probably just one option he had in mind, and it worked itself out this way. You know these *brass button* boys won't even take a jake unless they've got a backup plan."

"Yeah? Well I feel like I've just been *jaked* on. You know

I'll never get Honest Bob trained in three days, not in a way that'll stick."

"So what? It don't have to stick. Just get him to where Custer can make a lap or two around the parade grounds without the horse killing him. Then forget about it."

"But I hate to get the name of poorly training a horse."

Jack just looked at me. "Then you're as crazy as Custer. You just said the man suckered us."

"I know, I know." I shook my head, and we walked around to the corral on the other side of the barn.

That whole day I worked with Honest Bob, rigging a war bridle on him to keep him from reaching around and biting me when I tried to rein him sharp. Jack watched for a while seated on a corral rail, then when I rode Honest Bob past him and the horse tried to scrape me off along the corral rails, he stepped down and walked away dusting his hands together. "I'm gonna find Brazelton and his bottle," he called back. "If you'd like me to shoot that horse, and the general, too, just holler."

In the hottest part of the day I took off the war bridle, and as soon as I did, Honest Bob decided to go into a running spell. So I let him, cutting sharp on the reins, riding him in a figure-eight pattern back and forth across the large corral until he was covered with white froth. Then when I thought he'd gotten it out of his system and felt him giving me what I asked for on the reins, I reached down and patted his wet neck. "See, you know what to do when you want to, don't ya, boy."

But then as I nudged him toward the corral gate, he let out a long whinny and sat straight down on his rear haunches like a dog. Nothing I tried to do would move him. I slid down off the saddle and quirted his rump. He just rolled down on his side and lay there like a dead man. *Jesus.* I walked off and left him, and before I reached the corral gate, he flipped back up, shook himself off, and charged at me from behind like a bull. Sidestepping him, my hand shot out and caught a rein as he ran past me. He looped at the end of the rein and tried to kick me before settling down.

"Drug him," said Sergeant Griebs's voice from the corral gate. I caught the other rein, rigged the war bridle back on Honest Bob, and led him over. Griebs grinned. "I can get you something to smooth him out, laddie. Just say the word."

"What are you doing here, Griebs?"

"Staying close to my reward money," he said, swinging the gate open for me. "You'll never teach that animal anything," he said.

"We'll see. Tomorrow I'm starting from scratch with him, just like he's a young colt who's never been handled. I'll teach him something."

"I heard the general has you over the barrel on this one," he said. "Thought it might be a good opportunity to patch up our differences." He took note of my nose and added, "The word is, our young general gave you a little of the ole *one-two*, and has bullied you into training this beast for him."

"How in the hell do you even know about it?" I stared at him, leading Honest Bob back into the barn. "I only met with the general this morning."

"Laddie, there are no secrets a sergeant doesn't hear." He spread his big arms. "The army belongs to sergeants. It's our business to know everything."

"Well, then you know he's only given me three days to straighten this horse out. So if you'll excuse me."

"Don't forget my offer," he called out as I walked toward the stall. "A little shot of the right stuff and that horse'll stand up and salute the flag for ya."

"No thanks, Griebs." I called back to him, saw him shrug and walk away, and I uncinched the saddle and dropped it over the rail of the stall. "You heard him," I said to the horse as I dried him down. "If you don't start taking this as serious as I do, he'll light you up with morphine." He stomped a hoof and swung his head back toward me.

As I opened the stall door, he pulled back and shook his head. "Don't even think about it," I said, slipping my hand up to his bridle. "You're going in. I've had it with you." But he slung his head, nearly taking me off my feet. I yanked back on his reins and he let out a long neigh.

"Goodness, Mr. Beatty. What are you doing to that animal?"

I glanced around and saw Libbie Custer standing there in her long cape with the hood up.

Aw, naw. I ducked my head and glanced around to see if anyone was watching. "Ma'am, you shouldn't be here. Your husband made it very plain he doesn't want me around you."

"Oh, phooey on him. I know what he did, and I came here to tell you how terribly sorry . . . and *ashamed* I am." She stepped forward, pointing at the war bridle on Honest Bob. "Why are you doing this to him?"

"It keeps him from biting, ma'am." I stepped in and removed the rope war bridle. "Hate doing it, but the horse has to learn some manners."

"It looks so uncomfortable." As she spoke and idly laid her hand on Honest Bob's rump, without so much as a whimper the horse slipped into the stall. I just stared at him.

"Anyway, about today. Auddie—I mean, my *husband,* can be overbearing and abusive sometimes."

"Tell me about it," I said, facing her with my swollen nose.

"Oh, good heavens!" She swept the hood back off her head and reached out toward my face. "That must be awfully painful? He's *so-o-o* strong and agile, my husband. To think he would do such a thing."

My face reddened a little. "Well, I ain't been up to my game since the knife fight . . . and him being the first in his class and all." I shrugged.

She touched my cheek and left her hand there. "Mr. Beatty, my husband was never the first in his class at *anything.*"

"But he said—"

"I know what the general says. But he only says it to boost his self-confidence."

"It seems to work," I said, stepping back from her hand and turning to a wooden feed bin beside the stall.

"He'll hear from me about this, you can rest assured."

"To be honest, I wish you wouldn't mention it, ma'am."

"Ma'am, is it?" Earlier you called me Libbie."

"Things being as they are, ma'am, maybe it's better I don't do that anymore. The fact is, your husband really has me on the spot here. I've got to go along with him until we can work things out. It'd be bad if he even found out you came here."

"But he'll never know. He's out at the camp, applying the *Custer* principle to all his junior officers."

"The Custer principle?"

"Yes. He believes it's best to always go in shouting at his staff as if something is wrong. That way, whatever *might* be wrong is fixed immediately."

I shook my head. "Still, ma'am, it seems like gossip travels like wildfire around here." I stopped and looked at her as I reached over the stall rail to pour in a scoop of grain. Honest Bob batted it away with his nose. Grain flew. I just let out a breath and drew up another scoop of grain. This time he snapped at me and snorted in my face.

"Here, let me try," she said, reaching for the scoop in my hand.

"He'll bite you, ma'am," I said, even as she took the scoop, reached over the rail, and poured it in his feed trough. But the horse only sniffed at her hand and nuzzled it like a kitten.

"Oh, look, he seems to like me." She stood rubbing his muzzle as he crunched grain between his jaws. He even stopped eating for a second and let her scratch him under his chin. *I'll be damned . . .*

A woman's horse, I thought, feeling a little foolish that I'd never thought of it before. Hadn't any of his past owners ever thought of it? Evidently not. I hadn't seen it very often and wasn't convinced that I was seeing it now, but I knew of rare cases—especially when a horse had been raised by a woman—where the animal would become so greatly attached to a woman's handling that it would refuse to do anything for a man. If this was the case, it sure explained a lot of things about Honest Bob.

"He's only doing this to be vindictive, you know," Libbie Custer said as I stood there watching Honest Bob grow meek as a lamb.

"Pardon me?" I wasn't sure if she was talking about the horse or her husband.

"Making you train this horse for him. He's only doing it because he thinks you and I have become friends, and it makes him jealous." She sighed and pulled her hand back from the stall. "But perhaps you're right. If my being here with you causes you trouble, then I promise to stay away from now on." Honest Bob tried to reach his muzzle out for her to continue patting him.

"Uh . . . well, ma'am. Maybe I'm just a little tired right now and not thinking straight." A plan was starting to form in my mind, a way of turning Honest Bob into an *honest* horse. "I mean, after all, you've got a right to choose your own friends I reckon."

"But, if he should hurt you again, I'd never forgive myself."

"Neither would I—" I grinned. "—Forgive myself, that is." I took her hand and held it. "The fact is, I'd like to think you and I have become friends through all this. And I see no reason to let anybody change that." As I spoke, a twinge of guilt swept through me. Not that I was being dishonest with her. But I wasn't about to tell her that the key to training Honest Bob might be within her reach when it certainly wasn't within mine.

"Do you ride much, Libbie?" I asked, letting go of her hand.

"Oh yes, James. Not that I'm the greatest equestrian in the world."

"Good, then," I said, realizing I'd just started sounding like all the rest of Custer's men. "Why don't you join me here tomorrow. I have something I'd like for you to help try on Honest Bob."

"I'd love to. What might that be?"

I thought quickly and rather than tell her the truth, said, "I think if I could have you sit on his back while I work him around the corral, he might settle down and pay attention."

"Oh." She looked a little confused but didn't question it. "Well, certainly, if you think I can help."

"It would be worth a try," I said.

That evening, Jack and I sat eating a plate of beans we'd cooked over a fire outside the small stable behind the main barn. I happened to gaze up the slope to the main barn and saw a half a dozen armed soldiers lead Foxfire away in their midst. Jack saw me watching and said, "Best put it out of your mind. This whole bunch has turned into crack soldiers now that Custer is back kicking ass and taking names."

"I know." I let out a breath. "Seems odd, after all the

horses we've stolen, the very one I can't seem to get to is *my own.*"

"The more we dabble with this crazy general, the worse things get," he said. "Just do what you can with Honest Bob. If it don't work, we'll act like we're leaving, wait until they head out across the plains, then steal Foxfire right from under their noses."

"Yep." I spooned up a mouthful of beans and watched Roland Gaither walk toward us from the main barn. "Look who's coming here. I think I'll ask him about what Ebb Walker told me, just to see if he wiggles a little."

"Leave it alone," Jack said. "The man's aligned himself pretty strong with the upper brass. Why take a chance and get them all down on us?"

Jack was right, yet it kept eating at me what Walker had said about stealing the horse from three white men, one of whom just *had* to be Roland Gaither.

"So there you boys are," Gaither said, walking up, lifting his hat from his head, and running a hand across his forehead. "It's sure warmed up, hasn't it."

"What's on your mind, *Gateholder,*" I said, not sounding too friendly.

He spread his arms. "Must there be something on my mind? Can't I just stop by and say hello to the men I rode in here with? After all, I can't help but feel like you two should share in my good fortune."

"We're not investing any money in government beef, if that's what you came by to ask." I swallowed my beans and picked up my canteen of water.

"Too bad, then." Here was another one picking up the Custer line. I wondered if the word *then* might be habit-forming. "Most of Custer's staff officers are investing with me, you know. It's not so much that I *need* your money as it is that I'd like for you to take advantage of this wonderful opportunity." He grinned and hooked a thumb in his vest. "After all, you should make something out of all this, since your horse dealing doesn't seem to be working out so well."

I looked up at him standing there all full of himself, and couldn't keep from saying, "Speaking of horse dealings, I heard a strange story the other day."

"Let it go," Jack said in a low tone. But while I couldn't

help saying something about what Walker had told me, I did it in a way that made a point without really accusing him of anything.

"I heard about a man who came up here without a pot to piss in, just looking for a way to make some quick money. He ran into a fellow who had an expensive racehorse, and he decided to get in good with the guy and try to steal it while his back was turned. Can you imagine that?" I looked up at him from under my hat brim.

His eyes gleamed. "Go on . . ."

"Well, he hired a couple of men to help him steal the horse, but then while they were making off with it, a band of Indians hit them and stole the horse from *them.*" I grinned. "Kind of funny in a way, don't you think? Of course, the men he hired didn't think so, because he killed them when the going got rough."

The gleam left his eyes and his expression went flat. My story had struck a nerve. But I wasn't worried. He wasn't wearing his gun. I supposed a sidearm didn't fit his new business image. "What's your point, Beatty?"

I shrugged one shoulder. "None, really. Just wanted to pass that story along to ya. I reckon it shows how a man who's out to change careers might go through a lot of different ventures before he finds one that suits him." I sat my plate down and stood up facing him, dusting the seat of my trousers. "Also thought it might be a good idea to let ya know, that if *that* man ever came at me with a deal, I'd sure stay clear of him."

"Good, then." He smiled. "Point well understood." Then he added, "If I were a man like that and found something better for myself, the last thing I'd want to do is mess it up by trying to steal a horse, no matter how valuable it was." Now he glanced at Jack, then back to me. "I guess you can't really blame a man for trying whatever dirty business he has to, until he can get settled into something legitimate." He grinned. "I mean, we are all red-blooded Americans . . . and that is the American way, isn't it?"

He tipped his hat in a cautious manner, backed off a few steps, turned, and left.

"Looks like you were right," Jack said as Gaither walked out of sight around the corner of the large livery barn. "He was out to steal Foxfire. Probably spotted him on the train in St. Louis and followed us ever since."

"Yep. But why us, Jack? We don't look like the easiest people in the world to rob, do we?"

"I don't, you might." Jack smiled.

"No, I'm serious. Being an ex-lawman, you think he might know we're outlaws and figure if he stole our race-horse, what could we really do about it . . . legally, that is."

"Yeah, and he's just cocky enough, he probably thinks he could handle the likes of us if it came down to it. But I reckon if he did think that, he's found out different by now. Of course, he might know we're outlaws and wants us with him on this beef deal in case something goes wrong and he needs somebody to blame it on."

"Like taking off with everybody's money, and if he got caught he could always lay it on us? Or like hiding his investor's money, knocking himself in the head, and saying we robbed him?"

"Yep," Jack said, "the possibilities are endless out here, I reckon, once a man like Gaither wants to put his mind to it."

"Right, *then!*" I spoke in a mock-Custer voice, smiling my best military smile, putting a lot of chin into it the way everybody else did, and I turned back a sip of cool water from my canteen, gazing off to where Roland Gaither had disappeared around the barn. *That sneaking bastard . . .*

Chapter

20

---◆---

Riding with the lady in my arms . . .

The next morning, Jack stood up from beside our campfire outside Honest Bob's stable while the sound of reveille rolled throughout the fort. "Rise and shine," he said, holding up a pot of steaming coffee with his bandanna wrapped around the handle. "This better be some awfully good stuff. I just paid a cook ten dollars to slip it to me out the back door of the officer's mess."

"A stolen pot of coffee, for ten dollars?" I sat up, then pushed myself to my feet.

"To them it's called *procuring*. They don't call it stealing so long as it's government property."

"Then neither do I," I said. "Let's not spill a drop of it at that price."

Jack bent down beside the embers of our campfire and filled two tin cups. "You know, everybody here has a little trade of some kind going on on the side. The thing everybody seems least concerned with is fighting the Indians. You never hear them say much about it."

I sipped and hissed. "With an army this size, I reckon they already know the outcome. Why think about the killing until it comes time to kill?"

"Maybe that's best," Jack said above a rise of steam off

the edge of his cup. "Damn shame the Lakota don't have some spending cash. I figure if they could put enough money in the right people's hands, they could *buy* this war." He swished his cup of coffee and sipped it.

"Now there's an idea," I said. "Just *buy* a war, no fuss, no mess, no bodies."

"All wars are bought and sold," Jack said. "Problem with this one is it's gone too far past the dickering stage. Congress ain't offering enough for the land, and the Indians ain't willing to sell."

I sipped another mouthful of our stolen *officer's* coffee, noticing how much better it tasted than any I'd had for a while. "I don't think Congress *really* wanted to *dicker* with the Indians. They just wanted it to appear that way, so they could go about getting all this for nothing and still keep a clear conscience."

"That's your opinion, huh?" Jack stood up and stretched his back.

"Yep, for what it's worth." I sipped and looked up at him.

"Good, *then!*" He smiled the same mock-military smile. "Maybe you've learned something about it, dealing with the Custers."

"What's that supposed to mean?" I cocked an eye.

He chuckled and raised a hand. "Nothing, not a thing. I'm gonna scout around the fort while you and your *friend* do whatever it is you've got in mind."

"Don't start on me, Jack," I said, but he'd already slung his gun belt over his shoulder and walked away toward the main barn.

The main barn sat thirty yards uphill from the small stalls and breaking corral, and though the body of the fort lay out of sight from here, the sound of men and equipment drifted down to me as they came forward and went about their labors in the gray dawn light. Eerie in a way, I thought, hearing but not seeing the fort come alive up there. For a second I was swept by a dark premonition. But it passed as suddenly as it came, and I sat quietly and sipped another cup of stolen coffee.

When daylight had broken full and the morning sun began drawing waves of dancing heat off the rooftops of workshops and command buildings, I finished the last cup of coffee and walked up to the main barn. I washed in a water barrel, then went back to Honest Bob's stall, slipped a saddle and bridle on him, and led him out to the breaking corral. No sooner had the horse's hooves hit the corral dirt, he broke into a trot before I could even pick up the lunging whip from beside the corral gate, and I fed out the coils of lunge line until he was circling at the end of it twenty feet out.

"That-a-boy." He pranced and blew and trotted, keeping the lunge line just right, no slack, no tension, staying in perfect turn to the circle of corral railing. No need for a whip, I thought. For a moment it seemed that Honest Bob had forgotten all his craziness and had now attuned himself to the slightest flicker of my wrist on the line. But just as I started to cally the line and circle him back the opposite direction, he slid to a halt in the dirt, spun once, and sat straight down.

"Good morning, James," I heard Libbie Custer call out behind me.

So that's it? I shot the horse a dark glance before turning to her as she stepped through the corral gate carrying a small wicker basket. "I came prepared for a hard day in the saddle," she said, setting the basket down at her feet. I caught a glimpse of riding boots. Then, letting go of her cape and spreading it open, she added, "How do I look?"

My face reddened when I saw she was wearing English riding trousers and a billowy white blouse unbuttoned at her throat. "You're the trail boss, and I'm the hired hand, *podner,*" she said in a playful voice, slipping out of the long linen cape. "I'm so excited . . . I even had Martha prepare us something." She folded the cape and laid it on the wicker basket. "Nothing really, some cheese, some crackers, some sweetmeat, and a bottle of wine."

Oh, man! I ducked my eyes and glanced around quickly, grateful that no one could see us from the fort yard above. "Ma'am, I—"

"No, no." She cut me off, wagging a finger. "It's Libbie, remember? This entire day, I refuse to be *Elizabeth,* or *Mistress Custer,* or anyone else except *Libbie.* Now, as my friend, you must promise me . . ."

So I did.

When we'd taken the basket of food and her cape over and laid them both outside the corral, I gathered the lunge line as Honest Bob stood nuzzling and sniffing and poking his muzzle against Libbie's shoulder. "This might not be necessary," I said. "But let's keep the line on him until we see how he's going to act."

"You mean . . . you'd like me to ride him in here?"

"Yep, but don't worry, I'll have him in hand. We're just going to get him used to *you* on his back instead of me."

"I'm not worried. I think he's a darling." She smiled, rubbing his muzzle.

I shook my head, then reached my hands out, feeling a little awkward. "I'll . . . uh, need to help you up in the saddle."

"Of course." She put one hand my shoulder and her other on Honest Bob's withers as she stepped into my cupped hands and up into the stirrup. I started to put my hand on her hip to boost her, but stopped myself and stood with my hands an inch from her as she swung her leg over and seated herself. "My goodness." She wiggled into place on the saddle. "I've ridden sidesaddle so long, I've almost forgotten how good it feels to have this big living thing between my legs."

I looked away, feeling myself blush for a second, then turned back to her, realizing she had had no idea how it had sounded. "Okay," I said, as if I hadn't heard her. "I'll feed out the lead line, and you just ride him around the corral like you would any horse, until he acts up. Then we'll see what we need to do to correct him."

She tilted the reins, and to my surprise he collected himself up like a show pony. Then with the faintest touch of her boot heels, he stepped into a canter as I fed out the line and watched him fall into a smooth circle around the corral. "He rides *so-o-o* smooth," she called out, hardly drifting at all in the sway of his canter.

"Why, sure. I knew he would." I smiled, turning with them on my end of the line, all the while feeling like walking out and cracking him over the head with my pistol barrel.

But then I had to chuckle a little to myself, watching him show off now, loving every touch of her knees against him, making a little hitch in his gait now and then to bring her legs taut around his sides. Was he doing this on purpose? A way of feeling her, reminding himself she was there? Or was this something I conjured in my mind, maybe feeling close to her myself through the rise and fall of their bodies, swaying as one to the beat of the horse's hooves.

A woman's horse . . . after all this time. What would the auction crowd think of this? I wondered, and after a few laps, I brought them in, unhooked the line from his bridle, and said, "He's mellowed right down for you. Feel like taking over on your own?"

"Yes, I would love to." She patted Honest Bob's neck. He blew and closed his eyes for a second.

"Good, then," I said, smiling, but not putting a lot of chin into it. I'd have to be careful not to get into the habit of saying it. "Just take him around a few times. If he does good, I have something I want to try with him."

"What is that?" She looked down at me.

"Well . . . if you don't mind, I'd like to ride behind you for a few laps."

Her face seemed to flush a bit, so I said, "But if you'd rather not . . . ?"

She seemed to consider it for a second, then took a breath and said, "Yes, why shouldn't we?"

There was something in the way she said it that made me wonder what had just gone through her mind, but before I could read anything in her face, she gathered Honest Bob with a tilt of the reins and whisked him into a canter with just a tap of her knees and a kiss in the air.

Watching them make a couple of smooth laps, I called out to her. "Cut him left." And she did, effortlessly. With a light touch of the rein against his neck, Honest Bob turned sharply and precisely, yet with perfect balance, every muscle and nerve in him given to the care of his trust. "Now right," I called out. And again the horse swung, powerfully yet flawlessly, and with all the grace and ease of clear water over polished stone. His hooves seemed to dance for her at the whisper of reins against his skin.

I smiled, whispered *Jesus* to myself, and tossed my hands. "Ride him out, Libbie . . . do with him what you will." And I just stood there, almost in awe at the splendor of it—this magnificent ballet of woman and horse played out on a stage of dust beneath the hot Dakota sun. Here there were no wars or rumors of war, no sound of massing troops, no distant fields of reckoning from which the wounded fled. Here only was the wedded rise and fall of body and hoof, attuned to the pulse of earth and all that clung to it beneath heaven. Watching them, I lifted my top hat and let it hang from my hand.

"Hold this for me, please." She called down to me, pitching me the comb she'd taken from her hair as she cantered past, then tossing her head and letting her hair flow and sway to the beat of the horse's hooves as she rode on. How could a man study war, let alone traipse off in pursuit of it? I thought, picturing this woman alone, waiting, perhaps longing for the touch of a man— *Stop it.* I shook my head, realizing that I was becoming guilty of the very thing Custer had accused me of. But what man with blood in his veins wouldn't at least wonder, wouldn't at *least* picture it?

By the time she brought the horse down to a walk and drifted him to me across the corral, it seemed that time had passed with no regard to its framework. We could have been there an hour or a day. A quiet, heady peacefulness had settled over us. At first I wondered if it had only happened to me, in *my* mind, but as she stepped down from the stirrup and stood there silently with the warm wind licking her hair, we looked into one another's eyes and both of us smiled.

"Isn't this about as good as a person ever has a right to feel?" She spoke in a near whisper, careful not to disturb something, I thought, lest it leave us here in a circle of dust and be gone forever. I took the horse's reins from her hand without answering and walked over to the corral gate, still quiet, still savoring whatever it was that had settled over us.

We rested Honest Bob in the shade of a cottonwood tree beside the stalls where I'd dropped his saddle. He picked at sparse grazing in and along a rise of the tree's ground roots while Libbie and I ate the food and sipped the warm wine from two glasses she'd brought in the basket. After a few moments of silence, she sighed, leaned back against the trunk of the tree, and said quietly in the low purr of the wind, "So, is this the way a horse trader spends his days? If it is, I certainly envy you your profession."

Sitting cross-legged facing her, I smiled and picked a short blade of grass. "I call it my *trade*. But, sure," I shrugged. "This is all I ever do . . . what time I ain't getting cut or shot, or getting my foot stepped on or my ribs kicked in." I tossed a hand. "This is pretty much it, sitting in the shade sipping wine, spinning out a horse, or I *should* say, watching a lovely woman spin a horse out for me."

She gazed out across the open land beyond the rear of the fort and tossed her hair to the side. "I oftentimes wonder what life would be like for the general and me, should he leave the army and go into other pursuits."

The one person I didn't want to think about then was General George Custer, so I tried switching the subject around to her by saying, "I can't help but notice that anytime you talk about your husband, you always refer to him as *the general*. Makes him sound like somebody far away, or bigger than everybody else, or as if anything you say about him *must* be more interesting than anything about you. Personally, I'd rather hear about—"

"No, I don't . . . do I?" She smiled, cutting me off with a bemused look, as if she'd never realized it.

"Well, not always maybe, but most times. Not that I mind, except it would be nice to know more about you."

"I see." She considered it for a second, then said, "I'm sure it's only as a matter of propriety if I do. There's very little interesting about *my*, life I'm afraid, other *than* being the general's wife."

"See. You did it again, '*the general.*'" I smiled and put the blade of grass between my teeth.

"Then it's a habit I shan't break easily. Perhaps it seems so right to refer to him that way . . . it makes him bigger than life, and let's face it, generals *are* bigger than life. Wouldn't you agree?"

"Yeah, they are the nation's heroes, and we seem to need heroes. But what about you? Tell me about you."

"Well . . . let's see." She paused with a finger to her lips. "After the general and I married, we were stationed at—" She stopped and laughed. "I just did it again, didn't I? There just seems to be nothing about myself that doesn't revolve around *the general.*" She laughed again and looked a little embarrassed.

I stood and reached a hand down to help her up. "Come on, we'll give Honest Bob a few more laps while you think of something."

We led the horse bareback into the corral, and I threw his saddle blanket up on him and boosted her up. "Are you sure about this?" she asked as I handed her the reins.

"Not real sure, but we'll see how he takes to both of our weights." I didn't want to mention what was now becoming apparent to me, that he was a woman's horse through and through, and that the best I could hope for was to try and get him used to me on his back with her using the reins, then gradually take the reins from her. I knew it would work if given the right amount of time, but there wasn't much chance of it happening in two days.

"Hold him for me, now," I spoke, walking back behind him a couple of feet. Then I leapfrogged up on his back and felt him stiffen and step sideways, snorting and sawing his head up and down. "Easy, boy," I whispered, settling against her, feeling her hair sweep my face in a warm lick of wind.

She righted him and stood him still in the reins. "So far, so good," she said, her voice sounding a bit strained. She stiffened a bit herself as I placed my hands on her waist. "What now?" She asked.

"Now we ride. Just take it easy with him for a couple of laps, then we'll see how he takes to me handling the reins."

She hesitated for a second and cast a nervous glance up along the rise toward the back of the main barn. But then I felt her take a breath and let it out, as if having resolved something in her mind. "Good, then," she said in a soft tone, and she gathered the horse and touched her boot heels to him.

Chapter

21

Our welcome is overstayed. . . .

The midafternoon sun leaned west when I stepped down from Honest Bob and helped Libbie slip from his back. "I didn't mean to stay so long," she said, "but it has been such a wonderful day." The horse blew and shook out his mane. White froth streaked his sides, yet he stepped back and forth toward Libbie Custer with his head up, as if to say he had more to give. I patted his muzzle with a gloved hand and he stood still for it.

"Thank you. Kind of you to help," I said to her.

"Not at all. It's the least I could do, after all the difficulty you've had. But now I really must run. The general will be coming home shortly."

"If I could ask one more thing of you?" I said, leading Honest Bob by his reins to the corral gate. "I'm taking Honest Bob out to the camp tomorrow while your husband is there. I'd appreciate it if you'd be there and ride the horse for the general—just let him see how well he handles for you."

She smiled but with a hand on her hip. "I see. Show him that even a *woman* can handle the horse?"

I blushed. "It would mean a lot, I'm sure. Of course, he can ride the horse, too, if he needs to convince himself."

She stopped, picked up her cape from across a corral rail, and slipped it over her shoulders, tying it at her throat. "Certainly I'll do it, if it will help."

"I'm sure it will." Picking up the empty wicker basket, I handed it to her and smiled. "Libbie, it's been a most pleasurable day for me, too. One I won't forget."

She took the basket, swept a strand of hair from across her face in the warm wind, then let her expression turn slightly caged as she said, "The things I've told you about my husband and myself. I trust you shan't repeat them to anyone? Especially what I've told you about him? After all," she shrugged, "no one would take much interest in what I've said about me."

"You can count on my discretion." I cocked my head. "Although I don't agree that no one would find you interesting. I've certainly enjoyed hearing about your writing, your artwork. Who knows, someday when you're famous for your paintings or your novels, or both, I'll be able to say I knew you when you were a struggling horse trainer." I smiled.

She turned and walked with me to the stalls, Honest Bob clopping behind me on the end of his reins. "That may be true," she said. "Of course, painting is only something I dabble with . . . but as far as my writing, I feel almost as if it's meant to be. As if there's just some particular thing that must happen first, but once that happens, the words will just spill out and take shape."

"I'll keep my fingers crossed for you."

At the stalls, we stopped and said good-bye, and there was something awkward in the way we kept finding one more thing to say first, the way two young people might act at the end of a date. But when she did leave, and I stood watching the wind play at the hem of her linen cape as she walked up atop the sloping rise to the road out front of the main barn, I reached a hand under Honest Bob's chin, rubbing him, still picturing her and me atop him, riding circles as she spoke to me over her shoulder.

Somehow in the sway of the horse and the closeness of us there on his back, she revealed things about her husband to me. "He has absolutely no fear of death, you know," she'd said above the sound of the horse cantering beneath us. "He believes that his spirit will return here time after time. So, I suppose to him death is simply passage on to the next adventure that awaits him."

When no response came from me, she'd added, "That may sound courageous, yet I think it makes him reckless with *his* life and the lives of his men. Not to mention how little it considers *my* feelings should something terrible happen to him."

We had ridden on in silence for a few moments until I'd reached around her and taken the reins from her hands without breaking the gait of the horse. "That went simple enough," she'd said over her shoulder, whispering as if the horse might hear.

"Yes, but he knows the difference," I'd said. "It's just a matter of whether he'll accept it." Then she'd relaxed against me as we rode, my arms around her holding the reins, and I'd slowed the horse and turned him, stopped him, backed him, and heeled him forward again, time after time, until I'd felt that for then, at least, he had taken to the feel of me for the sake of the woman.

Now I stood there alone with the reins in my hands, the woman gone but the feel of her against me still lingering, the sound of her voice still clear in the passing wind. "Honest Bob, huh?" I spoke to him as I rubbed his muzzle and watched him gaze up toward the main barn, his nostrils searching for her in the wind. "A strange name for a strange horse," I added. "More *honest* than anybody ever thought."

After I'd dried him down, watered and grained him, I went outside, lifted the reins to my roan, and led him behind me up to the fort yard. A heavy wind blew in during the late afternoon by the time I found Jack playing poker on an empty barrel with two woman cooks and their helpers outside the officer's mess. The sky had suddenly turned dark and started to boil overhead.

"This place sure has taken on a change," Jack said, looking around the fort yard. Most of the supplies for the Seventh Cavalry, along with the soldiers and teamsters handling them, had gone out to the camp, leaving the fort quiet and the streets all but deserted. Only the garrison soldiers now remained, and they had taken shelter from the coming storm.

"Yeah, it has," I said, glancing up, then all around us. It felt strange walking along toward the livery barn, the sound of thunder rolling in from the direction of the Black Hills. Dust swirled up from empty supply lots where, only hours before, black cannon iron, crates of ammunition, and stacks of canvas bundles had glistened in sunlight.

Along the way back to the small stalls, with the hard dusty wind whipping Jack's duster tails, I told him what had gone on with Libbie and Honest Bob. "So you figure that'll do it, huh?" His voice rose above the roar of wind.

I only nodded, then added, "For now, anyway. Maybe her being around the horse will keep him straight for a while. But I'd hate to depend on him out there if the going gets rough." I paused while a hard gust of wind passed, then said, "I don't like doing business this way."

"I know, but they gave you no choice." We leaned against the stinging dust and made our way on.

Back at the small barn we swung the doors shut and sheltered our horses in empty stalls next to Honest Bob. "What a blow," I said, sitting down on an upturned bucket and shaking dust from my top hat. Jack took a candle lantern from a peg on the wall, bent down, leaned back against a stall door, and batted his dusty hat against his knee. "So," he said, letting out a breath, "Custer believes in reincarnation?"

"Sounds like it," I said, watching him dust off the lantern and raise the soot-streaked globe. "Whatever he *believes in,* I hope he believes in giving me Foxfire tomorrow and letting us get the hell out of here." Even as I spoke, I pictured Libbie and me atop the horse, and knew I'd miss her once we were gone.

"Yep." Jack touched a flaring match to the candlewick and lowered the globe. "Seems like we've spent a *lifetime* here ourselves. How's your wounds holding up?"

"Real good." I patted a hand against my side. "Looks like I'll carry a scar from this place for a long time, though."

"That's a good souvenir . . . a little reminder from now on not to get tangled up with the army."

I nodded, staring into the glow of the candlelight, picturing the woman atop the horse, seeing her freedom coming to her as she rode within the circled confines of the corral, the corral within the confines of the fort, the fort within the circled confines of the world around us. "Yeah," I said quietly, "life's full of souvenirs."

Throughout the night the storm blustered and raged, windblown rain pounding the small barn like a handful of steel darts, the wind lifting and drawing at the roof above us. Twice I woke up to the sound of the horses blowing and grumbling under their breath, growing frightened by the streaks of lightning flashing through the barn slats. But the storm had passed by morning, and as I swung open the barn doors, Jack had already saddled his silver gray and led it from the stall. Outside the sky lay low, swollen and gray, rain still falling, yet not driven by the wind. "Looks like rain all day," I called back to him over my shoulder.

"It's good luck when it rains on the last day of a visit," he said. He led his silver gray up beside me and gazed out through the steady downpour. "So let's get out of here today before the weather changes again."

"Getting superstitious on me?"

"No. Just telling ya it's time to go, while luck's on our side."

"Suits me," I said, turning to the stalls and picking up my saddle.

"Speaking of luck, I meant to tell ya last night. That whole *investment* deal of Gaither's ain't at all what he built it up to be."

"No kidding? How do you know?" I spoke as I saddled the roan.

"Heard it from one of the cooks. She said Gaither's saying he's got all the big brass investing with him, but the fact is, the *big brass* ain't giving him the time of day. All he's got is a bunch of Custer's junior officers sticking their pay into it."

"What's the difference? If all he needs is capital, their money is as good as the rest, ain't it?"

"Yeah, but she said mostly all he's got are their markers. Custer's holding up everybody's pay until they get out on the expedition . . . it's supposed to keep everybody from sneaking off to Bismarck and getting drunk. So it looks like Gaither has to ride out with them if he wants the money. Can ya beat that?"

"That's good enough for him. Gaither needs a little Indian-fighting experience." I made the cinch taut on the roan, moved him to the side, and put the lead rope on Honest Bob. "But we don't. Let's get on out to the camp, get Foxfire, and get out of here."

We gathered our gear, left the fort, and rode alongside the muddy trail out to the bivouac camp with rain pouring heavy and straight down on us. Hoofprint and wagon rut lay filled with water, and three times we passed muddy soldiers and teamsters standing calf deep in mud, whipping mules and shouldering wagon wheels that stood tilted and sunk to their axles. Soldiers cursed the teamsters, the teamsters cursed the mules. The mules brayed long and mournfully, veins in their necks swollen like knotted rope. They stretched out in their traces, their eyes wide and pleading to the dark sky. Water sprayed off their wet backs with each strike of the whip.

"Damned *dandelions,*" An old teamster shouted at us as we moved our horses past them.

"Mule killer," Jack called back to him over his shoulder. Glancing back, I saw the teamster wipe a wet hand across his muddy face and spit toward us. Jack shot him a one finger salute and we rode on. At the end of a lead rope, Honest Bob sloshed along behind me with his head held high, like a kid following an ice wagon.

At the perimeter of the camp, a guard looked out at us from beneath a rubber rain slicker and waved us on. Water ran in a stream from the lowered tip of his rifle. Inside the camp, soldiers shot back and forth from one tent to another. As we stood down from our saddles outside the command tent, a stooped figure with its arms full of blue clothes bumped into me, and as we caught each for balance, I saw it was Shotgun Tom. "Excuse me, sir," he said, and started to go on past.

But I caught his arm. "Tom? Man, look at you." Beneath his open rain slicker, he wore a uniform that could've fit him twice.

"Yeah. Look at my new boots." He raised a wet foot and a clump of mud dropped from his boot sole. He looked up at me and tried to smile, but it only twitched across his lips, then went flat on him. "Looks like I'm in the army now, huh?" He sounded unsure, as if he needed somebody to confirm it for him.

"Looks like it," I said. Jack stepped over beside me and we both looked him up and down. "Thought you had something worked out with Tom Custer. Thought he was gonna take care of you."

He leaned forward and ducked his head. "I think they've all lied to me," he said. Water dripped from the tip of his nose. "And now they're keeping too close an eye on me for me to sneak away."

"That's too bad," I said. "Maybe if you'd—"

"Move out there, Trooper!" A voice boomed from a tent where three heads stuck out looking toward us.

"See what I mean? Gotta go," Tom whispered. "Here, take this, keep it." He slipped his shotgun from beneath the bundle of clothes in his arms. "They won't let me carry it anymore." Before I could say another word, he splashed away in the rain, and I stood with the shotgun dripping rain from its barrel.

Jack and I just looked at each other and stepped under a canopy set up in front of the command tent. A young soldier came out of the tent carrying a coffeepot. He only glanced at us, ducked his head, and took off through the rain toward the officer's mess tent.

From inside the command tent, General Custer's voice said to someone, *"Good,* then! From now on, only write the truth as I interpret it to you! This ole *freedom of the press* malarky has pretty much outlived itself, wouldn't you agree, sir?"

"But, General—" It was Henry Brazelton's voice, and his words were cut short beneath the sound of dogs growling.

"Down, boys," Custer said; then his voice lowered a notch and he added, "That *will* be all, sir! And don't forget, make the news *good news!"*

I shot Jack a puzzled look. He only shrugged.

"Maybe you'd like to go in there with me?" I spoke in a whisper.

He chuckled under his breath, but before he could answer, Henry Brazelton came walking out through the tent fly like a man in a trance. His eyes swept over us with a glazed expression. "They were going to *eat* me . . ." And he staggered away in the rain with his notepad hanging from his hand. "I'm leaving *this* place. I'd do better drawing political cartoons in Chicago." One of his trouser legs hung in shreds from his knee to his boot. We eyed the neck of a whiskey bottle sticking up from his coat pocket.

Jack chuckled again, patted my shoulder, and said, "Good luck." Then he stepped out in the rain behind Brazelton, yelling, "Henry, wait up."

I stood for a second staring at the tent fly swaying back and forth— *Well, here goes*—then I took a breath, pulled it aside, and stepped through it.

General Custer looked from behind his folding desk with a long ink pen in his hand. Under the open front of his desk, his boots were crossed at the heels and on either side a skinny greyhound lay facing them. They craned their necks toward me and perked their ears. "Well, then! Mr. Beatty!" The general smiled, putting more than enough chin behind it. "I've been expecting you! Good morning, sir!"

"Good morning, General." I glanced around the tent, hoping . . . But I didn't see Libbie Custer, only the general, the two skinny dogs, and in the front corner of the tent, the Crow scout who'd stepped in the kettle of mush. He sat rigid on a folding stool with a war club across his lap. Bits of peeling skin hung from his leg as if he'd suffered a terrible sunburn. His eyes flared and seared into mine like branding irons.

"Looking for someone, Mr. Beatty?" Custer's smile broadened. He laid his pen down and folded his hands. He seemed to take no note of the shotgun hanging from my hand.

"No—I mean, yes—that is, I expected Mistress Custer to be here, since she *is* the one who bought the horse." I glanced around once more as if she might be hiding. The Crow lifted a dark eyebrow toward me the way an undertaker sizes a man for a pine box.

"Yes. Well, be that as it may . . . she shan't be joining us this morning."

"Oh . . ." I stopped myself from looking around one more time.

"Mistress Custer and I put away the ole board games last evening during the storm and had a lengthy discussion about *you* . . . you and your horses, and—" He tossed a hand. "—Well, life in general, you might say." His brow narrowed. "I know she rode the horse yesterday."

"Oh . . ." I said the word again, not sure just how much she'd told him, or *why*. I wasn't about to mention us riding double on Honest Bob. No way! Let him bring it up if he knew about it. His eyes bored into mine for a second longer. Then he said something in Indian to the Crow scout and the scout nodded, tilted his head back, and stared at the tent ceiling.

"I just told him this is a private conversation," Custer said. "So now we can speak freely. He won't hear a word."

"Some trick," I said, sounding a little skeptical. "But I don't know what you and I have to say to one another in *private*. I brought you the horse . . . he's ridable. I suppose your wife must've told you that?" *What else had she told him* . . .

"Yes, she did indeed. and I must say I am greatly impressed that you could do *so much* in *so little* time. But given your background with animals, I'm sure you're used to working under *intense* and *unusual* circumstances."

Custer let out a breath, reached into a file box on his desk, and pulled up the clipboard with Captain Hirshfield's report on it. It looked thicker now. "I've gone through this at great depth, sir," he said. "Apparently Mistress Custer has gotten tangled up with quite a character."

"I beg your pardon?" *What did he know here?* I slid a glance across to the Crow scout with his head thrown back, then just stared at Custer, feeling my wet hand tighten around the shotgun stock.

"I've put two and two together, sir!" He waved the report, dropped it on his desk, and used his finger to emphasize his words as he spoke. "A horse trader from *Missouri?* Yet your accent is pure backwoods *Kentucky*. The *glades* knife? The shoulder harness? My goodness, man! How blind do you think we are? You came up here and stole horses from *horse thieves!*"

He threw back his head and laughed. "Even had a knife fight with a *known* killer! And *lived!*" As he laughed, he slid the report around and flipped it open. There between the pages of Hirshfield's notes, I saw the wrinkled wanted poster of myself looking up at me. Under the sketch of my face was the name Miller Crowe in bold type. Boy, this looks bad, I thought.

In a flash, I saw how my life would end. I'd be hanged for killing one of the nation's leading military figures.

He must've seen the barrel of the shotgun edge up an inch, because he nodded at it and smiled. "And you may just as well lay that aside and put it out of your mind. You *will not* shoot me with it, sir."

I stepped to the side, turning just enough to keep both Custer and the Crow scout in sight. I fanned it back and forth. "Nobody make a move!" But the scout sat still as stone with his head thrown back. Custer sat smiling with his hands spread on his desk.

"Stop it, Mr. *Crowe!* One word in Egyptian and these dogs will come forth and rip your heart out!"

"Greyhounds? I doubt it!" I swung the shotgun down at the dogs, then back up to Custer. "Greyhounds don't attack."

"Oh, *really?* But then, graduates from West Point don't know how to fistfight either, do they?"

"I'm leaving here," I said, backing a step toward the tent fly. "Don't try to stop me."

He shrugged. "Good, then! But aren't you going to take your racehorse?"

I collected myself. "Okay, then. Let's say I am Miller Crowe, which I *ain't.* What happens now? I ain't surrendering. If you know anything at all, you oughta know that—not while I'm alive."

"Good, then! I would expect no less from one of the *James* Gang." He wiggled his fingers in the air, forming quotation marks. "But I have no desire to kill you, sir. Although, there's no question I *could.*"

I eased my thumb back from the trigger on the shotgun and cocked an eye toward him. "This ain't about reward money?"

He glanced at the wanted poster, chuckling, shaking his head. "It must be embarrassing . . . a mere *thousand* dollars?"

I blushed. "Well, it looks like an old poster."

"Indeed." He flipped the report shut. "I dare say, if *I* had chosen outlawry as my trade, there would be at least *twenty thousand* or more on *my* head! But then, I would have been much more than just the *horseman* for the gang. I would be at least the—"

"Spill it, Custer. What's on your mind if it's not the reward money? What do you want from me?" I sliced a quick glance at the scout; he still stared up at the ceiling.

"What *I want* from you, sir—" He jerked the pen up from his desk and scribbled as spoke. "—Is the very thing I told you before. Stay . . . away . . . from . . . my . . . wife!" He laid the pen down and raised from his folding chair, snatching up the note he'd just written. The two greyhounds stood up under his desk and raised their thin hackles. "Your presence here has been most distracting to her. She was upset when I told her who you are!"

The shotgun lowered in my hand. "You—you told her who I am?"

"Of course, I told her. Were it not for her, believe me, you would have been *shot* the instant you rode in here."

I stared at him as he walked around to the edge of his desk and faced me, rocking back and forth on his boot heels with his hands folded behind his back. "Is she . . . okay?" I asked before thinking of how it might sound to him. Then I steadied myself, expecting him to blow up over it.

But instead, he collected himself, cleared his throat, and said in a lowered voice, "Yes, she's fine. My wife can be very trusting at times. Now . . . things being as they are—" He brought his hand from behind him and held the note out for me. "—I want you out of here. Take this to Ole Nutriment, get Foxfire, and *go!*"

It dawned on me. Sure, he wanted me out of here. How would it look to the high brass: me, Miller Crowe, an outlaw, bringing him a horse, spending time with his wife, *alone?* This would make him look a fool if the word got out.

"Okay, General." I let out a breath and glanced down at the note. It read, *Give this man his——horse. Signed, General George A. Custer.* There was *that word* again! Maybe Libbie had learned it from him. "I see your situation. Just give me the seven hundred for Honest Bob, and I'll be on my way."

"Oh, now we're going to dicker about money? Good,

then!" His other hand came from behind his back, cocking the big army Colt on its way. "Let's see now . . ." He tilted his head and turned his eyes upward for a second. "I can let you leave as planned, discount the reward on you by three hundred dollars, and keep the seven hundred dollars for Honest Bob. *Or,* I can put a bullet through your brain, if you have one, collect the thousand dollars, and have you carried out of here on a board."

He spread the smile with lots of chin behind it. "How is your arithmetic, sir? Which would you prefer I do?"

I nodded, let the shotgun point straight down at the ground, and said, "You've got it, General . . . you've got it all."

PART 4

———◆———

Valley of Death
A Killing Wave
Atop a Bare Hill

Chapter

22

———◆———

An outlaw at the lady's beck and call . . .

The smoke in that Bismarck saloon hung low and thick. Two days of breathing it, breathing it to the beat of the madman's rattling piano, was enough to make a person want to draw a pistol and shoot the man sitting across the table. Especially if that man was palming cards, as this one was. Or as I *thought* he was. Maybe he wasn't. Maybe I just didn't like his looks, a broad, toothy smile, lots of chin behind it—the same kind of chin I'd seen too much of lately. *Maybe I'd just shoot him . . .*

Yep, that's what I'll do, I thought, swinging the pistol from my shoulder harness, cocking it, knocking over a bottle of rye on the way. His face went chalk white as the bottle busted on the floor. A spray of glass and whiskey rose and fell, and the rattle of the piano fell with it. "Here, now!" a bartender yelled. Then he dove to the side when my pistol swung toward him from the table and a glass jar of cigars exploded on the wall.

Jack moved quickly. When the bartender came back up swinging a shotgun across the bar, Jack shoved the barrel toward the ceiling. A belch of fire rounded out of the barrel. Jack twisted it from his hands, smacked him once with the butt, and dragged him over the bar top. "Stay there and be good," he said, shoving the bartender back against the bar. Drinkers scooted farther away, their beer mugs sounding like a low drumroll along the rough bar top.

"Now what the hell are you doing?" Jack's voice went low, stepping toward my table where I sat with my smoking pistol pointed back at the man across from me. The man's lips and eyes quivered, as if he tried to recall a time when he'd been any closer to dying than this second, and couldn't come up with one.

"He cheated." I spoke to Jack without taking my eyes off the man.

"He cheated?" Jack glanced back and forth between us.

"He might've."

"Might've?"

"Yep. If not today, then sometime or other. I guarantee ya, somewhere, sometime, he's—"

"Lord have mercy. Give me that." Jack's hand snapped out and down over my pistol, the bridge of his thumb wedging down between the hammer and the cylinder.

"Turn it loose, Jack." I hissed like a snake.

"You packing any iron, mister?" Jack's eyes snapped to the man.

"No, I never carry a—"

"There, see, he's unarmed. You ever shot an unarmed man?"

"No," I said flatly.

"Good, then!" Jack gave his best Custer impression and eased his hand off my pistol. "You'll never find a better time to start." He took a step back. The man's face turned the color of frog skin. Jack said to him, "Don't worry. If he shoots you, I'll crack this shotgun barrel over his head."

I looked at the man's pleading eyes, saw prayers run across his mind that he hadn't thought of since Sunday school as a child. "Damn it!" I uncocked the pistol and banged it down on the table.

"I ain't having this kinda shit in here," the bartender said, now that things had wound down. "What's wrong with him. Is he crazy?"

"Naw. He's just been fooling with the army the past

couple of weeks—trying to deal with General *Custer.*" Jack looked around at the drinkers.

"Awwww, well," came a low rumble from the drinkers. Their heads nodded. Jack unloaded the shotgun and pitched it to the bartender.

"Wisht I'd known before he started playing poker," the bartender said, catching the gun.

"Lord, me, *too,*" said the man across from me. He wiped a hand across his forehead. "I've never cheated at nothing in my life."

I just stared at him with my hand still covering my pistol. "Well, billiards once," he added with a nervous grin. "—Horseshoes a time or two when nobody was looking." He shrugged and wiped his head again.

I snatched up my pistol, sprang up from my chair, and stomped out onto the boardwalk. Behind me, Jack said, "If I'd known it was gonna keep eating at ya this bad, we woulda shaved his ass and painted it with roofing tar."

"What are you talking about?" I snapped back over my shoulder.

"Custer, damn it! Don't tell me that ain't what this is all about."

"I won't . . . but it ain't. I'm just sick of this place."

"Then let's go home! You're the one keeps finding stuff to do here—gotta see the new *firehouse* . . . gotta look at the *ostriches.*"

"So?" I stopped and turned to him, holstering my pistol. "I'd never seen an ostrich before, had you?"

"That ain't the point, and you know it. There's two trains out of here every day, anytime you're ready. You don't have to sulk around . . . wind up shooting somebody over nothing."

"The man's a cheat, Jack. I saw it in his eyes."

"Bullshit. You've just got a mad-on at the world because that Custer woman knows who ya are." He shrugged. "And why give a damn about it? That's *them* over there, in their world." He pointed out in the direction of Fort Lincoln across the river. "This is *us,* here." His finger pointed straight down. "Get it through your head, she's a marrie—" His words stopped. Behind him we heard a commotion from the saloon and saw the man I'd nearly shot come sailing out the door, off the boardwalk, and facedown it the muddy street.

"And don't come back, you son of a bitch!" somebody yelled, and a handful of aces flew out and showered down on him.

"Good, then." I put a little chin into it, turned, and walked off toward the livery where we'd quartered our horses.

"That was just a lucky guess, and you know it," Jack said, catching up, walking along beside me.

"I know it. It really *has* been bothering me ever since we left Lincoln. I can't stand Libbie Custer knowing I'm just a two-bit outlaw. I just keep wondering what's going through her mind about me." I shook my head.

"I wouldn't call the James Gang *two-bit*." Jack grinned. "At least we ride with the biggest and the best."

"If I just could have seen her, talked to her, explained it to her before I left," I said. "But no-o-o-o! *He* had to spill it to her, probably in a way that made her feel like a fool for ever dealing with me. There's no telling what she thinks now . . . maybe that I was out to do her harm. Who knows?" I tossed a hand.

"Who cares?" Jack spit as we walked along. "It was all for no good reason to begin with. We had no business coming here. She had no business buying him a horse. He had no business knocking up an Indian. You had no business falling in *'luuv'* with his wife." He chuckled. "It's all been Shakespeare stepping in horseshit, if ya ask me. Now you're dragging around like a mooneyed dog."

I swung the door open and walked into the livery barn. "I ain't in *'luuv'* with his wife. I just don't like thinking I've let her down, is all. The woman's had enough letdowns in her life."

"You don't know that, now do ya?" Jack swung the door shut behind us.

"No, but I feel it. I look into her eyes, and I just . . . *feel it.*"

"Yeah, well . . . stick your hand in your pocket and *feel* something else. We know where we live, don't we? You're so far from that woman's world, you couldn't reach it if she

"And after the terrible way the general treated you, I wasn't sure you would come—"

I shook her gently. "Calm down, Libbie. Of course, I came. Now what's wrong? Martha said you're about to traipse off after the expedition."

"Oh. Martha . . ." She took a step back with her fingers pressed to her chin. "Where *is* that woman?" For the first time, she noticed Jack there with me. She gathered herself, touched a hand to her hair, and said to him, "I have no tea prepared . . ."

"No, thanks, I never touch the stuff," Jack said.

"That's all right, Libbie. Martha said you needed me. Here I am. How can I help you?"

She started to speak, but then hesitated, shooting Jack a glance.

"Libbie, he's my friend. Anything you have to say can—"

"Never mind," Jack said, stepping away. "Just point me to the kitchen. I'd love a big strapping cup of Dettweiler's."

"It's always my favorite," Libbie said in a shaky voice, ushering him in the direction of the kitchen. "Would you be a dear?"

She stood watching him until he walked out of sight, then turned back to me with an urgent expression. "Oh, James! I've done a terrible thing. You must help me!"

"Of course, what is it?"

"The night of the storm, the general and I had an ugly fight over you. I told him I had ridden Honest Bob and that the horse was fine. But he forbade me coming out to the camp—said he would never pay you for the horse." She shook her head. "He said terrible things about you. I didn't believe them, of course."

I thought about the wanted poster. "That's okay," I said.

"We hardly spoke afterward, and when I packed his personal items for the expedition, I enclosed a horrible letter . . ." Her words trailed and her hand went to her cheek. "Now I don't know what to do."

I stared at her. "This letter . . .?"

"Oh, James, I was so angry. I told him I was leaving him, that I would seek a legal decree of divorce . . . that I never wanted to see him again." Her eyes filled; she chafed her hands together.

"Oh, I see." I waited for a second, then asked, "Did you mean it?"

"At the time, yes." She took a deep breath. "But the *letter*. That was a terrible thing to do. Now he's gone off to protect our nation with such— Such—"

She gave in to weeping, and I stepped forward and drew her against me. "I know, I know," I said. "It's a lot for him to deal with. But if you meant it, stick by it."

"But I can't, James. I can't do this to him. You must help me." She pushed herself back from me slightly, her eyes pleading.

"Of course, just tell me how."

"Please catch up to him for me. I've written another letter telling him it was all a mistake, that I didn't mean it. But I will not trust this letter to a dispatch rider. Please say you'll take it to him. I've made an awful mess of things. Please help me clean it up. Please?"

"Oh, I see . . ." It came to me, standing there looking into her eyes, that Jack had been right all along. Take away the emotion in her eyes, in her voice, take away the warm tears on my chest, and put this all on the level where it belonged: she was simply asking a chore of me. The general's wife, asking a gardener to prune the hedging. An *important* chore, but a chore nevertheless.

She must've sensed the change come over me, because she took a step back, her eyes searching mine. "What's wrong, James? Will you do it for me?"

For a second I tried to imagine how she would react when I told her *no*. Would she collect herself, step back, and say, *Very well, that will be all, James?* Would she dismiss me with the toss of a hand? Jack was right: this was *their* world; there was no place for me here. Realizing it, I tried to keep the bitterness out of my voice as I spoke. "You mean you would trust such a personal letter to me, to an *outlaw* like me?" I forced a smile. "Think how embarrassing that would be if anyone ever found out."

"Tea's up," Jack said from the doorway, standing there in his long riding duster and his sweat-stained hat, a beat expression on his face, a dainty teapot clutched in his gloved hand.

I glanced from him back into her searching eyes. "Outlaw? Why, whatever are you talking about, James?" She looked genuinely confused. "Did *he say* that to you? Is that what the general called you? *An outlaw?* Then I don't wonder why you left, refusing even to tell me good-bye. Then I'm surprised you even came back here . . ."

Whooa here. I shook my head to clear it as she spoke on. She didn't know, truly had no idea what I was talking about? He hadn't told her? ". . . When he said you were in a hurry to leave, I just assumed you wanted to get ahead of the rain. Why on earth would he call you an outlaw?"

"Tea's *up* here. Good, piping-hot—"

"Will you . . . get us . . . some . . . *cups? Please!*" I cut him off with a dark glance, then looked back at her as he turned and stepped back toward the kitchen. "Did—did he mention a report from Captain Hirshfield?"

"Hirshfield *always* has a report of some sort. There's one on the general's desk upstairs." She shrugged. "Why would he mention it?"

I shook my head. "Never mind." *The bastard!* He'd beaten me out of a horse, tricked me into training it for him, then blackmailed me out of his life, telling me his wife never wanted to see my face again. *The lousy, rotten . . . !* "Where's the letter? I'll take it to him, you bet." I couldn't wait to see his face, see the smile fade and the jut go out of his chin, when I told him I was wise to his game. *What's wrong, GENERAL? Are you so unsure? Is your position so shaky? Has the presence of one little ole outlaw got you so—*

"James? What is going on between you and the general?" I felt her shake my arm.

"Uh . . . nothing. Get the letter ready."

"Okay, we got cups, we got tea," Jack said from the doorway, looking around for a place to set the silver tray in his gloved hands.

"I have it here." She turned out of my view, slipped a green-trimmed envelope from the bosom of her dress, and handed it to me. It was sealed in red wax. "But if there's something wrong . . ."

"There's not." I looked past her at Jack, still turning, looking for a place. "Will you put it down, and *let's go!*"

He stiffened, shot me a smoldering glance, and set the tray down on the floor at his feet. "I fixed the——stuff, I'm drinking the——stuff."

There was *that* word! In the presence of a lady! She gasped; we both did. He'd used it twice! In the same sentence.

Chapter

23

Moving on winds of war . . .

We'd been gone three days, skirting the badlands along the Yellowstone River, making good time despite the land lying wet and soft beneath our horses' hooves. Each of us carried ten pounds of oats for our horses, extra cartridges for our rifles, and enough coffee, hardtack, and jerked beef to last us over a week. Jack had made me agree that if we hadn't caught up to some part of the expedition in a week, we'd turn back.

By the end of the second day, Jack had given up asking me why I had to make this trip or what I hoped to gain from it. By the end of the third day I'd given up asking *myself*. Yet I knew without doubt, of all the crazy things I'd ever done, or would ever do in life, this one ranked up along the top edge.

But I had to do it.

"I think you're attracted to Indian wars," Jack said, lying beside me along the crest of a ridge. I gazed out through the field lens we'd bought from a supply sergeant before we'd left Fort Lincoln. Everything at Fort Lincoln had its price. For enough money, we probably could've bought a cannon.

"Keep still," I said, scanning along the riverbank. "We've got movement out there. Two horses, two riders coming up out of the brush."

Beside me, I heard his rifle lever click. "Keep me posted," he said.

From a thousand yards I recognized Lonesome Charley Reynolds, the scout who'd sewn up my wounds. He rode with a Springfield rifle across his lap. In front of him rode a white man dressed in buckskins with an Indian headband drooped low on his bloody forehead. Their horse walked slowly toward the riverbank below us. "It's Lonesome Charley," I said, turning to Jack. "This might be a break for us."

"Good, then." Jack pushed himself up and dusted his trousers.

"I wish you'd stop saying 'good, then' all the time," I said, standing and collapsing the field lens. "It's getting to be a habit."

"I know it. It's just gotten stuck in my mind, you know, like a song you hate but can't quit humming."

I nodded. We mounted and followed a deer trail down around the ridgeline, keeping in view of Lonesome Charley should he look our way, and at the same time staying cautious about exposing our backs to the open land south of us. At the base of the ridgeline, Jack raised his arms and swung them back and forth and when we saw Lonesome Charley acknowledge us with one raise of a hand, we moved our horses into the brush and stayed hidden until we came out along the riverbank below.

He grinned, riding up to us. "You two coyotes are apt to show up about anywhere, aren't ya? What brings ya out here? *Go-o-o-o-l-d?*"

"Never got a chance to thank ya for sewing me up. Thought I ought to." I smiled, with my wrists crossed on my saddle horn, and noted the handcuffs on the man with the bloody head. The man noted me also, eyeing my doeskin shirt.

"Shoulda thanked me by mail," Reynolds said. "This is risky country here. You're too far from the fort one way and too far behind the expedition the other."

"How far behind—" Jack cut a glance at me, then back to Reynolds. "—More than a week?"

"Yep. Quite a bit more, the way you're going."

Jack looked at me with a smug grin.

"But it's a whole lot quicker by riverboat. That's why I'm here. Boat's coming through in a couple of hours. Caught sight of her rounding a turn a few miles back."

"Suppose we can ride on it?"

"Don't see why not," Reynolds said. "Army's paying three hundred dollars a day for the use of that boat. We'll just tell Captain Marsh you're with me. He'll let ya on."

Now I shot Jack a smug expression, almost said *good, then,* but stopped myself and said, "Thanks" instead. Then I nodded toward Reynolds's bandaged hand and asked, "What happened? Get yourself wounded?"

"Naw, we ain't had no skirmishes yet." He wiggled his swollen fingers. "Musta got a splinter in it. It festered, then got infected. I'd had it treated before now, but I struck out chasing this rascal and a couple young bucks. Figured it'd be closer now to go to the boat than it is to the scout camp."

I looked the prisoner up and down. He sneered and said, "That ain't your shirt."

"Pay no attention to Ridgely here. He's a squaw man, been living with Sitting Bull's bunch, stinking up their teepees."

"You don't know nothing, Lonesome Charley," the man said. "I been held captive by 'em, is all."

"Yeah." Reynolds reached out and poked his side with the barrel of his Springfield. "That why you and them bucks've been fanning our back trail?" He looked back at Jack and me. "Caught 'em lifting a pack that fell off a wagon. He's a squaw man, all right. Look at him . . . got himself a little taste of injun *puu-yaa* and ain't been able to turn it loose."

"Bastard," the man said. Then he let out a breath and looked away.

"Where you taking him?" Jack looked at the man, then back at Reynolds.

"Aw." He swiped his bandaged hand. "He ain't worth taking nowhere. Just wanted somebody to talk to till the boat came. Now that you two showed up, I'll let him go."

"Sure 'nough?" The prisoner perked up in his saddle.

Reynolds shrugged. "You can get down, take your moccasins off, and get outta here, far as I care."

"My *shoooes?* Hell, I gotta keep my shoes!"

Reynolds raised a boot and kicked him from his saddle. "You can keep *one* of them, then. You can even pick which one." Reynolds grinned. "Now get one off and skin out of here."

The man struggled to his feet and raised his cuffed hands. "What about these?" As he spoke, he stepped on the heel of one ragged moccasin and wiggled his foot out of it. "I can't make it out there with handcuffs on!"

"Keep 'em dipped in water, they'll rust off before ya know it."

"This ain't right! I gotta have a free hand."

"Then go somewhere and gnaw one of your paws off, like a wolf does." He grinned again and laid a hand on his knife handle. "If I take the cuffs off, I'll have to hamstring a leg for ya. Which you druther go with?"

"That ain't no choice," the man said.

"But it's all ya get. Now get away before these boys tie a rock to your head and throw you in the river. You don't know how mean these boys can get."

The man looked at Jack, then at me. "I know all about this one. He's the one Rain in the Face kilt in a knife fight. And that there shirt? He stole from Ebb Walker. Shore did."

"*Kilt*, huh?" I glared at him. "Do I look like I've been *kilt* to you?"

"Just as well be, when Rain gets a hold a ya. Better keep that bulletproof shirt on, is all I can say." He shook his head, stepping away, looking back at us over his shoulder with a worried expression.

"Watch this," Reynolds said in a muffled voice; and as the man reached the edge of high brush, Reynolds threw the Springfield to his shoulder. "Ridgely! Look here!"

The man turned and froze, a look of horror in his red-rimmed eyes. "BANG!" Reynolds shouted, and Ridgely swayed and nearly fell.

"Yeah, that's real funny, you asshole you." The man turned and scrambled off into the brush. Reynolds chuckled; I just stared at him.

"How long before that boat comes?" Jack spit, ran a hand across his mouth, and looked up along the high ridge atop the riverbank.

"Not long," Reynolds said. "We'll likely have some

stragglers come in to us by then. Don't go shooting at 'em thinking they're Indians."

We made a small fire and fixed coffee. Reynolds filled us in on how the expedition was going while we sipped, ate some jerked beef, and waited for the river boat. "You never said why you're really here." He spoke over a mouthful of jerked beef and washed it down with coffee made from muddy river water.

"Custer owes me for a horse," I said, not wanting to mention the letter.

"How much?" He chewed and stared at me.

"Seven hundred," I said.

He grunted and shook his head. "That ain't enough."

"That's what I keep telling him," Jack said. Seven hundred ain't worth the trouble."

"That ain't what I mean," Reynolds said. "I *mean* coming up here over a horse ain't enough reason . . . no matter how much money is involved. If I was you I wouldn't tell anybody that's why you're here. They'll think you're simpleminded."

Jack nodded. I avoided his eyes and asked Reynolds, "Just how bad is it looking out there?"

"How bad?" He sucked his teeth and considered it for a second. "You're a businessman, so I'll put it this way. In Sixty-six, it cost the government a million dollars a piece for every Indian killed. Compared to this, that was a *discount.*" He glanced around. "Where's your big racehorse?"

"I quartered him at the livery in Bismarck. Didn't want ta bring him up here."

"Good thinking." He picked a tooth. "I been backtracking and sidetracking for three days. I've never seen signs of so many Indians in my life. There's tracks coming from all directions. They started fanning our back trail nearly a week ago." He spread a wry smile. "It's bad enough to have them everywhere ahead of ya, but even worse when they're behind ya, too. They're awfully bold this time . . . awfully bold."

While we waited for the riverboat, Reynolds craned his neck at a rustling sound from within the thick brush. Jack's pistol was out and cocked, and my rifle had already gone up to my shoulder when Reynolds raised a hand toward us. "Easy, boys, I think it's some of us. Indians never make such a racket."

In a few seconds a black man wearing a faded red shirt stepped from the brush and grinned. "Don't shoot me. I've still got some money left from payday." Behind him, three haggard young soldiers staggered from the brush bareheaded, their clothes streaked with mud and picked full of briar holes.

"Get in here, Dorman," Reynolds said. "I oughta known it was you. Been hearing you for a mile, and smelling ya, for two."

"You heard them, not me." The black man gestured his rifle barrel at the three young soldiers. The soldiers dropped to the ground near us and stared back and forth.

"Deserters?" Reynolds eyed the soldiers and spoke to the black man.

"Naw . . . they just went to take a jake together and never found their way back." He grinned at them. "Right, boys?"

"It's the truth," a blond-haired boy of about eighteen said. "We got separated."

"Shut up, Joe," another one said. "We *tried* to desert." He looked around, then dropped his eyes to the ground. "Hell, we couldn't even do that right. Hadn't been for this Negro, we would've starved to death."

"No, you wouldn't," Reynolds said. "The Indians would've killed ya first. Where's your rifles?"

The three soldiers just looked at one another, then at the ground.

Dorman said, "They didn't take their rifles with them. Said that would be *stealing!*"

"*Well?* Wouldn't it?" The blond-haired boy looked up long enough to speak, then back down.

"In a manner of speaking," Reynolds said. He glanced at Jack and me, caging a smile.

"Will they hang us?" the blond-haired boy asked.

"That depends. Are ya ready to go back now and do your duty?"

"Yeah," they said in unison. "But General Custer says—"

"Never mind him. He's just the general." Reynolds and

Dorman shot each other a glance. "If you're ready to make amends, we'll get ya back in and fix things with your sergeant."

"We're ready," one of them said. "Ain't no way out of here, anyhow. Never knew there was so many Indians in my life."

"Did you see any?" Reynolds asked, with his brow narrowed.

"No. But the ground is covered with tracks everywhere we been."

Reynolds's gaze went to Dorman. Dorman nodded. "Twice I spotted some from a long way off. They're all headed the same direction, right into our laps." His eyes had a concerned look in them. Then he nodded toward Jack and me for the first time. "What about these two? They don't look like deserters."

"This is the one I sewed up a couple weeks back," Reynolds said.

"You're kidding?" Dorman looked at me again, paused for a second, then said, "You cost me two dollars. I bet Griebs over in H Troop that you wouldn't live the night through after the way Rain in the Face carved ya up. You sure fooled me. Must be tougher than ya look." He smiled a broad-faced smile.

"Thanks," I said in a wry tone.

"Geeeez," the blond-haired boy said, glancing at me. "You're the one who killed Rain in the Face? After him cutting you all to hell?"

I shook my head and looked away, and Dorman chuckled and said to the three young soldiers, "He also stole one of the Walker boys' shirts right off his back."

The three soldiers stared at me as if in awe.

"Get him to tell ya what he's doing up here," Reynolds said to Dorman. They looked at me, and when I didn't say anything, Reynolds said, "He's here because of a horse."

"Is that right?" Dorman lifted a brow. "Huh-uh. I don't believe that."

I just stared at him, and he cocked his head slightly to one side. "Custer's got you up here doing something for him. He does, don't he?"

I still didn't answer. He shook his head. "I never seen

nothing like him. He gets everybody involved some way or another. Everybody wants to do something for the general." He laughed, still shaking his head.

"It's the Custer way," Reynolds said, standing up and brushing the seat of his trousers. "Everybody wants to please the Custers."

Jack chuckled. "You've got that right."

"I wish somebody would do something to please him," Reynolds said. "I've never seen him act this way."

"How's that?" Dorman squatted down and touched a hand to the coffeepot as he pulled a battered tin cup from under his sweat-stained hat.

"He acts like he ain't paying attention," Reynolds said. "Talking to him is like talking to a stump. Something's got his mind ate up."

"Figure it's all the crap going on in Washington?" Dorman poured a cup of coffee. The three soldiers sniffed toward the coffeepot like hounds sniffing a smokehouse. "Word is, if Custer don't do something *big* and *bold* this trip, his career has about run its course. He's got more politicians out for his scalp than he does Indians."

"Yep. He's got a lot on his mind," Reynolds said. "I don't know who's got it the hardest sometimes, the soldier on top or the soldier on bottom." He looked at the three soldiers in their ragged clothes. "What do you boys think?"

"Shiiit," the blond-haired soldier said, rubbing his palms up and down his knees, staring at the coffeepot. "You *know* which one we think."

"Yep, I bet I do." Reynolds let out a breath, threw back a swig of coffee, and pitched his empty coffee cup to one of the soldiers. I did the same; so did Jack. They caught the cups and scrambled forward on their hands and knees, their lips quivering as they poured coffee with shaky hands. A hard life at best . . . soldiering, I thought; and we waited for another hour until the steamboat bobbed into sight above the frothy swirl of the yellow muddy river.

Chapter

24

Recalling tricks of the trade . . .

We spent three days aboard the riverboat, the *Far West,* a big triple-stacked twin-engine steamer with a broad, flat bottom and a five-foot piston stroke. The thrust of it pumped back and forth, strong and steady against the rush of the river. The boat would measure nearly two hundred feet from bow to stern, and according to the captain, a big man named Marsh, with steel gray hair and bushy eyebrows, this was the first boat ever to carry two steampowered capstans on her bow.

The boat was light but strongly built, and with plenty of speed for the waters of the Yellowstone, even with its two hundred tons of quartermaster stores, commissary goods, and a top deck bulging with tents, tarpaulins, and smallarms ammunition. Marsh and his crew of thirty deck hands had been busy for the past month, gathering supplies and pushing them upriver to stopping points along the way. They worked constantly, sweat streaking their backs as they hoisted and shifted cargo in anticipation of the turns and changing depths of the river.

We'd followed Lonesome Charley Reynolds's advice and told the captain we were two new scouts that'd just hired on out of Fort Rice. Nobody had questioned it, not even the staff of adjutant officers from General Terry's command, or the dozen or so soldiers who stood guard on the boat. I'd asked Reynolds if he might get in trouble for slipping us in. But he'd only grinned. "If Custer can invite his nephew along to do some sightseeing, I suppose a couple of Indian fighters like yourselves are always welcome," he'd replied.

Indian fighters? I'd shot Jack a glance, and neither of us said a word.

At first I thought we might've made better time by horseback; but as the boat wound along, I noticed the rugged forbidding land around and above us, and realized that this country would make quick work of both horse and man even under normal conditions, let alone with the chance of warring Indians waiting at every turn.

"If you was to change your mind, and want to go back right now, you'd never hear me complain about it," Jack said as we stood on the aft deck and watched the jagged ridgelines fall away behind us. Wind lifted a light spray above a churning wake of yellow water and swept it back across us. High up, a hawk soared and circled, then disappeared—gone off to tell other hawks about us.

"We're too far in to turn back now," I said. It flashed across my mind what Dorman, the black scout, had said about the Custers having a way of making everybody want to do their bidding. But I pushed the thought from my mind. "Besides, you wouldn't have missed this boat ride for the world, Jack, and you know it."

He'd sat in on a poker game the night before with three of General Alfred Terry's adjutant officers and won close to a thousand dollars off them. "Well, I can't say it's been bad up to this point." He chuckled. "Of course, winning money is one thing; living to spend it is something else altogether."

"You ain't getting worried, are ya, Jack?"

"Naaaw, worried about what?" He gestured a hand, taking in the country. "A beautiful day . . . a beautiful place. What difference does a few hundred Indians roaming around make, more or less?"

I grinned. "I doubt there's enough Indians in the world to stand off this army."

Jack chuckled wryly. "That's what I say."

"Reynolds ain't new at this business; neither's Dorman. As long as we can stick with them until we get there, I figure we'll be all right."

"Made any plans for our return trip?"

"We always make it home, Jack, don't we?"

"So far," he said. "And I guess if we didn't, we wouldn't know about it."

No sooner had he'd said it, something moved in the brush along the riverbank as I gazed past it. "Jack!" I swung my eyes back to the spot in the brush and narrowed my gaze on it.

"I saw it, too," he said beside me, and his rifle lever clicked. "Now it's gone." He spoke as we drifted along the rail closer to the shelter of some flour barrels stacked as a barricade. "It coulda been a deer." We'd seen dozens of deer along the ridges above the banks on both sides.

"That wasn't no deer," I said raising my Henry rifle from the cradle of my arm and leveling a round up in the chamber.

Above the pounding engines, a voice called out from the brush along the bank: "Give me my shirt, you son of a bitch!"

"Ebb Walker?" I glanced at Jack. He shrugged.

Then a bullet ricochet sang out against the rail of the boat and Jack I ducked back behind the flour barrels as a gray puff of smoke rose up from the brush. I caught a glimpse of Walker's head as it rose up, then ducked back down. "It is him! What's the odds of running into him again?"

"Pretty good, evidently," Jack said, peeping around me toward the bank.

Boots pounded along the walkway along the side of the boat. "Stay back," I called out to Reynolds and Dorman. They'd come running from the galley at the sound of fire, and now skidded to a halt beside us. I peeped around the barrels, saw Walker and two Indians rise up from the brush, running in a crouch, watching us, trying to keep up with the moving boat. They ducked down again when I pointed my rifle around the barrels at them.

"What have we got?" Dorman craned his neck and looked around me toward the bank. He had a big army Colt in his hand, cocked and ready.

"Can't tell how many," I said. "Counted three just then. Might be more."

Jack had slipped to the other end of the barrel barricade and got off a shot. The brush thrashed; a loud scream came from it. But then the boat had moved on enough that we were looking back as we started winding into a turn. Again Walker's voice called out, but this time it trailed beneath the engine's roar.

An officer came running back, pulling his galluses up over his shoulder. Behind him came two of the boat guards with their rifles at port arms. "What's going on back here?"

"Indians, Captain," Dorman said.

"Indians!" In his excitement, the adjutant captain said, "Here, give me that," and he tried to jerk my rifle from my hands.

I shoved him back. He looked embarrassed. "Well, goodness, man! Why didn't you shoot one?"

"They weren't cooperating, Captain." I shot him a harsh glance and jacked a fresh round into my chamber.

"Got to hand it to Walker," Reynolds said. "He ain't gave up yet. After all the beating he took back at Lincoln, he's still loose and in the game."

"Yeah, he's real partial to his shirt," I said.

"What do you mean?" The captain looked confused.

"Beatty here is the man who cut Rain in the Face all to hell, Captain. And he took Walker's medicine shirt from him."

The captain looked me up and down. "No wonder they hate us so."

Then he turned and walked away, the two guards scanning the riverbank as they followed behind him.

"Poor ole boy," Dorman grinned. "Probably just missed the only chance he'll ever get to shoot at an Indian."

Although the *Far West* intended to follow the Yellowstone all the way up and turn west onto the Big Horn River, Jack and I got off with Reynolds, Dorman, and the three deserters at a point just southeast of Rosebud Creek, where they expected to find a party of their Crow scouts protecting the rear of the expedition.

Reynolds pulled some strings with a sergeant aboard the boat, and had managed to get the deserters outfitted with rifles, hats, and travel rations from the supplies the *Far West* carried. No sooner was the boat out of sight, he gave the three men fifty rounds of ammunition apiece and three pounds of jerked beef.

"Can't we travel with you?" The blond-haired boy asked, looking up at us atop our horses.

"You've got all you'll get from us," Reynolds told him. "We're riding, you're walking. Follow our tracks or follow the creek bank. I'll square things with the sergeants, tell them you got lost and we found ya out here and have 'em send somebody back for ya. What you tell them then is up to you."

"Couldn't we just ride in on the boat?"

"How would that look? You leave for a week and show up coming upriver on a load of supplies. Who'd believe that?"

The three looked at one another, then nodded and stood watching us as we kicked our horses out and rode on ahead. "Seems harsh, leaving them here this way," I said to Reynolds as we rode off. I glanced back to where they stood with their rifles hanging from their hand. One of them raised a hand and waved good-bye.

"I know it is. If we had spare horses, I'd give them some." He shrugged. "But we don't, so that's all we can do. There's *six hundred* men up ahead waiting to hear what I've found out here. Which would you do, Beatty, look out for three deserters or six hundred fighting men?"

I only nodded without answering, and we rode on.

According to Reynolds, Custer's troops would follow the Rosebud all the way to the Big Horn River unless they made contact with hostiles and had to change their route. With any luck at all, pushing hard, we'd reach the rear of the expedition within a couple of days. Following the army's tracks wasn't hard, but the trick was to follow them and at the same time stay out of sight as much as possible. Although we'd seen no Indians other than the ones with Walker along the bank of the Yellowstone, now that we traveled Rosebud Creek their tracks were everywhere.

At first, Dorman had seemed a little leery of Jack and me

riding with them. But by the end of the first day, he began to see that we knew what we were doing. We worked a four-man pattern up and down the rolling land as if we'd worked together for years, alternating the front man to the rear every few hundred yards while the two in the middle fanned away to either side.

At no time was more than one rider visible, and only then if the land forced him to be, as he skirted close to the crest of a hill or as he rounded from one rise to the next. The only man at risk was the front man, which is always the case, and should he come upon the enemy and have to make a run for it, the two men in the middle were there to cover his flanks, hit his pursuers from both sides, then fall away, forcing the enemy to have to split their forces if they wanted to follow. Splitting forces was something no experienced fighters ever wanted to do, Indian or white.

Jack and I had learned these things riding guerilla with Quantrill—something I certainly wouldn't mention to them—and by evening we could both see that both the scouts were surprised, and a little curious about us. "Tell me what this looks like to you, Beatty," Dorman said when we'd stopped and gathered for a few minutes in a strip of woods near the creek bank.

I looked down at the wide path of unshod hoofprints less than a couple of days old. "Looks like more than twenty riders," I said, bending slightly and following the tracks with my eyes, back along the creek bank. "I'd say they're in no hurry." I straightened up and looked at him.

"Not bad," he said. "But the important thing is that they are right on the army's trail, right out in the open. Pretty brazen, wouldn't you say?"

"Not if they're well behind the troops. Not if they know they've got plenty of others around somewhere to fall back on—" My words stopped for a second. "Not if they know they're gathering for a battle anyway."

Dorman smiled a tight, wry smile. "There you are. That's how we've been reading it for the past week. That's why we can feel pretty safe out here unless we stumble onto them. They don't seem interested in three or four riders like they usually would be."

"If they did, we'd be dead," Reynolds said. As he spoke, he tried working his swollen fingers on his bandaged hand.

"So they're holding out for something bigger than a couple of horses and a handful of scrapes," Jack said, pushing up his hat brim. "They're getting ready to seriously put the hurt on somebody this time."

"Yep, this is the one Custer's been praying for, I'm afraid," Reynolds said. He and Dorman looked at one another for a second, then mounted up.

That night, we'd built a low smokeless fire long enough to make coffee, and after putting it out and brushing away all remnants of it, we sat in the darkness of a strip of woods, and Dorman said, "You boys seem to know how to hide your butts when you want to."

"It comes in handy," Jack answered, not sounding too willing to talk about it.

"Ever scouted for the army?" Now it was Reynolds's voice in the darkness. Somewhere a wolf called out, then another answered from farther away.

"Not until today," I said, my voice sounding no more eager to discuss it than Jack's had.

"I see," Reynolds said, getting the idea.

Then after a second of pause, figuring I should say something rather than let them think the worst, I said, "We were both up at Powder River back before the Fetterman massacre . . . rode awhile with Jim Bridger. So yeah, I suppose you could say we scouted some. Not enough to call ourselves scouts, though."

"That explains how come you can read track," Dorman said in a quiet tone. "I guess it'd be impolite to ask where you learned to fight with a knife, huh?"

When a few seconds passed without my answering, Jack chuckled and said in the darkness, "Reckon if we all sit here explaining where we've been and what we've done, it'll be a long time before morning, won't it?"

Another silence passed, then it was Reynolds's voice speaking in the darkness, changing the subject. "Dr. Porter told me on the boat that he wasn't gonna let me go back until my hand got well. Even had Captain Marsh try to talk me into staying on board." He chuckled. "I told him I've never needed but one hand to fight with. Can you imagine how I'd feel, laid up with a sore hand after waiting and getting ready for this expedition for two years!"

"Maybe you shoulda stayed back a few days and missed it," Dorman said. "This might turn into a *two-handed* battle before it's over."

"Miss it? I'd sooner die than miss it. When a man can't fight, what else is he good for?"

Chapter

25

On the trail of the guidon . . .

The next morning, after a handful of jerked beef and cold water, we headed out, quiet as ghosts, and by the time we recognized the army trail in the grainy morning light, we'd traveled fifty yards above it on a higher rise of ground. With Dorman riding point thirty yards ahead and Reynolds in the rear at about the same distance, Jack and I were riding fifty yards apart in the middle when I heard the sound of metal on wood coming from the trail below.

I froze, slipped down from my saddle with my rifle in my hand, and stilled the roan, searching the gray light until my eyes stopped and fixed on the sight of three Indians, one holding reins to their horses while the other two squatted down in the middle of the trail, chopping on a wooden crate with steel tomahawks. *Jesus!* Without making a sound, I backed the roan away, out of sight beneath the crest of the rise, dropped down beside him, and raised my rifle over my head, swinging it back and forth for Jack to see.

When Jack saw me signaling him, I raised three fingers to show him how many Indians I'd spotted. He raised his rifle, waved it once to tell me he'd understood, then turned his horse quietly and headed back toward Reynolds in the rear. While I waited for Jack and Reynolds to get to me, I crept close enough to the crest of the rise to keep the three Indians in sight, and I scanned the clump of brush and trees a hundred yards away for any others until Reynolds slipped up beside me. Glancing around, I saw Jack take up the reins to my roan and hold them along with his and Reynolds's army bay.

Without a word, Reynolds nodded and slipped his field lens from inside his buckskin shirt. He watched them up close through the lens until they gave up on opening the crate, hefted it between the two of them, and carried it over to the horses. "Bold as hell," Reynolds whispered almost to himself. In a few seconds they'd managed to get it tied on the back of one of the horses, then they rode away, two of them double now on one horse, the other leading the packhorse with its load. We watched, me with my naked eye and Reynolds scanning the distant brush with his lens for a full minute after they'd disappeared into it.

"Damned army packers," Reynolds said just above a whisper, when he'd lowered his lens. "That's the third pack we've dropped that I know of in the last week."

"Did you see any more Indians inside the brush line?"

"Nope, but it's full of 'em. You can bet on it."

I let out a breath, looked around at Jack, then back to Reynolds as he said, "You can bet we're close to the troops, too. Close enough that they must've dropped that pack late last evening. Otherwise the Indians would've already had it and gone."

We both turned and looked out across the slope of rise behind us a hundred yards. "We gotta get off this rise pretty quick before full light, in case there's more over there." Reynolds shoved himself to his feet, closing the field lens. "We're gonna have to hit it hard from here and get on in. This place is getting too busy for my liking."

"Think we better go one at a time till we get off of here?"

"Yep. Dorman will keep heading straight on unless somebody relieves him on point. That gets him out. You two decide which of you will go next. I'll pull out last and keep your backsides covered."

"No deal," I said in a whisper as Jack came leading the horses to us. "It was time to rotate positions, anyway. *You* go on, we've got *you* covered. If the troops are close, you're the one needs to report in, anyway."

He hesitated. "Are you sure about this, Beatty? This is no time to get heroic. You men *are* civilians."

"Yeah, we are, but there's nothing *civil* about us," I said, taking my reins from Jack. "Get going now. We'll catch up."

Reynolds shot Jack a questioning glance. "You heard him," Jack said just above a whisper. "It ain't often he's in such a generous mood. Probably wants to stay back here and have a nice hot breakfast with 'em."

Reynolds offered a tight smile and shook his head. "I can't come back for you, ya know. Give me a ten-minute lead, then haul outta here."

"You know it," I said as he took his reins from Jack. "Tell the cooks to have us some coffee ready."

He slipped atop his horse and nudged it forward quietly, keeping it checked down until a short distance away. Then we lowered with our rifles across our knees, and I held my breath when he batted the horse up into a hard run. We watched the brush and trees in the distance on both sides until he faded into the grainy light, and listened with our ears tuned to the silence of morning for a full five minutes or so before we stood up to leave.

"Hold it," Jack's whispered, and I stopped with my foot already reaching for the stirrup. "Get 'em down, now!" His whisper turned urgent. Without even seeing why he'd said it, I hooked the reins on the roan, threw an arm up under his neck, and brought him down on his knees, then over on his side. I dropped down and peeped over his side toward the distant brush line. Beside me, Jack had downed his silver gray in the same manner and swung his rifle up over it.

We waited, watching, scarcely breathing, as a band of warriors walked their horses out of the grainy light from within the brush and trees, and moved with the silent stealth of mountain cats along the edge of the rise, less than a hundred yards away. The roan lay beneath my rifle barrel as still as death. I counted them emerging into sight like apparitions stealing into a nightmare. Eight of them, then twelve, then a half-dozen more until at the rear came the three who'd taken the crate from the trail below us. They'd been the front scouts, I thought. Now they'd circled and gone to rear. The same pattern we'd used, only with more men to keep it rotated.

Their faces fixed in the direction Reynolds had taken, as if they'd heard his horse's hooves and come forward now to see about it. Two of them looped their big ponies forward and out to the spot where I knew they would see his prints and the prints of Dorman gone on before. Light was breaking fast on us. Another few minutes and Jack and I would stand out like tin ducks at a shooting range. I glanced at Jack and saw his rifle at rest across the silver gray's back, his eyes given to the determination of a man unafraid, *unafraid!* And intent on staying alive.

His right hand lay along the rifle stock, his glove off and lying at his side. His trigger finger rested an inch from the trigger guard. He could have been a statue save for his gloved left hand moving slowly, caressing the silver gray's neck, soothing it, bringing it peace, keeping it calm before the storm. I almost shook my head looking at him—my partner, always cool, always out front of that tightly stretched wire that runs quivering and humming from a man's brain to his nerve endings when life and the taking of life stood before him. *Quiet Jack . . . you bastard. I always envy you that . . .* Always the one left standing when the killing stopped.

What went through his mind? I wondered, looking away from him, letting *my* hand relax on the rifle, back to where the two Indians leaned down in their saddles of fur and blanket and studied the prints beneath them. They spoke between them, looking down, one of them letting his finger point from the prints back, following the path Dorman had made earlier. Behind them the rest of the party moved on slowly, their mounts strung with fresh game, the blood of deer running dark in wide streams down the horses' flanks.

The two rose in their saddles, looking all around, their eyes sweeping ever toward us. *Here goes.* My finger tensed once more on the trigger. But then their eyes moved on back across the grassy rise, and they spoke again, then spun their horses, kicking them into a loop and headed back, following our scattered prints.

I breathed easier, but only for a second, knowing that at

any minute the two would come upon all four sets of prints and decide which ones to follow. Then it would be a matter of luck whether they followed mine and Jack's and rode straight to us, or picked up Dorman's and Reynolds's leading off the rise toward the rear of the soldiers. I didn't feel lucky.

As soon as the last of the party topped the crest of the rise and disappeared over it, Jack and I raised our horses, slipped atop them, and headed down toward the wide army trail below us without saying a word. At the bottom of the steep slope we swung out onto the trail and batted our horses into a run. Only when we'd gone nearly a full mile did we stop long enough to look back. "If those two are on us, it's best we stay here and kill 'em," Jack said, spinning his silver gray with his rifle in his hand, scanning behind and around us.

I slacked my reins and let the roan blow and step back and forth in place, settling down. "They mighta gone on Dorman's tracks; that'll take them back to their party. One shot out here will bring the whole country down on us."

"You've got your knife," he said, his eyes locking onto mine as he stilled the silver gray. "We can get covered and jump them when they come by."

"*If* they come by," I said. "I'd just as soon outrun them."

He swung the silver gray closer to me. "If you're gonna get squeamish about sinking that blade in somebody's heart, you shoulda thought of it before we left Bismarck. We're in it now, up to our asses."

"Damn it, Jack! We don't know for sure they're coming this way. Give it another mile or two, then——"

"Stand down, there," a shaky voice called out from behind a low spill of rocks alongside the trail.

What the——*!* We both spun our horses toward the sound. There stood a young soldier thirty feet from us, up from behind the rocks, with a Springfield trembling against his shoulder. Beside him, another soldier stood up slowly with a pistol drawn. Jack and I shot each other a puzzled glance. "Told ya this was a good place to jump somebody," he said under his breath.

"Drop those weapons," the soldier said.

"Easy, young man," I called over to him. "You don't see

no feathers in our hair, do ya?" I knew they were both wondering about my medicine shirt, so I spread my arms a bit. "We're new scouts for Lonesome Charley. You can ask him."

One whispered something to the other, then the one with the rifle said, "Oh? Well, how come we've never seen ya before?"

I started to answer, but Jack jerked his horse forward a step and said, "Because we're *new*, damn it! Can't ya hear?"

"Don't come any closer," the one with the pistol called out, his gun hand shaking like a man with palsy. "Drop the rifle."

"Bullshit! You're talking crazy." Jack stepped his horse closer. "We got Indians dogging us behind, and more flanking us atop that rise. You wanta stand here and dicker all day, that's up to you. We're heading on in." He nudged his horse on as if they weren't there. I followed.

"Wait," the one with the rifle called out. "We'll get our horses and stay behind you. Don't try nothing funny. We're watching."

"Good, then! You see anything *funny*, you tell us," Jack said. "We ain't had a good laugh all morning."

"Saaay. I *have* seen you before," one called out as they mounted and swung their horses in behind us. "You're the one who killed Rain in the Face, aren't you? Took his shirt right off his back!"

I looked at Jack and batted the roan into a trot. "What are you two doing out here?" I asked as they caught up to us.

"McDougall sent us back after that damned box of hardtack. One of the packers lost it last night coming. They sent us because we fell asleep last night in our saddles."

The other soldier chimed in, "Hell, ya can't blame us, can ya? We only stopped long enough for supper last night, then rode till daylight. A man needs a little shut-eye. Now I guess we'll catch hell 'cause the Indians found the hardtack. But we couldn't help it. They was there when we got there. Lucky they didn't see us."

"How much farther to the rear guard?" Jack asked over his shoulder.

"Five miles, more or less. You guys gonna be fighting with

us? We've spotted a big encampment twenty miles ahead. They say there'll be plenty of injuns for everybody."

I judged that dropping down and taking the army trail might have caused us to ride four or five miles farther, but with the party of Indians above on the rise, it was four or five miles we'd gladly give them. By the time the sun stood at midmorning, we'd come upon the rear guard, seeing them at first as dark specks on a hilltop four hills away in this high roiling. We worked our way to them with caution, one of us riding to the next peak, checking it, then signaling the other three ahead. I'd ask one of the soldiers what they knew about scouting forward, and he'd told me they *didn't know nothing about nothing, except getting shot at and shooting back.*

The first living thing we came upon was a ragged army mule standing balked in the middle of the trail with his pack straps hanging in the dirt. A hundred yards ahead a short column of soldiers flanked the trail on either side, watching as we pulled up to the mule. Dried sweat covered the animal in long white streaks, but his head was up and his ears flicked back and forth at me. I gathered his reins, held him by his rope bridle, and crossed my horse in front of him, turning his head back and forth, confusing him, making him forget why he'd refused to go forward. He resisted for only a second, then fell into a walk for a few feet, then into a trot as I fed out his reins and led him behind me.

A muffled cheer went up from the soldiers when we looped up to them. One of them dropped down, ran forward, and took the mule's reins from my hand. "You vant a yob, drivink dese mules?" A stocky soldier ask in a heavy German accent, smiling as I spun my roan up beside him and a rough-looking captain with bloodshot eyes. The captain saw my confused expression and said as Jack and the two soldiers came sliding in, "That's Windolph." He nodded toward the smiling German. "He shoots better than he speaks English. He asked if you want a job driving mules?"

"No, thanks. The mule was just worn out and needed to rest," I said. "Now that he's rested, he came right along."

"Yes, we know. But the problem was getting someone to go back and get him. Even a few yards has turned into a dangerous proposition. Windolph was just getting ready to go back for him when we spotted you men." He shot the two soldiers a glance. "Where's the hardtack?"

"Indians took it, Cap'n McDougall. And that's the gospel truth," one of the soldiers answered. "You can ask these guys. We ran into them along the road."

Captain McDougall lifted an eyebrow, and I understood his question. "We were riding in with Dorman and Reynolds, got separated a couple hours back, and had to swing wide of a hunting party—the ones who took your box of hardtack."

He nodded, satisfied with my answer, and gestured off to the left with a yellow-gloved hand. "We saw Reynolds and Dorman ride around us earlier, heading up front to the command. How many Indians did you see back there? How are they armed?"

"A dozen, maybe," Jack said before I could answer. "Most of them carrying bows—a few older rifles. Nothing strong."

The captain bit his lip, considering something, then said, "General Custer is going to blow his top when he hears about the hardtack. They know we're here now, no question about it."

I looked at Jack with a bemused expression as I spoke to McDougall. "Captain, they've known it all along. You've cut a path twenty yards wide. Indians ain't stupid or *blind*. They've seen you long before now."

"I know. I'm part Indian myself, sir. But the general doesn't look at it that way. He feels the big encampment ahead has had no warning of us. But if that hunting party is headed there, he'll realize our cover is blown."

I just shook my head and let out a breath. For the first time since we'd left the riverboat, I thought about the sealed letter in my pocket and said, "Captain, with your permission, we'll ride on ahead to command and join Reynolds and Dorman."

"Of course." He turned to the German. "Windolph, go with them. You need to be up with H Troop, anyway." He looked back at me. "Please stay to the side of the trail. I can't have anybody slowing down these mules. You've seen what happens once they stop."

"Thanks, Captain." Jack and I backed our horses enough to let Windolph the German fall in ahead of us. Then we followed him off to the side of the trail, riding alongside it until we started moving past a long string of mules with their tails swishing beneath heavy loads of rations and ammunition packs. Alkaline dust swirled around their hooves and drifted over in our faces.

Chapter
26

A promise is kept to the lady. . . .

With the army on the march, it took us over an hour to reach command at the front of the long, winding line of mules, wagons, and mounted troops. Riding beside the trail, seeing them through a heavy veil of dust, they looked like ghosts of some ancient army long past, yet doomed to ride these rugged hills forever. Windolph fell back beside us, speaking with his yellow bandanna tied up across his face. Jack and I had covered our faces in the same manner, and our words sounded hollow and distant as we spoke.

When I asked Windolph what had become of Roland Gaither, he said the man had collected only a small amount of investment capital from the troops at the end of the first day when they drew pay fourteen miles out of Fort Lincoln. Hardly enough to support his cattle venture. After that, Gaither had disappeared. "Vat a foolish man he was," Windolph said, shaking his head. I found it odd that in the thick dust, with a bandanna over his face and the sound of an army clinking alongside us, his words became more understandable.

"He should have known that zoldiers alvays plan to invest their *next* pay. But ven it comes time to go to battle, dey alvays change dere minds and send it home to dere family, or dey save it for to drink on when the battle iss over." He laughed; dust bellowed from his bandanna. "Dis man did not know dis . . . he vas foolish, yaa?"

I smiled beneath my bandanna, and Jack and I both nodded. "Been in the army long?" I asked him.

He shrugged. "Vat iss *long?* In ze army, it iss alvays *long."*

Riding on, Jack asked him what he thought about the coming battle, but he wagged a gloved finger back and forth. "Never do ve talk about ze battle . . . until aftervards. For today, ve talk about ze beer and ze women. I talk about ze time when I vaz a boy in Bergen . . . about ze flowers zat grow vild along ze old stone road. I talk about them because zey vill be there long after zis battle, whether ve live or ve die."

I shot Jack a glance and we rode on in silence. Finally, out of the blue, Windolph said without facing us, "How vonderful ve must look, on a bold horse, with our carbine and our revolver . . . a hundred rounds in our web belt. Zere iss no prouder life than for us, the zoldier."

It was nearly noon when we came upon a gathering of scouts just out of the rising dust off to our left, lounging against a rise of rocks with canteens in their hands. I didn't see Reynolds among them, but Dorman's faded red shirt and his sweaty black face stood out, sunlight glistening on his bare head as he lifted his hat and ran a hand across his forehead. I motioned toward him, and Windolph fell in with us as we cut our horses and rode over.

"See you two made it all right," Dorman called out. He gestured a hand toward a battered coffeepot at their feet. "Got some coffee, but it's cold . . . brewed from alkaline water. Probably make you pitch up your breakfast."

"What breakfast?" One of the scouts grumbled under his breath.

"No, thanks," I said for all three of us. "Where's Reynolds?"

"Up at command. I came on back here. Reynolds told them about the hardtack." He shook his head. "Sure wish he hadn't. Terry wanted us to wait until Gibbons brings up his troops on the other side and box that big encampment in. Now Custer's jumping the gun because of that damned hardtack. He told Reynolds we gotta hit on our own, before they run away from us."

"But ve have been marching all night," Windolph said beside me. "Our horses are vorn out . . . ze men are vorn out."

"Jesus," I said. "What good will it do to hit 'em? If they *do* run, ya can't chase them down on worn-out horses?"

"You're not saying anything that the men haven't said all morning, Beatty. "Maybe *you* can convince Custer. Nobody else can." He rubbed his sweaty head with a dark laugh and looked off toward the distant sky. "Maybe we'll be lucky. Maybe they *won't* run."

A Crow scout sprang to his feet, swinging an arm wildly toward the land before us. *"Otoe! Otoe Lakota!"* He pounded himself on the chest. "I see *otoe! Otoe Lakota!"*

We stared at him. Dorman cocked his head at us, shielding his face with his hand against the sun glare. "He says many Indians out there. Too many to count. Seems real excited, don't he? If you plan on getting your horse money from Custer, you best get ta doing it. Reynolds is already giving away all his belongings."

"Doing what?"

"Yep." Dorman shrugged as he pushed himself forward, dusted his trousers, and reached for his dangling reins. "Says he won't need none of his stuff after today."

Jack sidled his silver gray up against my roan, pulled down his bandanna, and said in a caged voice just between us, "Let's go home."

"In a minute, Jack." I turned back to Dorman as he stepped up in his stirrup. "Think you can get us up to Reynolds? Get me in to see Custer before he pulls out?"

"I doubt it."

"Will ya try?"

He shrugged again, turning his horse toward the front of the endless line of billowing dust. "Sure, I've nothing planned."

We batted our horse and rode on behind him, and an hour later we reached the point where the front of the line had stopped and began to bunch up on itself. The dust had thinned down and troopers stood near their horses watching us pass by. "Windolph, over here." A voice called out, and the German turned toward it.

"It is my own H Troop, moving up," he said to me. "I go to join zem now."

I nodded and had turned back to rein forward when a thick hand reached out and grabbed my reins. "Ahhhh, laddie. What on God's earth are ye doing here?"

I looked down at Griebs smiling up at me, and remembering in a flash how he'd set me up with Ebb Walker and the reward money, I jerked the reins. "Get off my horse, Griebs."

But he held firm. "Don't tell me you're still sore about the reward money, laddie. If it does you any good to know . . . the general canceled the request for it."

I eased up a bit on the reins. "Well, good enough, then. Let's let bygones be bygones."

"Yes. I would feel much better." He grinned. From the group of gathered soldiers, Corporal Dammio stepped up beside Griebs leading a big gray gelding and carrying a bugle in his free hand. He looked up at Jack and me, blushed, and looked away.

"Didn't know you were musically inclined, Corporal." I grinned at Dammio, and his face reddened.

"Okay, I blowa the bugle. Bigga deal! Thata don't meana nothing."

"What are you so touchy about?" Griebs asked him.

"Nothing." he ducked a glance past me, then looked back to Griebs. "I'ma gonna be riding dispatch alla day long. So don'ta nobody give-a me no shit. Okay?" Behind them, boots reached up into stirrups and the whole gathering of men began to mount in a creaking of leather and clink of steel.

"So," Griebs said, turning loose my reins. "Will you lads be joining us this day?"

"No way," I said. Beside me Jack added, "Sure hope not, even if I have to crack his head to get him outta here."

Griebs and Dammio both stepped up and swung onto their horses. "How are the odds running on this one, Griebs?" I asked. "Anybody betting any serious money one way or the other?"

"Shhhh!" He ducked his head, raising a gloved finger to his lips. "This is no gambling matter, Beatty. All the betting, the drinking, the wheeling-dealing. That's all just grab-arse and passing time. It all stops once the orders are drawn. Today we go to the sacred trade of war . . . so, mind you keep a civil tongue in your head." He winked, wagged a finger, turned his horse, and called to his men in a hushed tone, "Column of twoooos, move out."

They formed up in a swirl of dust, and Dammio swung his gray horse over to us with the bugle strap hanging from a saddle ring. He looked back and forth between Jack and me and said, "I justa wanta tell ya. I gotta nothing againsta how you live. This isa bigga world, and I don't judge nobody."

We just stared as he turned, kicked his horse into a loop and headed off toward the officers gathered an eighth of a mile farther up the line. "What the hell did he mean by that?" Jack squinted, scratching his head.

"I don't know, Jack. Maybe he thinks we're Mormons."

We followed Dorman's red shirt in the swell of dust that rose up in the wake of H Troop riding off behind a stocky gray-haired captain and two scouts. Ahead of us in the dust, I thought I caught a glimpse of General Custer at the edge of the trail, but I wasn't sure. If it was him, his hair had been clipped short and he wore a wide-brimmed flat-crown hat. Just as I gestured toward him and motioned for Jack to follow me, Reynolds came sliding his horse out of the dust before us and spun it sideways, blocking us. "Hold it, you're not going anywhere." Even as he spoke to me his eyes stayed off toward the dusty horizon.

"Is that Custer?" I pointed past him, craning up in my saddle. "Did you tell him I was coming?"

"Yeah, I told him." He looked over at Dorman and said, "Head over to C Troop. They need you on point." Dorman touched a finger to his hat, spun his horse in the dust, and rode off. Then Reynolds turned back to me, still looking away. "You must be out of your mind, Beatty. Maybe I sewed you up too tight and cut off the air to your brain."

"Did you tell him? What did he say?"

"He said if I laid eyes on you, to shoot you with no hesitation. And I said I would. But I'm not laying eyes on ya." He still gazed off as he spoke. "He says you're Miller Crowe the outlaw. Is it true?"

"If it was, would I admit it?" A sweat bee zinged in near my ear. I slapped at it and heard it whine louder.

"Fair enough, then. I haven't seen ya—don't want to—ain't going to. Forget about your horse money and skin out of here, whoever you are."

I shot Jack a glance, then said to Reynolds. "Listen to me. I lied about the horse money. I came to give him a letter. A personal letter from his wife."

"Aw, shit, what's the difference? I'm dead today, anyway." He tossed his hands, glanced back in the direction of Custer, then looked at me. "So, now you're saying you're some kind of mailman? Aw . . . well, everything's fine, then. I'm sure the general will want to—"

"Listen to me." I cut him off. "They had some ill words, him and her. She sent me because she didn't want to take a chance on somebody seeing the letter. It meant a lot to her . . . probably will to him, too. We've got to get it to him."

"Beatty, don't I look a little busy right now? He's not concerned about some damn love letter. I've tried to tell him for the past hour that we've got nearly three thousand Indians less than miles from here. He won't even listen to that. Instead, he's so worried about the hardtack being found, he's split the whole Seventh up into *four* separate outfits!"

"You're kidding?"

"Sure, I am. I always kid about stuff like this when I'm getting ready to die." He grimaced. "Now get out of here."

"He's right," Jack said. "Let's go."

"Hunh-uh. I'm taking it to him." I jerked my horse to get past Reynolds, but he stepped his horse with mine, blocking the trail.

"Okay, Beatty. Give me the letter. He'll get it, I promise ya. First chance I get, I'll slap it into his hand and see he reads it."

I started to jerk the horse again, but he anticipated me. "I mean it, Beatty. That's the best we can do here."

I let out a breath, looked at Jack, then back to him. "All right. As long as he gets it . . . that's the main thing." I took the wax-sealed letter from inside my shirt and handed it to him. He tapped it on his hand, then shoved it under his hat.

"Now, will you two get out of sight? I really *do* need to go fight this war."

"Thanks, Reynolds. I owe you a lot," I called out as he turned his horse back into the swirling dust. "I'll buy you a beer when this is over."

"Not me, you won't. I ain't coming back. But you can buy one for every man in the Seventh, if any of them make it back to Lincoln."

"You've got it." I called out to him, then looked at Jack as Reynolds disappeared back into the dust he'd came sliding out of. "He's serious, ain't he? He don't think he's gonna make it."

Jack spit and pulled his bandanna back up over his nose. "Sounds like it," he said.

Chapter

27

Searching for a peaceful way home . . .

We'd stepped our horses off the trail and ridden a few yards out of the settling dust. I sat atop my roan with my wrists crossed on my saddle horn, feeling relieved that it was over for us. I didn't clearly understand why I'd had to bring the letter up there in the first place. But now that I'd done it, I felt better than I had in a long time, even though one army of young men had just marched off in a swirl of dust to slay another army of young men in an act of nature too dark to discern, yet in the same nature, too ancient to deny.

Gone now were the troops on horseback, and in their place came the creaking wagons and the mules with their heavy burdens, their tails swishing and their mallet-shaped heads low and bobbing as Captain McDougall's rear guards trudged forward, restirring the dust. A wagon rolled out of formation and up near us. A broad-chested teamster sat back on the brake and pulled his bandanna down from his bearded face. It was the same man who'd called us *dandelions* the day Jack and I had passed him, stuck in the mud. He stepped down from his wagon, rolling up his dusty shirtsleeves. "I see you two assholes everywhere I go . . . and I've yet to see either of yas hit a lick."

"And?" I cut my roan sideways to him.

"And I'm gonna kick whatever ass you've got all over this hillside," he said, rounding his finger toward us. "Now climb on down here." Behind him, a little red dog jumped up on his wagon seat and started spinning in place, yapping at us.

Jack kicked his silver gray closer and dropped his boot from his stirrup. Sunlight glinted on the rowel of his spur as he cocked his leg back. "Hold it, Jack! I'll take a couple of minutes and teach this rude bastard some manners."

But just as I started to swing down from my saddle, Captain McDougall called out from the edge of the dust. "You, men! What's going on there?"

He loped forward on a blood bay gelding. "Don't ask us, Captain. This baboon just rode up and started in on us, wanting us to kick the hell out of him, I guess."

"I'm sick of looking at them!" the teamster yelled above the yapping dog. "They don't *work!* They're good-for-nothings!" He pointed a thick finger at Jack. "That one made an obscene gesture at me the other day whilst I was stuck in mud."

"Stand down, man, and shut that dog up!" The captain's voice boomed; he swatted a hand at a sweat bee. "We're supposed to keep quiet back here." He looked at Jack. "Did you do that?"

"No. He has me confused with somebody else." He glared down at the man. "But I'll be glad to straighten the matter out with him."

"That's quite enough!" McDougall pointed at the teamster. "Now. You. Shut that dog up before I strangle it. Get your wagon back in line." The teamster grumbled, turning, and stepped back up on his wagon, backhanding the dog over into the wagon bed. It yelped once and fell silent as stone. McDougall looked at us. "Shouldn't you be out front of one of the columns? You *are* scouts, after all, aren't you?"

I cleared my throat. "Well, no, Captain. The fact is, we never got the job. The general had Reynolds come tell us he had all the scouts he needed. Damn shame, too. We really need work."

"Has *all* the scouts he *needs* . . ." McDougall pinched the bridge of his nose with his gloved fingers and shook his head. Then he collected himself and looked up. "Well. You can't wander around during an Indian battle. Why don't you stay back here with us until we reach the *Far West*? She'll be meeting us over on the Big Horn River in a day or two."

"Thank you, Captain. But if it's all the same, we'll just ride on over and wait for her. Too much dust here to suit me."

"Sorry." He shook his head. "It's too dangerous right now. You'll have to wait. Fall back with the mules until we hear how things go out there."

Jack and I slid one another a glance and nodded. "Anything you say, Captain," Jack said as we reined our horses around toward the rear of the pack animals. They moved as if having to force themselves through the thick veil of dust.

"We're out of here, first chance we get," Jack said as we rode back pulling up our bandannas. "Can you believe that teamster? Wants to start a *fight* at a time like this."

"Probably got himself all worked up, knowing there's a war and he ain't fighting it," I said. "You know how teamsters can get."

"I didn't know you had anything against teamsters."

"I don't. Some of my best friends are—"

"Psst! Beatty, over here." A voice from a tall clump of grass cut me off. We swung toward it and saw Shotgun Tom poke his head up, then drop back down.

"What are you doing out here, Tom?" Jack looked down at where he lay huddled in a ball. Dust streaked his face in long lines of sweat. He stared wild-eyed at us.

"I quit," he said. "You got to help me get out of here!"

"Tom, Tom, Tom . . ." I shook my head, stepped down from my stirrup, and placed a hand on his damp, dusty shoulder. "I told ya before, you can't *quit* the army. Do you know what they do to deserters?"

"No worse than what the Indians will do to me if I stay." He nodded toward the distant horizon. "Ain't the Canadian border up that way somewhere?"

I smiled at Jack, then pulled Tom to his feet and dusted his shoulder. "Yeah . . . a couple of *million* miles up there somewhere. But you don't want to go to Canada. There's nothing there. Weak whiskey, cold weather . . . you'd have to learn a whole new language."

"Don't they speak English?"

"Well . . . if you want to *call* it that." I looked all around. "Where's your horse? Your rifle?"

"I left my horse tied to the rear wagon with my rifle and equipment on it. I couldn't steal government property, could I?"

"Jeeez! Somebody needs to talk to all you deserters. You can't strike out to the border on foot . . . no weapon, no food. How was that gonna work?" I reached a hand up to Jack and he stuck a canteen in it. The sweat bee hovered close, as if watching my every move.

"I don't know, but I ain't gonna stay here. You can't make me. I'm a ballplayer, not a soldier. They lied to me!" He snatched the canteen from my hand, twisted off the cap, and threw it up to his mouth.

"The army *always* lies to you to get ya to join . . . it's like a tradition." I patted his shoulder. "But listen to me. When we met ya, you weren't no ballplayer, you were a prospector, remember? Then you decided to be a soldier . . . now you're gonna desert." I shook my head. "Hope you ain't turning into one of those people who can't make up your mind—"

"I ain't going to fight Indians! They never done nothing to me!" Water spilled from his lips and ran down the dust on his uniform. "Don't try talking me into it!"

I let out a breath, looking up at Jack, seeing him nod as his eyes met mine. "All right, Tom. Take it easy. If you really want to desert, we won't try to stop ya. Stay right here. We'll get your horse and come back for ya."

"Will ya? Really?" He clung to my shirt with his dust-streaked hand. "You're not lying to me?"

"No, Tom. We'll be back. Just keep your nose down behind the grass and wait for us."

At the rear wagon, we just untied the reins to Tom's horse and fell back with it as the wagon rolled on. A few yards behind came a man leading two mules, and he looked up at us through one dust-shot eye with tears streaming down his cheek. His other eye had long been sealed shut by a terrible scar that ran from his forehead to the corner of his mouth. "I know what ya'll are thinking," he said with a crafty grin. His bandanna hung just below his lips and strings of saliva filled with dust clung from lip to lip as he spoke.

"What?" I asked cautiously.

"You're thinking, *'what'll we do if they go to scalping us whilst we're still alive?'* He made a strange giggling sound and lifted his floppy hat above a shaved head. "See. If you was smart, you'd do what I done—shaved that sucker last evening, eh?"

Jack sidled close to him as I led Tom's blood bay gelding. "That wasn't *real* smart, ole man. If an Indian wants to lift some hair, he'll lift it. Get my drift?" He patted himself on the crotch and grinned at the man. The man swallowed hard; his face turned a strange color as we fell back past him and swung over to the edge of the trail.

Twenty yards back, the mounted rear guard took note of us riding away from the trail, but we turned and waved, and they returned our wave with uncertainty as we rode on. When we reached Tom, both of us stood our horses between him and the rear guard until he mounted. He lay low in his saddle and riding between us, both of us keeping him shielded from the soldiers. We rode up, topped the steep slope, and rode a few yards down the other side. "You can get up now," Jack said.

"Aw, man!" Tom sat up and ran a trembling hand across his face. "I thought I was a goner, for sure. I never want to see this place again."

"We ain't home yet," I said, batting my roan into a trot. "We could run into Indians twixt here and the river. Keep that Springfield close at hand."

He fell his blood bay in between Jack and me and looked back and forth at us. "Fellas, I'll be honest . . . I don't think I could kill somebody if it came down to it. It made me sick killing that mule and Boston Custer's horse—and that was accidentally. Don't know what I'd do if—"

"Put it out of your mind until the time comes," Jack said, cutting him off. "If you think about it too much, it'll make ya crazy."

"But what if we *do* run into trouble?" he asked as we trotted along at a steady clip, following the same path

Custer and his five troops had taken. We would cut off it and over toward the river a couple miles ahead, I figured.

"If it happens, just think of it as a ball game," Jack said. "You're on the mound, ball's in your hand, it's the last inning, the score's tied, and there goes a runner from third base to home. You've *got* to stop him, right?"

Tom nodded; Jack grinned. "That ain't so bad, is it?"

"Naw, except if my pitching hadn't gone to hell on me, I wouldn't be here in the first place."

Baseball . . . I gigged my roan, riding on, scanning the rise and fall of this rugged land, wondering how far Custer and his men had made it by now. I pictured him somewhere up there, perhaps reading Libbie's letter right then, reading it and feeling a little better now. It had to be bearing heavy on his mind, getting the other letter, thinking that she was leaving him. Yep, I'd done a good thing, I thought, coming up here . . . although I still wasn't sure why I did it.

"I'll tell you one thing," Tom said as we rode on toward a narrow stand of trees at the bottom of a draw. "These men are all nuts. We marched all night without a wink of sleep. Now they're going right into a battle. That's no way to live."

"That's how war goes," Jack said. "You go for weeks with nothing to do, then *bam,* you've got both hands full and no place to drop it. Yeah, maybe you're doing the right thing, *quitting.*"

"I know I am. The general's a wild man. Came out ranting and raving this morning . . . twice he got thrown off the horse you sold him."

"You don't say?" I winched hearing about it. The whole horse transaction was bad from the start.

"Yep. Maybe that's why he's got such a mad-on at everybody," Tom said. "Maybe that's why he wants to rush in and get this over with so bad. Nothing like getting thrown off your horse to ruin your whole day."

"Don't say that, Tom," Jack said in a low tone. "He's got other horses. He didn't have to ride Honest Bob."

"That's right, he didn't," I said, gigging my horse a little harder and riding on ahead of them.

Chapter
28

Fleeing into the valley of death . . .

It was afternoon when we saw a party of at least two dozen Indians watering their horses at a thin creek a hundred yard below us. Tom hadn't been able to get the hang of riding in a scouting position, so we were side by side when we came upon them. The sight of them caused Tom to yank so hard on his horse's reins, the horse whinnied loudly and nearly fell back on its haunches. Jack snatched the horse by its bridle to help Tom settle it. But it was too late. I looked down and saw the Indians stand up, looking right up at us.

There in full view above them, before turning my horse, I saw, of all people, Walker and Rain in the Face. Walker's finger came up pointing, and even at a hundred yards, I thought that he must've recognized his medicine shirt. He yelled something in Indian. I spun my horse. "Come on, Jack! They saw us!" Again Tom's horse let out a long whinny. It tried to rear, but Jack caught its bridle again. "Slack off the reins, Tom! Jesus! Can't you ride a horse?"

We spurred hard, getting as much distance between us and them as we could before they hit the top of the rise. For all the mountainous rolling land around us, we happened to be on a short stretch of flatland headed west. Two hundred yards ahead the land broke upward in a steep slope. Behind us, we heard them squalling out war cries. Jack rode close beside me, both our horses stretched out, bellied down, taking long strides of earth beneath their hooves. We kept Tom in front, goading his horse on if it slowed for a second.

Tom wobbled in the saddle, flopping back and forth, out of control, not helping the animal a bit. Jack shot me a glance as we ducked low on our horses, his silver gray pounding neck to neck with my roan. I knew as well as he that if Tom came off that horse, he was on his own. A rifle shot popped behind us, but we hadn't heard the whistle of lead go past us. My eyes searched the crest of the slope coming up before us, looking for cover, seeing none.

At the top of the slope, Jack and I stopped and spun our horses, slipping our rifles from their scabbards. Tom went over the crest and down the other side, letting out a long cry as the horse swerved and pounded on. "What do you think?" Jack yelled at me, throwing his rifle to his shoulder. He pulled off a round and one of the front riders rolled backward off his horse. But the party fanned out, starting up the slope. They'd be around us in a half circle by the time they reached the top.

"Run!" I yelled without getting off a shot, and we spun and gigged our horses down the other side, following Tom's blood bay as it hit the bottom of the slope and headed up another. We'd caught up to him by the time we topped the next hill. Jack spun and fired again. I scanned the land back and forth, searching for a position. Where would three men go to hold off two dozen? *Jesus!*

Then, past the next rise, a lower hill than the one we'd just raced up, a drift of dust hung in the air, stretching back a long ways toward the place where we'd left the rear guard. *Custer's troop? H Troop?* Behind me, the warriors cried out like wolves. Jack's rifle barked again. "Better find something quick," he yelled. I glanced back, saw them starting up the hill, no closer, but farther away. If we could outrun them another few minutes . . . The army had to hear the rifle fire.

"Come on!" I yelled, pointing out the rise of dust as I spurred the roan and we caught up to Tom at the bottom of the hill where he'd managed to stop the blood bay and had it turning in place waiting for us. He gigged it as we came past him, and the horse shot out alongside us. He managed to raise a hand and point toward the rise of dust. "I know," I yelled. "It's our only chance."

By the top of the next hill, I felt the roan tiring. This was torturous land for horses. But if ours were tiring, so were theirs. This time, when Jack spun and fired, I fired also, having caught a glimpse of the column of cavalry topping the next hill and heading down it, coming our way from out of the rise of dust. "Hold them?" I fired three shots one after the other, but saw no one fall. Jack's shot took another one off his horse and flung his body into another rider. They fanned out wide, coming up toward us.

"Can't you *hit* anything?" Jack bellowed. Pistol shots whistled past us. A rifle shot blew up a clump of dirt. We backed our horses, still firing. Another rifle shot, this one barely missing me. I caught a glimpse of Walker dropping down from his horse, his rifle coming up again as he hit the ground. I glanced back. The soldiers were gaining ground. Tom was down the hill and headed straight at them, his arm waving in the air.

"One more run, Jack. We'll be there!" We ducked in the hail of gunfire, spinning our horses, kicking them out down the hill. Glancing back as we reached the bottom of the hill, we saw the Indians stop short and scatter as the cavalry's pistol fire whistled over our heads from one hill to another. Tom had loped his horse over into a coulee out of the fire. "Give them hell, boys!" I yelled as the cavalry descended on us. But they seemed to not even see us as they sped past and up the other hill, us spinning in their midst, their army Colt revolvers exploding in one long hot hail of fire.

We cut over to where Tom had gone into the coulee and tried to catch him racing along across jagged rocks and spilled clumps of sun-hardened dirt. "Easy, Tom, you'll break a leg," I called out to him as Jack and I checked our horses down, but he neither slowed down nor looked back. He pounded out of sight, the big bay swaying and zigzagging across dangerous ground. "He ain't gonna make it, Jack. The boy's too spooked for this kind of situation."

"Hush! Listen!" Jack raised a hand. We stopped and heard in the distance the sound of rifle fire. It started with a few scattered rounds, but in an instant it grew and swelled into a full raging battle. "Something big's going on."

"Yeah, not far from here." My voice sounded strained to me. I swallowed hard and edged my horse along the coulee a few feet. "They must've found the big village."

"If they did, it must be bigger than they thought." Jack's voice took on a tone of awe. "The battle ain't moving away from the army. It's moving *toward* it."

"Let's find Tom and get out of here, Jack. This don't feel right. We're in a bad spot."

We eased along the coulee, hearing the big battle rage on one side of us, less than a mile away, I figured, and the sound of pistol fire dying down on the other side of us where the soldiers had just come through and saved our behinds. "Maybe we better stay close to them," I said, nodding in the direction of the soldiers above us, hearing them move off in the same direction Tom had taken. We could hear them shouting orders back and forth. Walker and his Indians had scattered. Now the soldiers were regrouping, probably wondering the same as we were: what all the firing was about on the other side of the hills toward the river.

"Let's stay still here," Jack said, looking up, his eyes running along the edge of the coulee. "If everybody's fighting a big battle, maybe we'll slip around it unnoticed."

"Yeah, maybe." I also scanned the edge above us. Then I moved my horse forward along the coulee. "Let's see about Tom."

We rode along the winding ravine as it widened downward, the sound of battle growing more intense to the left of us, and to our right, nothing, not since the soldiers' horses had pounded off ahead of us. It felt eerie, as if we might climb up on the right and enjoy a peaceful picnic lunch while gazing across the coulee and watching hell spill up and swallow the rest of the world.

"Tom," I called out ahead of us. "Tom, it's us, come on back."

We waited for a second. "Come on," Jack said. "He's gonna have to sort this out for himself."

"Wait. I heard something, did you?" Farther down the coulee I thought I'd heard a low rumble. The sound of horses? Men running?

Jack shrugged. "No. But if you want to stay and—"

Before he could finish, his words were drowned by a

rising wall of sound coming up along the coulee, a sound of explosions, men screaming, yelling, horses whinnying. It swelled and rolled toward us in a great and terrible wave. We stared at each other for a second, our faces drawn pale as it dawned on us what it was.

"Ho-o-o-oly!"

We swung our horses, almost too late. "Yiiiiii!" Tom came screaming around a turn in the ravine, his boots pounding, arms outstretched, his hair blowing straight back, his mouth open wide, seeming to fill the whole ravine as he came upon us. Behind him came the roar, the shooting, the screaming, the pounding hooves swelling, rushing toward us like a mighty river through a broken dam. *"Climb!"* Jack bellowed and swung his horse, its hooves digging at the steep bank of rock and dirt, raising dust, crawling up it on its belly. Bullets tore chunks of rock and dirt off around him in a spray.

"To-o-o-om!" I threw down my hand and caught him under his arm as he tried to speed past me. His weight swung him up against my roan's side. Coming at us was a swirling red-gray cloud; within it were blue uniforms churning, belches of pistol fire exploding, tomahawks and sabers flashing. A horse tumbled forward with a long pitiful scream, blood spinning and spewing from its neck.

The roan crawled and scraped behind Jack's silver gray. I spilled from the saddle but grabbed a handful of mane and hung on, my right hand holding, my feet scraping upward with the horse through loose rock and choking dust, my left hand holding Tom's shoulder by his army shirt, in a death grip. He screamed, climbing with me, his boots scraping up and down the pit of blood and fire beneath us.

A young warrior scrambled up and over Tom's back. But as he rose to swing a war club, his face exploded onto me. The bullet that killed him whistled past my ear, streaming a hot wake of blood. A soldier rose up from the swirl atop a big sorrel horse with his pistol raised. A naked arm swung in, as if conjured from the dust, and buried a hatchet in his neck. Blood sprayed.

Had it not been for Jack grabbing me as the roan spilled over the edge and scrambled to its feet, I would've hung from its side forever, suspended there, entranced by the spectacle beneath me. Tom rolled away on the ground. Jack spun with his pistol drawn and shot a warrior in the chest as he leaped screaming toward us from the back of his big pony. He sailed out and down into the coulee, seeming to toss and bounce atop the raging battle before sinking into the cloud of dust and flashing steel.

"Come on!" Jack yelled, pulling me up. The roan stood shaking himself off. Dust billowed. I snatched my pistol from the holster beneath my arm. Fifty yards away, Indians came running on foot, swinging rakes, army swords, a three-legged milking stool. Jack snatched Tom up and shoved him to me. I caught him and swung him up behind me as Jack sprang up on his silver gray and kicked it out and away from the coulee. I followed, Tom hanging against my back, yelling his brains out. Less than a mile away, dust rose above the sound of heavy fire. *Custer's troops?* If so, they had their hands full.

I'd lost my top hat and noticed that Jack had lost his hat as well. We got ahead of the main body of Indians as they raced toward the fracas in the coulee, and we pounded on toward a hill high above the swirl of dust from the battle going on. A few Indians on horseback and a few stragglers on foot ran right past us, waving weapons and yelling. Only a few even looked toward us, and those who did only shot a glance at Tom's uniform and kept going. Their eyes appeared to be glazed over, as if intoxicated by the headiness of battle.

"Get your shirt off, Tom," I called back to him. Although his uniform was so dusty and streaked with mud it was hardly recognizable, getting shed of it seemed like a good idea. In a second, his shirt spun away on the wind, and we topped the high hill and fell from our horses, gasping fresh air in and out of our lungs. Our horses shook and blew and snorted dust from their nostrils in long strings of brown saliva. Tom rolled on the ground gagging, his arms wrapped tightly around his stomach, his undershirt wet with sweat, clinging like a loose layer of skin.

The hilltop lay empty save for the three of us, but looking back the way we came up, we saw soldiers stagger and crawl from the edge of the coulee and pressed toward the battle on the other side of us. They fired, fell back, and fired again, trying to regroup, but each time leaving a scattering of dead and dying Indians and soldiers between them and the Lakota warriors pouring up from the coulee.

From above, I saw that the coulee we'd been in led down toward the river and narrowed into a buffalo path at the river's edge. At a bend in the river stood a heavy grove of cottonwood trees, their leaves shimmering in sunlight, and visible through them lay the bodies of man and horse alike. Dead littered the river and its banks. The river ran clear and shallow across, but a spread of blood encroached downstream, growing wider as it flowed.

Looking down, the world below seemed to be ending in violence, violence cloaked in a sea of dust. Jack pitched me the field lens and I wiped dust from it, dropping down on my knees and looking out at the battle raging in the valley farther down the river. "My God, Jack!" It was Custer's troops, all right, moving back beneath a thick onrush of Indians.

On the end of the battle near the river, soldiers fell like wheat beneath a sickle; on the other end of the strung-out body of troops, two flags waved, a Seventh Cavalry regimental flag and an old Third Cavalry battle flag. The troops pressed, fighting, then rushing back, toward a hilltop two hundred yards away. At the head of the rush, I saw Custer on Honest Bob, surrounded by a tight group of officers fighting their way up the hill. *Jesus* . . . As I turned and adjusted the lens, I saw Honest Bob rear and spin, and saw Custer spill back and roll across the ground until two soldiers grabbed him and pulled him to his feet. Honest Bob bolted and ran away.

"What's going on?" Jack said beside me. Even as I watched, it ran through my mind. Had Reynolds gotten the letter to him? Had Custer read it?

"Uh . . . nothing, Jack."

"Nothing? Are you out of your mind?"

"I mean, here, look for yourself." I handed him the lens. "But hurry up. We've got to get out of here."

Jack whistled low, then turned to me from the field lens. "We got to get them some help down there or they're finished."

"I know." I looked all around. "H Troop and the rear

guard have to be over on the other side by now. Think they hear what's going on?"

"Unless they're stone deaf, they *have* to hear it." He pushed up from the ground. "Wanta make a run to them? In case they don't know?"

"We gotta do something. Two more guns down there ain't gonna help much."

"Nope. Let's get to H Troop." Jack stood and gathered his reins, lifting Tom by his forearm. "You gonna make it, boy?"

"Yeah." Tom staggered to his feet, and we helped him up onto the roan. The horse stepped back and forth and shook out his mane, ready to make another run. *Hell of a horse . . .*

I climbed up behind Shotgun Tom and batted my boots to the roan's sides, and in a second we'd headed wide behind the rising dust of battle and across the rise and fall of hills and rock in the warm afternoon sunlight.

We rode at a flat-out run until ahead of us we saw a single soldier on horseback top a rise on our right and come bounding toward us. "You men waita fora me!" It was Corporal Dammio waving his hat back and forth. We slowed long enough to let him fall in with us.

"What're you doing out here?" Jack asked him as we all kicked our horses forward in a trot. I saw blood streaming down the rump of Dammio's big gray gelding.

"Takinga thisa message backa for Custer. They needa some packs anda reinforcements."

"You're telling us," I called over to him. "We just saw them. They're getting pounded out there."

"Oh, no! Now I suppose-a I'm gonna getta jumped on. I can't getta thisa horse to go no faster."

"He's shot in the ass," I called out to him. "Didn't you know?"

He glanced back at the blood, then thumped himself on his forehead. *"Mama mia!"*

We slowed enough to let Dammio keep up with us, but by the time we came upon a column of soldiers, all three horses had given all they had to give. When we spotted the soldiers and they began waving at us from a hundred yards off, we tried to hurry our horses toward them, but the tired animals only grunted and strained. They couldn't move a second faster. The last few yards, Jack, Tom, and I dropped down and walked the rest of the way in. Dammio rode on in on the wounded gray and handed his dispatch over to the captain of H Troop.

"Are you men from the *Far West?*" The gray-haired captain looked up at us from the paper in his hand as we walked up to him. We shook our heads. "Then who are you?" He raised a bit in his saddle.

"We're scouts," I said. "Or we would have been. We came in with Reynolds this morning, but Custer said he didn't need us."

"It'sa true, Captain Benteen," Dammio said. "These-a men beena around awhile."

"General Custer doesn't hire the scouts, sir," he said, ignoring Dammio and looking down at me.

I shrugged. "Evidently not. He didn't hire us. We came to tell ya, him and his troops are getting the hell kicked out of them, over that way." I pointed, realizing as I did so that it was unnecessary. The sound of battle was clear and the rise of dust visible.

He shook the paper in his hand with a wry, tight smile. "We've been getting rumors to that effect. He says here to bring packs. Sounds like he has them on the run." He craned slightly and gazed toward the distant thunder of gunfire.

"Then it's gotten worse since that dispatch, Captain. If he can't get some help over there, they're done for."

"I see." He rubbed his chin for a second, then added, "Your horses look blown. Take them forward." He looked closer at Shotgun Tom and said, "What are you doing out of uniform? Are you one of Reno's men? Where's your horse and weapon?"

Tom looked stunned, so I spoke up for him. "Captain, this man found us a couple of miles from here. Hadn't been for him, we'd never have made it. He fought off five or six warriors, *hand to hand.* Now I think he's in some kind of shock from it." I tapped a finger to the side of my head.

The captain nodded. "Go with them, Corporal Dammio. Get this soldier gathered and have him report to Major Reno. He'll need everybody he can get on a position. We anticipate a rough evening." He pointed toward the front of the line of unmounted soldiers, where the sound of pistol and rifle fire popped sporadically. We turned and walked forward, leading our horses.

The line of unmounted soldiers stood holding their reins and watching us, many of them reaching out and slapping Tom and Dammio on the shoulder as we passed. "Way to go, Private," one of them said. "Good work, Corporal," said another.

At the head of the column, the trail stopped at the edge of a long steep hill, and in the valley below, less than a mile away, hundreds of Indians roamed back and forth on horseback on both sides of the river. They fired at stragglers who fought their way across the valley floor trying to make it up to the hilltop where we stood. We all four ducked as a bullet spun over our heads with a flat twanging sound.

"Get down!" a voice called out from amid a group of dirty bloody soldiers huddled together behind a short rock facing. "They've gotten some of our Springfields now."

We looked at the sweat-streaked face of a major with a yellow bandanna tied around his head in place of a hat. "That's right," he added. "They can't hit anything, but they get lucky now and then."

"Major Reno," Dammio said, "are you hit?" He bent down, moving to him. Against the rock lay half a dozen wounded soldiers. The coppery smell of blood was strong around them.

"No." The major fanned him back. "We just made it in. We took a beating, Corporal. Where have you been?"

"I bringa back a message from the general . . ."

As they spoke, Jack and I gazed along a skirmish line set up along the edge of the hill. Dusty soldiers lay behind anything they'd scrounged up for cover. One of them had three slabs of greasy bacon stacked in front of him. Flies swarmed. A bullet whined off the rock facing. "So, you men are scouts?" Major Reno looked at Jack, Tom, and me, as if sizing us up. "We can use some *scouts.*"

"Uh . . . no, Major. We came up here to be. But Custer didn't need us."

"Ha!" He shook his head. "Well, the poor bastard *needs* you now." It was plain he'd been terribly shaken by battle.

That must've been why he, a major, was scrounging in the dirt up front, while Benteen, a captain, sat at the rear in a command position.

"If you don't get some help over to him, all he's gonna need is a shovel and a preacher. Last we seen, he—"

"Scouts, man!" He cut me off. "I need scouts out there! Didn't you hear me?"

"No, Major." I shook my head. "We just came *in* from out there. We saw what's going on. We're not on the payroll here. What about Reynolds? Bloody Knife? What about Curly?"

"See this?" He gestured a hand down the front of his grimy, stained shirt. Flies rose and scattered. "This is Bloody Knife's splattered brains, sir." He was near hysterical. "And Reynolds is hanging dead over a cottonwood stump!"

"Reynolds? Dead?" I swallowed hard. "Did he—did he ever reach Custer . . . before they went into battle?"

"Oh-h-h-h ye-e-e-es!" He hissed. "Reynolds kept his nose up the general's rear end all morning, I'm sure." He rose to his knees and leaned forward, taking my shirt in both hands. His eyes were wild and desperate. "Now, you three *scouts . . . form up!* Blast your hides! We've got to get out of here!"

I grabbed his wrists; we leaned nose to nose. The sweat bee swung in and whined, suspended between our foreheads. "Now you listen good, Major—"

Beside us a shot spun up from the valley. A side of bacon bounced and blew apart, and the soldier behind it rolled screaming with both hands thrown to his bloody face. His body bucked and squirmed in the dust, his boots scraping, until two soldiers scrambled in, pinned him down, and dragged him away.

I turned to Jack and Shotgun Tom and swallowed hard, seeing the look in their eyes. Tom reached over to a wounded soldier and lifted the bloody Springfield rifle lying near his side. He took the soldier's dusty hat and put it on. Then he turned and looked back at me. "Jesus . . ." I whispered under my breath.

Chapter
29

Scouting the eve of destruction . . .

The afternoon sun still burned warm and high, but leaned west as the three of us crawled like snakes from one clump of grass to the next, working our way northward. Most of the warriors had moved away toward the sound of battle raging off to our right, but a few remained, and they'd gotten more familiar with the Springfield rifles they'd taken from the dead. They had good sniper positions now, scattered out across the valley floor. They worked in close enough to call out and taunt the soldiers.

We'd turned our horses over to Dammio, and before leaving on foot, I'd taken Tom's old shotgun from my bedroll behind my saddle and pitched it to him. "In case that Springfield gets a little hard to aim."

He'd caught it, grinned, and run a hand down it. "If I can't shoot nothing with it, at least I can swing it like a ball bat . . ."

Now I looked back at him, lying there beside Jack in a swirl of bent grass. His lips trembled as he stared back at me. "Get ready," I said, my voice sounding a little weak. "Are you ready?"

"Yes, damn it!" Jack answered in a low tone. "You don't have to ask us that every time!"

"All right, then," I snapped back at him in a harsh whisper, then peeped above the edge of grass and watched the two warriors gather their army web belts of ammunition and slip away. I could've shot them, I thought, as close as they were. *But . . . I don't want to shoot no Indians . . .* I shook my head to clear it. *Don't want to shoot Indians . . . don't want Indians shooting soldiers!* "Man, this is the thing I don't like about war," I whispered before realizing I'd spoken aloud.

"Oh? Really?" Jack looked at me with a flat expression. "And what *thing* about war *do* you like?"

I let out a breath, rose slowly just above the grass, waved an arm toward D Troop, who'd taken front position and waited out of sight for my signal, then dropped back down, and whispered, "I don't like nothing about war."

Jack chuckled. "There's always Canada."

I blushed a bit and said, glancing back at Tom, "Well, there's nothing *really* wrong with Canada. They make good *smooth* whiskey. They get along with the Indians better than we do . . . that's a fact. It gets a little cold there, but so what?" I shrugged and turned, gazing out at the column of troops moving toward us at a cautious pace. "Cold weather never killed nobody."

"Why don't you just shut up," Jack said. "You don't know more about Canada than I do about *Russia.*"

"Russia, huh? Jack, I could tell you things about *Russia* that would curl your hair, terrible things."

"Good, then. I need some excitement in my life."

"What's wrong with you two?" Tom whispered, and Jack said back to him, "Aw, it's him. He gets like this when he's scared. He'll get religious if he ain't careful."

"So? There ain't a damn—I mean, *darn* thing wrong with religion. Everybody ought to believe in something, I reckon."

"See?" Jack whispered. "Scared shitless."

"Pay attention, Jack, they're moving up the wounded."

We lay there still as stone until the column made it halfway to us. Then we moved forward on our bellies. "This ain't what I call *scouting,*" Jack said behind me. "This is what I call *live bait.*"

When we reached a wide clearing and saw no Indians in

any direction, we signaled in D Troop and lay back against a deadfall of cottonwood until they moved in and spread out into a skirmish line. A captain by the name of Weir led the first troops in and swung his horse over to us. "Good work, men. But I must tell you, since you weren't officially hired in, I'm not sure how you'll be paid." The sweat bee rose up from somewhere near me and circled Weir's head.

"That don't surprise me a bit." Jack spit and looked away. Tom and I stood up without answering, dusted our trousers, and walked over to a water cask atop a sweaty mule.

We sipped and watched as the rest of the soldiers came in. At the rear came the rest of the pack mules. The soldiers struggled to keep them quiet as they balked and brayed and swung their mallet heads. A tired, sweaty company of men led their horses in and collapsed on the ground with their reins in their hands. Some of their horses staggered in place; others dropped to the ground beside the soldiers. No sooner had they'd stretched out to rest, Captain Benteen came riding up swinging a quirt over his head.

"You men! Get up! Get those horses up *now*, or they will never get up!" He spun his horse toward a lieutenant, almost trampling over him. "Godfrey! Get them up! Get these men out there on foot and form an advance perimeter!"

The lieutenant scrambled to his feet. "You heard the captain, men! Let's go! Every fourth man hold horses. Rest of you! Move out!" The men groaned as they rolled to their feet. One of them wept aloud, cursing and stomping a foot on the ground.

"Jesus," I said to Tom, "think they could get any louder?"

"This is the bravest team of men I've ever seen . . ." His voice trailed. His eyes appeared to have glazed over. *Team?* I sipped water and stared at him.

"You there, *scout!*" Benteen dropped from his saddle and walked toward me, pulling a tin of powdered cornstarch from inside his tunic. "Do you realize what you've done?" He stopped, ripped the top off the cornstarch, held out the waist of his trousers, and dumped a load of the powder down into his crotch. Powder billowed around him.

"No need in thanking us," I said. "We just did what we—"

"Thank you? Thank you, my fine-galled arse! Now we're scattered all over hell's half-acre! Look around at us, sir!"

I did. He was right. The troops had spread and each of them had taken position here and there, strung out in every direction. "Damn it, Captain. We didn't tell them to do this! Why didn't somebody stop them?"

"Why didn't *you,* sir? Instead of plopping your dirty behind down and resting on it! You better hope to God we don't draw fire here! Now get out front of Lieutenant Godfrey's men. See what's out there."

Jack and I collected our horses from one of the packers and led them out through the cottonwoods where Lieutenant Godfrey and his men had formed a forward firing line. Captain Benteen had snatched Tom by the arm, chewed him out good, and sent him off with Windolph, the German we'd met that morning. "For two cents I'd put a bullet in Benteen's galled ass," I said to Jack as he walked off.

"Maybe you ain't noticed it," Jack replied, "but he's the only officer left here that ain't shook senseless by all this. Reno's a wreck, and the junior officers can't believe what's happened yet. They're stunned by it. Indians ain't suppose to *win,* you know. They're just supposed to be targets in all this."

When we got to Godfrey's line, he looked up at us from the cover of a brush pile. "Would either of you happen to have a chew of tobacco, of some fixin's, or something?"

"Sure." Jack sat stooped down on his boot heels, fished a pouch of tobacco from his pocket, and pitched it to him. "Chew it or smoke it. Pick your pleasure," he said.

The lieutenant grinned. "Any paper?"

Jack fished out a pack of papers and handed them to him. "What are you two doing out here?" he asked as he rolled a quick one and slid it in and out of his parched lips. A few feet away lay a dead warrior in a pool of blood. Flies swarmed. Three yards past him lay a dead soldier with his own snarl of flies around his bloody head.

"Scouts," I said, letting out a breath.

He lit the cigarette, sucked in a deep draw, and let it go in a long stream. "Oh. Well . . . I suppose we shall die together out here. My men have sworn to give up nothing more today than we have given already. They've struck their positions, and they *will* die there if need be."

I looked at his face, saw the slightest twitch in his jaw. "We're going on out there . . . take a look around. Now that the shooting's stopped, I'm afraid to guess at what we'll find of Custer's troops."

He formed a sad smile. "Oh, they're dead, right enough. I've concluded that over the past two hours. This is the day of the Indian, sir. We can only hope to take as many with us as God will allow, for Custer . . . for the dear ole Seventh."

"That's one way of looking at it," I said.

He let go another stream of smoke. "When you're given the advance position on a day like today, it's the *only* way to look at it. How do you *scouts* see it?" He spread a dark disturbing smile.

We stood without answering. Then Jack said, "Keep the tobacco—I been trying to quit. Watch out that you don't shoot us on our way back in."

"Your way back *in?*" Again the dark smile. "I salute you, gentlemen." He nodded and smoked as we walked away.

"Jack, are you all right here?" I asked in a serious tone.

"I've felt *better* about things . . . but I'm okay. Why?"

"Well, Reynolds started giving *his* stuff away, and . . ."

Jack lifted an eyebrow. "Oh, you figure I think I'm gonna die just because I gave away my tobacco?"

"Just wondering, Jack. I—I feel kinda bad that I got ya into this, you know."

"Do ya really?"

"Yeah, I do." We walked on through the grass and brush, seeing in the distance a fresh stir of dust turn into a long sheet that stretched across the horizon. All about lay the bodies of Indian and soldier alike. All at peace now—all akin on some distant level past the snarl of flies and the smell of stale blood.

"I don't think we're gonna die here," he said, letting out a breath. "I always figure when I die, it's gonna be in a big four-poster bed." He grinned and stretched his hands wide. "I'm talking a bed two or three times bigger than I need. I'm talking flowers blooming outside the window, birds singing. All like that. Not out here . . . not in something like this." He tossed a hand. "So put all that *dying* crap out of your mind. I'm okay. Take my word on it. Besides, we've been in worse spots, ain't we?"

I stopped and scratched my head without answering. "What exactly does Benteen want us looking for out here? He *knows* there's Indians out there. What are we doing?"

"You don't know?" Jack chuckled. "Like I told ya. This ain't scouting. We're *live bait*. We're just a warning bell. The advance line hears us fighting, they get ready. Benteen hears it and knows it's time to get his men out of here." He chuckled again. "You didn't know that?"

"Sure, I knew it." The roan stepped up beside me, nudging my shoulder. I stilled him with a hand beneath his muzzle, scratching his chin as I gazed out and up at the sheet of dust growing closer over the hills.

Chapter

30

One fine day for dying . . .

We'd taken position a hundred yards ahead of Godfrey's advance line, just the two of us out there in the open, lying on a bald knob, our reins in our hands and our horses downed on their sides for cover. The sheet of dust thickened before us, moving closer, until beneath it we heard the low rumble of horses' hooves. "Getting ready here," I said, rising up with my Henry rifle in the air.

If we truly were nothing more than a warning bell, it was my intention to ring that bell as early as possible and make a dash back to Godfrey's advance line—for whatever that was worth. From the thundering sound of hooves and the tremble in the ground beneath us, making it back to the troops would mean only a few more moments of life at best. Nothing would stop what pounded toward us beyond the hill. We raised our horses up and watched for another second. Then the earth began to tremble harder. "Here goes, Jack." I levered up a round to fire in the air.

"No! Not till they top the hill. They could turn away. Don't fire until we're sure they're charging."

Above the thunder of hooves a child cried out, and above the crest of the hill a naked Indian boy came wobbling over the edge and sat straight down. "Aw, naw, Jack! Look at this!"

A few yards away, a woman appeared from a clump of grass. She ran out as the sound of hooves grew deafening, snatched the child up, and ran back with him under her arm. I glanced around at the clumps of grass everywhere around us. Did every one of them shield an Indian? We looked at each other and stepped up in our stirrup. "Okay," Jack said, raising his rifle with mine. "Do it now."

We fired two shots each as the endless line of horsemen spilled over the hill. They spread down it like a dark pool of melting sky, and within that dark pool pounded the heart of the beast, a terrible monster come to face the terrible monster that lay in wait before it. Seeing us, they yelled and fired, and the front of the line swung toward us as we batted the horses and raced away, back to Godfrey and his skirmish line. His *dead man's line,* I thought.

Of all the things I'd ever done that required the service of a fast horse for my getaway, never had I worried more about a horse going down, faltering over a rock, or snapping a leg as I did at that second, glancing back at our wake of dust, and behind it the screaming jaws of death. Before us, the soldiers' rifle shots blossomed along deadfalls of cottonwood and sprung out from the sides of standing trees and clumps of dirt. We didn't even flinch as these shots whistled past us, as if *these* bullets had not the power or purpose to separate our lives from our bodies.

As my roan sailed up over a gathered pile of brush and downed branches, I felt the Indians were within arm's reach behind me; yet as Jack and I both spun our horses, the mass of horse, dust, and man came charging from two hundred yards away. "Hold steady, men, men!" Godfrey's voice boomed among the cottonwood grove, above the hail of fire. A few feet away, a young soldier cursed and sobbed in anger and fear as he worked a knife blade back and forth, trying to free a swollen shell from his rifle chamber.

Dropping down from our horses with our rifles up, I noticed that the soldier finally broke the knife blade, then tossed the rifle away and snatched out his revolver. He swung the pistol out from behind his tree, and each time it bucked and exploded it appeared too large and powerful for his small hand. Now, as pistol shots spun forward from the pounding mass and nipped at tree bark and spit up dirt,

Godfrey turned to us with his rifle smoking. "Scouts! Report back to command!"

Jack and I glanced at one another, crouching, moving up toward Godfrey. "Are you crazy," I shouted. "They *hear* what's going on!"

"Get out of here!" he screamed, his rifle swinging toward us. "You did yours! Now we do ours!"

Like hell . . . I threw my Henry rifle up, taking aim. But Jack grabbed my shoulder and yanked me back.

"Come on! You heard him! Let's go!"

I looked out again as we scrambled for our reins, the horses stepping in place, nervous, snorting, pawing dirt. The ground trembled. Now Jack sat atop the silver gray, grabbing my shoulder, pulling, shoving me until I spilled into my saddle, swinging the roan around, my rifle swinging freely in my hand. Then I collected, closed my knees on the horse, and slapped the rifle barrel back against its flank. The roan shot away like a dart.

I looked back, pounding toward the main body of troops, and saw the great swell of man and horse roll back upon itself in a hail of fire from Godfrey's rifles. How could this be? An unstoppable wave had just stopped, men and horses spilling out of it and spreading forward like froth on a beach, while the crest of it rolled upward and back in a mass tangled of horses' hooves clawing at the sky, and of men and weapons flying in that terrible sea of dust.

Nothing could live through that, I thought. Yet even as I thought it, turning and pounding forward, Godfrey's voice called out, "Fall back!" and I caught a glimpse of Indians springing forward from the downed horses, screaming, sailing forward as if on wings. Before us the next skirmish line held fast, holding their fire, staring glaze-faced at the battle, waiting for their part in it.

"Steady, lads." It was Griebs's voice. He stood and stepped forward, a pistol raised and cocked, glancing up at me as I shot past him, his bloodshot eyes as steady and calm as pools of smoldering steel. "Let's not go shooting our own here." Behind this firing line lay another line twenty yards back, and beyond it, Benteen sat atop his big blood bay, spinning it, swinging the riding quirt, and yelling orders, forcing the broken line of mule and man back toward the hill from which we came.

Jack slid in on his silver gray, and together we batted our horse over to Benteen. "Where have you *scouts* been?" He bellowed before either of us could say a word, then swung the riding quirt past our faces and shook it toward the line of tired, dirty troops. "Get to the front! Get them back up on the hill!" Veins stood out on his brow.

"Captain, we—" Behind us, Griebs barked a firing order and the line exploded, drowning out my words.

Benteen's lips moved, but we heard nothing above the rifle fire. "Come on!" Jack leaned over and screamed in my ear just as a bullet kicked up dirt near Benteen's horse's hooves. He spun, ducking, still yelling at the troops. I kicked out the roan and followed Jack along the line of men and mules, back to the same hill we'd tried so hard to get away from. Behind us the battle raged.

Along the line, men dropped and fired from their knees, then hurried on toward the hill. Indians with rifles had spread out from the main body and taken position out in the cover of grass and rock. Shots zinged in. A mule lay upturned, braying, its hooves pawing in the air. Two soldiers struggled to free up the load of ammunition that had shifted to its bloody side. We rode and fired, dropped from our saddles, and ran in a crouch, pulling our horses forward. A soldier stumbled and fell against me. I shoved him away only to see that his face was gone.

"Jack!" I screamed as a naked warrior hurled himself up out of the grass, swinging nothing but a short stick, and Jack turned, catching him by the throat in midair. A hole blew open in his back, and he fell away from Jack's smoking pistol. And we pressed forward to the front of the line.

At the base of the hill, we covered the oncoming line with rifle fire as soldiers ran the last few open yards under heavy fire. They dropped beside us, firing as they came in, and in moments we'd established a strong skirmish line, while back in the distance Godfrey's advance line and Griebs's two lines fought on, giving up ground inches at a time, leaving bodies strung out behind them.

We edged backward up the hill and held, letting the rest of

the men and animals seep through us and climb up into position atop the hill.

Then, as suddenly as the great charge had began . . . it ended. The mighty wave of man and horse seemed to melt back and spread out. Save for a few random shots, and the catcalls and tauntings of the warriors, a silence set in. "Jack, it's over." I let go a tight breath and ran a sweat-soaked sleeve across my face.

"Nope," he said, "it's just changing." He glanced behind us up the hill, then all around. "They've got us where they want us now. We're stuck here."

"Shit. You never see the good side of nothing, do ya?" I squinted up into the evening sun. It had grown large, turning red and sinking, spreading out along the horizon. Benteen and Reno came riding past us and stopped, spinning their horses and looked back and forth along our line, still firing, but not in long volleys now. They covered the stragglers coming in two and three at a time. Griebs came limping along, a bandanna tied around one of his legs, a young soldier's arm looped across his shoulder, the soldier screaming as blood ran down from his forehead.

Jack and I stepped forward, him taking the soldier and me catching Griebs as he stumbled forward. "Are you hit bad?" I asked, throwing his arm across my shoulder and hurrying up the hill with him.

"Naw, laddie, just both of me tired ole legs here. But was that a scrape, or what?"

"Yeah," I said, "quite a scrape." I glanced back, still hearing rifles firing, still hearing bullets spin past us. "I hadn't seen ya for a while. Didn't know what became of ya."

He sat down just over the rim of the hill and grunted and squeezed both his legs. "Aye." He let go of a leg and raised a bloody finger. "The *trick* is to never be where they want you to be. Just always be there when they *needs* ya." He winked and ran his bloody hand back across his head. "But the ole sarge held his lines, did he not, laddie? I'll be drinking free on this one for a long time to come, eh?"

"I'll sure buy ya a round," I said, my voice a bit tight.

Chapter

31

❖❖❖

An angry call from the stands . . .

There was no cover atop that bald hill, except for the upturned rock facing where Reno and the wounded had lain when we'd met them only a few hours ago. *How many hours?* I had no idea, but it seemed like a lifetime. I lay flat on my back with my rifle across my chest, hearing the shots pop in from a higher hill east of us and zing up from the valley below. Darkness would come in another hour or two, yet it was hard to look even an hour into the future with men and animal falling, rolling, and screaming all around.

Around the rim of the hill, H Troop had posted riflemen twenty feet apart. Behind them, soldiers moved back and forth, crawling, scrambling, digging the hard earth with rifle butts, with spoons and mess kits, with bare hands. Even in the heat of it, they'd managed to set up a spot in the center of the dished hill where they'd stacked boxes of hardtack, saddles, bacon slabs—anything that would stop or slow down a bullet.

The mules and horses had been gathered there also, and they milled and whinnied loud when another of their number dropped in their midst. When my rifle had cooled, I rolled back over beside Jack and looked down my sights, waiting for a sniper to give me a glimpse of his head or shoulder.

"Reno's ready for a big charge," Jack said. "But I got news for him—" He aimed his rifle and pulled off a round. Somewhere out there a voice yelped, then stopped abruptly. "—There ain't none coming."

"You don't know that, Jack. What makes you think so?" I tensed at the flicker of a headband behind a clump of brush, then let down when it disappeared.

"Because if I was them, I wouldn't charge. I'd keep us here just like this, and pick us down to nothing."

Something scraped in the dirt beside me, and Lieutenant Godfrey came sliding up between us with a pistol in his bandaged hand. "Thought you might want this back," he said. He pitched Jack's tobacco to him.

"Thought you were dead," I said, looking at his crusted, sweat-streaked face.

"So did I. But we made it . . . most of us, anyway. Quite a soldier, that young ballplayer, Corporal Stovine."

"Corporal? Tommy?" I looked at him, stunned.

"Yes, he is now. I asked Reno to promote him. He even carries a shotgun, you know."

"Yeah, well . . ." I shook my head, not knowing what to say.

"Here," Jack said, passing both Godfrey and me a thin cigarette. I took mine and twirled it back and forth in my fingers while Godfrey lit his and took a deep draw.

"Thanks, Jack, but I'm more of a cigar man myself."

Jack reached over, shielding a lit match. "We're fresh out of cigars right now. Maybe these warriors will bring you one."

Behind us, Major Reno's voice called out, "Griebs, Windolph, Godfrey, Dammio! Back here, quick time!"

"Gotta go," Godfrey said, sliding back. "Thanks for the smoke."

"Where is Griebs?" Reno's voice called out.

"Wounded, sir," a soldier's voice answered. A shot pinged off the rock facing and spun upward. From the valley came a rising war cry, and in seconds the clumps of grass below spilled forward a charge of thirty or more Indians.

"Guess you were wrong," I called to Jack as we leveled our rifles down. "Here they come."

"This ain't nothing," he called back to me, firing down into them.

And he was right. They ran in a few yards firing and yelling, then fell back, taunting and calling out from behind cover. A tall naked warrior jumped up yelling, shaking himself back and forth at us, then dropped down just as a dozen rifles opened up. "Hold your fire," a voice called out. Another Indian sprang forward running flat out. He came in close, yelling, tapping a stick on one of the dead soldiers at the bottom of the hill. Rifles cut him down when he turned to run away.

"It's gonna be a long night," Jack said, taking a deep draw on his cigarette and flipping it out over the edge. And so it was.

The sun sank down into a rosy pool until the last glow of it called forth the chilled Montana air. With no moon and no fires to light or warm us, blackness closed around us like a thick glove. Soldiers spoke back and forth quietly until at length a voice called out in a hushed tone, "No talking on the line." For a moment the hilltop fell silent as a tomb, save for the groaning wounded and the clink of a canteen. Into that silence came the beating of tom-toms and shouting and wailing on all sides of us from the valley floor. Then a voice that sounded a lot like Griebs let out a dark chuckle and said from among the wounded, "May as well get a good sound sleep, lads. They don't attack at night."

Hushed laughter spilled and rippled along the line, and out across the valley floor, I stared as fires struck up here and there almost as far as the eye could see. From those fires rose the laughter and singing, the long yells of celebrated victory, a victory long awaited. As I listened, I thought about the Lakota we'd met and come to know at Powder River a few years back—good men, *friends* of mine and Jack's, and it was easy to see their faces out there now, the fire light flickering on them, their women and children at their sides. "Jack," I said in a whisper. "Know what I was just thinking about?"

After a second, he said, "No, what?"

"Remember Brown Horse and the others? Remember Red Cloud? I was just wondering. Do you suppose any of them are down there? Think maybe they're—"

"Don't do it," he said, cutting me off. "Quit *thinking;* get some rest."

Jesus . . . Rolling onto my side, gazing out across the valley, I raised a hand and passed it back and forth between my eyes and the distant firelight, just to see something of *myself* in the swallowing black night.

During the night, while Jack snored and I shivered in the cool air and rubbed my hands together to keep them warm, I thought of the hopelessness of our situation. Then, just as I realized that things couldn't possibly get any worse—it rained . . . of course.

Jack groaned beside me as cold rain pelted down on us. "I can't believe this shit," he said. "If I ever get to heaven, I'm gonna talk to God about his *strange* sense of humor."

"Don't talk like that, Jack. Not now. Not here." I stood up clutching my medicine shirt closed at my chest.

"Oh, really? What's he gonna do? *Punish* me?" He chuckled, and even in the pitch darkness, I caught the slightest glimpse of him, a dark *substance* in the otherwise darker *essence.* His arms spread upward and dropped. "Come on, let's find a blanket or something."

Groping forward in the darkness, hearing Jack beside me, we moved toward the breathing and milling of horses until Jack stumbled and cursed. "Who goes there?" A voice called out in a hushed tone.

"Scouts," I said. "We need blankets from our saddles. We're freezing . . . getting soaked."

Benteen's voice spoke now. "Why didn't you think of your blankets earlier?"

"Don't start on me, Captain." It was hard to keep my voice under control. "We've been *busy.*"

"Can't you just bunch up near the barricades? It shan't rain long."

"How . . . in . . . the . . . *hell* do you know how long it's—"

"Easy, Jack," I said in the darkness. "Captain, we need something here."

"Oh, all right. Wait a minute." In a second a match flared,

and I almost flinched back from it. Behind us men grumbled along the line. "As you were," Benteen said to them. A hat brim came down over the match, forming a dome over the light, and moved over to the pile of saddles stacked in a barricade. "Hurry up," he said as Jack and I rummaged for our bedrolls. "It doesn't have to be *your* blanket, does it? Any blanket will suffice."

"Got it," Jack said just as the match went out.

I snatched at anything I could grab, worked out a rolled-up wool cavalry coat from the pile, and put it on. "Thanks, Captain."

"Since you're up for a *stroll,* anyway," Benteen said, "go join Corporal Dammio and his men over on the south edge. We'll need you there come morning."

"How are we gonna find them, Captain?"

"Just keep walking. If you fall over the edge you've gone too far."

Damn it! I stumbled forward, hearing Jack walk on in front of me, but I stood there for just a second longer and heard Major Reno whisper to Benteen behind me. "Think they heard us?"

I froze there, listening.

"No," Benteen whispered. "But it doesn't matter. I won't be a part of leaving the wounded here to die. If you go, sir, you go without me."

"It's just one idea," Reno whispered. "What are some others?"

"Find Custer's troops," Benteen said, "if they're alive."

"Oh, I'm certain he's alive. That fine-haired bastard. Rest assured he's met Gibbons's and Terry's troops. He's sitting somewhere now with his boots propped up and—"

"Sssh!" Benteen hushed him, then called out in a low tone, "Who's there? Is someone there?"

I moved forward without a sound and didn't stop until I bumped into Jack and fell over him. He cursed under his breath. "Are you gonna wander around all night?"

"Damn, Jack." I sat up wiping mud and rain from my face. "This ain't where he told us to go."

"To hell with him. I'll sleep where I want to."

It stopped raining sometime in the night, and morning broke in a silver haze, to the sound of renewed firing all around us. Starting with a shot here and there from the valley floor, it soon spread around to some sharpshooters on the hillsides above us. They fired long-range buffalo rifles into us from up to a thousand yards away. Springfields couldn't reach them.

Jack and I had dug in with Dammio, Windolph, and rest of H Troop along the south side of the hill, and as the morning wore on, when it looked as if we'd be overrun any second, Griebs came crawling over from the wounded with both trouser legs cut off above the knees. Bloodstained bandages wrapped his thick, hairy legs. "One dollar to the man who bags the ole sarge one of those sharpshooters," he said.

"Griebs, you've got no business here," I called out to him, as a bullet thumped the ground a few feet from him.

"My *business* is where I find it, laddie." He chuckled and crawled in among us. "Awww, now look at the bunch of yas." He pointed at Dammio. "My good corporal looks as if he'll cry his dear Italian heart out most any second."

"Don'ta come around witha your bullshit, Sergeant," Dammio said, making an obscene gesture with his hand. "I'ma inna charge here."

"Aye you are, Corporal. And yet I hear no plans of your coming attack. I hear nothing said about getting down there and fetching water for the wounded. Alls I see are a few naked Indians kicking your sweet Italian arse. Has my dear H turned into a group of schoolchildren? Now how will this story sound back in the taverns along Lancaster Square?"

I started to say something, but Jack grabbed my forearm.

"You thinka we're afraid to getta some water?" Dammio's nostrils flared. "You thinka we won'ta charge-a these bastards?"

Griebs grinned and shook his head. "Never you mind, Corporal. I'll tell the captain you're simply not up to it."

"Wait, Griebs, you shot-upa bastard, you." Dammio turned, crawling, and caught up with him. "Don'ta you dare saya we won'ta make a charge here! We just wasa saying maybe we go getta some-a water, eh?"

"Were you, now? Well, I don't see why not. It's just a short jaunt down yon gully to the riverbank."

"*Shorta jaunt?* You're outta youra *mind . . .*" They bickered and argued and crawled off toward Benteen and Reno at the center of the hill.

I looked at Jack and nodded toward Griebs. "Can you believe that?"

"It's his job," Jack said.

We hugged the ground under heavy fire, knowing the Indians were moving up, but unable to stop them. The best we could do was get a quick shot in, then duck back down as lead rained past us. For few minutes a group from north of the hill ran in, firing a hard volley that forced the Indians back down in their cover. As soon as the firing lulled, Captain Benteen came walking along the line, straight backed and without so much as a flinch when a bullet slapped the dirt at his feet.

"Volunteers for water detail, step forward," he called out. The men all turned to one another with a curious expression. "That's right," he called out. "The wounded need water. Let's get them water!"

Windolph the German looked up at him. "Captain, get down. Zey vill kill you!"

"Don't worry about me, Windolph. Will you provide decoy and cover for a water detail?"

Windolph rose slowly to his feet and nodded his head. "There now," Benteen said to the others. "He'll do the hard part. All I need now are a few water carriers."

We watched, and Griebs came crawling in beside me as volunteers stood amid the fire and marched off with Benteen and Dammio. "Isn't that a proud thing they do, these troopers. I'd rather be a miserable soldier in the dirty desert than the finest *count* in the queen's court." He gigged me and chuckled.

"Then you must've found your proper calling, Griebs," I said.

When the water detail went out, Windolph and three other German boys covered them as they worked their way down a gully that ran from the hilltop to the river below. For more than twenty or thirty minutes, the four of them stood among heavy fire, punching out round after round until the water detail ran back in, many of them wounded, all of them spent and gasping for air. Dammio lay a few feet from me, and Griebs crawled over, patted his arm, and said,

"Good show, lad. Now prepare a strong attack, and we'll call it a fine day's work for dear ole H Troop."

Dammio looked around at him, sweat streaming down his face. "Why don'ta you crawl off anda choke youra self to death?"

"That's the spirit." Griebs laughed, and crawled back toward the wounded.

"See," Dammio said, shaking his hand. "He's gotta keepa his hand in."

They did attack. Captain Benteen led the charge. With some of Reno's M Troop falling in with them, H Troop pushed hard against a swell of warriors who'd fought their way up the hill and taken strong rifle position, some of them so close they had started shooting arrows and hurling in lances and rocks. But the charge cleared them back a hundred yards, leaving dead on both sides strung along the slope of the hill. Then, as quickly as they left, the soldiers came back in, dragging their dead and wounded, and once again we lay beneath rifle fire—not as heavy now from the valley floor, yet just as accurate from the sharpshooters on the higher ridges.

I lay cooling my rifle when *Corporal* Tom Stovine came sliding down beside me. A bullet whined in and kicked up a chunk of dirt near his feet. "Jeez, Tom! Be careful here."

He grinned. "I guess you heard about my promotion?"

"Yeah, congratulations." I smiled, hugging close to the ground.

"Looks like I'll be staying after all."

"Looks like we might *all* be staying," I said, squinting up at him. "Why don't you get down before they nail ya."

"I'm okay. Look." He rose almost to his feet and made a stupid sound out across the valley. I sliced a breath in half and snatched him down beside me. A bullet slapped the side of an empty ammunition crate. "Sorry," Tom said. "That was stupid of me." He dusted his sleeve and adjusted his hat brim. Griebs came crawling over from the wounded.

"But, I have to be honest with you. This army is where I shoulda been a long time ago" He saw the look in my eyes and shrugged. "I know, it's taken some getting used to. But, *damn!* This is like the feeling ya get playing in a big game somewhere. You know, bases loaded, score tied . . . everybody waiting for that one big play."

"What if there's no big play coming?" Behind him Griebs crawled closer.

"There's always a big play coming." He grinned as another shot whistled in, this one high and to our right.

I shook my head. "Tom, I'm sorry about all this—"

"Naw, don't be."

Griebs came in, reached out, and rested a hand on Tom's calf. "Captain needs a corporal over there, quick time."

"Right away, Sergeant." Tom pulled back, low now and out of the fire. "Just wanted to let ya know, if it hadn't been for you I might never have—" He grinned and bucked forward an inch. I smiled back at him, then noticed he'd gotten stuck there. Something went wrong? He'd forgotten his words? Something about his eyes?

Griebs let out a yelp and rolled away with his hands against his face, blood spewing. I shot him a glance, then looked back at Shotgun Tom. He sank forward, the grin still there, but a big part of his heart blown out through the front of his shirt. "Awww, Tommy!" I screamed, grabbing him, pulling him against me, his grin there on my chest, but flat, with no life behind it, and I saw Jack and two soldiers pin Griebs down and drag him off toward the wounded. He cursed and fought them until they disappeared with him behind a stack of crates and saddles.

"Awww, Tommy, look at you! Look at you!" His blood ran warm down my chest. *"Damn it, boy!* This ain't baseball! This is no *ballgame!*—no game . . ."

Dammio crept in, laid one gloved hand on my shoulder, and with his other pulled Tom's body away from me gently, almost cautiously, as if lifting something from my pocket without my knowing it. "Leta him go, he'sa dead. He's a soldier . . . he belongs to us now. We take-a care of him."

"They're firing the grass!" Someone yelled as I let Shotgun Tom slip from my arms into Corporal Dammio's.

"Get down," Jack said sliding in beside me. I started to say something, but he stopped me with a raised hand. "I know. I saw it. The same bullet got Griebs. Damndest thing . . ." He shook his head.

"Griebs? Dead?"

"Naw! Hell, no. Just grazed his temple, just enough to let the blood fly. You can't kill that ole Irish sergeant." He tapped a finger against the side of his head. "You know this vein that runs from here down to—"

"Don't tell me, Jack, okay?"

"By Gawd, sir! They are *leaving! Leaving, I tell you!*" Benteen's voice was something between a sob and plea to heaven. Jack stood up and pulled me up with him. We gazed out across the valley floor at long lines of men and horses leading off and joining a larger line, forming a main body and moving off, out, and over a hilltop, as if walking off into the sky.

"They left?" Jack slumped with his pistol hanging from his hand. "But—but they won. They had us." He turned to me with a strange expression, while past him smoke from a licking sheet of fire rose and drifted between us and the endless streams of warriors. His gun dropped from his hands and he turned, looking out across the valley with his fists raised. "What *the hell* do they mean? *Leaving!*"

The soldiers had already started rolling, bucking up and down, some of them jumping up, knocking each other down, yelling, hugging, kicking dirt at one another, and above it all came a long whine like that of a beast—the beast as a child—crying out softly for its mother's arms.

"What is going on out there?" Griebs's voice bellowed from over behind the barricade. "Somebody tell me something. I can't see from here!"

"It's over, Griebs!" I yelled at the top of my lungs. "They're gone! You've got to see this for yourself."

"Haaa! I do, laddie. Now I do. I see it as plain as the nose on your face. Now go find General Custer and his men, and we'll call it a good day's work."

PART 5

————◆————

How Pale They Are
The Shirt off My Back
Gift of a Horse

Chapter

32

Who among the living could say . . .

We waited, all of us baffled but relieved. An hour passed, then another, and by midafternoon, when Captain Benteen and Major Reno convinced themselves that this was no trick, that the Indians, for reasons known only to them, had actually pulled stakes and left the valley, we gathered our gear and our wounded, buried our dead in the trenches we'd carved for fire holes, and walked down to the river. A quiet hung about us like a funeral shroud. The warriors had gathered their dead along the way. Their travois poles left trails from one spot to another until the trails ran out into the distant hills.

"I'll never figure this one out," Jack said, standing up at the river's edge with his canteen dripping cool clear water. "They had us by the short hair, and just—just turned us loose."

I smiled. "You can't stand being wrong, can ya?"

"I wasn't *exactly* wrong. They didn't attack."

"Yeah, but you wasn't exactly *right*. They didn't keep us pinned and pick us down to nothing, either."

"What's the difference? We're alive."

"Yeah, we are," I said, letting out a long breath. The rest of the troops watered while the wounded filed in; and we stood watching man and animal drink side by side. "Even our horses made it. Even this worthless ole roan." I patted the horse on his withers as he drew water. He turned his muzzle up toward me with a long stream running from his mouth, as if asking what the hell I wanted now.

Benteen rode over to us with a lit pipe in his teeth. I thought it peculiar that he stepped down from his horse and squatted near us at the edge of the river. "Scouts, huh?" He cocked an eye up to us and let go a stream of smoke. A slight smile twisted around the pipe stem. Back with the troops, Reno had once more taken charge, his voice sounding more sure and steady now as he pointed and called out orders to the junior officers.

"Well, Captain, like I said. We *would've* been, had the general hired us."

He brushed a hand in the air. "Doesn't matter. You did the best you could, under the circumstances."

"We only led them where you told us to, Captain. Sorry it didn't work out."

"A good scout doesn't necessarily *do* as he's told." His smile spread, and I realized this was his way—his only way—of saying he'd made a mistake. So why push it?

"That's good advice, Captain. We'll remember it in case we ever do something like this again," I said.

He pushed himself up on his feet, and looked at both of us. "Better hope to God you *never* do something like this again." His eyes turned caged, and he added, "The army teaches us everything about battle except how to lose one. We learn that in the field, it appears."

"You didn't lose, Captain. You just didn't win. That's a brave bunch of boys there." I swung a hand toward the dirty, wounded, hungry troops. "Who knows. The Indians mighta left just as an act of honor to them. Indians ain't without heart, you know. And they damn sure ain't without respect for courage."

"Yes," he said, almost whispering, "who will ever know?" He puffed the pipe, gazed away for a second, nodding, then looked back at me. "You heard something last night in the dark, didn't you?"

I just stared at him; Jack lifted a brow toward me. "I

know you did," Benteen said. "But just realize this . . . men say things they don't always mean under extreme circumstances."

"I know." I nodded, glancing upstream at Major Reno atop his big blood bay, then back at Benteen. "But don't worry . . . I never heard a word of it." Jack stared back and forth between us with a curious expression.

"Very well then, sir," Benteen said. His tone of voice went back to being an officer. "I know you two are probably wanting out of here, but I'd like you to do one more thing." He pointed with his pipe stem. "Ride forward. If you come upon Custer's command, tell him we're on our way. *Ask* him to *please* wait for us."

"We'll do that, Captain. Then we're cutting out of here."

"I understand." He stepped up into his saddle, and I saw a white stain of sweat and cornstarch on the seat of his trousers as he swung his leg over. He looked down and smiled a military smile. "By thunder! It's been rough as a cob."

"It has that," Jack said as we collected our reins and stepped up. We sat our horses for a second longer, watching him ride back to the troops, and as we turned, Windolph, Dammio, Godfrey, and the others looked up from the river, the clear river from which we'd all drank. We held up our fists in the air toward them—the sign of a warrior. They stood and made the same sign in return. And we turned, batting our horses off along the riverbank. Across my lap lay *Corporal* Tom Stovine's shotgun.

It was no great surprise to us when we came upon the small hill littered with the naked white bodies of Custer's men. We'd followed the smell of death for the last mile, and rode among naked dead for the last hundred yards. We stopped at the edge of the hill long enough to draw our bandannas up across our faces, then stepped our horses quietly toward the center. "So there you have it," Jack said, and we sat there, watching a bloodstained dollar bill stir on a gentle breeze and dance away across the grass. "This will be talked about for a long time to come . . ."

I could not look at any of the bodies for more than a second. It didn't seem right, somehow, staring down at them, some of them badly carved, their insides exposed to the open sky. I *did* look long enough at General Custer to recognize him, lying there as if asleep, naked and white and with nothing to distinguish him from any of the other dead. No dashing Western hat perched on his forehead, no buckskin trousers covered his manhood. All things personal of him were gone now, save for a dirty sock that lay inches from his foot. The sweat bee lighted for a second on his stiff white toe, then careened away.

After a second of silence, we turned, reined our horses carefully through the dead to the edge of the hill, and rode away. I have no idea how far we rode without speaking. It might have been a few minutes . . . it could have been an hour. But as we skirted along the edge of a dry creek bed lined with aspen and cottonwood, I said to Jack, "Naw, this won't be talked about for long. In a few months, he'll just be one more dead soldier. There's nothing to tell here. They fought . . . they died."

"You're wrong," Jack said in a quiet tone.

"No, I'm not. What's gonna be talked about is what happened back there . . . those brave men left hanging on that bare hilltop." I shook my head. "There's a soldier's tale if ever there was one. Wouldn't surprise me if somebody writes a book about it."

"We'll see." He shrugged.

We'd ridden on another few yards and slipped inside the trees to rest our horses out of the sun, when all at once Walker's voice called out behind us. "Up your hands, you sons a bitches! I got yas now."

We raised our hands a few inches and watched as he stepped around in front of us. He grinned, nodded back toward the hill where the dead soldiers lay, and said, "Did we kick your asses, or what!"

I let out a breath. "Yeah, it was a big day for the Indians. No doubt about it." He wore the battered top hat I'd lost running from the coulee.

"Damn right it was. Did you see what ole Rain in the Face did to Tom Custer's body? Carved him open from asshole to appetite." He giggled and ran his free hand across his mouth. "He ate his damned heart."

"No," I said, "we didn't see it." Watching him, I saw one of his shirt pockets bulging with bloodstained dollar bills. In his other pocket I saw two green-trimmed envelopes, and had to stop and look at them twice. *Could they be?* Had he taken them off Custer?

"What now, Walker?" Jack said. "Anything else you want to say before I close your stupid mouth for you?"

"Ha!" He stiffened and wiggled the big army Colt in his hand. "You don't seem to know who's got the advantage here!"

Jack sliced me a glance and a flat smile. With just the touch of my boot to the roan's side, the horse drifted sideways a step, then another, opening the distance between Jack and me. Walker jerked the pistol back and forth. "Now hold it, damn it! I see what you're doing."

"What's that in your pocket, Walker?" I smiled at him. "Tell me, and maybe we won't kill ya."

His eyes widened. "Are y'all crazy? Look at this." He shook the gun in his hand.

"Yep, you've got a gun all right." The shotgun rose from my lap, cocked, and pointed at him from six feet away, so slowly and smoothly it seemed to happen before he noticed.

"I never said you could do that!" He batted his eyes. "I've got you covered here!" He yelled and jumped back a step. But it was too late and he knew it. The open end of the eight-gauge must've looked like a field cannon staring at him.

"You hesitated, Walker. You oughta know better. Now you're gonna have to drop your gun. Feels foolish, don't it?"

"Aw, hell!" He lowered his pistol and stomped the ground. "Y'all *are* crazy."

"After three days of hard killing . . . you're out here picking a gunfight. And you call *us* crazy? Now pitch it away before I make soup out of ya."

He uncocked the pistol and pitched it on the ground. "Alls I wanted was my shirt back," he grumbled, looking down. Jack covered him while I stepped down and over to him.

"That's my hat you're wearing," I said. On his wrist I saw the severed metal handcuffs.

"Then take it and give me my shirt." His eyes lit up for a second as I glanced at the hat and the greasy hair hanging beneath it.

"Naw, I reckon not." I pulled the two envelopes from his pocket, looked at them, and felt my heart jump in my chest. It *was* Libbie's letters. Both of them! And I turned them over in my hand and saw that neither of them had ever been opened. The wax seals were still in place. "I'll be damned. You took these off Custer's body, didn't ya?" I glared at him.

"So? He's got no use for them, does he? Any more than them boys back there need this money."

"Can't argue that with ya." I turned the letters back and forth in my hand. *Jesus* . . . Custer hadn't even bothered opening the first one, let alone the second. Libbie's handwriting was on them. The first one was addressed to *The General;* the one I'd brought up simply read, *Dear Auddie.* "How come you didn't open these, Walker?"

"I meant to. Would've sooner or later." He clucked his cheek. "Boys, it's a hard thing to do . . . opening another person's mail."

"Yeah, it is." I looked at Jack as he stepped down from his silver gray and walked over with his pistol cocked.

"Y'all ain't gonna kill me, are ya?" Walker's eyes widened more.

I sighed. "There's been enough killing, don't you think?"

"Oh yes, absolutely! I know I'd just as soon go get a beer and put all this behind us."

"Where's your horse?" I asked him, glancing around the sparse woods.

"Uh . . . I ain't got one."

No sooner had he'd said it than as if on cue, the neighing of a horse came from deeper in the woods. "Shit. This just ain't my day, is it?" He tried a sheepish grin. "See why I need that shirt back?"

"Are you riding the general's horse, Walker?"

"Well . . . yeah, one of them, I am. One of the ones you took from me. Some Arapaho took his other horse. It's headed all the way up to Canada."

"Come on, let's go get it." We walked deeper into the aspen and cottonwood, and there stood Honest Bob, sawing his head against his reins, tied to a tree, looking no worse for the wear of battle. "What're you doing here anyway, Walker?" Jack asked him as I reached out and tried to rub Bob's muzzle.

"Uh . . . nothing." His eyes darted back and forth.

"Tell the truth, now," Jack said. "I hate wasting a good bullet on ya."

"All right." His shoulders slumped. "I'm waiting for my brother Rance. He's supposed to meet me here."

"He won't sneak up and shoot us, will he?"

"He might. I can't promise nothing. He knows what ya look like. We split up at the coulee battle. He went over and did some sharpshooting."

For a second I thought about Shotgun Tom and wondered if that had been Rance Walker's work. But then I put it out of my mind. The battle was over. The killing had to stop somewhere.

"What if we just take the horse and these letters, and let you go?"

"Hell, that ain't fair. I had the drop on you—coulda killed ya!"

"But ya didn't, see?" I spread my hands. "You can't just point a gun and expect everybody to do what you want. What kind of world would this be?"

"It works on most people—" He looked embarrassed. "—If ya catch them *unaware*."

"But not us." I grinned. "We're horse dealers. We never get caught *unaware*."

"That's it, brag about it, just 'cause you got the upper hand here." He looked back and forth between us. "You ever think how I feel? Every damn time I run into yas, I lose more of my stuff."

We stared at him for a second, then I let out a breath, reached over, and flipped open my saddlebag. "Tell ya what I'm going to do, Walker." I pulled out the shirt Libbie Custer had brought to me in the hospital, shook it open, and hung it on my saddle horn. "You really think this medicine shirt is bulletproof?"

"I *know* it is. You didn't get shot, did ya?"

"But neither did I," Jack said as I reached down and skinned the shirt off my back.

"There's things about Indian magic ya can't explain," Walker said. "Maybe just being close to him kept you alive."

I shook the shirt and slung it over his shoulder. "Here, it's yours . . . if you promise not to dog us from here back to Bismarck."

"You mean it?" He looked as if he thought there was trick involved.

"Take it and go." I gestured a hand as if sweeping him out of the woods.

"Hot damn!" He grinned, snatched off the top hat, slipped into the shirt, and put the hat back on. "You ain't too bad a fellow after all."

"I like to think so," I said and we walked back to where he'd dropped his gun. I led the roan in one hand and Honest Bob in the other. Jack picked up his pistol, unloaded it, and shoved it down in Walker's holster.

"I'm leaving on foot, but at least I got *something* from ya this time." The sweat bee circled in and landed on his cheek. With a swift slap, he flattened it and shook it from his hand. "Hate these aggravating little bastards." Then he'd tipped a hand to his hat, turned, and had walked about three steps out into the clearing when a rifle shot exploded and flipped him backward.

We cowered down between the horses, our pistols drawn, and waited for more rifle fire. But none came. After a few seconds, we heard the sound of hooves pounding away, and we eased to the edge of the tree line just in time to see Rance Walker top a hill and disappear from sight. "Lord have mercy . . ." I looked back inside the woods at Walker's crumpled body, at the hole in his chest that only a buffalo rifle can make. "Did he think it was *me?*" A few feet from Walker lay my battered top hat, upturned as if laughing at the sky.

*"May*be . . ." Jack looked back at the empty hill, then back at Walker's body. "His Indian shirt got him killed?" He stepped over slowly, reached out with his boot toe, and tipped over the laughing top hat.

"Was it the *Indian* shirt or the *white man's* hat?" Jack looked at me as if he needed me to say something more on it, something that put in its right perspective. But I had nothing for him. So I shrugged and said, "Or . . . maybe he just didn't *like* him."

Jack lifted an eyebrow with a bemused look on his face, and I added, "I know they're *brothers,* but not all brothers get along."

His expression didn't change, so I shrugged again. "They *should,* of course. But they don't . . . always."

He *still* just stood there staring at me. I spread my hands. "Jack. What do you want from *me?* What do you want me to say?" With Libbie's letters in one hand, I gestured with both hands toward Walker's body on the ground, then out toward the hill, then back. "Crazy stuff happens in a war."

Finally he rubbed his neck and walked over to the horse. "I know one thing," he said, stepping up in the stirrup. "I'd give a hundred dollars for a hot bath."

Chapter

33

Mercy from an angel of keep . . .

The *Far West* arrived at Bismarck two days before we did, and that was for the best, I've always thought. It would have been terrible, bearing the bad news to all those wives and families.

I dreaded visiting Libbie Custer, but it was something I clearly had to do. So as soon as we got to Bismarck, I rested a couple of hours, cleaned up, shaved, put on a new change of clothes, and went alone over to Fort Lincoln—carrying the two unopened letters inside my shirt.

On the way there, I ran it back and forth through my mind, trying to decide what would be the best thing to tell her. Would it do well to just tell the truth, that her husband hadn't read either of the letters? Or would that just compound the hurt? Maybe I'd just tell her I didn't get to him in time. *Hunh-uh, that was bad, too.* I still had no idea what to say as I raised the door knocker and brought it down.

Inside the house, Martha closed the door softly behind me and led me into the parlor without a word. Open trunks sat here and there with folded blankets and household goods packed in them. A big clock ticked back and forth slowly in a corner. The general's wife looked up from a piece of needlework in her lap and started to stand up as I stepped over toward her. But I raised a hand, stopping her. "No, please," I said in a quiet voice, and she sank back on the chair and folded her hands across her lap.

"Oh, Libbie, I'm . . . *so* very sorry." I kneeled slightly there before her, prepared, perhaps, for her to fling herself against me and sob her heart out. Yet she only sat there, composed, resolved. Her eyes looked weak and drawn, the crying part all ready behind her, I thought, at least for the sake of appearance.

"Yes, thank you," she said.

I gazed around awkwardly, then back at her. "I—I see you're packing?"

"Yes." She sighed. "My tour of duty here has ended. I shall travel to my father's house . . . and just rest for a while."

"Sure." I nodded. "Rest always helps." We looked into each other's eyes in silence for a second. I thought about the letters inside my shirt and started to reach for them, still not sure what I would say once I brought them out.

She must've seen something stir in my thoughts, because she reached out and took my hand, stopping me. Then she said, "Dear Mr. Beatty, my angel of keep. Tell me that you found my husband in time. Pray tell me that you gave him the letter, and that all was well between us. I could not otherwise bear to think—"

"Sssh." I squeezed her hand gently, stopping her from speaking. "Of course, I got to him in time. Of course, I gave him the letter." I offered a trace of a smile. "What kind of angel of keep would I be if I hadn't done that?"

She settled a bit, and I added, "Everything was fine, Libbie. He understood."

"I see. Thank you. It helps to know that. I've waited to hear from you, hoping, praying . . ."

"I know. We came here as soon as we could. I wanted you to know just how much he loved you, how he spoke so much about you the night before the battle."

"Oh? Did he?" Her eyes lit, just a little but enough to let me know it was the right thing to say.

"Of course." I took a breath and built the story word by word as it spilled from my lips. "He read the letter right there, with me in the tent, and you could just see how relieved he was. He spoke on and on about you . . . about you and him, mentioned a—a vacation you'd both talked about, I believe." I stopped and placed a finger to my lip as if trying to remember."

"Cape Cod? Was it Cape Cod he mentioned? We'd talked about going there . . . afterward." I saw her spirits sink a bit, realizing there would be no *afterward,* other than this one at hand.

"You know, it *was* Cape Cod, I believe. Yes, I'm sure it was. But anyway, the main thing is . . . the general loved you, Libbie. And everything was fine. The letter must've made all the difference in the world to him."

"Good, then." She patted my hand and let it slip from hers, and I stood up and stood back, and finally folded my hands when I could think of nothing else to do with them. "I've decided to write about him, you know. After everything settles down. I shall write and tell the world about my dear husband, my *Auddie.* I think the world should know how kind and warm and wonderful he was." She looked at me, her eyes searching mine for some kind of acknowledgment, some kind of support, a sign perhaps, since giving a sign was something an angel of keep would surely do.

"That would be good," I said, nodding, "real good."

We talked on for a few minutes while the clock ticked in the corner and I told her that Honest Bob was in the livery station in Bismarck, that I'd brought him back to her because the general so loved that animal, and had ever since the day he'd seen him in New Orleans at the horse auction. And *yes,* he'd paid me for him, and that there before the end I felt like her husband and I might have gotten close to making friends with one another.

Then, when we'd said all we needed to say and I was ready to leave, she said quietly, "Yes, my Auddie must have had a great deal of respect for you."

"Oh?" I just looked at her, knowing there was more to come.

She glanced around as if making sure no one else could hear, and said in a lowered voice, "I found that terrible wanted poster and destroyed it. That is what he would have wanted me to do, isn't it?"

"Uh . . . yeah! Yes, I'm sure it is."

"So, you see. He must've thought highly of you, or else he would have turned you in. My Auddie was, above all else, a law-abiding man." She smiled. "And never worry, my lips are sealed. You'll always be my angel of keep . . . and what others don't know about you—" She shrugged. "—Well, perhaps they *shouldn't.*"

Once again I left the Custer house with my head spinning just a little, and back in Bismarck I went straight to Jack, thinking that even though she'd said her lips were sealed . . . well, you just never know. I could see the air getting too hot around there if we stayed much longer. Besides, my cousin had been talking about robbing a bank over in Minnesota. We didn't want to miss that. So when I walked into the saloon and saw Jack leaning on the bar talking to an old man with a handlebar mustache, I cut right in and said, "Amigo, let's go home."

But he and the man both turned to me, and as they did, I caught a glimpse of a badge on the old man's vest, and froze. "Wait a second," Jack said, smiling. "The sheriff here has something I think you oughta hear."

Before I could move or say a word, the old sheriff said, sizing me up and down, "So you're Beatty? I've been looking for you for a week, sir. You left a horse boarded at the livery here a couple weeks back?"

"Uh . . . yeah? And?" I slid a glance across Jack's smiling face, knowing it couldn't be too bad or he would never have brought me into it. "What is it? Didn't I pay his board in advance?"

"Sure did, but this ain't nothing about that." He wagged a hand. "The fact is, we caught a man stealing your horse! Got him over in jail waiting to hear from ya. Said he's a friend of your'n and it's all just a misunderstanding."

I just stared for a second, then it all started peicing itself together in my mind. *Gaither! That rotten, lousy . . .* "No kidding? Is this a tall feller? Thin mustache? Well dressed?"

He was taken aback a step. "Why, yes, that's him. So he does know ya?"

"Know me? Ha! You bet he does! Was he carrying a hefty roll of money, new bills?"

The old sheriff's eyes widened. "He dang sure was . . .

twenty-one hundred and seventeen dollars, to be exact. Why?"

I slapped a hand down on the bar. "That's correct, Sheriff, twenty-one hundred and seventeen dollars! Every dollar of it he stole from me! Robbed me in my sleep. Must've found the receipt for my horse being at the livery and decided he's just come steal it, too. What kind of world *is this,* Sheriff? Can somebody please tell me?"

"By God, don't you worry, son. We don't catch 'em all, but we sure caught this one."

I sighed and let go a breath. "Then God bless ya, Sheriff."

Sitting against the edge of a battered oak desk, I counted the money, folded it, signed a receipt for it, and shoved it down in my pocket. Then I looked at Jack, smiled, and said to the sheriff, loud enough for Roland Gaither to hear me from his cell. "Will I have to come back for a trial? They do still *hang* horse thieves, don't they?"

"Naw, not in a case like this. We'll just call it robbery, give him a few years to think things over, see if he can be rehabilitated."

"I always thought *hanging* was a good idea. What happened to that? Ain't we getting a little too liberal with these *rogues?*" Again my voice rose for Gaither's benefit.

"Yeah, but times are changing, Mr. Beatty. Folks like us just have to bite our lip and go along, I reckon. But, yes, you will have to come back here and testify in a couple of months. It'll be that long before a trial . . . with everybody being so broken up over Custer and all."

"I understand." I cleared my throat and asked, "What happens if I can't get back here?"

His eye grew wide. "Surely you'll be back! If not, this scoundrel could actually walk free after all he's done."

"All right, then, I'll be here. You've got my address in Missouri. Just let me know." I leaned slightly so Gaither could hear me. "Sure wish they'd give *hanging* a little more consideration, though, don't you, Sheriff?"

"Beatty, pleeease!" Gaither called out from the dark end of a long row of cells.

"Shut up, boy," said a deep voice. "Give me your cornbread."

When Jack and I left and got back to the saloon, a lot of businessmen had stopped by to drink and talk about the terrible thing that had happened to the Seventh Cavalry. We drank and listened, and drank some more. A big man in a green plaid suit bought a round for the house just to make sure everybody would listen to him, and he laid his big derby hat on the bar, raised his shot glass, and said, "Here's to 'em, boys. And may we not rest so long as one heathen Indian still lives on this earth."

Most of them muttered *Hear! Hear!* and threw back their drink, but Jack and I just looked down at ours, then at each other, and tapped our fingers on the bar. Jack must've read what was running through my mind, because he said quietly between the two of us, "You can't hate folks for what they don't understand, can ya? It's like smacking a pup for pissing on the floor. You just get a sore hand, and the pup don't know why you did it."

"Yep." I stopped tapping my fingers, wrapped them around my shot glass, and raised it. "So here's to pups."

"And hands that ain't sore," he added, raising his glass as well.

"And a floor full of piss," I said, chuckling.

"Hear! Hear!" Jack laughed and we threw back our drinks while the rest of the crowd looked at us—looked at us as if we might've been two poor souls just blown in on a hard cold wind from a place too far away to matter.

But we stayed a little longer while the sun set, and the man went on and on about the battle. By the fourth or fifth drink, he'd gotten so caught up in it, it sounded like he'd been there. Maybe by then he thought he had. "It's not the damn Germans, the Italians, the Negroes, or even the dirty Irish I'm talking about here. By God, gentlemen! There were *good American boys* slain there, too."

"Not to mention all the Lakota, Arapaho, Cheyenne, and the—"

Jack gigged me in the ribs to shut me up. I mighta been a little drunk. They all looked at me, didn't get the gist of what I'd started to say, nodded in agreement, and turned back to the big green suit. "See, Jack. I don't start no trouble. They don't even hear ya less you're saying what they *want* to hear." We chuckled between ourselves.

"There was even a fine young baseball player who died up there," the man said, his eyes getting a little misty from bourbon and memories he wished were his own. "He died right by Custer's side, swinging a saber like he'd swing a ball bat. Can't remember his name, though . . ."

A hush fell over the crowd while they considered it for a second, and a bartender filled their glasses. "It was Tom Stovine," I said, hearing my voice take on a whiskey slur.

They looked at me. "Oh . . . was it?" The big man's voice went a bit flat, and he ran a hand back across his hair. "I didn't know it was *him* . . . but it was a damn shame." He threw back his drink and the bartender poured him another.

"Yep, that's who it was," I said, looking from one to the other. "He was a fine boy, fast, a good batter, a damn good sport, all around."

"Well, to be honest, mister," the man said, not facing me as he spoke, "I'm not saying he wasn't a good soldier—I mean, it's a damn shame he died and all—but the truth is . . . hadn't his pitching game pretty much gone to hell a few years back?"

I stood for a second, staring at him, then turned to Jack and said, "Finish your drink. I'll go get the horses."

It was dark, and my mind had cleared some by the time I got Jack's silver gray, Foxfire, and the Gypsy roan and led them back toward the saloon. The piano had started up, and I could hear it rattle as I walked along the empty mud street. A man sat huddled just off the boardwalk, and all I saw was a broad floppy hat above a ragged blanket as I walked past him. But then his voice called out as soft and cool as an updraft from a deep well of water. "Want to buy some crackers? Some peaches?"

"What?" I froze in my tracks, steadied the horses, and turned back to him. "Are you talking to me?" I eased forward a step, dropping the reins in the dirt.

"You were there. I saw you there," his voice said, a voice I'd heard but couldn't quite place. But then I began to realize who it was as I stopped, squatted down in front of him, four feet away there in the mud street, and tried to look up beneath his hat brim.

"You didn't see me there. I wasn't there."

"Neither was I."

"Rain in the Face? Is that you?" I'd heard no sound of threat in his voice, but it was good to know that my glades knife lay up in the well of my boot a few inches from my lowered hand.

The hat tilted up enough to show a glimpse of his dark face, then lowered. "The day after we fought, I got up, went out, and shot a buffalo, then dragged it back with my bare hands."

I considered it for a second, then said, "Yeah? I went out the next morning and broke six green horses for the army, then loaded a freight wagon full of flour barrels."

A silence passed—two of us there in the pale moonlight, squatted down, four feet of muddy street between us, lying about how tough we were, while up the street the madman rattled his piano. "When Custer fell, I said to the others, 'This is the end for us. Now the soldiers will not stop until we are wiped from the earth.'"

"Yeah, they're pretty fired up about it." I glanced back and forth along the empty street. "Ain't it risky, you being here? After all that's happened?"

"The others go to live in the land of the Great Mother. But I am an outlaw. I live where *I* live, until I die where *I* die. Want to buy some peaches?"

I thought about the money in my pocket, this deserted street, one *bad* knife-swinging Indian, and I said, "Not me. I'm broke. If you're smart, you'll get out of here. What are you doing here, anyway?"

"I brought your spirit to you. Want it back?"

I tensed, thought about the knife in my boot, the pistol up under my arm, the rifle in my saddle scabbard. "Not if one of us has to die," I said, forgetting all those weapons of ill intent and letting out a breath. "I don't think I want to fight anybody else for a while."

"Good, then." A dark chuckle came from beneath his hat brim, and I sensed that he had just breathed a little easier himself. "What will you trade me for it? What is your spirit worth?"

"Right now, I ain't sure. But I'd rather trade than fight. What can I trade you?"

"I have no horse. You are a horse trader. Give me a horse," he said, and the way he said it let me know that nothing else would do.

Aw, man . . . I looked around at Foxfire and the tough little roan, and bit my lip. I'd wanted a horse like Foxfire all my life, but after what that roan and I had gone through . . . I couldn't give him up. As I thought about it, as if reading my mind, Rain in the Face added, "Give me your best horse."

I stood up. "Couldn't you use a few bucks? Say . . . a couple hundred? Some traveling money?"

He shook his head back and forth slowly. I turned and stepped over to the horses. It wasn't because I was afraid of him—I could've turned and shot him and nobody would've said a word. But there was something larger at work here. So I took a deep breath, slipped the saddle from the roan, pitched it over on Foxfire, and rubbed the roan's muzzle one last time. *What a horse* . . .

I led him over and dropped his reins down beside Rain in the Face. "He's the best . . . there ain't none better."

He didn't move. After a moment I stepped away, then turned and said in afterthought, "You better cut out now. Everybody's heard what you did to Tom Custer. They'll go hard on ya."

"I didn't do it," he said.

"Walker said ya did."

"Walker lies. That is why I will not ride with him again."

"You can believe you won't," I said. "His brother shot him."

"Always thought he would," he said.

I picked up the reins to Jack's horse and Foxfire, Foxfire not looking as good now that I'd given up the Gypsy roan. I couldn't bear to look back at the roan. So I didn't. "Do you know what it means to give a man your *best* horse?" His voice rose slightly as I made the cinch on Foxfire and tested the saddle.

"Yep," I said, although I really didn't, except that it meant I was now a horse short. I stepped into the stirrup and swung up.

"It is not true that I killed a buffalo the day after we fought," he said. "I was hurt bad."

"Me, too," I said, "and I didn't break no horses the next day. Take care of yourself, Rain."

"Take care of yourself, horse trader."

When I walked into the saloon, Jack turned to me and saw the look on my face. He threw back his drink, and we both turned toward the door. "What took ya so long?" Behind us the piano rattled.

I stopped just inside the door and said, "Jack, I just been talking to Rain in the Face."

"Sure you have." He grinned and started out, but I stopped him.

"No, Jack, it's true. That's where I've been. I saw him plain as day."

He pushed up his hat brim and laid a hand on my shoulder. "Listen to me. You're drinking some. You and that Indian damn near killed each other. You probably *did* see him. I imagine both of you will be seeing each other for a long time to come. Get what I'm saying here?"

"Yeah, you're saying I'm truly *crazy* and seeing things . . . is what you're saying." I trailed behind him as he stepped out on the boardwalk. "But you're wrong. I saw him. Hell, I gave him my roan."

"You did, huh?" Jack turned in the doorway, grabbed my arm, and pulled me forward. "Then what's this?"

There at the hitch rail stood the Gypsy roan next to Foxfire and Jack's silver gray, and I swayed and caught myself against the doorjamb, wondering if maybe I was losing my mind. Jack walked over to the edge of the boardwalk and looked down, shaking his head. I walked over beside him and looked down, too, at the big can of army peaches sitting in the street by our horses' hooves. "What's wrong? Are you afraid they won't feed us on the train?"

"Uh . . . yeah," I said, and I glanced up and down the empty street. Behind us the piano stopped for a second in a hail of laughter and applause, then peeled right into another rattling tune. "I thought we might get hungry on the way."

Epilogue

Jack was right about Custer's battle being talked about for a long time to come. But I noticed over the passing years that the ones who talked about that battle and seemed to know the most about it, were the people who'd never been there. The ones who'd been there didn't talk much about it at all, unless they had to. Ain't that how it is with most battles? Long after the bones of the warrior have turned to dust, the armchair heroes fight on, a blazing cigar in one hand, a brave glass of bourbon in the other. And so goes the heritage of war.

I never knew what happened to most of the men who walked off that bare hilltop with us, although I read somewhere that Windolph, Dammio, and the rest of the water detail received the Congressional Medal of Honor for heroism. I was glad to see that they didn't win it for killing some great number of Indians, but rather for an act of mercy—bringing water to wounded men.

I also read somewhere years later that Rain in the Face was pardoned, settled down from his outlaw ways, and lived the rest of his life in peace. Although many people accused him of cutting Tom Custer's heart out, he always denied it. As a former outlaw myself, I could see why he would, whether he did it or not. History doesn't have to know everything. Even the ones who write it change it a bit here and there to suit themselves. Elizabeth Custer did.

Everything she ever wrote about her late husband made him out to be a saint. Maybe it was because I'd lied to her, telling her how much he loved her—not that I'm saying he *didn't*. It's just that in her state of grief, the picture I painted of him that day might've stuck with her so clearly that she forgot all else about the man and saw only what she wanted to see. Who knows? I saw her only once more after that. It was years later, in New York, during the holiday season, and we didn't talk much about *him*.

She was there signing books, and I was there to invest some money in a deal Jack had going. It sounded crazy, but Jack had found some ole boys who'd supposedly built a machine that flew through the air like a bird. It sounded too crazy to be real, but I figured, what's a few dollars more or less, since his hunch *had* been right about telephones.

As I passed a small bookstore, I saw her through the window and had to look twice just to make sure it was her. It was getting late, and inside, I stood back from a small group of people gathered around her until the last one had left and a clerk walked over and turned the sign on the door. It was a nice little place, all done up with Christmas decorations, candles gleaming on polished wood, with rows of Poe, Twain, and Stevenson all flickering in the soft light. *Her* kind of place, I thought, watching her place the cap on her ink pen and put it away.

She glanced up, recognized me after a second, and seemed real glad to see me. She stood up, we hugged, and as she stepped back, her fingertips brushed softly across my temple beside the patch on my eye. "Why, James, you've gone and gotten yourself injured, I fear."

"Yeah. Lost it years back," I said, not wanting to talk about it. "But just look at *you*, Elizabeth. You haven't changed a bit." I craned a look over her shoulder at the stack of books on the table. "A *writer*, I see! I'm happy for you."

She tossed a hand. "Yes, a *writer* . . . Gracious sakes, the stories I could tell you about *writing*."

I smiled. "Will you sign a book for me?"

"Of course. Here's some already signed . . . I'll just add a special little notation to you."

"Already signed?"

"Yes. I always sign a stack of them before I leave." She glanced around, then leaned near and whispered, "Once I sign them, the bookstore feels obligated to purchase them from me." She winked. "It's a little trick of the trade."

"A trade? I would call writing a profession."

"Yes, but a profession is only a *profession* to an outsider looking in. I've found that once you've become something, it's simply another *trade* from then on." She smiled. "Perhaps that's sad in a way. But I may have learned that from you . . . you and your *horse dealing*. Do you still do that?" She lowered her voice, formed her dainty hand into a pistol, and snapped her thumb back and forth. *"That . . .* and the . . . *other?"*

"No, no." I spread my hands. "I still dabble in horses, but the other . . . I quit that years ago."

"Good, then!" She smiled, reached around, picked up one of her books, and looped her arm in mine. "May I take you to dinner, Mr. *Beatty?"*

I chuckled. "I remember what happened the last time you took me to dinner." Loneliness flashed across her eyes, and I added quickly, "But, of course, you can. I'd be delighted."

And we left the store and walked along the quiet street in a soft-falling snow. A few silent seconds passed as each of us searched our memories for something to say, realizing perhaps that aside from the brief terrible time we'd shared, we were not much more than strangers. Then for some reason, she stopped and looked at me. "You realize, of course, that no one will ever take the general's place. I wouldn't want to mislead you . . . again."

Again? It was a strange thing for her to say, but I smiled, brushed a drop of water from her cheek where a snowflake turned to rain, and said, "You've never misled me, Libbie. We both knew where we lived." I breathed in the cold air. "But I have to admit, I was stricken by you. You are quite a woman."

She linked her arm in mine, satisfied, and we strolled on together along the cobblestone street, beneath streetlamps that formed halos on and around us, halos that swirled of snow, and of snow turning to fine rain. Ahead on a corner a harmonica played. Strange, I thought, out here in the snow on this empty street.

"You know, it took me a long time to get away from the army," she said. "I didn't realize how deeply I'd become ingrained in it. The pageantry, the protocol . . . and with it, of course, the discipline, the sacrifice." She sighed as we walked, and the harmonica became clearer as we drew closer. "It's all behind me now."

"Yep," I said, "it's a hard life at best . . . soldiering."

She stopped again, tilting her head slightly. "What an earthy way to put it. 'A hard life at best . . . soldiering.'" She repeated the words almost under her breath, then said, "I like that. Are those your words?"

I shrugged. "Well, I suppose so. I've said it often enough."

"Do you mind if I use it sometime?"

"I might use it myself," I said. "I've been thinking about writing a little about my friend and myself, back when we were, you know . . ." Now I made *my* hand into a pistol and clicked my thumb.

"Oh really! Why that's wonderful! Then you shall be using the line yourself?"

I blushed a little, seeing her make such a big thing out of it. "Well, I've never been that good with words. Just thought I'd try my hand at it. I'll tell you what. You use my line about soldiering . . . and if I ever really write anything, I'll use the line you told me once about two hands reaching for one another through a bead of dew. Deal?"

"Yes, certainly." She slipped her arm back in mine.

"Good, then," I said, patting her forearm. The harmonica broke into a soft version of "The Girl I Left Behind Me" as we drew nearer.

"Oh, my goodness, listen to it." Her voice turned softly reminiscent. "The very song I heard the day the Seventh left for the Big Horn River."

I hugged her arm in mine. "Are you okay?"

"Sure. It's a beautiful song."

As we neared the corner, we saw the old man huddled against a wall of stone with the harmonica against his lips. His hair hung long and matted from beneath a ragged old garrison cap.

"I *do* hope that someday you will write, perhaps about me, perhaps about the general? Write the things I couldn't say? But be kind?"

I reached inside my coat for some money to drop in the old man's cup; yet even in doing so, I saw no receptacle for my charity down there on the snow-covered sidewalk. The old man sat on a worn wooden pallet with rags tied around the stumps of missing legs. He was blind, but he turned his blank eyes upward past us in the falling snow, and as if reading my mind, he said, "'Tis not for the ring of coin I play here, but for the sound of my song on this harsh night."

His voice sounded familiar. I looked at him closely. "And it's a soldier's song?"

"Aye, laddie, for I play no other." He smiled across broken teeth. *Griebs? Could it be? Could God in some fit of mocking humor* . . .

"James? What is it?" Libbie's voice spoke softly as she looked at my face.

Jesus. I rubbed my eyes and looked back down at him. *Could it be?* "Uh . . . nothing," I said to her and the old man lowered his blind eyes and held the harmonica near his lips with hands clad in ragged gloves. And I said to him, "Can't I give you something? Buy you a drink? Help you home? It's getting bad out here." *Was it Griebs?* I couldn't tell.

"My pension buys my whiskey, and where more at home can an old soldier be than with his back against a hard wall and the unseen world before him?" He chuckled and coughed. "I tell you, laddie, these stumps have walked the world and back . . . these blind eyes see it all as it is." He pressed the cold metal back to his lips.

Could it be? God, I thought, don't let it be! It can't be. I didn't want it to . . . and so it wasn't, as we turned and walked away along the cold night street.

"Anyway," she said, taking up where she'd left off, "I should like to think that if you ever *do* write . . . that in some small way I might have inspired you." Behind us, the old man struck up a sweet, mournful version of "Gary Owen," and it drifted along with us.

I glanced at her and suddenly felt like stopping there on the street and pressing her to me to taste her lips and feel her hair against my cheek. But it would not be the kiss of the woman who'd ridden with me bareback on a crazy horse in the South Dakota sun. It would not be the hair that flowed so freely that day for those brief moments in the circle of corral, within the confines of the fort, within the circle of the world, the confines of our universe. *Always the general's woman* . . .

I smiled and turned with her, and we walked on. "If I ever *do,* Libbie . . . you most certainly *have.*"

Behind us the song seemed to circle and swell high above the dome of the streetlamp's glow, and higher yet above ancient fields of battle. Lord, I thought, to take the sound of one old soldier's song, and to pen it to paper the way it was played, played from the earth's womb this harsh hollow night—therein would lie the trick of *every* trade, therein would two hands touch as one through the bead of dew . . .

Someday? Maybe?

I smiled to myself, thinking how good that would feel. But I wouldn't kid myself about it. There wasn't yet enough in my ole outlaw soul to move the heart or stir the spirit, or to know what snow or wind or dust it must take . . . to cover the grave of even one warrior's bones.